Praise for Kate

'Kate Fenton's forte is sharp, contemporary comedy'
Elizabeth Buchan, *Mail on Sunday*

'The perfect summer read'
Company on *Lions and Liquorice*

'Kate Fenton on sparkling form . . . A funny and highly
engaging novel'
Woman's Journal on *Balancing on Air*

'A sparkling, frothy tale, lively, intelligent'
The Times on *Lions and Liquorice*

TOO MANY GODMOTHERS

Kate Fenton

flame

FLAME
Hodder & Stoughton

First published in Great Britain in 2000
by Hodder and Stoughton
First published in paperback in 2001
by Hodder and Stoughton
A division of Hodder Headline

A Flame Paperback

10 9 8 7 6 5 4 3 2 1

A CIP catalogue record for this title is available
from the British Library.

ISBN 0 340 76914 9

Typeset by Palimpsest Book Production Limited,
Polmont, Stirlingshire
Printed and bound in Great Britain by
Mackays of Chatham plc, Chatham, Kent

Hodder and Stoughton
A division of Hodder Headline
338 Euston Road
London NW1 3BH

For my friend, Lynne Tommony, in fond memory of pantomimes past.

Also, with gratitude to Fizz, the borrowed dog, for walking a thousand miles and more with me in the ravelling of this plot – and surviving.

Chapter One

Once upon a time – we open in the time-honoured way because, in spite of all the evidence to the contrary, there are certain people who *will* insist this is some kind of fairy tale – thus, once upon a time, a full two years before our story truly starts, and so very long ago a Tory government was still clinging to office in Merry Olde Englande by its much-bitten fingernails, there lived within convenient reach of the Palace of Westminster a spinster by name of Dunstan. Miss Theodora Elizabeth Fortescue Dunstan if you want the full moniker. Teddy for short.

It would be nice to continue that she was young, vivacious, beautiful and all the rest. Nice, but untrue. She was thirty-five even then, and, as she would be the first to tell you, no great shakes in the looks department. Five foot two, eyes of blue, damn little of the coochy-coo. Observe that sturdily erect spine, that elongated nose and stubbornly jutted chin. Here is no modern *Ms*, no dizzy-dazzling, thirty-something swinging-single in designer labels and emotional turmoil. Here, unmistakably, is an old-style *Miss*, who thinks labels are for jam pots and angst is a furring of the coronary arteries.

In fairness, she's not so much uncomely, as uncommonly lacking in the talent or will to make more of her modest assets. A pretty thatch of fair hair is chopped into a brutally sensible bob; a rosily clear complexion endures daily soap and hard water while her meagre make-up bag is mislaid for weeks on end, and bosoms a cup size too large for her diminutive frame make her look more stocky than voluptuous because she hasn't a clue about clever clothes. That her favourite outfit is a seventeen-year-old pair of cords teamed with a much-darned cricketing pullover says everything.

She would also freely inform you that she's neither brainy nor accomplished. She possesses three O-levels, a silver medal for life-saving, and a magnificently embossed certificate in Cordon Bleu cookery from a wonky so-called finishing school on the south coast which went bust soon after she graduated. Little does she suspect the upheaval in her life which will soon be prompting her to frame this document for public display. At present, however, she employs respectable typing and shorthand qualifications in a job as secretary to the backbench Member of Parliament for Tadstone West. Conservative, it goes without saying. This is the daughter of a baronet and the great-niece of an earl: heart of oak, vowels of glass, handbag of granite – the latter wielded without compunction in disputes over the neckties, grammatical constructions and non-executive directorships appropriate to an aspiring politician. Is Teddy Dunstan bossy? Is the sky blue?

(But only with the best of intentions. Was not the said Member for Tadstone West being tipped for a junior ministership? And would this have been the case had he appeared in public sporting lime-green polka dots around his neck? Thank you.)

One of the few attributes she does claim for herself is common sense. Common sense she has by the bucketful. Also, she sincerely trusts in this degenerate age, a staunchly old-fashioned armoury of moral principles, so anyone hoping for scenes of exotic hanky-panky is likely to be in for a thin time. In fact, one is almost tempted to pack in this story altogether, because it cannot be denied Miss Dunstan is decidedly unpromising as the heroine of a romance. Not that she would dream of casting herself in such a guise. The very idea. Romance, in her view, is an affliction of the teenage years not unlike acne, and she's happy to say she has never suffered from either. Perhaps her only qualification for this leading role is her lively desire to get married.

After all, dear reader, marriage can be the only satisfactory conclusion to a tale such as this – can it not? – and it is safe to state that few heroines in the entire annals of romance have been keener to hasten towards that happy consummation than Theodora Dunstan. What is more, unlike so many modern fictional females, she feels no obligation to waste two hundred and fifty pages flying the sex-equality flag by composing symphonies, founding commercial empires or navigating polar wastes before plighting her troth. Her view is that if God intended her to do any of the clever stuff, He would have supplied the cerebral wherewithal. As it is, her ambitions are more Jane Austen than airport bonkbuster. Give her a small house in the country (six bedrooms quite adequate), a brace or so apiece of well-trained children and dogs, a decent garden, a paddock for the ponies and a few civilized neighbours, and she confidently guarantees to live happily ever after.

Did she forget to mention the husband in that list? Ah yes, well, a husband is obviously required to sire the sprogs and foot the bills. Being neither bright nor beautiful herself, she doesn't demand an Adonis or an Einstein, still less a combination of the two, just an average, respectable, decent sort of chap with a glimmer of potential and a healthy share of ambition, whether his field be diplomacy, law, industry at a pinch – or even, perhaps, the Tory party. Having secured such a promising specimen, she is prepared to devote herself to the smoothing and advancement of his career. Dinner-partying, shirt-pressing, diary-scheduling – you name the support service needed by a man-on-the-make, Teddy is equipped to supply it. She is also sound on blocked drains, income tax returns and cantankerous elderly relatives. Yes, on the very cusp of the twenty-first century, Teddy Dunstan is quite archaic enough to believe her natural vocation is that of the proverbial woman behind a successful man.

As to precisely why she has yet to assume her chosen role, why Miss Theodora Dunstan remains unwed at the embarrassingly advanced age of thirty-five, well, she would prefer not to go into that. If you don't mind. Suffice to say there is a man in her life. This gentleman has figured large in her life for several years, one way and another, is part of the furniture, really, only not – yet – her lawful wedded husband. Which is utterly maddening, if you want the truth, because he never seems to be around in those parts of her life where a chap is really needed. Certainly, since one can only carry old-fashioned principles so far these days, he is regularly to be found in her bed – but what, pray, is the use of that? Where is he when an obstinate pickle jar requires opening? When one wants towels retrieving from the top shelf of the airing cupboard? Where is he, more to the point, when one needs a little support to endure the more gruesome rituals of family life, such as the funeral of one's father?

For this is where we – if not he – first join Teddy. On a brisk March day, with daffodils dancing and clouds scudding like lambs across the sky, we find ourselves in the North Riding of Yorkshire at Langley Hall, distinguished ancestral pile of the Dunstan family, on the sad occasion of Sir Theodore Dunstan's obsequies. And while Sir Theo's life – in spite of sturdy efforts in the vicar's address to suggest otherwise – may have failed to create much of a ripple in the great wide world beyond Langley-le-Moor, the events set in train by his passing will be quite another matter . . .

Chapter Two

Teddy thought she had brushed through the actual service pretty well – managed not to blub, anyhow – but the ensuing knees-up back at the Hall was proving more than averagely poisonous. At every turn, she found herself being cornered by deaf and mothball-stinking ancestors, jovially demanding to be told, at foghorn pitch, when she was going to get herself hitched. With clenched smile, she kissed her way round the scrum, endeavouring *en route* to chivvy half-baked waitresses and even dopier brothers into doing their duties likewise. She had just seized a platter of distinctly unappetizing sandwiches from one of the former when she collided with her sister-in-law, Isobella, now Lady Dunstan.

'This bread's stale.' Bella, lush as a ripe plum in tight ebony velvet, balancing on the spindliest of stilettos, nevertheless helped herself to a further quarter. 'And they've been jolly stingy with the smoked salmon.'

'Sorry?' Teddy was scowling across the crowded room, signalling her younger brother towards a doddery great-aunt. 'Sandwiches? Oh yes, absolutely. Bloody awful caterers. I shall complain.'

'Darling, you look shattered.' Wresting the sandwich plate away and dumping it on a nearby table, Bella wrapped an arm around her sister-in-law's shoulders and lowered her voice. 'Seriously, now. Have you had a good weep?'

Teddy blinked. 'Weep?'

'Vital. You mustn't bottle grief up. Causes cancer, spots, terrible things, all that poison bubbling away inside. You have to let it flow.'

'Honestly, Bella, you do talk rot.'

'I believe you're in shock.'

'Course I'm damn well shocked – aren't we all? Pa popping his clogs like that, without so much as a word of warning.' For one treacherous second, Teddy's eyes moistened. 'All by himself, silly old fool, holed up in that damned Mill House. I wouldn't mind so much if one could be sure he didn't suffer at the end, didn't—' She broke off, sniffing ferociously.

'Don't hold it in, my poppet, let go.'

Red-eyed, Teddy glared back. 'All one can do is thank God Lily Rowbotham happened to be passing. Otherwise – otherwise one doesn't like to think how long he might have been lying there, stiff as a plank . . . Oh, knickers.'

'That's right,' crooned her sister-in-law in triumph. 'You just bawl your poor little heart out.'

But Teddy grabbed a paper napkin from the table and trumpeted determinedly. 'Where's Ma?'

This diverted Bella from grief counselling. Her face darkened. 'Holding court in the Gold Drawing Room, telling all and sundry she expects to be turfed out of her precious home within the week by her heartless bitch of a daughter-in-law.' Her voice dropped to an enraged whisper. 'Honestly, Teddy, it's so *bloody* unfair. It's not as though Charlie and I have any choice about coming back here. Anyway, she doesn't have to move out – well, not immediately – and Mill House is heavenly. Of course I've only ever known it as your papa's den – so sweet the way he was forever scurrying off to his bolthole by the river, just like Ratty, don't you think? But it always used to be a sort of dower house, didn't it? Elephants' graveyard for elderly rellies?'

Teddy flinched at a turn of phrase only too apt given that her father had been found stone dead in his bed at the cottage in question, but her sister-in-law, unheeding, swept on.

'And even if the place has got a bit run down, that's no excuse for calling it a rural slum. Besides, since she's spent her entire married life and most of your father's money doing up this place, I thought renovating Mill House might give her a new interest. I told her I was sure she could make it absolutely charming. Which is when *she* said, if it was so lovely, why didn't we go and live there ourselves? But, truly, Teddy, with four children, not to mention the animals, Charlie and I simply *couldn't.*'

'Of course you couldn't. Ma's talking through her hat.'

'But she keeps saying—'

'Charlie must take a firm line with her, for once in his life. Forgive me, Bella, I ought to circulate. And, oh Lord, there's Lily over by the door. I insisted she come up to the house and she might be feeling a bit adrift.'

'Lily?'

'Lily Rowbotham. You know, the one who found Papa, bless her heart. Used to work here when I was a child: cook, babysitter, surrogate mother, absolute salt of the earth. I must have a word.'

Her progress across the room was slow, however. More kisses had to be exchanged, more hands shaken, the proper inanities uttered: yes, it was a decentish sort of service, all things considered, although the new vicar was a tad on the high side, in Teddy's view, definite whiff of incense in the nave. There were condolences to be suffered, cousins to be enquired after, glasses to be filled, reminiscences to be endured, and lavatories to be identified. Worst of all, there were questions to be answered. No, of course Cousin Julia had not been omitted from the guest-list to Teddy's wedding. There hadn't been a wedding, not so far.

How old was she now? (*Honestly* . . .) Thirty-five last birthday, she was afraid. Truly, because Charlie was thirty-nine. Indeed, Teddy found it as hard as Miss Lewisham to believe that this lolloping, overgrown schoolboy was now *Sir* Charles Dunstan. (Too much to hope he might sprout a brain along with a title.) Jeremy? Well, one must remember that Jez was the baby of the family, years behind her and Charlie. Yes, she supposed he'd made a competent job of reading the lesson. (And so he jolly well should after three years at drama school.) No, Baby Bro wasn't married either, perish the notion. Time and plenty to think of that when he was earning the money to support a wife. (Fat chance.) Was he still on the television? Not since that hospital series finished. He seemed to have some wild idea of taking himself over to America, to try his luck in Hollywood, so perhaps they might yet end up with a movie star in the Dunstan family. (And pigs would fly over Sunset Boulevard.)

What was that? Oh, absolutely, Teddy herself was still down in London, typing her fingers to the bone at the House of Commons. *Boyfriends?* Gosh, surely Uncle Roly would agree she was a bit long in the jolly old tooth to talk about *boyfriends* . . . No, she most certainly was not one of these trendy lesbians – Uncle Roly had clearly been watching too much daytime television. She would have him know she was blessed with plenty of friends of the opposite sex. Well, if he insisted, one chap in particular. But if he would forgive her . . .

'Lily?' she called, waving desperately.

Great-uncle Roland, however, was not to be deflected. Teddy found herself having to explain that this one particular gentleman friend couldn't be present today, unfortunately, because . . . because what? The bleary old eyes did not waver from her fast-reddening face.

'Because – it's all been so unexpected, hasn't it?' she managed to stutter. 'Pa dying so suddenly.' An ill-chosen tack, because just thinking about her father's lonely demise brought the salty tears crowding back into her throat, and the only defence against a humiliatingly sodden collapse was to gibber on about his having had his three score and ten, about a heart attack being a mercifully quick way to go, at least one prayed it was, and—

'He went out quiet as a light.' A plump hand with pearly pink nails had closed over her shoulder and a gruff voice familiar from childhood was whispering in her ear. 'You listen to me, chuck. Your dad were fast asleep and didn't know a thing. So give over fretting yourself.'

'Lily!' With a hasty apology to her great-uncle, she turned to embrace the newcomer. 'Sorry, silly of me, blathering on, it's just—'

'I know what it is,' interrupted Lily Rowbotham. 'And you can tek it from me, he didn't suffer.'

'You think so?'

'Know so.' As if sensing Teddy's doubt, she added testily, 'I found him, didn't I? Here, you look proper buggered, let's get a drink.' With a swing of her capacious hip, like a queen cow clearing a path through the herd, Lily led the way to a waitress, plucked two brimming glasses from her tray and told her they'd hang on to the bottle and all, ta very much.

'You rescued me in the nick of time from Uncle Roly,' said Teddy, accepting her glass. 'Nosy old goat. Honestly, what is it about funerals that inspires ancient relatives to grill one so mercilessly about one's personal life?'

'Human nature.' Lily sighed philosophically and downed a swig of wine. 'Funerals is the only chance us oldies get to do a stock count round the tribe.'

For a women on the wrong side of sixty, Lily Rowbotham was a notably handsome creature. Her white-blonde hair was swept back in bouffant waves, her plump body upliftingly corseted and her feet, in spite of her bulk, were squeezed into the most delicately high-heeled of sandals. Doubtless in honour of her former association with the Hall, she was decked out for the present sad occasion in a flowing black georgette two-piece, scarcely less impressive than the Dowager Lady Dunstan's weeds. Moreover, in contrast to the widow's flawless maquillage, Lily's mascara was noticeably blotchy. This did not surprise Teddy, because Mrs Rowbotham had ever been a warm-hearted friend – had mingled her tears copiously with Teddy's over the demise of a pet hamster – and, Lord knows, had more than enough to blub about in her own life. Her husband was a miserly old despot who had been demanding an invalid's privileges for years as he threatened to die and failed to do so. She also had two lumpish bachelor sons in their late thirties still living under her roof, while a much younger and gloriously pretty daughter had run disastrously off the rails at art college, falling pregnant by some layabout hippy teacher twice her age. That the scoundrel had married Lorette in time for her to produce twins, poor child, did not mitigate his villainy because the escapade rightly cost him his teaching job and, by all accounts, he had not done a day's work since. Oh, in Teddy's view, poor Lily had plenty to cry about.

'Married, is he?' she was asking now.

'I beg your pardon?' About to enquire after Lorette and her renegade husband, Teddy blinked. 'Who?'

'This here gentleman friend of yours, the one you was doing your best not to tell your uncle about. No, don't try fibbing. Answer's written plain across your face.'

'*Lily!*' Teddy looked round frantically.

'Keep your hair on, they're all deaf as posts.' She shook her head. 'Lumme, a married man. Never thought you were the type.'

'I'm not.' Teddy flushed, lowering her voice to an urgent whisper. 'Look, I don't want to talk about this, but believe me, it's – it's not what you might think. You know me. I have – I have very strong views on, well, on that sort of thing.'

'Sounds like it and all.'

'God's sake, Lily, you don't think I'm some cheap marriage-wrecker?'

'Not the marriage I'm bothered about, you daft lummock.'

'I never intended . . . I mean, she'd left him before anything happened.'

'Only, let me guess, she came back.'

'Temporarily. There were – are – circumstances . . .' Teddy was growing redder by the minute. 'But you've got to understand the marriage was over before I came along, truly, dead in all but name.'

'Aye, and the patron saint of wedlock should be Lazarus. Kids?'

'I'd rather not go into it.'

'What's his excuse? Waiting for his children to grow up before he makes an honest woman of you? And don't give me that hoity-toity stare, Teddy Dunstan, I've known you since you was knee-high to a coal scuttle, and it sounds like you're not much wiser now. What happens if his missus pops another bun in the oven while you're sitting around twiddling your thumbs?'

Teddy spilled half her drink. 'Another child?'

'Happens.'

'Don't be absurd. The boys are in their teens. She was forty last birthday.'

'How old were you when your mum had Jeremy? And she

was across forty, wasn't she? So were I, nearly, when I fell with our Lorette.'

'Possibly, but John and his wife don't – well, you know. Packed all that sort of business in years ago.'

Lily snorted. 'Sez him.'

Teddy's face was puce. 'Can we please change the subject?'

'By gum, there's times when you're the living spit of your old dad. Any road up, if you want my advice—'

'I don't,' snapped Teddy before, with an effort, she caught herself up and continued more moderately, 'Lily, look, I'm sure you mean well, but you couldn't possibly understand—'

'Oh yes I could,' growled Lily Rowbotham with sudden ferocity, 'I understand better than you've ever dreamed of, chicken. So if you want this fella, tell 'im to stop piddling around with excuses.' She gestured round the sombrely clad throng and, all at once, she looked older and very weary. 'A do like this makes you realize. Wait too long and one day you might just find it's too bloody late.'

Chapter Three

———◦◦◦———

'I mean, how long has it been now?'

Teddy, two days later, was briskly smearing reduced-fat spread on to a slice of toast before handing it across the table of her Pimlico flat. The question was rhetorical. 'Six years we've known one another, damned nearly three since we, as it were, got together.'

Some women might consider moonlight, Moët and Mozart appropriate to the issuing of a proposal of marriage, but Miss Dunstan was a morning person, so it was tea, toast and the *Today* programme as usual. Anyway, this was *not* a proposal. This was simply a clarification of a long-standing, if unspoken, understanding between herself and Mr John Blackwell. Have we got that clear? Fine, then we will not be surprised to learn that she was clad – just as she would be any morning, post-bath – in her sturdy old tartan dressing gown. And you can be very sure she wasn't tarted up with make-up, perfume or any of that nonsense. Mascara at this hour? She would as soon pour crème de menthe over her cereal. 'I mention it only because, frankly, I think the time has come to – to regularize our situation.'

Her beloved stumbled to his feet with a mumbled expletive. 'Dropped the bloody toast on my trousers.'

'Chump.' Teddy rose too, seizing a cloth from the sink. 'Lord, what a mess, jam everywhere. Come over to the French windows so I can see what I'm doing.'

Now, one of Teddy's few vanities – perhaps her only vanity – was a reluctance to admit she required spectacles. She owned several pairs, but could not be convinced that she did not cut a comically absurd figure in all of them. Some people, she claimed, were simply unsuited to glasses. Look at the Queen, God bless and protect her. Was Teddy the only loyal subject to have noticed that nothing had gone right in the royal family since the day Her long-suffering Majesty had first felt obliged to perch those ludicrous reading specs under her crown? Not that the travails of the Windsors could be blamed on failing eyesight, exactly. Teddy's downfall was to be a different matter.

Finding the light even by the window inadequate, she kicked open the door and tugged her inamorato out into a patch of watery sunshine. (This was a ground-floor flat, with secluded, tree-lined garden to the rear, but since she is not to occupy it for much longer, we need waste no time on topography).

'Ouch!' yelped Mr Blackwell, as she thrust a hand deep inside his waistband to isolate the stain. We need expend little time on Mr Blackwell's charms either, and for much the same reason. Suffice to say he's passable on the eye, if no maiden's dream, and, while unlikely to qualify for Mensa membership, combines sufficient ambition with irresistible helplessness – irresistible, at any rate, to a woman of Teddy's managing disposition. He is generally known, moreover, as a good-natured fellow, even if his easy-going amiability was a trifle strained at that moment. 'God's sake, woman, let me undo my flies before you castrate me.'

'It's your own fault for putting on weight,' she muttered, clicking her tongue as he fumbled with hook and zip. 'Never mind, soon sort that out when we're married.'

'Married?' he gasped, at a pitch that suggested castration was under way.

Teddy, vigorously applying cloth to trouser leg, paused. You must not think she had allowed herself to be alarmed by Lily Rowbotham's warnings as to the perfidy of the male sex. Being of the officer and gent class herself, she naturally held that a chap's word was his bond, even when that word was, so to speak, unspoken. If challenged, she would probably claim it was just the whole ghastly business of Pa's death which was prompting her thus to push for legally married status. There is, after all, something about funerals that tends to concentrate the minds of those of us who remain, making us uncomfortably aware of just how swiftly *tempus* can *fugit*. Not least, in Teddy's case, overhearing a prune-faced spinster aunt congratulate her mother on the possession of an unmarried daughter to care for her in her old age. A chill hand had clutched Teddy's heart, and an iron resolution had hardened within her.

So now, still gripping the sticky patch of navy pinstripe, she straightened and looked her intended squarely in the eye. 'We are *going* to get married, aren't we, John?'

Give him his due, he didn't suggest otherwise. Mind, it would take a brave man to meet that steely gaze and demur. As it was, with a few caveats and provisos only natural to a man of his calling, Mr Blackwell gave Teddy to understand that his longstanding commitment to the proposed course of action remained unswerving; on this policy above any other a U-turn was unthinkable; but that it wasn't fudging any issues to point out certain major obstacles remained, with the interests of other parties demanding to be weighed in the long-term balance . . .

'John, you've been shilly-shallying over this divorce for years.'

. . . *however*, as Teddy well knew, he had never regarded these obstacles as insuperable; and while he was sure she would agree that precipitate announcements would be ill advised in the present uncertain political climate, he confidently predicted they could look forward, in the not too distant future, to embarking on a new and public era of partnership. All being well.

'Get the election out of the way and heigh-ho for the altar?' enquired Teddy.

He swallowed. 'In a word.'

'Good show,' she cried, and was actually moved to toss aside her dishcloth and plant a kiss on his flushed cheek. It was the most chaste and innocent of pecks. Thereby, however, she released her grip on his unzipped trousers, which, with the inevitability of farce, crumpled to his knees. Unwisely, he tried to step forward, and would have plummeted headlong to the flagstones, had he not clutched Teddy for support. Or rather, he clutched her dressing gown, which burst open and slithered to her waist.

'Great fat fool,' she squawked, because it was not a morning clement enough to be exposing one's naked bosom to the air. She was vainly tugging back her clothing while he, protesting equally vociferously, hopped around with ankles shackled in navy superfine, when all at once there came the most terrific cracking and crashing from the branches of a chestnut tree in the neighbouring garden.

And somehow, the next minute, there was a little man squirming in the middle of Teddy's herbaceous border, moaning that he'd broken his fucking leg. A leather-jacketed little man, with a very large, black, telephoto-lensed camera.

Fortunately, the injuries to the photographer proved minimal. Less fortunately, there was no damage at all to camera or film.

Chapter Four

You probably don't remember the story – at least, Teddy devoutly hopes you do not. After all, it was a full two years ago, at a time when the newspapers were chocker with bonking MPs.

Ah yes, the truth is finally out – as if you hadn't guessed. John Blackwell was none other than the Honourable Member for Tadstone West, and Teddy that hoariest of parliamentary clichés, a secretary who was also mistress to her employer. Or rather, former employer – indeed former Member, since, not long after the events in question, Mr Blackwell lost his seat in the Labour landslide. It was the imminence of that election which had inspired a tabloid newspaper to stake out Teddy's flat for more than a fortnight. Such liaisons between politicians and their secretaries are rarely as secret as the participants imagine, even if they are not as ubiquitous as the tabloid press would have us believe. The exposure of this one offered unusually juicy pickings: a vociferous champion of family values caught, not just literally with his trousers down, but sporting a patriotic pair of red, white and blue boxer shorts – putting the flag in *flagrante* as one Wapping wag expressed it – along with a baronet's sister, spectacularly bare breasted. The headline writers were spoiled for choice here, given a topless toff and all the rib-tickling variants on 'Teddy' and 'bare'.

Still, as we say, that was two years ago. The whole grisly business is now in the past, thank you very much, and Teddy has a new home, new occupation, new life . . .

. . . although, while we're on the subject, she would just

like to make clear that those Union Flag underpants were a joke, a foolish Christmas present (from his wife, adding insult to injury); that the riding crop was purest journalistic invention; and as for the banana – well, *really*. She's here to tell you she would have referred that banana to the Press Complaints people had she not been advised that least said meant soonest forgotten. The story might have been forgotten sooner still, however, if her fatheaded elder brother had not taken it upon himself to punch the nose of the erring Member for Tadstone West in a well-frequented Belgravia restaurant. One of the more memorable headlines ran 'BARKING BART BOPS BONKING BLACKWELL'.

Thereby, the barking baronet nearly earned himself a black eye from his sister, but was unrepentant. This bounder had promised to marry Ted, yah? Had been dipping his ugly little wick round there for yonks, right? So what the hell was he doing with his wife and sprogs on the front page of the *Daily Telegraph* (an organ to which Sir Charles accorded the reverence due to Holy Writ), the front page of the *Daily* bloody *Telegraph*, no less, grinning like a Cheshire Cat, claiming that his affair with Miss Dunstan had been a brief, stress-induced fling?

Their engagement was certainly brief. Teddy calculated it endured some ten seconds, and naturally her job expired along with it. All in all, the experience was . . . character building. A lesser female might have felt impelled to unburden her soul to the female columnists clogging her doorstep and telephone line. Naturally, Teddy resorted to nothing so vulgar, and was rewarded by reading luridly fanciful descriptions of her emotional devastation, along with some uncalled-for comments on her taste in dressing gowns. It seemed to be widely held that a mistress in frumpy old tartan could not expect to hang on to her man.

The press coverage provoked fierce indignation elsewhere.

'Bloody disgrace,' snorted Lily Rowbotham to the son-in-law she happened to be visiting at the time, thrusting the offending rag towards him.

The son-in-law, swabbing congealed scrambled egg from the mouth of a toddler, glanced up. 'Ace pair of tits,' he grunted.

Thus spoke a typical member of the Great British Public. You will not be surprised to learn that if Teddy has one overmastering wish in life these days, it is that she should never, *ever*, feature in the pages of a newspaper again. Even now, two years on, she finds strangers in a street or shop eyeing her curiously, as if trying to place the face.

Otherwise, as we say, that whole chapter of her life is closed, and she would be obliged if no further reference were made to it. Whatever twaddle her sister-in-law may spout about emotional scars and festering psychic wounds, Teddy is quite recovered, thank you very much, and has stoically observed to Lily Rowbotham – if to no one else – that the fault was hers for tangling with a married man in the first place. She will not make that mistake again. New home, new job, new life. On a fine summer morning, we find her once again in North Yorkshire.

She was resident up here now, having yielded to a natural instinct to bolt homewards in time of trouble. She was not living at Langley Hall, however. A mere month in the ancestral home had convinced her that alternative arrangements were needed if she were not to spend the remainder of her days mouldering in gaol for matricide, fratricide or whatever murdering one's sister-in-law was called. Besides, she had a living to earn. Thus, after selling the flat in London, she had settled herself in the picturesque Market Square of Langley-le-Moor. While the eponymous market, to the oft-expressed disgust of right-minded denizens such as Teddy, had long ago degenerated into a weekly craft fair ('organic joss sticks and crumpled scarves . . .'), the square remained a relatively bustling hub of activity, so much so that (again to the disgust of right-minded locals) a one-way traffic flow had recently been introduced. The right-minded brigade, you may be sure, were now permanently on guard to protect their stone-built, curly-roofed and charmingly crooked village from the imposition of any further suburban horrors.

Immediately behind one of the offending new traffic signs stood a handsomely green-and-gold-painted shop called The Pantry. Teddy was the proud proprietor of this establishment – a delicatessen, for all she insisted on calling it a grocer's. She lived in the two upper floors, while, from a large and shiny, steel-and-tile kitchen concealed behind the quaintly cottagey shop, she also ran an outside catering business. Prices supplied on application for dinner parties, buffets, private and corporate hospitality. Shooting lunches a speciality.

Her first customers had consisted of old family friends who assumed memories of dandling the infant Theodora on their knees entitled them to generous discounts. These she was soon granting only by dint of adding correspondingly hefty mark-ups to her initial quotations – and was surprised and gratified to discover this turn for commerce in herself. Customers now came from much further afield. After two years with barely a day off, the bookings diary was crowded, her bank account healthy, her VAT up to date, and she modestly believed she could claim her enterprise was doing rather well. Jolly hard work, of course, but hard work never hurt anyone, did it?

Bella, watching her sister-in-law labouring all hours in her steamy kitchen, would sigh gustily and urge this poor little Cinderella to abandon her labours and have some fun before it was too late, while, in the same breath, booking her services for another dinner party. At the usual discount. A keen amateur psychologist, Lady Dunstan would tell you in strictest confidence that all this frenetic work was a textbook case of displacement activity, an attempt by Teddy to bury the pain of her disastrous affair with that funny little politician, and (much though she hated to say so) she feared Teddy might never trust another man enough to embark on marriage.

Teddy (were she given to discussing such intimate matters, which she was not) would tell you this was hogwash. Two years on, her desire to settle into six-bed, five-acre, two-child, two-dog nuptial bliss was as keen as ever (she would even settle for four bed without paddock) and she anticipated no difficulty in trusting any man equipped to provide the same. The only difficulty lay in finding that man. She was thirty-seven now, with a biological clock not so much ticking as doing a tap dance, and she was certainly no airy-fairy Cinderella, sitting around in her kitchen waiting for Prince Charming to gallop along. Fat chance. Apart from Prince Charming types being guaranteed to gallop straight past the unprepossessing likes of herself, she would have you know single men of *any* type were proving to be about as common in rural North Yorkshire as pink zebra.

But was she downhearted? She was not. At this very moment, in the 'H' section of her filing cabinet, between herb-growers and hygiene regs, there was tucked a list she had recently drawn up of every unattached male she could think of locally who could conceivably be considered husband material. Refusing to be dispirited by the brevity and frankly unpromising nature of this list, she was applying her mind to devising some subtle method of improving her acquaintance with these gentlemen. At least, she *would* be applying her mind to it, if she had not a business to run and a witless, warring family forever demanding her attention.

'*Honestly*, Ma,' she hissed into the telephone, clenching it tighter between chin and shoulder and grabbing her mixing bowl.

'Poor Charles looked stunned.'

'Charlie always looks stunned, he was built that way.' Teddy cracked an egg into the bowl and began to beat. 'Goodness, Mother, she wasn't serious. Even Bella wouldn't want a male stripper at her birthday party.' Her whisk paused momentarily in mid-air, then resumed beating. 'No, of course she wouldn't. Just her idea of a joke. Anyway, what party?'

'Exactly, darling.' There was a silvery sigh, eloquent of sufferings unspeakable. 'Not that I expect to be consulted, because it is made clear to me at every turn this is no longer my house. As you know, I never complain but . . .'

Since the complaints her mother never uttered could be depended upon to last several minutes, Teddy put down the phone and stuck her head between the louvred doors to check all was well with Beryl in the shop, before retrieving a pepper grinder from the shelf over the cooker. When she returned, her mother's voice was still trickling out of the receiver.

'. . . beyond surprise at a woman who can stand a video-taping machine on a Hepplewhite cabinet, even so . . .'

Apart from interpolating bracingly that Ma would be spared such barbaric spectacles by her imminent removal to Mill House, Teddy said little. Informed that her darling papa was spinning in his grave, she did not point out that, in accordance with his instructions, his cremated remains had been scattered by the said Mill House, she just beat her sauce a little more briskly. Besides, the saintly and devoted soul mate to whom her mother, since being widowed, made such frequent and loving reference bore no resemblance to the shambling old sot Teddy remembered. She could see him now as, eyes rolling in alarm, he lurked behind a door in a puddle of Labradors, waiting until Ma's footsteps had tip-tapped safely by. Or slumped at the dinner table for what he called one of her smarty-arty parties, blearily enquiring whether this Inigo Jones ran on the flat or over the sticks. To his wife's often-expressed disgust, he was much happier eating sausage stew off tin plates in the company of what she frigidly termed 'society's unfortunates' at the annual camps for city children he insisted on permitting in the grounds. Teddy, who had loved her father very much, rarely bothered to argue with her mother's fluent rewriting of history – unlike Bella, who had been known to protest indignantly that the longest and most intimate exchange she had ever witnessed between her in-laws was a request to pass the marmalade.

'. . . with a big red bow tied round his private parts.'

Teddy dropped her whisk. 'I beg your pardon?'

'Darling, I told you. Isobella said that if Charles was too blankety-blank stingy to pay for a blankety-blank party, she'd just have the stripper instead, with—'

'Thank you, I got that bit.'

'And she wouldn't listen when Charles said they couldn't afford a party at present. Of course, I make it a rule never to come between husband and wife, so I just told Bella – jokingly, you know – that I didn't think my own life had been permanently blighted by the lack of a fortieth birthday party, and that, if I were her, I wouldn't be so keen to advertise my age.'

'But you did have one,' said Teddy, for once moved to expostulate.

'I beg your pardon?'

'You didn't let on it was your fortieth, but you had a whacking great do, with a houseful of guests. I've never forgotten, because you made me come down in a pink frock, all ghastly frills and tucks, and that frightful Irishman pinched my bottom. You remember, the poet chap. Ginned up to the eyeballs the whole weekend. Lord, what was he called? Big cheese in his day, but he must have been about a hundred and two by then.'

There was a frigid pause. 'I really cannot recall.'

'Well, I can,' retorted Teddy, with spirit. 'Disgusting old goat. Hugo something . . . Macaulay? Maloney? Fell off the perch not long afterwards. I remember seeing the obits and boggling that we'd had this celebrated geezer playing footsie under our mahogany. You can't have forgotten, Ma. He wasn't invited, he just rolled up with the Blaydon-Shawes.'

'The point is, if I had a party at all, it was a small and civilized gathering of like-minded friends,' stated her mother. 'Whereas Bella seems intent on rolling back the carpets, hiring a discothèque and throwing open the doors to the world and his wife. Charles, perfectly reasonably, asked whether she didn't think she was rather old for that sort of bun fight.'

'Charlie's an ass,' muttered his sister, groping for the salt. 'Red rag to a bull.'

'Darling, I'm not surprised he's upset. If it's not male strippers, it's the new under-gardener. Isobella gives the impression of being totally fixated on sex.'

'Just her way. Doesn't mean a word of it.'

'Exactly what I tried to tell poor Charles last night. "Take no notice of her, my love," I said, "or you could end up convincing yourself this party is simply an excuse to fill the house with every Tom, Dick and Harry who's ever taken her wayward fancy."'

'Mother, how *could* you?' Teddy went on to inform her parent that the sooner she left for Mill House, the better it would be for everyone – but with something less than her customary robustness, because her mind was elsewhere. It was occurring to her that a birthday party was indeed a first-class pretext for filling one's home with any number of promising Thomases, Richards and Henrys. To that sort of free-for-all bash, one could legitimately invite chaps one hardly knew from a bar of soap. Except her own birthday was six months away. Besides, she loathed party-parties: noisy, plate-juggling scrums, hopeless for conversation. Dinner parties were infinitely to be preferred, but she couldn't fit more than six around her table without tangling the cutlery, and inviting a strange man to so intimate a gathering would look undesirably pointed. So much for that bright idea. 'Sorry, Ma?'

'I said, that was when Bella began to talk about divorce again.'

'Drunk as skunks, I suppose.'

'However, Charles seemed to feel he should meet her halfway. He hasn't spoken to you yet?'

'No, and if he wants me to come running up to the Hall to play piggy-in-the-middle, he can forget it.'

'I gather a small supper party is the compromise they've settled upon.'

'Oh, *terrific*,' snorted Teddy. 'Cooked by guess who? At rock-bottom price, with my labour thrown in for free. Well, you can tell Charlie—' All at once she halted.

'Darling?'

There was a pause. Teddy tapped her front tooth with the hilt of a spoon. 'On second thoughts,' she said slowly, 'perhaps I will come up to the Hall. Bella likely to be around at lunchtime, do you know?'

Chapter Five

'I'll kill her,' growled Bella, clutching a packet of frozen peas to her head. 'One day, so help me, Teddy, I will throttle her. Oh, why do I feel so *bloody*.'

The younger Lady Dunstan was seated at one end of a long refectory table in what had been, in balmier times, the servants' hall at Langley Hall and now served as the family kitchen. A golden sun streamed heartlessly through mullioned windows, plates winked merrily on bleached-oak dressers, baskets of dried flowers clustered lusciously in every available corner, and a plump pair of Labradors snoozed in front of the Aga. Less conventionally, a white rabbit was lolloping across the flagstones, and a small grey monkey hung upside down from a light fitting, thoughtfully scratching one buttock. Although it was nearly one o'clock, the chatelaine was still huddled in a towelling robe which, for all she was built on splendidly Junoesque lines, was nevertheless several sizes too large. Long, wavy mahogany-brown hair, of a lustre which had once moved her husband to declare she reminded him of his favourite spaniel, hung lank around features twisted in anguish. An Alka-Seltzer fizzed in a glass at her elbow.

'Self inflicted,' said Teddy callously, plonking her own mug of coffee on the table. Before sitting down she shook from the chair what appeared to be a squashed currant, but caution was advisable in this household.

'She'd drive a saint to the bottle. And I ate a whole bucket of ice cream, too. Can you believe that? Half a litre of Belgian chocolate at half past one this morning. I can feel my thighs *exploding* with cellulite. God, I hate myself. I'll never get into my black dress and it cost a fortune.' She squinted at her sister-in-law from under the frozen peas. 'And you can stop pulling faces, I have to shop. It's a substitute for sex.'

'Look here, Bella, Ma phoned me and—' Teddy broke off. 'It's *what*?'

Bella tossed aside the pea packet. 'Totally kosher, darling,' she said animatedly, 'I read about it. Sublimating one's urges, you know, and it's *so true*. Think about it. That dizzy infatuation as you glimpse some divine little number across a crowded shop, the illicit thrill of stripping to try it on, even though you know your credit cards are screaming, the orgasmic release when finally—'

'You do read some tripe.'

Pouting, Bella wilted again. 'I have to find my kicks somewhere. You wouldn't believe how long it is since Charlie and I got it together. I've said I'll ask the doc about Viagra if he's too shy, but he won't hear of it.'

Teddy flushed. 'I really don't want to know this.'

'Anyway, the problem isn't physical, it's *her*. She inhibits him. Shimmers into our room at all hours, pretending she's forgotten it isn't darling Theodore's any longer. Darling Theo, my foot. You can bet your life she never shimmered along in her nightie when he was in residence. If you ask me, he hadn't had a sniff of the oats bucket for centuries, poor sausage.'

'She was forty when Jez was born,' observed Teddy fair-mindedly, 'so he must have. And speaking of being forty . . .'

'Don't remind me. Besides which, even when she's not actually invading, Charlie can *sense* her, lurking about the place like a vampire bat. One creak from a floorboard and *clunk!* Limp as a curate's handshake.'

'Bella, honestly, he'd die if he heard you.'

She hunched a sulky shoulder. 'It's grounds for divorce, non-consummation.'

'Not after four children it isn't. When are they home, by the way? Must be end of term soon.'

'I may be a mother,' declared her sister-in-law tragically, 'but I am also a woman. And a woman has needs.'

'Lord, water his whisky, can't you? Or get yourself a good detective novel.'

Unexpectedly, Bella's face softened. 'Is that how you manage? Oh, you poor baby, I'm such a self-obsessed cow, moaning on about my troubles, when you've been totally manless all this time. You must be climbing the bedroom walls.'

'Never give it a thought,' snorted Teddy with perfect truth, sex in her view ranking well below pickle-jar opening in the fringe benefits of matrimony. 'But . . .' She hesitated a moment. 'As it happens, that's not entirely unconnected with why I'm here.'

'Sex?'

'Can't you ever think about anything else?'

'You sound just like your mother. No, sorry, dreadful thing to say; only joking, darling, but she will go on as though I'm some kind of free-range nymphomaniac.'

'Listen, *please*. The thing is . . .' Unaccustomed as she was to public soul-baring, however, Teddy hesitated. 'Look, this is totally confidential. You must absolutely swear not to breathe a word to a soul.'

Lady Dunstan's face brightened. 'Sounds serious,' she said, hauling herself to her feet. 'Shall we take a little walk in the garden?'

'He must know,' said Teddy impatiently, as Bella, with a shifty glance upwards at the massed windows of the Hall, put a light to her cigarette. 'The stink clings to everything.'

'If he ever got close enough to smell it.' Settling herself on the shallow stone parapet surrounding the lily pond, Bella wrapped her dressing gown more tightly over her bosom, and fixed expectant eyes on Teddy. 'Now then. Tell all.'

'This supper party, for your birthday.'

Her face fell ludicrously. 'That all? I suppose Charlie's been bending your ear. You know *why* we can't afford a decent party, of course? It's because we've spent a king's ransom on bloody Mill House for your bloody mother, but will she move down there? Her latest excuse is that she's waiting here to welcome the prodigal son back from the States.'

'Jez actually is coming home, is he?' said Teddy, momentarily diverted. 'Broke again, I suppose. When?'

'Three weeks tomorrow. And Charlie has promised he'll make her pack up after that, *promised*. Which means,' she added, with a sigh, 'I've let the brute whittle me down to a crummy spag. bog. for twenty. God, what a gateway to middle age.'

'He can run to a couple more then. That table seats two dozen easily. Were you thinking of anyone in particular to partner me?'

Bella blinked. 'But, darling—'

'You'd assumed I'd be cooking? Thank you, but I spend quite enough of my evenings sweating in other people's kitchens. This time I'd prefer to be above stairs.' She clicked her tongue. 'Don't *fuss*. I'm not saying I won't lay on the grub, just that someone else will have to man the hobs on the night, Lily with luck, if her back's better. What's more, this is going to be a nice, civilized, sit-down job. Tell Charlie he can have the full five courses at cost – under certain conditions.'

'You mean I can have that fabulous chocolate pudding thingy? Well, it beats spaghetti. What conditions?'

'You can invite a man. For me.'

'You've got a lover tucked away?' She squealed delightedly. 'You dark horse.'

'Don't be ridiculous. That's the whole point.'

Bella stared back blankly. 'Point of what?'

The moment for disclosure now being inescapable, Teddy squared her jaw and fixed her gaze on the distant pinnacle of the stable-yard weathervane. 'It occurred to me that a dinner party is the best opportunity one gets, at our age, to meet someone. That is to say, a man.'

'Oh, I don't know. You should try advertising for an under-gardener. I've found the most divinely chunky little chappie . . . Sorry, sorry. Go on.'

'Do I need to spell it out?' growled our heroine, flushing. 'Isn't it perfectly obvious? I've been bridesmaid so often I have more satin slippers than Imelda Marcos, and enough godchildren to stock a sizeable junior choir, but none of my own. I'm not just unwed, I'm unattached, un-anything, with a sell-by date zooming up faster than a sign on the motorway, and since

27

I'd rather not end up as a batty old maid, breeding smelly Pekingeses and wearing my tiara to breakfast like Great-aunt Lottie, I'm suggesting you could lend a hand by inviting an eligible prospect to sit next to me at dinner. That's all. And frankly,' she finished furiously, 'if anyone in this family ever gave half a thought to anyone's problems but their own, you'd have bloody well suggested it yourself.'

After an instant of stunned silence, Bella overflowed with contrition and sympathy. Her sister-in-law was absolutely right, she should have been racking her brains for some gorgeous hunk – what sort of chap did Teddy have in mind? And she was most impressed when Teddy produced a piece of paper on which were jotted the names of a few possibles.

'God, you're always so organized. When I was on the loose I just bounced around like a balloon from one hopeless rotter to another. Until I met Charlie, of course,' she added hastily. 'Because whatever the old witch says, I do love him, you know, truly, madly, deeply.'

'Yes, yes. Concentrate.'

Bella twitched the list out of her hand. 'Let's see, Martin Luscombe, who he? Oh, I know, Daffy Luscombe's bro-in-law; sorry, not met him. Simon Hertingbury, never heard of him unless . . . no, can't be. George Beresford – *George Beresford?* Teddy, he's practically drawing his pension.'

'Fifty-four.'

'Exactly, far too old and so unutterably boring he could . . . *The Revd Timothy Lighthope*, darling, you cannot be serious. The vicar?'

Teddy bridled. 'Tim's under forty. And perfectly presentable.'

'And a raging poofter.'

'You don't know that.'

'Oh come on, all these high churchers are the same: smells, bells, frilly knickers under their surplices – he's more likely to fancy the choirboys.'

'All the more reason for him to settle down with a wife,' Teddy declared austerely. 'That's if he wants to get on, because

I should think Lambeth's pretty damn chary of promoting bachelors nowadays. And,' she continued, with the air of one who had given consideration to the matter and decided a bishop's palace would suit excellently, 'I don't see why Tim shouldn't go far, with the right help. He prays very nicely.'

'But imagine waking up with that in your bed. No, really, darling, forget him – all of them. Give me a couple of days and I promise I can come up with *hundreds* of better ideas. I'm sure I know lots of scrummy-delicious sex-starved males.'

'Give me strength,' hissed Teddy. 'You're *totally* missing the point. This isn't some kind of – of fantasy fornication league. I'm not looking for a muscle-bound Adonis with the libido of a Friesian bull.'

'If only.'

'Exactly,' she retorted stiffly. 'I fully realize I can't afford to be choosy.'

'Darling, I didn't mean *that*.'

'Just someone steady, respectable, ready to settle down.'

'How depressing.'

'And while we're on the subject, no married men. I mean, obviously not married men, but I can do without fresh-bleeding divorcees, either.'

'Well, that cuts the field by about ninety per cent. Widower?'

'Possible.'

'Not that I know any.'

'Ideally without young children – I should rather not play wicked stepmother for the next umpteen years, because whatever people say it isn't the same without blood ties. Oh, and I suppose I'd prefer a non-smoker.'

'Anything else?' muttered Bella mutinously. 'Eye colour?'

'Although a pipe is marginally less offensive, but one can always sort out details like that. Solvent, it goes without saying. Age immaterial, really, as long as he's not too old to start a family.'

'Do we ask for a banker's reference and a sperm count before we issue the bloody invitations?'

'Bella, really—' But then she broke off because a soft masculine chuckle was emanating from behind the hedge.

'Charlie!' squawked Lady Dunstan, and plunged hand and cigarette together into the lily pond.

'Nonsense, that wasn't Charlie's laugh.' Teddy strode across to the curlicued gates, which gave into the park, and saw a stranger rising from a bench in the shade of a beech tree.

He was a tall, lean, olive-skinned man in his mid-thirties perhaps, clad with notable elegance in a linen suit of Italian cut. Strikingly, in his swarthy complexion, he had eyes of a pale and steely green. More strikingly still, above his left eyebrow, shone a streak of silver in his otherwise black and impeccably sculpted hair.

Now, since this stranger is tall, dark and quite passably handsome, tiresome misunderstandings will be avoided if it is pointed out immediately that he sported a discreet enamelled brooch in the shape of loop of red ribbon on his lapel, and carried tucked under his arm, along with a slim sheaf of estate agents' brochures, a copy of *The Gay Hotel Guide*. This will suggest, to the sophisticated eye, that he is unlikely to figure as the romantic hero of our story – even if these nuances passed unnoticed by Teddy or her sister-in-law. Not that any such bird-brained fancy would cross Teddy's mind anyway. If she were expecting tall, dark, handsome strangers to wander uninvited into her life, she would not be here arguing guest-lists with Bella.

And when, with a dawning smile of recognition, he began to exclaim, 'Is it . . . ? Course it is, I'd know you anywhere. Talk about Fate . . .', she did not flip back her fringe and run a tongue over her lips as Bella was hurriedly doing, two steps behind her. On the contrary, with a glare which would have blast-frozen a shed full of turkeys, she informed the stranger that she very much doubted it, wished him good day, turned on her heel and stomped back into the rose garden.

'What was all that about?' protested Bella, trotting in her wake. 'Do you know him?'

'Don't be ridiculous. Never seen him in my life.'

'Well, he seems to know you. Look, he's waving goodbye. I wonder where he's off to across the park?'

'The only strange men who think they recognize me,' stated Teddy tight-lipped, 'are readers of tabloid newspapers with long memories. And he obviously heard every word of our conversation, dammit.'

'So?'

'I prefer not to advertise my private concerns.'

Suddenly, Bella let out a gurgle of delighted laughter. 'Wow, amazing,' she cried, 'that's it. That's your answer.'

'What is?'

'Newspapers – advertise!' Bella spluttered. 'You know, for a husband. Oh, what a blissful thought. *You* in a lonely hearts column.'

'Hysterical,' said Teddy. 'Oh, for God's sake, Bella, put a sock in it.'

Chapter Six

This, however, was too rich a joke to be abandoned readily.

They parted on a compromise, agreed by Teddy only because she was late returning to work, that no invitation would be issued to the vicar until her sister-in-law had been given a chance to apply mind and address book to alternatives. Thus for several days, and invariably at inconvenient junctures, she found herself being telephoned not merely with the names of possible dining partners, but also with supposedly humorous suggestions for a lonely hearts advertisement.

Cuddly Supercook seeks big bucks Superman, however, was not her idea of a priceless witticism, with a shop full of customers and four dozen choux balls in the oven. Nor could she tell Bella exactly what she thought of Gerald 'Gazza' Cole and dear old Piggy Gloucester with her shop assistant Beryl interestedly eavesdropping on her indignant protests.

When returning such calls, though, in the evening and the privacy of her own sitting room, she had less restraint.

'You're impossible,' wailed Bella. 'Here I am racking my brains to shreds and you contrive to find some nit-picky thing wrong with every single suggestion.'

'Myself, I don't call incipient alcoholism and two ex-wives a nit.'

'Well, perhaps not Gazza. But Piggy—'

'If Piers Gloucester was the only boy in the world and I were the only girl, I'd build a one-woman convent. Fortified.'

'I don't know why I'm bothering.'

Teddy, who was concluding that involving her sister-in-law

had been a grave error of judgement, cordially invited her to pack it in.

'Absolutely not. What are family for? We'll just have to go for the lonely hearts then.'

'Bella—'

'If you like, since you're so squeamish, I'll do the dirty work for you.'

'Bella, it's half past ten, I've a stack of invoices to type and I'm in no mood for jokes.'

'I'm not joking. As it happens, I have the *Dales Gazette* here in my hand, and there's a whole page called *Heart-to-Heart*, did you know that? Such a hoot, local papers: *plumber, enjoys the rumba*, do you think that's supposed to rhyme?' A lubricious laugh gurgled out of the telephone receiver. 'Tell you what, I'll place the ad, audition promising candidates and draw up a shortlist.'

Teddy rolled her eyes. 'When I want to rumba with a plumber who's probably unemployed with six children and a beer gut, I'll call you.'

'Knowing you,' said Bella grumpily, 'he'd have shed four stone, gained a Norland nanny and be running ICI by Christmas.'

The ridiculous thing, the truly maddening thing – the thing that would afterwards make Teddy want to scream and drum her heels – was that she never for one second supposed her sister-in-law was in earnest about placing such an advertisement. Never. It was only Bella's cock-eyed notion of a joke – and even she wearied of it.

By the end of a week, her suggestions for dinner guests were interspersed not with cuddly cooks and fun-loving plumbers but with renewed suspicions about her mother-in-law ('. . . plotting something, I could tell by the way she smiled when she opened her post . . .'), along with the usual complaints about her husband ('. . . and I said to him you'd better just give me a big black vibrator then, and he said, *hergh* – you know that stupid noise he makes – *hergh*, haven't we got enough bloody animals in this bloody house already? So God knows what I'll get for my birthday, probably a gift-wrapped boa constrictor

33

. . .'). Bella even conceded, albeit with reluctance, that she supposed they had better fall back on the vicar, if that was what her sister-in-law really wanted, although it seemed pretty pointless when Teddy was forever bumping into the Revd in the course of her duties as churchwarden.

Teddy retorted that discussing flower and brass-polishing rotas was quite different from sitting down at a dinner party and, thank you, Tim would do nicely. She would doubtless have hounded Bella into issuing the promised invitation had she not been so busy. And much though she would have liked to blame her sister-in-law for what ensued, she could not. There was no wriggling out of the responsibility. She got into the mess all by herself.

It happened late on a Friday afternoon. Teddy was in the shop, totting up the till, while Beryl spooned marinated cherries into jars. Since the proud proprietress would undoubtedly be offended if we hurried on without so much as a glance at her emporium, your kind indulgence is begged for a swift guided tour.

Please note the handsomely carved counters and shelving – solid oak, she's happy to confirm, with the original brass fittings, salvaged from a former chemist's shop. These shelves are now tight-stacked with jewel-bright jams and chutneys; with every shape and shade of pasta from spinach green to squid black; with fancy teas, hand-made biscuits, herb-infused oils, fruit vinegars – and yes, Teddy is aware such items are all non-essential luxuries. She takes very seriously the provision of essential services in rural areas, and would have you know she was prepared to continue running this business as the catfood-and-cornflakes general stores it had been when she bought it from Miss Fletcher – if the ungrateful locals hadn't made abundantly clear they were still going to drive hundreds of polluting miles to giant supermarkets for their Whiskas and bog-cleaner. Thus, as she'd tactfully had to explain to Miss Fletcher, the elderly spinster who, together with her sister and late brother, had once run both this shop and the now-defunct butcher's next door, she had found herself driven willy-nilly into this ritzily up-market niche. That she rather enjoyed dealing in hand-blown flasks of walnut oil as opposed to square tins of the all-purpose household lubricating variety was neither here nor there. Teddy had strong views on community responsibility.

On that sultry July afternoon, her shop smelled powerfully of fresh-roasted coffee beans, cinnamon, garlic and a camembert so ripe it was singing an aria. There were bunches of herbs rustling from the rafters, boxes of wine stacked on the terracotta tiles, voluptuous slabs of baked meats basking in the blue glow of the chiller cabinet, and a spread of empty baskets, gingham-lined, waiting for tomorrow's delivery of loaves. Today's woman cannot live by sliced white alone, she needs stone-ground, olive, pumpernickel and ciabatta. And for all it went against the grain, because Teddy naturally also had strong views on the sad degeneration of working rural communities into prettified tourist traps, she turned a handy profit on fancy fudge, Italian ice cream and novelty chopping boards, the last of which added a colourful touch to the window display, which was looking particularly smart that afternoon, if she said so herself.

Having admired both premises and stock, then, we can move on. Teddy was just reaching across this window display to pull down the blind – bottle-green, lettered in gold, which she flattered herself was distinguished, even if a tad reminiscent of House of Commons livery – when she paused in mid-pull. Leaning against the litterbin a few yards along the pavement was – a gorilla.

No, truly. Not only did this creature possess the authentic concrete-mixer torso of a patriarch silverback, he had the square, close-cropped head to match. The hair on the rest of his uncommonly hirsute body was appropriately black, and far too much of it was revealed by a skimpy T-shirt, which might once have been white but appeared to have encountered a red sock in the wash. He even had the curving, long-fingered hands of a great ape, presently cupped round a match flame as he lit a cigarette. A tripper obviously – the village was overrun with coachloads of undesirables at this season – but there was something about this particular chap's manner that struck her as . . . shifty? Yes, shifty. It was the way he kept glancing around – not at her, he was turned away, oblivious of her scrutiny – but at the shop next door. He gave the impression of a man steeling himself for action. If she hadn't known that the former butcher's was long since stripped of its contents while the Misses Fletcher bickered over its fate, she would have suspected him of casing the joint. As it was, she jerked down her own blind with a loud rattle, to let him know there were watchful neighbours about. Then she returned to her conversation with Beryl.

'So Lily didn't say anything about coming back to work?'

Beryl, a wiry busybody of sixty-odd with a crisply corrugated perm, gave it as her opinion that Lil didn't know whether she was coming or going. Just last night, at the bingo, she'd said . . .

Teddy listened with only half an ear because she believed she was tolerably abreast of Lily's troubles, amongst which she naturally did not include the recent demise of her husband. Any friend of his wife could count Stanley Rowbotham's long-overdue expiry only as a blessing, but in tending him through his final days poor Lily had strained her back, and was thus temporarily invalided away from work.

'I think the doc told her to keep it rested another week or so,' offered Beryl.

'I'll be glad when she's better,' sighed Teddy.

Lily Rowbotham, inevitably, had been her very first employee. These days, she also paid Beryl full-time to manage the shop, and, after a few dispiriting experiments with gum-chewing youth trainees, a select squad of other equally doughty Yorkshire grandmothers to assist part-time with her outside catering operations, every one as capable of scrubbing a floor as of knocking out a feather-light meringue. Lily, however, remained her trustiest henchwoman. No one could sergeant-major a humming kitchen like her. When she swore – which at times of drama she did with exuberant fluency – not just the waiting staff but the very pots and pans rattled to attention. Teddy had been so overstretched in her absence, she'd had to miss Stan's funeral which, for Lily's sake if not that of the deceased, she would certainly have attended, had it not coincided with a wedding breakfast for two hundred in Pickering. Instead she'd dispatched Chrysanths, apologies and two sherry trifles.

'It's the money,' proclaimed Beryl, with gloomy relish.

'Money?' said Teddy in some surprise, because not the least benefit to Lily of her husband's death had been the astounding discovery of some forty thousand pounds cash in the battered old tin box Stan kept under his bed. No mention of this bounty had been made in his will, probably because – as Lily darkly opined – the old bugger'd been salting lolly away from the taxman since the year dot, and the least said the better. It was perhaps fortunate no employees of the Inland Revenue were resident in Langley-le-Moor, because Teddy had subsequently heard of this secret stash from at least four sources, with the sum escalating at every turn. Of course she had heartily congratulated her old friend on such good fortune – and silently and unworthily hoped it would not tempt her to retire from work.

'She's handing the lot over to the boys,' explained Beryl, demonstrating why she was frequently known as the *Langley Chronicle*. 'On condition they use it to get a place of their own. You want the cherries under the counter?'

'Please. *All* to Brian and Colin?' Relief at learning Lily planned to give away this potential retirement nest egg was superseded by astonishment. 'I gathered when they were round here rewiring they were inheriting something, but surely not the whole lot?'

'She reckons they earned it, running their dad's business between them all this time. I mean, when did you last see Stan with a screwdriver? All the old buzzard did was count the takings.'

'Well, very possibly. But what about Lorette?'

'*Exactly.*' Teddy's assistant pursed her lips. 'Twenty thousand each to her sons and not a penny-piece to the lass. She's saying she'll square up accounts when she passes on herself. Small wonder Lorette's up in arms.'

'Lily probably doesn't want her frittering it away on that airy-fairy waster of a husband.'

'No, it's not that—'

But Teddy's head was buried in a chiller cabinet and she swept on unhearing: 'Frankly, I don't blame her. Lily doesn't talk to me about it, because she knows my views, but Brian obviously can't stomach the chap. Said his brother-in-law hasn't worked since the day they wed. Lord knows what they've been living on.' She emerged with a weighty round of Stilton clutched to her bosom. 'I mean, he may be unemployable as a teacher now, but whose fault is that?'

Beryl put her head on one side. 'Lorette was no innocent chicken.'

'She was eighteen and a student. Disgraceful behaviour. And then to cap it all, one gathers he claims to be an artist, if you please, and declines to sully his lily-white hands doing anything else. Or so Brian says. Well, I have no patience with that sort of high-falutin' nonsense, as I frequently tell my little brother. All very fine calling yourself an actor or an artist, but it doesn't butter any bread if no one wants to employ you. Jez, however, doesn't have a wife and two children to support, thank God. And for all I wouldn't dream of saying so to Lily,' Teddy concluded, seizing a cloth and wringing it out over the sink, 'because she's a loyal old soul, bless her heart, and devoted to those grandchildren, I'm not surprised her precious son-in-law never shows his face in this village.'

'Only because he couldn't take Stanley,' said Beryl fair-mindedly. 'Can't blame him for that.'

'I can, when he's forever summoning Lily over to Huddlestone at the drop of a hat. And always,' she added feelingly, 'when we're rushed off our feet here.'

'Not any more,' declared her assistant, allowed a word in at last.

'I'm sorry?'

'They've bust up, him and Lorette.'

Teddy looked up from her labours. 'No, have they really?' She hesitated only for a moment as abstract principles governing the sanctity of marriage warred with personal prejudices about layabout so-called artists. The latter won. 'Good,' she pronounced. 'Because, for all divorce is regrettable with young children involved, I'm sure no one could condemn Lorette for wanting out.'

'Lily does,' retorted Beryl grimly, stripping off her apron. 'She's mad as a hornet, and that's why she reckons she's not giving her daughter any money.'

'Dear me.' Teddy dropped her cloth and walked over to unbolt the door for her assistant. 'I dare say she doesn't mean it.'

'Very fond of her son-in-law is Lil.'

'Lily is too soft-hearted for her own good,' declared her employer austerely. 'People take advantage of her. Do you think she might feel up to managing a dinner party at the Hall on the thirty-first?'

'Can but ask.' Beryl plucked her mackintosh off the peg and joined her at the door. 'Lorette's home with her now, of course, and if them twins are running her ragged, she might be glad to get out.'

'I must call round. I wonder when would be a good time?' Pondering this as she rebolted the door, Teddy did not notice the gorilla was still lurking on the pavement.

Having extinguished his cigarette, he was now squinting into the windows of the adjoining shop, which, since they were blank and empty, was a highly suspect activity. If Teddy had observed him, she would have suggested he move along sharpish. The shop might be empty, but Connie Fletcher stubbornly lived alone in the terraced cottage beyond, in spite of her sister's oft-repeated wish they should join forces in her own modern bungalow. Since the resident village bobby had long since been replaced by an occasional sweep with a patrol car, public-spirited residents – amongst whom Teddy naturally numbered herself – had an extra duty of vigilance.

As it was, having flipped the sign to 'Closed', she cast one final look around her counters, twitched a pile of leaflets into order, snapped off the display lights and retreated through a side door into her living quarters.

These comprised an airy and pleasant sitting room, a cramped apology for a dining room, the usual offices and three decentish bedrooms spread over the two upper floors. A narrow and rather dingy hall and staircase ran alongside the shop, connecting the apartments above to a private front door, which gave onto the pavement beside the shop frontage. Not for the first time, Teddy resolved that something needed to be done about this gloomy hallway. A mirror perhaps? Or just some bright paint? If only she had the time. It was a fortnight now since she'd managed to give her front door a coat of gloss, and she still hadn't screwed back the brass fittings.

She was reminded of this because, as she placed a foot on the stairs, there was a rude thumping on the door panels. The brass bell and knocker winked at her reproachfully from the hall table where they clustered in a soup-plate along with assorted screws and a curlicued figure seven. One of the drawbacks of living, literally, over the shop, was the temptation it offered to regular customers to bash on the door out of hours. And unless this was a *very* regular customer, with a damn good reason for knocking, thought Teddy, they could go hang because she was locked up and cashed up.

Thus, she strode down the hall and flung open the door, framing the words 'I'm sorry but . . .', only to shut her mouth again. This was no regular customer. This was the gorilla.

He seemed to plug the entire doorway with his hairy bulk: not so much a visitor, more a temporary eclipse of the sun. Since he was now presented close up and full frontal, she was able to see that in addition to the pinkish T-shirt and convict crew-cut, this unsavoury specimen also sported too-tight jeans, clod-hopping workman's boots, a chunky gold wedding ring on one of his long, prehensile fingers, and an earring – yes, an earring – in one lobe. He had lugubrious brown eyes (as gorillas generally do), a slightly stumpy nose and a square chin, close-shaven, but nevertheless dark with incipient stubble. There hung about his person a faint aroma of tobacco and – Teddy's nostrils twitched – alcohol.

She drew herself up to the full five feet two, but even so was level only with his slate-coloured jaw.

'Can I help you?' she enquired, in the frigid tones which had seen off many an importunate constituent.

The gorilla, for its part, gaped down at her in seeming bewilderment. 'Yeah – no. Well, I 'ope so but . . .' He sighed. 'Look, I prob'ly should've given you a bell first off, but I forgot to get the number. And I was only intending to buzz daun and recce the patch, know wot I mean?' The beast's native habitat was evidently the uncharted jungles of Sarf London. 'Fing is, once I got 'ere, I sez to myself . . .' At this point, however, he broke off, and eyed her more closely. 'Hang abaht,' he said, 'you know somefink, you got a real look of—'

That was all she needed. A *Sun* reader. Teddy was about to slam the door when he finished, '—my daughter.'

'I beg your pardon?'

'Sorry, suddenly struck me. Floss sticks her chin out just like that when she's in a strop. No, don't flounce off, no offence. I haven't told you why I'm here.'

Teddy, with no good grace, paused with the door still ajar.

He leaned forward confidingly. 'I know you haven't actually agreed to place the ad, not yet, but I wanted to get a word in first – you know, ahead of the stampede.'

'What advert?' And no suspicion of treachery on Bella's part crossed her mind. Indeed her only thought was that this must be a rep from the *Dales Gazette*, in which she bought an occasional quarter-page, touting for extra trade. Before she could articulate her views on such high-pressure sales tactics, however, he was assuring her he realized she was in two minds, but that her sister had urged him to drop round for a chat.

'Sister? I don't have a sister.' But a dark worm of suspicion began to wriggle. 'You don't mean, that is to say, we can't be talking about my *sister-in-law*?'

'In-law job, is it?' he exclaimed, seemingly much relieved. 'Yeah, well, that explains a lot. I mean, I was thinking to myself she couldn't hardly be your sister. She's dead keen, mind. She tipped you off about me yet?'

'No . . .' breathed Teddy. 'She wouldn't – *couldn't*.'

'Before you say a word, let me just tell you she's filled me in, and I know you're iffy about the whole idea. No, listen,' he continued rapidly, as, gasping in stunned indignation, she groped afresh for the door. 'I can imagine how you feel, sweetheart, honest to God, I can. Bound to seem like a jump into the unknown, bloke like me, not at all the kind of set-up you'd got in mind, I dare say, but if you're prepared to take a chance, I promise I'm your man. Steady, free whenever you want, and ready to settle down, get stuck in and work like stink to make a go of it. It'd be a helluva jump for me too, I don't mind telling you, but I'm not some dodgy fly-by-night. I've got kids,

I gotta think long-term, get my drift?' At which the gorilla's face split into a grin, and he thrust forward his hairy curving paw. 'Blimey, here I am doing the old sales spiel and I haven't even introduced myself, have I?'

Miss Theodora Dunstan, ladies and gentleman, the time has come to meet Our Hero. Yes, that's right. Prince Charming he most certainly ain't, but he's all we've got. So stick out your hands, please, and give a big, warm Langley-le-Moor welcome to our own – our very own – Mister Bill Smith.

Chapter Seven

Stone the fucking canaries, thought Bill Smith, what've I said *now*? Because this little comedian was glaring like she was Queen Victoria and he was the farting footman. He'd been warned she could be a bit touchy, but all the same . . .

'Is this a joke?' she squawked.

'Not to me, it ain't. Twenty-two carat serious. Look, your sister says—'

'Don't tell me what my lunatic sister-in-law says!' she bounced back furiously. You had to hand it these aristos, in Bill's view. Barely topped his shoulder and still she was managing to look down her nose at him. Takes centuries of in-breeding to learn a trick like that. 'Advert my foot. Of course it's a joke, and I realize full well it was she put you up to it. Who are you, the new under-gardener?'

'What?'

'Only I suppose you're going to tell me you're a – you're a rumba-dancing plumber?'

We've a right one here, he said to himself; Community Care's got a lot to answer for. 'Painter,' he offered warily. 'Leastways, I was, and I'm hoping—'

'Ha,' she cried, and let out a kind of laugh. The kind the Demon King gives when he pops up in a puff of green smoke. 'An unemployed painter and decorator. Perfect. Complete with wedding ring, I see, and obviously working on the beer gut.'

'Here, do you mind?'

'Six children?'

'Just the two.'

43

'You amaze me. Well, you can tell Bella with my compliments—'

'Who's Bella?'

'—that I wasn't fooled, not for one tiny minute. My word, she really has gone too far this time. Is she paying you extra?'

This, no kidding, is how the conversation ran – and Bill would like to make it clear he wasn't pissed. OK, so he'd had a couple of pints, but so what? Highly stressful time in his life, and here he was, just trying his humble best to haul himself back on the old straight and narrow, and look what happens. He's not ashamed to tell you he had a quick butcher's round the square for help in case she turned violent. He did, seriously. Pint-sized she might be, but this one wasn't just off her trolley, she was clean off the planet. 'And what would, um, Bella be paying me for?' he enquired gently. Humouring her, like you do.

'For taking part in this ludicrous charade,' she whipped back. 'Lonely hearts, indeed. She should be ashamed of herself.'

'*Lonely hearts?*'

'And what's more—' At which she stopped dead. Just like that. As if someone had pulled her plug out. At least it gave him a chance to stick his twopenn'orth in.

'Pardon me,' he murmured, ever so polite, 'but if I could just mention, I haven't a fucking clue what you're on about.'

And for the first time in his life, Bill knew what people meant about silence being deafening. Her mouth dropped open, but no words were coming out. Just a sort of faint gargling. What's more, while a second ago her little face'd been purple with temper, she'd now bleached out paler than a ghost.

'You – haven't?' she finally managed to croak. And you could tell it hurt. The words were emerging slower than wisdom teeth. 'Why – why exactly did you knock on my door then?'

''Cause I want to rent the joint next door, of course, what'd you think?' But the old light was dawning at last. 'Lonely hearts?' he echoed, thinking to himself he must have misheard. Only, seeing that look on her face . . . '*Lonely* bleedin' *hearts*? You don't mean . . . ? No, you never, you wasn't imagining me . . . and *you*?'

★　　★　　★

Which is how, at six o'clock on an otherwise unremarkable summer evening, Miss Theodora Dunstan found herself compelled to deal with a drunken gorilla enjoying noisy hysterics on her doorstep. The beast guffawed, hooted, slapped his beefy thigh – damn nearly fell over, so riotous was his amusement. Serve him right if he did. She would cheerfully have slammed the door and left the buffoon to rupture himself, had she not spotted Mr Kendall parading his terrier round the War Memorial. Worse still, Mr Kendall saw her – her and *it* – and was tangling lead with walking stick as he swerved round to discover what the fuss was about. In an arctic whisper, she requested Mr Bill Smith (a name so commonplace anyone could be forgiven for assuming it was a pseudonym) to stop making an exhibition of himself. As well try plugging a nuclear meltdown with a wine cork.

'I do not believe it,' he roared. 'Here's me rabbiting on about – about how you wanna give me a whirl, with you perched on your little step like Lady Muck, thinking—'

'Will you shut up?'

'—I'm the lonely heart from Hell, come in answer to your advert.'

'I never placed any such advertisement, you fool. I just thought—'

'Poetry. It is, honest, the thought of . . .'

'Evening, Mr Kendall. Yes, hasn't it been a warm day? No, this – this *gentleman* just wanted some directions. To Miss Fletcher's, I imagine.' She lowered her voice to a hiss. 'And if you don't shut up and stop sniggering, so help me, I won't be responsible for my actions.'

'You gotta admit, Duchess—'

'Don't call me Duchess.'

'Sorry, sweetheart. No, no, Gawd's sake don't look at me like that or you'll set me off again.' He swallowed manfully. 'Let's get this straight. You aren't Connie Fletcher, and I guess this isn't number nine neither?'

'Seven, like my shop.' It did not improve her temper to have to add: 'I took the number off for painting. Miss Fletcher lives on the other side of the butcher's, beyond the alley. But,' she added firmly, 'if you were hoping to rent the shop, you're wasting your time.'

'Oh?'

'Several people in the village have expressed an interest, but she and her sister can't agree.'

He touched a finger to his nose, with such a knowing grin, her hand positively itched to punch that stumpy protuberance. 'Leave it to me. The sister's already in the bag.'

'I beg your pardon?'

'Took quite a fancy to me.' He grinned even more broadly at the expression on Teddy's face. 'No accounting for taste, huh? So I'd better go see if I can sweet-talk this Connie, too.'

'I doubt it,' she said frigidly, stepping back into the doorway.

'Oh, I dunno.' And he actually winked at her. 'Sorry I'm not the man of your dreams, babe, but with a bit of luck you might cop in for me as a neighbour.' So saying, the gorilla sketched a flourishingly satirical bow, blew a kiss and loped off down the pavement. 'See you around, Duchess.'

The only comfort Teddy could draw from this farce was a cast-iron certainty that she would not be acquiring Mr Bill Smith as a neighbour.

Connie Fletcher was a cussed old stick who had been turning away would-be buyers and renters of the butcher's shop for years. Among the most recent, as Teddy knew for a fact, were Lily Rowbotham's sons, awash with their inheritance. During the course of the interminable week they had not long since spent rewiring her premises, they had, to her dismay, discovered irresistible potential in the adjoining property. The shop itself was of only marginal interest to them, although – as Brian had explained at ear-numbing length – it would serve conveniently enough as a base for their electrical business, while the living accommodation above was, in his phrase, more than adequately commodious. The real attraction, however, was the spacious, stone-built outhouse that lay to the rear of the premises, across the cobbled courtyard shared with Teddy's property. This structure, which in long-gone times had served as a slaughterhouse, would apparently provide perfect housing for their model railway. As he had informed Teddy, and doubtless Miss Fletcher also, their network was one of the largest in private hands in the county and had long since outgrown their mother's double garage. That it occupied this building she already knew from their mother's regular complaints. Fortunately, Miss Fletcher proved to share Lily and Teddy's jaundiced view of grown men playing with trains, and had sent Brian away with a flea in his ear, telling him she intended the shop to remain a shop, not be turned into an office-cum-storeroom. Until now Teddy had believed there could be no more hideous prospect as neighbours than Brian and Colin Rowbotham. She now realized she had been wrong. At least, though, there was no chance of this gorblimey gorilla succeeding where two such eminently respectable local citizens had failed.

By the following evening, as she climbed into her van to visit Lily, her face was still liable to burn if she chanced to recall the encounter on her doorstep, but she was determinedly suppressing such flashbacks. To be sure, she'd made an ass of herself, but it didn't matter so long as no one knew. And having pondered long and hard without identifying a single acquaintance, employee or customer who had ever mentioned an out-of-work decorator called Smith with a Sarf London accent and a marked resemblance to a great ape, she believed she was in no danger of becoming a local laughing stock. All she had to do was forget the episode. As quickly and completely as possible. Totally. *Finito*.

'. . . and when our Bill told me,' hooted Lily, within a minute of Teddy's entering her kitchen, 'I knew straight off it had to be you. By, I nearly put my back out again, I laughed that much. You've got to laugh, haven't you?'

Teddy felt no such compulsion. She stared at Lily in stunned disbelief.

'You know, *Bill*. Bill what's married to our Lorette, although not for much longer, more's the pity. Lad's gone back to Huddlestone this morning to sign off on the house sale, and start packing up.'

'The—' Layabout, she nearly said. 'The artist?' *Painter*: the brute had actually told her he was a painter. Oh Christmas, Bill Smith. How often had Lily bent her ear about her precious son-in-law? With Teddy, perfectly reasonably, visualizing some effete, long-haired hippy in velvet jacket and cloud of patchouli. Not a muscle-bound ape in road-mender boots and a miasma of strong beer.

'Best husband a girl could wish for,' Lily declared stoutly, 'and I've told our lass she'll be sorry. Well, she's sorry already, now she's seen the money going to her brothers, and if that doesn't teach her, nothing will. I dunno, you do your best for your kids, and what happens?' She sighed, shaking her head. 'I just hope it's not my fault them busting up, because I can't deny it were me pushed Bill to think about moving over here. "You can't go drifting on forever, love," I says to him at Stan's funeral. Mind,' she added fiercely, as though forestalling protest, 'I'm not blaming Bill. He hasn't had it easy this past five years, but, as I said to him, with Stan gone, there's nothing to stop them settling this road, and if I lent a hand with the kids, maybe he could get some work going. Only that's when young madam in the next room starts stamping her foot, saying that really is the final straw, no way is *she* ever living in Langley again, and Bill says, well, they've *got* to sell Huddlestone, and before you know it . . .' She rolled her eyes. 'Still, you didn't come round to hear my troubles, love. And I'm proper glad to hear you're doing summat about your own love life at last.' She chuckled. 'Although I were surprised at you putting an ad in the papers.'

This jolted Teddy back to life. 'I did no such thing,' she cried. 'Bella did – at least, she didn't, I just thought . . . Goodness' sake, Lily, it was all a misunderstanding.'

'Oh aye?'

'Honestly, I would never—'

'Give over, I'm all for it. As I said to Bill, you need to find yourself a nice fella after the runaround that scallywag in London give you.'

'Lily, *please*.' But she was prevented from arguing further by the entry of Lorette. Bashing open the door from the lounge with one swing of her shapely hip, she tottered over to join them at the kitchen table, carrying a phial of nail varnish between the carefully straightened fingers of one hand, and a copy of *Hello!* magazine under her elbow.

'What d'you reckon?' she enquired, thrusting glossy green fingernails towards Teddy. 'Think I'd sooner have blue myself. I'm not asking her,' she added, with a pout in her parent's direction, 'because I'm not speaking to her.'

We must break briefly from our narrative here to take the measure of Lorette Smith, née Rowbotham. The lovely Lorette is quite accustomed to having that effect. She has the kind of looks which stop breath, traffic, and dicky pacemakers, never mind a tuppenny stretch of dialogue. Legs like a clothes peg, face of a Madonna, eyes the luminescent turquoise of the Aegean, with yards of Titian hair tumbling and tangling down her swan-curved back – Lorette would be something quite extraordinary even in the shiny pages of the magazines she devours so avidly. And in mundane real life, in a melamine and chintz kitchen, she shimmers like a being beamed down from another and infinitely glitzier planet.

'Hello, Lorette,' said Teddy distractedly. 'How are you keeping?'

Teddy, you might be surprised to learn, had rather a soft spot for Lorette. Not just because she'd known her, off and on, since the girl was a ravishing cherub in rompers, but because, having not the remotest pretension to beauty herself, she took an uncomplicated pleasure in other people's. Looks such as Lorette's seemed a rare blessing from Heaven, like sunshine in February. The girl was a ninny, of course, head in the clouds with not a jot of common sense, but Teddy had been surrounded by air-headed ninnies all her life – look at Charlie, look at Pa – and thus had a high tolerance of brainlessness. Besides, there was no malice in the child, in general an admirably cheery little soul, even if she was now declaring herself halfway round the twist with boredom, swearing that a prolonged imprisonment in Langley-le-moronic-Moor would end up with her sticking her head in the gas oven.

'It's electric,' said her mother. 'Any road, what's keeping you here? Not me, for sure.'

'Where can I go when I'm completely skint? I keep telling

you, if my dad was here he wouldn't have given all that money to Brian and Colin.'

'And I keep telling you, if Stan was around, it'd still be stashed under his bloody bed and no one the wiser.'

'But—'

'But nothing. You know the answer. Shouldn't have left your husband.'

'Shouldn't never have married him, more like. And if you give me any more grief about trying again, I'll scream. Even Bill says it's too late now. Ask him.'

'He's not here. Anyway, Teddy doesn't want to hear this.'

'I just hope he's sorting out the house sale quick,' muttered Lorette, 'because I need my share right now.'

Her mother retorted she'd no right to demand any money at all from her poor husband, but Teddy paid no heed. Only now, having seen Mr Bill Smith with her own eyes, was the full enormity of the mismatch between him and Lorette sinking in on her. This foolish, pretty child had been chained for five years to that hairy, oafish thug. Good God, it was like Beauty and the Beast. King Kong and whatever the witless blonde was called. Her bubbling tide of indignation was stemmed only by Lorette's suddenly looking up from her fingernails with a merry giggle.

'Dead funny about you and Bill last night, by the way, weren't it? I bet you nearly died when he said he was only after renting the butcher's. You had anyone decent reply to your ad yet?'

Thus was it borne in upon Teddy that, not only was the whole Rowbotham clan acquainted with this splendid joke, but also – since Lorette kindly assured her that Brian, at least, had had a real go at the rest of them for laughing so much in the pub last night – most of the clientele of the Fox and Grapes. Which meant that very soon, if not already, the entire village would be chuckling over the news that Miss Theodora Dunstan was advertising herself in a dating column. She could no more squash the story than gather up the proverbial feathers. Moreover, Lorette assured her that Brian had said if only he'd known Miss Dunstan was feeling the need for male companionship—

'I am not,' she snapped.

'No, no one could be that desperate,' agreed Brian's sister cordially.

'I must go,' croaked Teddy.

Whereupon, to set the seal on everything as she hastily gathered up handbag and car key, she learned that the cause of her humiliation – that grinning gorilla, that King of all bloody Kongs – had, according to Lily's jubilant account, charmed the socks off Miss Connie Fletcher (Teddy could only assume her elderly neighbour was suffering from hitherto undiagnosed Alzheimer's), had negotiated a five-year lease on very favourable terms, and was set to move in as her next-door neighbour.

Not so much the final straw, more the entire bloody haystack.

Chapter Eight

You may well feel Teddy was making a fuss about nothing. After all, books, newspapers and magazines these days are awash with thirty-something spinsters bewailing their manless plight, only too keen to detail their ploys for trapping a mate. It's the new urban cliché, isn't it? The latest fashionable victim cult?

Not to Teddy's way of thinking, it isn't. She abhors the contemporary mania for airing private affairs in public. When the late sainted Princess cared to share her marital troubles with the world on telly, Teddy had to bury her head under the sofa cushions, choking with horror. She would no more bare her own soul than her breasts. And we must not forget she has already done the latter, very publicly, in the pages of a tabloid newspaper. Perhaps we must allow she has more justification than some for preferring to keep her private life private.

Shame there's no chance of her doing so, then. She is henceforward a marked woman in Langley. The Squire's sister is after a man.

'*Hergh* . . .' (Sir Charles Dunstan always preceded tricky utterances with this noise, a sort of throat-clearing operation, which, according to his sister, represented the sound of brain cells meshing into gear once the mouth was ajar.) '*Hergh*, good of you to drop by, old thing. Wanted a quiet word. Enough ton. in that gin?'

A couple of days after her unsettling call on the Rowbotham household, Teddy was back at the Hall in response to a plaintive summons from her brother. And yes, truly, on the very cusp of the twenty-first century, Charles Dunstan really did express himself in such *I-say-old-thing* P.G. Wodehousery, in a tenor voice that appeared to have been passed through a mangle. This walking anachronism, this one-man argument for the abolition of hereditary privilege, was clad that evening in the mossy tweeds, faded checks and balding cords one would expect, with Labradors sniffing round his highly polished brogues, and a hefty tumbler of whisky in his fist, as he sprawled in a venerably scuffed wing chair in the library of Langley Hall. In spite of a certain ruddiness the Scottish wine had lent to his complexion, and a slight thickening around the waistline incurred since quitting the army, Sir Charles was a not unattractive specimen. Tall and otherwise spare-framed, he was blessed with his mother's aquiline profile and superbly chiselled cheek bones, softened in his case by an air of sweet bewilderment in his pale blue eyes, inherited from his father. Even though his carroty hair, also inherited from Pa, was receding faster than was fair in a chap of forty-two, it would be a mean-spirited soul who did not concede that he still cut a handsome dash. Not even his most generous friends, however – and he was blessed with many – would describe him as one of nature's intellectuals. His affectionate regimental soubriquet had been 'Plank'. Thus the noble brow furrowed now as he continued: 'By the by, what's this cock-and-bull story Bella picked up about you and, *hergh*, some painter chap?'

'Exactly that. Cock and bull.' Teddy was irritated but unsurprised. Her sister-in-law had already telephoned after finding Maurice, the milkman, regaling Mrs Boardman, house-keeper at the Hall, with this choice titbit of village gossip.

'. . . but you mustn't worry, darling. I barged straight out of the back door to tell them they were talking nonsense – I mean, it is nonsense, isn't it? Yes, of course it is. Anyway, that's what I said to old Mouldy Milk and the Aga Queen. I was absolutely upfront, told them I had myself jokingly suggested dating columns to you, and that you were shocked to the jolly old core.'

'Thanks,' Teddy had said. 'Though I don't suppose it will do much good.'

'And that you wouldn't touch them with a bargepole, however desperate you were to settle down and make babies. Teddy? Teddy, is something the matter?'

'If that's all you wanted a word about,' she now informed her brother tersely, 'you can forget it. I can do without any more help from my family.'

Sir Charles blinked. 'Lord no. Couldn't make head nor tail of it.'

'Fine.'

'Doesn't sound your type at all, an artist. Long hair, I suppose?'

'Can we drop the subject? By the way, is Bella around? I'd better have a word about her blessed party.'

'Bella, birthday – yes,' said her brother. 'That's it. Hit the nail on the head.'

Teddy curbed her impatience with the ease of long practice. 'What nail?'

'Birthday pressie, fortieth and all that. Got to push the boat out. These, um, past couple of years haven't been easy for the old girl. One way and another. With, you know . . . *hergh* . . .'

'Mother.'

'*Hergh*. Quite. Reckon she deserves something splosh, and frankly I'm stumped. Any bright ideas?'

Even though her brother's eyes were the washed-out blue of a spring morning, they fixed on her with a pleading expression remarkably akin to that of the chocolate-orbed Labrador whose dribbling jowls were propped on her lap. 'Not a clue,' said Teddy, taking a swig of gin. 'Don't look so glum, I'll think. Plenty of time yet. Anyway, so long as you've got Ma packed off to Mill House, Bella'd be happy with a packet of bath salts.'

'More than Mother will,' sighed Sir Charles, swirling his whisky. 'Chap feels a bit of a heel, you know, shoving the ancient parent out on her ear.'

'You're a softy, Bro, always were. She twists you round her little finger. Stand up to her, man.'

'The removal wallahs are booked for a fortnight today. Once old Jez is safely home and settled in.'

'That's the ticket. I suppose you've thought about jewellery?'

'Sorry?'

'Birthday present.'

He looked aghast. 'Choose it myself?'

'Well—' Teddy had to abandon the topic, however, because Mungo the monkey scampered across the rug and bounded, screaming, onto the chimneypiece, which meant her sister-in-law couldn't be far behind. Sure enough, with a hoot of greeting, a kitten curled into the crook of her neck and a pot-bellied pig trotting on a lead, Bella cantered into the library. Her voluptuous form was vacuum-packed into shocking pink trousers and a low-cut white T-shirt, with a broad black belt yanked breathlessly tight around the waist.

'Darlings!' she cried, depositing the kitten in her husband's lap and shooing the piglet towards the fireplace. 'Don't look at me like that, Teddy, pigs are perfectly clean once they're house-trained, and Chalfont and I are working on that, aren't we, my pet? He's amazingly intelligent, you know, all pigs are.'

'Ow!' muttered her husband, sucking his thumb. 'Bloody cat scratched me.'

'This house,' observed Teddy acidly, 'gets more like a zoo every day.'

'Child substitutes,' responded her sister-in-law instantly. 'Now my babies are all growing taller than me, I need something to cuddle. As well as you, of course, my precious.' So saying she leaned low over her spouse to drop a kiss on his balding pate, thereby plunging his face into her cleavage.

'Steady on,' he gasped. 'Nearly choked on my Scotch.'

'Don't pretend, I know you're longing to ravish me on the spot, you gorgeous hunk. Oh stop, huffing and puffing, Teddy doesn't mind. Anyway, you're quite safe. I'm not here to rape and pillage, I want to know if you've discovered what she's up to.'

Charlie directed a puzzled look from wife to sister. 'Ted?'

'Your mother, dimbo. Trotting around upstairs with poor old Mrs Boardman and a hundred and fifty cardboard boxes.'

'Packing her bits and pieces, ready for the off?' he offered hopefully. 'Isn't she?'

'Ha!' cried his wife. 'That's what we're *supposed* to think. So tell me this. Why is she taking the Crown Derby?'

'The old green and yellow service?' said Teddy. 'Lord, you don't mind that, do you? It's hideous.'

'Exactly. She can't stand it, I know she can't. So why is Mrs Boardman wrapping it in newspaper at this very minute? And,' Bella swept on, 'two continental quilts were delivered from Harrods this afternoon, when you know she insists on sheets and blankets. No, Charlie, don't interrupt. She's been rootling around in those attics for days, collecting all sorts of oddments. Pictures, vases, you name it.'

'Saving money?' he suggested. '*Hergh*, Lord knows, we've spent enough kitting the place out already.'

'Your mother saving money? Don't make me laugh. She's up to something,' said Bella darkly, 'and it's your duty to find out what.'

Charlie's eyes rolled beseechingly towards his sister.

For all Teddy retorted that she'd more than enough on her plate already, and they could jolly well sort it out themselves, she would normally have felt duty-bound to initiate a few enquiries into the odd nature of Ma's attic gleanings. Not only because she was, as she would be quick to assure you, unutterably devoted to both brother and sister-in-law (in spite of their being total idiots), but also because she was acquainted of old with her parent's wiles. Over the following week, however she found herself preoccupied with the prospect of a house-removal closer to home. It soon became clear Mr Bill Smith intended to waste no time in taking up residence next door.

One might be pardoned for wondering what somebody calling himself an artist (Teddy was not actually acquainted with any artists, but she was sure none worth the knowing could possibly resemble Bill Smith) might want with an empty butcher's shop. She did not hesitate to ask Miss Connie Fletcher exactly this. And learned that Mr Smith intended to open a gallery, if you please. The lofty white-tiled space (reminiscent of nothing so much as a giant public lavatory, in her own view) was apparently tailor-made for the exhibiting of art. Which surely told one everything one needed to know about his sort of art. Formaldehyde cows would be quite at home. What was more, he had convinced Miss Fletcher that the former abattoir, so coveted by the Rowbotham boys, would convert into an ideal studio for him to create his masterpieces.

Frankly, Teddy was disappointed in Miss Fletcher. Had they not often bewailed together the way real shops were vanishing from rural communities, chased away like red squirrels by the voracious grey tree-rats of the tourist grot emporia? Her neighbour had stood firm before now in saving her premises from just such a fate, had even refused to allow Brian and Colin Rowbotham to install their electrical business, which, while not a shop exactly, supplied services a damn sight more useful than the lumpy pots and stinky candles stocked by your average so-called gallery. What on earth had made her cave in to Bill Smith, who wasn't even a local?

Possibly a little taken aback by the ferocity of her neighbour's indignation, Miss Fletcher replied that she had not sold out, only granted Mr Smith a lease. But he seemed such a good-hearted, friendly sort of gentleman, you couldn't help but warm to him . . .

'Wotcher, Duchess,' bellowed the good-hearted, friendly gent, as he swung himself down from the cab of a hired van, parked slap-bang across her shop frontage. 'Found your Mr Right yet?'

Chapter Nine

'Can we get one thing absolutely straight?' growled Teddy, marching up to the door of the van. 'I only ever mentioned lonely hearts columns because I thought you were taking part in a practical joke—'

'Cool it, babe,' he murmured, grinning encouragingly. 'Nothing to be ashamed of.'

'—dreamed up by my sister-in-law, Bella Dunstan, which was foolish of me, I grant.'

He jumped down to the tarmac with a heavy thud. 'Everyone's at it nowadays, by all accounts.'

'Are you listening?' she squawked furiously. 'I did not place any such advertisement. And what's more, I never, ever, not in a million light years, would. Is that clear?'

'Oh,' he said. And eyed her warily, rather as a bull mastiff might survey a particularly yappy Yorkshire terrier, aware that a substantial size advantage is no defence against a nasty nip on the nose. 'Yeah, well, probably wise. Always struck me as a dodgy way of getting yourself a fu—' He cleared his throat. '*Friend*. Look, not in your way here, am I? Only I don't fancy manoeuvring this bugger down the alley.'

Then and throughout the remainder of the day, Teddy judged it preferable to preserve a dignified silence. She did not complain about the vehicle blocking her shop frontage. She ignored Mr Smith's occasional smiles and nods as he squeezed his bulky form past her window while unloading, and did her best to repel friendly overtures.

'Look, we seem to have got off on the wrong foot,' he ventured, when she was unwise enough to emerge into the rear courtyard and found him squatting on an upturned wooden box, with a can of beer in one hand and a cigarette in the other. 'Bit of a misunderstanding, I realize that now.'

'Shame everyone else doesn't,' said Teddy tightly. 'Since I gather you all had a jolly good laugh about it in the pub.'

'What? Oh . . .' He shrugged sheepishly. 'Look, I'm sorry, OK? It just seemed so funny, you and . . . I mean, if only I'd realized from the start you was this Teddy Lil's always going on about – she thinks the world of you, you know.'

'She speaks very highly of you, too,' hissed Teddy in tones that suggested this devalued the compliment to vanishing point.

'I can see why you got so mad, thinking I was just trying to wind you up. And,' he continued placatingly, 'why you're a bit paranoid about gossip after what you've been through.'

Teddy's glare would have stripped paint. 'I beg your pardon?'

A lesser man might have been deterred. But Mr Smith ploughed stoically on. 'You know, that run-in you had with the pillock in the Union Jack drawers?'

There was no immediate escape route. Teddy was holding a bulging rubbish bag and the route to the bins lay directly past him. 'If,' she said, stepping carefully over his outstretched boot and striding on, 'you are referring to my former employer, I prefer to believe most people have forgotten that unfortunate episode.'

'Yes,' he said, gulping, 'I mean, no. I mean, I'm sure they have. I had, totally. Lil reminded me, but it never crossed my mind when I saw you on the doorstep, honest . . .' A faint chuckle, however, was bubbling irrepressibly. 'First time in my life I could honestly say I didn't recognize someone with their clothes on.' Catching Teddy's eye he converted the laugh into a cough. 'I shouldn't worry about it. No one remembers the garbage they print in the papers, and you can't believe a word, can you? I mean, that bit about the banana . . .'

There was a bang as the kitchen door shut behind her.

Bill Smith blinked and chucked away his fag. 'Well, don't say I didn't try.'

Teddy took a perverse satisfaction in monitoring the shifting piles of furniture outside her shop window: a motley cocktail of junk-shop pine and curly chrome modern. Not a single decent piece, of course. She also began to notice that amongst the smaller items – boxes, black plastic sacks, potted plants – there was a marked absence of pictures. This was surely surprising in anyone claiming to be an artist. Not one canvas did she spot. Perhaps the odd specimen slipped through while she was in her kitchen, but she chose to doubt it, largely because she had never believed this thug could be a painter – she could as soon believe he was a ballet dancer – and she had his own brother-in-law's testimony that he had produced nothing since marrying Lorette. And while would-be actors could argue that no one was offering them work, painters had no such excuse. A painter could pick up his brush at any old time, in any old corner. By the end of the day her suspicion that her new neighbour was not so much an artist as a thoroughgoing con artist had been confirmed. How? Because his own children told her as much.

Teddy might be keeping a frigid distance between herself and Mr Smith, but she could not apply the same policy to Florence and Ferdinand who tumbled into her shop squealing with pleasure and a request for toffee-crunch ice cream from Ferdy, along with dignified apologies for her brother's rudeness from little Florence. Teddy, of course, had become well acquainted with the twins over the past two years in the course of their regular visits to Lily, and found them a most delightful pair – surprisingly delightful, considering they were the grandchildren of the late and unlamented Stan, buds off the same tree that had produced such uninspiring specimens as Brian and Colin. Having now met their father, she was inclined to think, as they clustered beaming up to her counter, that their flourishing health and happiness were little short of miraculous.

'No, Ferdy,' said his sister, hauling him away from a pyramid of Chardonnay bottles.

'Gerroff,' said Ferdy, and fixed a gap-toothed grin on Teddy. 'Do you want to see my dog?'

'I believe I already have,' said Teddy, who had indeed observed a shaggy cur prancing around the side of the removal van. Ignoring the bellows of Mr Bill Smith, it had made a near-suicidal dive into the path of a tractor, before he managed to bundle the creature indoors. At the time she had remarked to Beryl that people shouldn't be allowed to keep dogs if they were incapable of controlling them, but, confronted with Ferdy's glowing face, she felt obliged to say she was sure it was a most agreeable animal.

'It's a she, and she's called Birdie,' stated Ferdy. 'Dad said she's a lia-fucking-bility, but,' he continued, happily oblivious of Teddy's face and Beryl's stifled gasp, 'she's a sort of spaniel actually. She'd like it in here.'

'Dogs aren't allowed in shops,' said his sister, bestowing upon Teddy a confiding aren't-boys-silly? grimace.

Florence was an admirably sensible child. Teddy had remarked this long since, when, on a visit to the shop with their grandmother, she had calmly extracted a glinting cleaver from her twin's clutches and restored it to the counter before anyone else had noticed what that cherubically beautiful little fiend was up to. The two were not in the least alike. Where Ferdinand was a Titian-haired, turquoise-eyed, gazelle-limbed replica of his mother – and every bit as feather-brained – Florence had inherited what Teddy now recognized as her father's build and colouring, poor mite, being dark, square-faced and stocky. No one could fail to be charmed by young Ferdy, Teddy included, but being herself a plain female cursed with handsomely witless brothers, she felt a fellow-sympathy for his commonsensical sister.

Thus, declaring their father was doubtless too busy to feed them, she ushered the neglected infants into her kitchen, perched them on stools and plied them with ice-cream sundaes and Coca-Cola. Not that she was remotely interested in what they had to tell her about their home-life, not at all. She simply let them chatter, as she chopped and mixed and seasoned a terrine, and was not wholly surprised to learn that Dad didn't do anything, really, just mucked around the house all day. According to his son.

'Mum's always going on about it,' he added, mouth dripping with ice cream. ''Swhy we've got no money.'

'Only because he's too busy looking after us,' excused his daughter, with touching loyalty.

'Nonsense, he must do something,' said Teddy. 'He, ah, paints, doesn't he?'

'Everywhere,' said Florence, with pride. 'He did my room yellow and green with a big lion over the bed.'

'He draws good monsters,' conceded his son, adding in a startling non sequitur: 'They came and took the big telly last week in a van, and the video. Dad was dead mad.'

It only needed Beryl to offer, in a whisper with many a sympathetic glance towards the children, that she'd heard the Smiths' house in Huddlestone had been sold within a hair's breadth of repossession, for Teddy to deduce conditions of Hogarthian depravity. Visualizing the gorilla slumped in a drunken stupor under the kitchen table – because, as became ever clearer, the notion of a father going out to work was quite outside the twins' comprehension – she simultaneously thanked Heaven they were escaping such a slum, while blaming their feckless papa for depriving them of it. Likewise, while believing the loss of such a resident role model could only prove a blessing to impressionable infants, she did not hesitate to condemn him for exposing them to all the well-documented evils of a single-parent upbringing. That they spoke about the impending divorce with unruffled composure only illustrated how little the poor mites understood their plight. She was even reluctant to assume Bill Smith had moved to Langley in order to stay close to his children, because Lorette had made clear she intended to move on as soon as he supplied her with the means to do so. Far more likely, having lost home and most possessions worth the repossessing, he was here to sponge on his long-suffering mother-in-law. By the time Bill Smith trudged across the courtyard to stick his head round her kitchen door, she would not have been surprised if that head had sprouted horns.

'Come on, brats,' he said. 'Your mum's showed up.'

The swift grimace of dismay between the twins – obviously prompted by their father's appearance – confirmed everything for Teddy. She replied to his thanks for looking after them with stony politeness.

He gave what he presumably imagined was a grin of sympathy. 'They been driving you up the wall?'

'They have behaved charmingly,' she stated. 'As always.' At which moment, the putative spaniel bounded through the open door, skidded along the polished floor into a crate of milk bottles, and bounced high into the air yelping joyously.

'Christ's sake,' groaned its owner, shutting his eyes.

'*Down, sir!*' roared Teddy. The animal juddered to a halt at her feet, and flopped on its belly, panting.

'Bloody Nora,' breathed Bill Smith. 'She never does that for me.'

It got worse.

Late into the evening, bangs and thuds continued from next door. These Teddy could tolerate – moving house entailed noise. What she found less acceptable was the accompanying counterpoint of enraged human voices. To be *perfectly* fair, the raised voice most in evidence was female. But it is well known high voices carry more penetratingly than low. And she was left in no doubt by his wife that Bill Smith was a selfish monster, that he'd been a complete let-down as a husband, from start to finish, that Lorette didn't know why she'd ever married him – there was a particularly long bass rumble at this point – followed by a scream that she never flaming would've done if she'd known they'd end up like this. The nub of the dispute, Teddy gathered, was the division of marital assets. Outrageous as it seemed, not to say illegal, Bill Smith had evidently told his wife she would not be receiving a penny from him. With two children to rear single-handed? Teddy was strongly tempted to march round and ask him if he had ever heard of the Child Support Agency. The only point on which she had to agree with him, albeit reluctantly, was when, in one of his few audible exchanges, he suggested they think of the bloody kids, and keep their voices down.

And, just in case you should be imagining otherwise, Teddy was *not* eavesdropping. That she heard so much of what was going on next door was not, believe her, from choice. She was trapped in her kitchen preparing a finger buffet for a civic reception the following lunchtime and could not help but overhear. She tried shutting door and windows to block out the noise, but the kitchen soon became unbearably sultry. Having thrown them open again, she clearly heard a gasp of sobbing – Lorette, poor girl – and even more clearly Bill Smith's enraged snarl that he could throttle her sometimes, so help him, he would happily swing for—

Teddy's telephone rang. Seizing it, she hurried through to the shop to escape this distressingly audible Grand Guignol. Only to be confronted with yet more sobs down the telephone line. Sobs so thick and choking she couldn't immediately identify the caller and, indeed, for one alarming instant, thought it was Lorette phoning from next door. With a last, desperate appeal for help, as her husband's hairy fists tightened around her slim throat . . .

But Teddy was not fanciful. 'Who's that?'

There was a gasp. 'I can't – oh Teddy, I can't bear it.'

'*Bella!* Heavens, what's up?'

'Sorry.' A shuddering wail of anguish. 'Sorry.'

Terror clamped Teddy's fingers to the receiver. 'Not Charlie?' She could hardly get the words out. 'One of the children? They're all home from school now, aren't they? Pity's sake, tell me.'

'It's – it's her. Your *bloody* mother.'

Not merely did her fingers slacken, Teddy's whole body slumped against the wall in relief. Not that she didn't love her mother. Naturally she did. As one does. But Bella wouldn't be hysterical if there were anything amiss with Ma – quite the contrary – so, wedging the phone under her chin, she returned to the kitchen to resume her labours, and invited her sister-in-law to spill the beans. This Bella was unable to do immediately, and since there was real distress in her sobbing, Teddy did not chivvy her, just emitted occasional clucks of sympathy as she carried on gutting tomatoes. Meanwhile the shouting next door was gathering fresh volume. At least, she reflected, this indicated her neighbours were both still alive and kicking, but what with their din in one ear and Bella in t'other, she was beginning to feel she was the only sane soul left in a world run mad.

''S Charlie's fault, much as hers,' Bella gasped at length. 'She knows she can get away with anything. He's hopeless – useless.'

'By and large,' said his devoted sister, and yelped as something crashed against the wall. 'Sorry, go on, only the idiots next door.'

'He'll never stand up to her.'

'For a chap with medals for bravery, he is the most snivelling coward,' Teddy agreed, prodding an aromatically garlicky mixture into a tomato shell. 'Mind, I still say he only crossed that minefield because he can't read maps.'

If this was an attempt to lighten the mood, it was ill judged. 'This is *serious*,' wailed Bella, her voice rising. 'I won't put up with it. I'll – I'll – oh God, I don't know what I'll do. She won't be happy until she's broken us up.'

'Oh, I don't think so,' said Teddy fair-mindedly. 'I don't think she's got anything against you, *per se* – well, except for believing no woman could be good enough for her son, but isn't that mothers-in-law the world over? Oh, and I don't suppose it helps these days hearing people talk about the ravishing Lady Dunstan, and realizing they aren't talking about her.'

But even this blatant appeal to Bella's vanity failed to elicit more than a further burst of choking.

'It's the Hall, that's all,' continued Teddy briskly. 'She's mad as all hell about giving up her house. Simple as that.'

'Exactly,' wailed her sister-in-law, 'and if I leave Charlie, she'll get the beastly place all to herself again, and – and—'

'Calm down. Keep reminding yourself she's off to Mill House soon.'

Bella's voice rose to a shriek. 'But she *isn't*. That's what I'm telling you. And all *bloody* Charlie says is, it's her *bloody* house and he can't stop her installing anyone she wants . . .' The sentence disintegrated into desolate tears. 'What's the use? 'Stoo late. You can't do anything about it. No one can.' And with that, the line was dead.

Teddy licked a smear of stuffing off her wrist and studied the phone thoughtfully. Conscience and family duty warred with three pounds of unstuffed tomatoes and four dozen anchovy puffs. Conscience, inevitably, won.

Minutes later, she was hurrying out to her van, checked only by a startling vision in the neighbouring window of Mr Bill Smith waving a large pair of scissors in one upraised fist. Pausing just long enough to ascertain that his intended target appeared to be a credit card, rather than his wife, who was dancing around him, trying, unavailingly, to reach the shears, Teddy clambered into the driving seat, reasoning with herself as she drove at reckless speed up to the Hall that, fond as she was of Lorette, she could only referee one marital battle at a time. Storming into the house, she informed her brother, who was closeted with a whisky bottle in the library, that he seemed to have been behaving even more idiotically than usual. Then she stuck her head round the door of the family sitting room to find a leggy tangle of nephews, niece and dogs sprawled across floor and sofa, engrossed in a gore-splattered movie on the television.

'Pay attention, you square-eyed vultures,' she barked, adding, as they surged towards her in a noisy mêlée of youthful enthusiasm, canine hysteria and frog-voiced teenage cool, 'hush, hush, we'll have to save the big welcome home number for later, I'm on a peace mission. Gosh, Jake, haven't you grown again this term? Hello, Pelly darling, Ben . . . Yes, sweetie, you can tell me all about the new pony later. Look, anyone know where your mother is?'

While his elders shrugged and capsized back onto their sofa, Teddy's youngest nephew, Harry, a curly-mopped urchin of nine, informed her with the weary stoicism of a trench-hardened veteran that Mummy had slammed off upstairs. Again.

'They don't mean it,' offered Jake kindly, a handsome youth of fifteen, with his mother's brilliant eyes and a modicum more sense than could have been hoped for, given his parentage. 'Only their way of communicating.'

'Doubtless,' hissed Teddy. 'I just wish they wouldn't use me as medium. Oh well, here goes. See you chaps later.'

Finally, having bawled up the magnificently carved stairway

to Bella that she was to keep her chin up, Teddy marched along the marble-tiled hall and flung open the doors to the Gold Drawing Room.

'Mother,' she cried, 'what in God's name have you been up to this time?'

Chapter Ten

Teddy, of course, is familiar with her surroundings and, besides, has pressing business with her mother, but we first-time visitors may well fail even to notice the diminutive figure of the dowager as we marvel at the splendours surrounding her.

It has, after all, been widely agreed for years in those shiny publications dedicated to the decorative arts that Evelyn, Lady Dunstan, has wrought miracles at Langley Hall, with the Gold Drawing Room representing arguably her greatest triumph. That plasterwork, those mirrored sconces, the cascading hangings around the windows: breathtaking, are they not?

When she married Sir Theodore, his enchantingly proportioned home had been neglected by generations of chatelaines more interested in dogs and do-gooding than pilasters and paintings, and although the new Lady Dunstan embarked on her campaign of restoration with zest, it is surely monstrous to suggest – as some mean-spirited souls have been known to do – that this talented decorator was marrying a house with husband attached, rather than the more customary reverse. Likewise, while it is undoubtedly true that the Dunstan coffers have been depleted by her labours – how could it be otherwise? – and beyond dispute that the silk damask lining this very chamber was woven to her express direction in France (by nuns) it is scandalously unfair to claim that this alone necessitated the sale of two farms. Only one tumbledown farmhouse with adjacent tied cottage went under the hammer, and who, admiring the incomparable sheen of these walls, could dispute the proceeds were wisely invested? Who, also, could fail to sympathize with

Lady Dunstan's stubborn reluctance to quit her magnificent creation?

Still, we are not here to admire the furnishings any more than Teddy is. Moreover, Evelyn, Lady Dunstan, in a grey dress of superbly simple cut, with hair coiled into a chignon as fine as spun sugar, is quite as worthy of note as her surroundings. Although she is recognizably Teddy's mother – the small stature, the aquiline nose, the bright blue eyes being common to both – Teddy is more her father's sturdy daughter, while there is a fragility about her ladyship's tiny person which borders on the ethereal. Age has withered the alabaster complexion a trifle – although the effects have been mitigated by the discreet scalpel of a very good man in Harley Street – but the bone structure endures triumphant. You may well be charmed by this fairy-like little old lady – people are – but, as storybooks show, it pays to be wary of fairies.

When Teddy burst into the room that evening, she was seated on a spindly-legged sofa with the upright poise of one taught to curtsey balancing a Bible on her head. There was a thimble-sized cup of coffee at her elbow, and *The Times* crossword open upon her lap. Propelling pencil in hand, she looked up and surveyed her daughter thoughtfully.

'Darling, I don't think you should wear that shade of green. It does so accentuate a high complexion.'

'If I'm red in the face that's because I've driven up here like what's-his-name Schumacher,' retorted Teddy. 'And that's because Bella phoned, in such hysterical floods of tears, I couldn't make head nor tail of what she was saying.'

'Can one ever?'

'Although I'm sure she's got the wrong end of the stick this time.' She eyed her mother sternly. 'She seems to think you're lending Mill House to someone.'

'Lending my delicious Petit Trianon?' The dowager's laughter tinkled innocent as a carillon of silver bells. 'Heavens, the girl must be mad.'

'Well, quite,' agreed Teddy, but she was not reassured.

Possibly this was because such blithe good humour in her mother invariably seemed to coincide with corresponding levels of misery in those around her. Not that, in the general way, Lady

Dunstan actively wished ill upon anyone. On the contrary, her failing was that she scarcely seemed to be aware of other people at all. Think Tinkerbell – think Titania even. Your typical fairy is a charming creature, but egocentric to a degree undreamed of by we ordinary mortals. She is not simply selfish, she is honestly and sublimely blind to the interests of anyone other than her adorable self. 'I want,' runs her amoral creed, '*ergo* it must be right.' Grasp that, and you have the measure of Evelyn, Lady Dunstan.

Such a feat of character analysis is, of course, beyond her elder son, and her younger – imminently due to return from California – is too much like her to worry his pretty head about such things. Her daughter, though, understands her well, and much though Teddy deplores the modern passion for psycho-babble and still more the habit of blaming every defect from peanut allergy to a penchant for mass murder on faulty upbringing, she is prepared to concede Ma's early life has much to answer for. After all, as she briskly puts it, if you've been Queen Bee for sixty-odd years, from petted popsy-in-the-cradle infancy to celebrated diva-of-the-dinner-table maturity, via a belle-of-every-ball débutancy, it's hardly surprising that you end up with the totty-headed notion that the rest of the swarm exists only to buzz around your lovely self.

Even so, she was never able quite to abandon the notion that her parent, like a spoiled toddler or ill-disciplined dog, should be trainable to heel by firm and fair handling. Thus she eyed her mother austerely.

'Of course, we all appreciate it's a wrench for you, uprooting from this house. But when all's said and done, Pa's been gone for more than two years now, and Charlie and Bella have got to take over some time. They need to make the place their own.'

'To turn it into a zoo?' enquired Lady Dunstan, with a shade less good humour.

'There'll be no monkeys or pigs to worry you at Mill House.'

'And barely space to swing a cat.'

'Three bed, two bath and a jolly decent drawing room now you've knocked through into the old kennels. Be fair, Ma, Charlie's let you fritter an absolute packet titivating the place.'

'I'm afraid the bills do seem to have escalated out of all proportion to the size of the property,' conceded Lady Dunstan. 'Still, I flatter myself the end result is quite a success.'

'Gorgeous.'

'In its own little way.'

'And ready for you to move in.'

Her mother's eyes opened very wide. 'But darling, no. That's the whole point.'

'But you said—'

'Heavens, I wouldn't dream of simply lending the place to anyone, not after spending so much. I assure you, it's been worrying me terribly. No, I realized it was my duty to recoup some of poor Charles's investment for him, and I had the cleverest idea.'

Teddy would have said that nothing her mother did could ever surprise her. She found she was wrong. 'Ma, what are you saying?'

'Why, darling, that I've let it.'

'You've *what*?'

'To a hairdresser from London. Isn't that hysterical? As a weekend retreat, one gathers. I didn't actually meet the chap when he came up to view, naturally. Once I'd placed the advertisement I left all the business side to the agent, and I must say he negotiated a very handsome sum for the year. I understand my tenant takes possession tomorrow.'

'Tell me I'm not hearing this. You've signed away Mill House for a year, and you're intending to stay on here with Charlie and Bella?'

'One must be prepared to make sacrifices for one's children, and although a single year's rent will by no means cover our costs, every little helps. Besides which,' Lady Dunstan continued with a sigh, 'I fear marriage is no longer the sacred bond it was for my generation. Who can say what may have changed here at the Hall in twelve months' time?'

It was well past midnight when Teddy trudged up the stairs to her own bedroom. She had failed to lure Bella out of hers at the Hall. Bella had bawled through an implacably locked door that she was not going to be reasoned with, that she intended to get her own back, in her own way, and she would be grateful if Teddy could tell her *bloody* brother that he could sleep where he liked, but if he tried stepping over the threshold of the marital chamber he was a dead man. Teddy, in fact, had a great deal more she wished to impart to her brother, but since he had already soaked up most of a bottle of whisky, she merely informed him that drastic action was required and commanded him to report to her shop for a discussion of tactics at noon sharp, the following day.

Only after she had returned to stuffing tomatoes at home did she realize she would be out serving the damned things at noon on the morrow. Sticking a Post-it reminder on the microwave to call in on Charlie in the morning *en route* to her buffet, she resumed her labours and told herself to keep things in perspective. This row between Bella and Charlie would blow over, just like all the others. Absurd even to think about divorce. It was only because she was so tired that she found herself fretting over quite how *resolute* Bella had sounded, how uncharacteristically unbending . . . Nonsense. She must finish these tomatoes, and get on with the salmon.

At least her kitchen was now quiet. Not that the gorilla next door had retired to his roost – lights were still blazing from the uncurtained windows, and there was the odd thump and creak as of furniture being shifted – but the battle seemed to be over. Obviously Lorette had taken herself and children back to Lily's, and a good thing too, poor babies. It was undoubtedly only weariness combined with the sultry summer night which, by the time Teddy stuck her last greasy fork in the dishwasher, was beginning to make the silence feel . . . unnatural.

Reaching her bedroom and kicking off her shoes, she padded over to yank open her window – Lord, this weather was stifling – and then she paused. There was movement in the yard below.

Across the cobbles loomed the gloomy shape of the old abattoir. It was the double doors to this that the gorilla was now, after much clanking with keys and rusting padlocks, heaving open. The yard was stygian, but there was no mistaking his bulky silhouette. Nor, had there been any lingering doubt, his whispered obscenity as the door shrieked open. A very odd hour to be inspecting his supposed studio, in Teddy's opinion, particularly since the outhouse, far from being empty, was a repository for generations of household junk and did not, to her knowledge, possess a working power supply. She was not surprised to see him immediately re-emerge and lumber back to his kitchen. Leaving the doors swinging open, she noted.

Having ascertained that it was not a prowler on the property, she would have retreated from the window and switched on her bedside lamp, had she not observed him hauling something out from the inky shadows below across to the abattoir. Something very large and very long – at least, as far as she could see. The thing was shrouded in black plastic, evidently, because slivers of moonlight suddenly glanced off its surface as a breath of wind made the wrapping billow. He was certainly handling his burden with slow, grunting care. But the next minute he – and it – had disappeared into the outhouse. What was more, he hauled the doors shut behind him. Yellow light, as of a torch, percolated dimly through a grimy window.

Nothing remarkable about this, one might think. No doubt some piece of household rubbish – some particularly *large* piece of household rubbish – he wished to add to the existing dump. So one would expect him to reappear more or less immediately. He did not. Teddy was not going to hang around by the window. She repaired to the bathroom, sluiced her face and brushed her teeth. When she returned, some instinct impelled her still to desist from flipping on the lamp by her bed. Instead, she tiptoed across to peep round the curtain again. The dull light still glimmered behind the filthy glass of the outhouse window. And distinct sounds of heavy objects being shifted reached her ears. A screech of metal on concrete, a clang, another curse. Finally, when he must have been in there a full fifteen minutes, the torch beam and Mr Bill Smith emerged into the yard.

'And as far as I'm concerned,' he declared, every word damningly audible, 'you can stay buried under there until you bloody well rot.'

Whereupon, snapping off the torch and clapping his hands together, as if to remove some lingering dirt or stain, he stumped back into his house.

Chapter Eleven

Teddy, as has been said, was not a fanciful woman. Not remotely. Other people might be tempted into all manner of lurid conjectures after witnessing this scene; Teddy well knew that bodies were buried only in the pages of detective fiction. However, when Ferdinand informed her, in a thrilled whisper, that Dad had hidden Mum in the shed, she did experience just the *faintest* twinge of anxiety.

This was the following morning. She was loading the chilled boxes and crates containing the civic buffet into the back of her van. Having supposed the children would have returned to Lily's with their mother the previous night, she was mildly surprised by Ferdy's gambolling out into the yard with the dog – and considerably more so by this confidential disclosure.

'Your papa has *what*?' she exclaimed, glancing round, sure she had misheard.

'Ferdy!' hissed Florence, following hard on her brother's heels. 'Dad told you it's secret.'

But as Teddy was swift to assure herself, no one ever murdered his wife, informed his five-year-old children where he'd buried the body, and swore them to secrecy. She smiled brightly. 'So where is Mummy this morning?'

The boy shrugged and tossed a stick for his cavorting dog.

'Nanna's?' offered Florence. 'Come on, Ferdy. Dad's got breakfast.'

Naturally Lorette was at her mother's. And why should she not leave the children overnight with their father? Teddy had no intention of allowing her imagination to run riot.

'You won't tell anyone what Ferdy said, will you?' whispered sturdy, *sensible* Florence, after shooing him into the house. 'He's useless at secrets.'

Lily Rowbotham was a little startled to receive a flying visit from her employer just as she was lighting her post-breakfast fag. Moreover, it was clear to her from the moment Teddy hurried in that the lass had her knickers in a twist about something – and not just this birthday dinner of her sister-in-law's neither, for all she gabbled on about having forgotten, the last time she called, to ask if Lily would be fit for work by then. And why, when that was settled, she wanted to know whether Lorette was home was anybody's guess.

'I were out at the bingo last night, so I've not clapped eyes on her since, oh, yesterday afternoon,' declared her mother comfortably. 'Still in bed, I shouldn't wonder, lazy little bugger. She was going round to Bill's, that I do know. Settling in all right, is he?'

Teddy's brilliant flush puzzled Lily still further. And she began blathering on about the extraordinarily fertile imaginations of young children, even while complaining how run off her feet she was, because she had to call in at the Hall before she could deliver her buffet, and – Heaven help her – she'd another lunch party tomorrow. The charity ladies at Thorpeness Grange again, did Lily remember them? Pernickety diamond-studded coven?

'I'd give you a hand if I could,' began Lily, distressed. 'The back's a lot better, whatever that old nanny of a doctor says, but tomorrow I've promised the twins—'

'No, no,' interrupted Teddy, looking most peculiar, 'I wasn't hinting, truly. It's just, well, if you happen to see Lorette . . .'

'Bit hard to miss her in a house this size.'

'Of course, yes, silly of me.'

'Something you wanted to tell her?'

'Oh . . . doesn't matter. Another time will do. Must dash.'

★　　★　　★

'Good of you to call.' Bella responded to Teddy's appearance with regal dignity. For once – following what anyone would agree was extreme provocation last night – Bella Dunstan would like it known she was not in the least hung over. What was more, even though it was barely nine-thirty, she was fully dressed, immaculately made-up and sitting at her desk, pen in hand.

'Actually,' said Teddy, pecking the air beside her distractedly, 'it's Charlie I'm after. He about?'

Bella's face froze. 'I have no idea. You might try the library floor. I understand from Mrs Boardman he spent the night there.'

'Already looked. Place stank like a distillery. Oh damn, is that his car going down the drive?'

'Just don't ask me to take a message.' Bella was turning back to her desk when a thought stopped her. 'Actually, I'm glad you dropped by, it will save me a phone call. I wanted to ask about that printer chap you use for leaflets and so forth.'

'This is for your benefit, Bella. I told Charlie to come round today so we could discuss this Mill House fiasco.'

'Too late. And quite unnecessary now.'

'Unnecessary?'

'I shall be making Charles *very* sorry. Also, I shall quite probably be leaving him. After my birthday party.'

'Look, I understand how you feel but—'

'No one can understand how I feel.'

'Lumme, I haven't the time for high drama. Look, can you just give me a piece of paper? I'll leave a note for him.'

'Not that.' Bella snatched back the sheet. 'That's my list. Will he do it the same day?'

'Who?' Teddy nibbled her pencil. 'Tomorrow instead for Charlie? Hell, no, the charity ladies. Thursday?'

'Your printers.'

'What? Oh, if you twist Ernie's arm, why?'

'Nothing in particular.'

'I warn you he stops for his dinner at twelve on the dot, so catch him early.' She scribbled rapidly. Then paused. Glanced at her sister-in-law who had returned to her own writing. 'What is it they say? Ninety per cent of murders are committed by members of the family?'

'I shouldn't be in the least surprised.'

'And one imagines most of those are between . . . husband and wife.'

'Believe me,' said Bella, 'I nearly added to the statistics last night.'

'Not really. I mean, one *says* that kind of thing. I do myself. But nobody – nobody one knows – would ever actually, so to speak, act on it. Obviously.'

'If I do, I expect you to appear as character witness, to explain I suffered provocation beyond bearing.' Bella eyed her sister-in-law rather pointedly. 'But I'm sure you didn't call in to discuss murder statistics. Was there anything else? Only I'm fearfully busy and if I'm to catch your friend Ernie before noon . . .'

'Oh, I've asked Lily, and she says she'll run the kitchen for your thrash, thank goodness. Have you invited the vicar yet?'

Bella promptly scribbled a note. 'It shall be done.'

'And we should talk menus, only I really must be moving.'

'Don't give it a thought.' Her smile was sphinx-like. 'Plans for my party are moving on apace.'

It says everything for Teddy's distracted state of mind that she did not question this interesting pronouncement.

A day's industrious labour, however, helped to put the previous night's events into perspective. It's hard to entertain suspicions of buried corpses when stacking hot curry balls onto silver salvers, tucking dill fronds under smoked salmon boatlets, and desperately puffing water vapour over fast-desiccating sandwiches. Teddy felt pretty desiccated herself by the time she drove home, late that afternoon, her van now rattling with empty crates, greasy dishes and cress-spattered trays. All was empty and still as she manoeuvred the vehicle round to her side of the yard. Only one sound assailed her ears as she climbed out: a dog was howling. Not just any dog. The Smiths' dog. And the sound was coming from the abattoir.

Teddy glared at her neighbour's kitchen door. How typical of him just to leave an animal to fret. She bustled into her own premises. Everything was fine, said Beryl. A Mrs Hawkyard had telephoned, and there were one or two other messages. As she rattled through them, Teddy trotted to and fro, offloading equipment and stacking the dishwasher, while the dog continued to howl.

'Been doing that for ages,' commented Beryl. 'Enough to give you the screaming hab-dabs.'

'Why don't they see to it, then? The poor beast's probably dying of thirst in this heat.'

'Out. They all went off in his creaky old car, oh, best part of an hour ago.'

Teddy put down the plastic tray she was holding. 'All of them?'

'Bill, isn't he called? And the twins.'

'Not Lorette?'

Beryl blinked. 'Haven't seen her since yesterday. The kids have been in once or twice looking for you, little beggars.'

'Ah,' said Teddy. 'Ah . . . Perhaps I'll just go and check if that dog is all right.'

'Watch yourself. Sounds quite savage to me.'

The savage beast flung itself at Teddy with passionate delight as she nudged open the door of the outhouse, and cavorted round her legs as though being rescued from years of miserable incarceration. As a matter of fact, Teddy could not but note there was a comfortably upholstered dog basket installed under the window, together with a variety of well-chewed toys and a large bowl of water. Nor was the temperature in here stifling. The stone walls held a refreshing chill.

'So what's all the fuss about?' she said, fondling the dog's ears absent-mindedly and glancing round. It was a big room, but choked with junk. Old bedsteads, a defunct radiogram, lengths of planking, the rusting hulk of a car engine, broken chairs: here was the lumber of a lifetime, looking as though it had lain undisturbed for decades. Except in the far corner.

The tramways in the dust over there were clearly visible,

even though a muddy tarpaulin seemed to have been spread specifically to conceal them. With an air of nonchalant disinterest, Teddy strolled across. This panelled door and mossy mattress had been freshly stacked. She was no detective, but anyone could see the dirty tidemark where they had previously rested against the wall. Now they fell a clear foot short, propped out at an angle, creating a large gap behind. A gap in which something quite sizeable could be hidden. Something wrapped in shiny black plastic which, by the oddest coincidence, she could see glinting down there.

All at once, the spaniel snaked past her legs and plunged into the hole, tail wagging wildly.

'Idiot,' she cried. 'You might get trapped.'

But the dog continued to squirm determinedly behind the foully stinking mattress – Lord, was it only the mattress which was stinking? – until Teddy managed to grab its flanks and yank it backwards. As she did so, the dog's claws caught in the black polythene and ripped it across, while she herself stumbled against the mattress which wobbled, buckled and flopped into the surrounding junk with an almighty crash. And Teddy found herself staring down at a tangle of Titian hair, a gaping expanse of pearly pink flesh, and a pair of dazzling turquoise eyes – which were smiling right back into hers.

'What the bloody hell's going on in here?' roared a voice from the doorway. 'This is private property.'

For an instant, Teddy thought she might faint, something she had never done in her life. But then, never in her life had she uncovered a naked corpse. Of course, within the same split second, and feeling unutterably foolish, she had recognized that the said corpse was no more than a painting, if a disconcertingly life-sized and life-like painting, by which time its owner – even, conceivably, its creator – had arrived, to find her standing amid the wreckage of his carefully constructed hidey-hole. She gulped, averted her eyes from the damage, and turned to face him.

Bill Smith was bulging out of a greying singlet, with a massively studded belt strapped around his jeans and the inevitable clonking great boots below. He was glowering like fury – looking every inch, she thought indignantly, the potential wife-batterer. 'Blimey, it's you, Duchess,' he said, scowl lifting. 'Hullo, babe. What you up to?'

Good question. 'The dog,' she said instantly, whereupon inspiration ran dry. Teddy had never been a creative liar.

'Don't tell me she's been digging the wife up?' He picked a path across the junk to her side, and let out an exasperated snort as he saw the exposed canvas. 'Terrific. You would not believe the trouble I went to, hiding this bloody thing last night.'

'Oh, I would,' began Teddy, before deciding she would be wiser not to pursue this.

'God knows why I bothered.' He kicked a broken chair leg away. 'If the bailiffs do turn up, you can bet your life old Ferd'll lead 'em straight to it.'

'Bailiffs?'

'Debt collectors. The heavies from the collection agency, you know.' He grimaced, patting his pockets for a cigarette packet. 'At least, no, you wouldn't know, would you? Come as a bit of novelty to me, matter of fact, but I'm learning fast. I thought I'd got them off my back, but along with the batch of bills Cuckoo produced last night, there was a couple of shirty letters, and for all I've sent off the dosh now . . . Well, better safe than sorry, know what I mean?'

'I – suppose so.'

'That's if I don't get banged up for murder first.'

'*Murder?*'

He was cupping the lighter flame in his hand and glanced round, grinning. 'I caught Ferd just now whispering to the woman in the paper shop that I'd buried his mum under a mattress in the shed. I tell you, she gave me a very funny look.'

'You don't say,' croaked Teddy. 'What – what a scream.'

All at once he eyed her more keenly. 'Something the matter?'

'Gosh, no. Look, sorry for, um, knocking these things over, I'd better get out of your way.'

'Hang about, hang about.' He put his head on one side, and there was a distinctly satirical glint in his eye. 'You wouldn't by any chance be snooping round here on account of my boy having had a little chat with you too, would you?'

'Ferdy?' She could feel the incriminating flush blazing up her face. 'No – at least – I told you, I heard the dog howling.'

'Sure.'

'Howling her poor little head off,' she protested. 'Of course, I never for one moment—'

He let out a shout of laughter 'Bleedin' marvellous. You know, first time we met, I had you down as two spoons short of the full canteen.'

'I beg your pardon?'

'Asking me if I was a plumber, abusing me left, right and centre – now you're telling me I'm a wife-murderer. 'Strewth, Duchess, what you going to come up with next? Satanic rituals?'

'Don't be ridiculous. I – I never imagined anything of the kind.'

'You're a bloody terrible liar, babe.'

Teddy was cross enough with herself for having yielded – momentarily – to such a lunatic fancy, but that Bill Smith seemed to find the situation so amusing made a certain redirection of her wrath almost irresistible. 'Well, what was I supposed to think? After the way you and your wife were screaming blue murder at one another last night?'

'Sorry if we spoiled your beauty sleep. Anyway, ex-wife.'

'Exactly,' she said hotly. 'Your squabbles over your divorce are none of my concern but . . .' Here, with a heroic effort of will, she caught herself up.

'Go on,' he prompted, grinning even more provocatively. 'Get it off your chest. Feel free.'

She might not have availed herself of such an invitation, but for a childish squeal of protest from the yard outside which recalled to her the innocent victims of the situation. She lowered her voice pointedly. 'I just think you should consider your children. This business must be causing them enough distress without that sort of behaviour.'

'You reckon?' Someone less ruffled than Teddy might have noticed that Bill Smith seemed not quite so amused by this. 'I'd say they was coping pretty well, considering.'

'I dare say you would, but—'

'Dad?' Florence appeared in the doorway. 'Dad, Ferdy's putting his Rollerblades on, and you know what Nanna said.'

'With you in a tic, Floss.' He turned back to Teddy. It did flit across her mind that, rather than a gorilla, he reminded her at this moment of a shorthorn bull of notoriously unpredictable temperament they used to keep on Home Farm. Rex was wont to breathe through his nostrils at her in just such a ridiculous fashion. He waited until Florence was gone before growling. 'I believe you was saying, Duchess?'

She could have made a dignified exit. What business, after all, was this of hers? But Teddy was no coward. Nor was she one to balk at plain speaking. Moreover, and perhaps more to the point, she was dog-tired, mad as a hornet and quite frankly longing to give this ape the benefit of a few home truths. Even so – and with commendable restraint under the circumstances – she confined herself to a lofty observation that, however inadequate the parents in question, she had always believed children were better off with two.

He snorted. 'Which cracker did that gem fall out of?'

'You asked.'

'She's the one leaving me, sunshine.'

'What difference does that make?'

'Fuck of a lot, from where I'm standing.'

'I meant from the child's point of view,' snapped Teddy, gesturing out towards the sunshine, where Ferdy and Florence were bickering innocently beside their father's car in the alleyway, while the dog pranced around them. 'They're very young to lose their father.'

Judging she'd said enough, and perhaps rather more than enough, she had turned to go, but a roar stopped her in her tracks. 'Lose their *father*? Are you completely barking? They're stopping with me.'

She spun round in horror. 'You can't be proposing to take them away from their mother?'

'Bet your bloody life.'

'She won't let you.'

'Like hell.' With a glance towards the twins he dropped to a fierce whisper. 'Cuckoo doesn't want kids spoiling her fun.'

'Nonsense,' she snapped, ruthlessly suppressing a memory of Lily observing that her daughter had taken to motherhood like a duck to concrete. 'Anyway – anyway, if Lorette doesn't feel she can cope, God knows how you think you can.'

'I've done it five years.'

'I'm sure,' she responded witheringly, throwing any last vestige of self-restraint to the winds. 'While their mother sat around twiddling her thumbs?'

We mustn't be too hard on Teddy. After all, in her own family life, it's probable the most ambitious flight of masculine domesticity she had ever witnessed was Sir Charles attempting to brew tea. But Bill Smith was not to know that. If this was a bull, it was clear she had just brandished something in the nature of a red marquee.

'How the hell d'you think they've got this far?' he bellowed, striding after her into the yard. 'You're looking at a man what had vomit stains on his shoulder – both shoulders – for two solid years. Who'd you suppose changed every nappy, sterilized every sodding bottle . . .' Teddy caught a flicker of movement beyond his shoulder, a whisk of the dog's tail, a whoop from Ferdy, but her neighbour was unstoppable. 'And I tell you I could take a master's degree in Thomas the fucking Tank—'

'Oh, my giddy aunt,' she shrieked, and flung herself past him.

Chapter Twelve

For an instant, Bill Smith stood baffled. There she'd been, giving him grievous bodily earache, little sod, then all at once – oomph. Vanished. Nearly knocked him flying, what's more. He turned, blinked, and that's when, suddenly, everything seemed to be running in slow motion.

She'd gone pelting off into the square along this cranky little alley, right? So narrow you could hardly get the motor down. So narrow, Bill could barely squeeze past his car after her. Because he was hearing a horn honk – and a scream of brakes. Christ, what a scream. Went on for hours and hours. He was rupturing his shin on the bumper, castrating himself on the wing mirror, blundering finally out into the square to find blinding sunshine and – he'd swear – silence. Total, sudden, sodding silence. Your olde worlde, dead-from-the-neck-up English village. Shops shut, few birds round the War Memorial, scatter of parked cars . . . and one car skewed at a crazy angle across the road. With a little figure spread-eagled next to it. Oh, sweet Jesus. A frail, redheaded little body, with thumping great skates on the ends of spaghetti-thin legs.

'Ferdy!' roared Bill. Only it didn't come out as a roar, because all of a sudden he had no breath in him. He could hardly raise a squeak. And at that very moment the little body stirred, jerked bolt upright and let out a blessedly lusty yell.

'She *pushed* me!' Ferdy was wriggling to his feet, arms and legs windmilling furiously. 'She made me cut my knee.'

Bill pounded over and gathered him up. 'Oh my baby,' he gulped, clutching him to his chest. 'What happened?'

All hell broke loose then. People were materializing out of the emptiness like flies round a jam pot. Bill became aware there was a bloke nearly falling out of the driver's seat of the skewed car – for a second he thought the guy'd cut his head open, but no, thank God, it was only a funny white flash in his Barnet – and he was gasping, was the kid OK? Bill could barely answer because Ferdy was kicking him in the balls with his Rollerblades and yelling at him to stop slobbering; some elderly geezer with a shopping basket was declaring the car was going the wrong way round the square; speeding and all, agreed his wife, adding that yon lass deserved a medal, so she did . . .

'Dad!' piped up a breathless voice amid the chaos. 'Over here.' With Ferdy still clamped to his chest, he turned. Floss was squatting on the opposite kerb, one fist knotted in the neck fur of the panting dog. Beside them, in the road, face down and still as a tombstone, lay Miss Theodora Dunstan.

'I – I don't think she's dead,' whispered his daughter, looking scared out of her wits. 'Is she?'

'Course not,' barked an autocratic voice, to Bill's considerable relief, although the words were indistinct because her ladyship's nose was pressed into the tarmac. 'Per-fly fine. Just – need minute. Get my breath.'

Bill planted his protesting son in the arms of a bystander with a grunt of apology, and hurried across. A cluster of onlookers was already gathering round the prone body.

'Shifted like greased lightning, she did.'

'The lad'd've been a gonner, other road.'

'Anyone called t'ambulance?'

That stirred Miss Dunstan into animation. Heaving herself up on one elbow, she declared that she didn't need ambulances. Bill dropped to the tarmac beside her. She stared at him defiantly, if lop-sidedly, one half of her face being black and bloodied where she'd hit the road. That could be Ferdy, thought Bill, crushed, bleeding . . . 'You saved my boy's life,' he whispered, so choked he could hardly get the words out. 'And there was me, giving you what for on what an ace parent I am. Jesus—'

'Shut up and – and give me a hand,' she croaked. 'So I can get up. Making exhibition of myself here.'

'You stay right where you are.' He thrust an arm round her shoulders and looked up at the ring of gawpers. 'Someone go ring for this flaming ambulance, will you? And give us a bit of space.'

'Let – me – go,' she squawked, outraged. 'I'm not wasting time going to hospital. Business to run, big lunch tomorrow.' So saying, she shoved an elbow sharp as a bayonet into his chest and was halfway scrambled to her feet, when she let out a little yelp and crumpled again.

'You silly bugger,' he wailed, scooping her up in his arms and cradling her to his chest.

'Put me *down*,' she snapped, faint but fighting to the last. 'Think the car must've – slightly – run over my foot.' And with that, she passed out.

Now, it would be delightful to report that when she returned to consciousness mere seconds later and found herself clasped in two brawny arms tight to the nakedly hairy bosom of this glorious hunk of masculinity, she fell instantly, irrevocably and dottily in love. Nice, but . . .

Sorry, what was that? No, your eyes do not deceive you. 'Glorious hunk of masculinity' were the words employed, and they were selected with care. For goodness' sake, hadn't you twigged that yet? My dears, Bill Smith is simply to die for. Oh, he may lack the regularity of feature required for mere handsomeness, but what he does have – and, girls, he has it by the truckload – is pulse-quickening, breath-shortening, one hundred per cent knicker-twanging sex appeal. And we're not just talking big, brute body. There's a warmth, an animation, a *joli-laid* quality to that face which, rest assured, would make any sensible female fall right back into a swoon were they to wake up and find those Guinness-coloured eyes gazing tenderly down into theirs.

'What d'you think you're doing?' snarled Teddy, squirming furiously in his embrace as he carried her to the pavement. She even went on to inform him it was a well-known fact accident victims should not be moved – as any fool should be aware – which was pretty rich considering she'd propelled herself off the ground in defiance of his express wishes. The words 'ridiculous buffoon' may have passed her lips. One is forced to conclude that she is in no immediate danger of succumbing to the gorilla's charms.

Sadly, we can't even claim that Mr Smith, who, being by all accounts an artist, might be expected to possess a more romantic soul, had instantly felt the thwack of Cupid's arrow, either. Fine bloody time to be thinking about crap like that, he might retort – with some justice, given that he's standing here with herself in his arms firing non-stop abuse, while a million nutters are swarming round, offering tea, chairs, blankets, witness statements, apologies, cold compresses, contradictory advice and (a neighbour of Lil's and the only one of these motormouths with an IQ in double figures) an offer to deliver kids and dog safely round to their grandmother's.

Ordering the Duchess to cop that wet cloth tight to her forehead – and she could stop telling him it wasn't no good for concussion, it wouldn't do any harm, would it? – he again yelled for the crowd to disperse, accepted the offer of childcare with harassed thanks, and wondered aloud where the medicos were coming from to take so long, Charing bleeding Cross?

Anyway, do him a favour, would you? Even without her face half-black, one eye squinting shut, and a trickle of blood from the corner of her mouth, Theodora Dunstan ain't exactly in the Miss World class, is she? Not that Bill makes any claims for himself in the looks department, course he don't, but, be fair, he's a very visual person, know what he means?

So, no. No romantic notion crosses his mind, either, which is a pity, because one cannot help thinking this is a delightfully promising clinch. Well, except perhaps for the quirk of fate that seems to have landed our heroine in the role of swashbuckling rescuer, and left our hero soggy with the tears of gratitude. Still, we mustn't let that worry us. This is an equal opportunities fairytale.

Nor must we entirely despair. There is more than mere gratitude – massive and heartfelt though that gratitude is – in the care Bill is taking of Miss Dunstan. His respect for this little madam is increasing in leaps and bounds as she exasperatedly insists, through a jaw swelling faster than a balloon, that she did nothing remotely clever, it was what anyone else would've done if they'd happened to be looking in the right direction, she doesn't want to hear any more of this baloney, will someone for God's sake go and check that the poor bloody driver is OK, and tell him she's fit as a flea – and *what*? Look, if Bill Smith thinks she's getting in that ambulance, he's got another think coming. A nice cup of tea and she will be—

Bill Smith, though, is not lacking in heroically masterful qualities when the need arises. Or, at the very least, in low cunning. Teddy most certainly *is* getting into the ambulance, he announces, and when she tries to bully the bemused paramedics, he simply lifts her in himself, and plonks himself on the bench opposite. You bet your life he's coming along, too. Just in case she makes an escape bid on the dual carriageway. He wouldn't put anything past this one.

'You family, sir?' enquires the ambulance man.

'How dare you?' hisses Teddy.

The ambulance man pulls a face. 'Well, in that case, sir, I'm afraid the policy is—'

Bill rises, thrusts himself between his charge and the man and leans forward. 'Not – legally related, if you get my drift,' he whispers craftily.

The man shrugs. 'Partner?'

'If that's how you like to put it,' agrees Bill, with the smugness of a man who has not actually uttered one untruthful word.

Teddy, who, to be fair, is feeling a bit ropey, takes a minute or two to absorb the import of the negotiations being conducted over her head. When she does, her jaw drops. Not far, because she has a large bandage tied round it. But the horror in her face is priceless. 'Are you . . . You cannot be—'

'Now then, my little prairie flower,' interrupts Bill loudly, wrapping her hand in his. 'Mustn't get hysterical, or they might have to give you a jab to knock you out.'

'You – you—' She can literally find no words. Since one eye is wadded in lint, she squints malevolently up at her protector through her remaining orb. But it's too late to object, the vehicle is moving (with blue light flashing), the gorilla is aboard, and the paramedic is filling out a form on his clipboard. Probably inscribing 'common law husband' in the appropriate column.

Bill sighs and settles back in his seat with the air of a man who has pulled off a very tricky mission.

'You *bastard,*' hisses Teddy.

'And I love you, too, sunshine,' he says.

Chapter Thirteen

In one of life's interesting little coincidences, even as Teddy was searching for Lorette Smith's dead and buried body, what was exercising Lorette's own mind was the fear of ending up buried alive. Her very words. By this, of course, she was again referring to the dread prospect of a prolonged sojourn at her mother's house in loathsome Langley-le-Moor. 'Fate worse than death' was another favoured phrase as she bewailed her plight to her brother Brian that afternoon.

Behind her, meanwhile, her mother was spitting and tutting even more venomously than the liver and onions she was frying for tea. Lorette ignored her. What could she do, she continued plaintively into the telephone, with the monster she'd been stupid enough to marry grabbing every last penny, and all Dad's money coming to Brian and Colin?

'No use trying to wheedle your way round your brothers,' Lily shouted across the kitchen, 'That money's for them to set up in a place of their own and I can still tek it back. Bloody ridiculous, having them under my feet at their age.'

'It's not fair,' she squawked.

'Don't you talk about what's fair and what's not when you're walking out on Bill and the kids. Just because he's hit hard times is no excuse. And you shouldn't be mithering Brian at work neither.'

Hunching a shoulder, Lorette carried the phone outside the door, only to reappear within minutes and announce, in some triumph, that there would be no takers for the liver and onions tonight, ta very much, because her brothers were treating her to dinner out. So they could talk things over in private – at least *somebody* sympathized with her. And where was her white skirt?

By the time the ambulance with Bill and Teddy aboard was flashing and wailing its path to the General Infirmary, Lorette was walking into the public bar of the Wheeltappers and Shunters Arms in nearby Boroughby. Her glow of triumph, however, was fading. Not merely had she been forced to travel here in her best Calvin Klein on the stinking, rattling, chewing-gum-spattered bus – her pig of a husband having swiped the car along with everything else, and her mother refusing to lend hers on the piffling grounds that it wasn't insured for under twenty-fives – Lorette was belatedly wondering whether Brian and Colin's notion of a good night out was likely to correspond with her own. This hostelry did not bode well. She tip-tapped across the pockmarked lino in her new platform mules with the caution of an explorer traversing an alligator-infested swamp. The Wheeltappers and Shunters Arms. That name said it all. Was this, she gloomily mused, hauling herself on to a stool by the bar and adjusting a microscopically short skirt over her tanned thighs, the shape of things to come?

A barman with fresh-blossoming acne, a lively Adam's apple and a baggy T-shirt claiming *Steam Men Do It the Old Fashioned Way*, stumbled over a beer crate in his anxiety to reach her end of the bar.

'Pardon?' said Lorette, inspecting the contents of her purse with disgust.

'Get you a drink?' he managed to utter.

Lorette, who found men dissolving into slobbering puddles of lust at her feet as unremarkable as most women find paving stones, declared without enthusiasm that she would have a cider. Half. And a packet of prawn cocktail crisps.

'I'm meeting my brothers,' she added, drawing a magazine from her bag and spreading it on the bar. 'Only I'm early on account of the lousy bus.'

'Bad day, huh?' enquired the acned youth, with the air of a movie-addict who fancies himself in the role of bar-tending philosopher.

'Bad five years,' responded Lorette, who also watched a

great many films and was in need of just such a sympathetic innkeeperly ear. 'Honest to God, if I'd known it'd end up like this, I'd never have chucked my pills down the bog.'

The Adam's apple bounced. 'Pardon?'

She took a swig of cider. 'Too young to know different, that's the problem. You got kids?'

He shook his head.

'Very sensible,' she said darkly. 'You would not believe how they change people.'

Busily polishing a glass, he mumbled something bashful about her not, um, looking like your average mother.

'Not me, *him*. Not that I don't love my kids,' she added in a burst of belligerence so unexpected he nearly dropped his glass, 'because I do, course I do, but they're better off with him. As I've told Mum, but will she listen?' She downed another gulp of cider and braced her shoulders. 'Still, water under the bridge. Thing is, to learn from your mistakes.'

'Life is a big box of chocolates,' he offered soulfully, 'only we've lost the lid telling us which is which.'

'You're not kidding. And I keep ending up with the flaming nougat.'

This stimulating exchange was interrupted by the arrival of more customers, and she fell to studying her magazine. In her present mood, the glossy pages were enough to make her weep. Parties and premières, penthouses and yachts, polo fields and catwalks . . . Just where, Lorette would like to know, had she gone wrong?

And surely we must accord her a little sympathy. After all, it doesn't take any great leap of imagination to visualize this delicious creature sashaying down a red carpet in Versace safety pins and a shimmer of flashguns. She wasn't asking for the moon. She had never aspired to star in the movies she watched with such passion, nor to top the pop charts she followed so avidly. All she'd ever wanted was the odd guest ticket into that star-spangled, paparazzi-popping wonderland, a chance to adorn a famous arm or two, before she was too old and her tits sagged. Which, at twenty-four and three-quarters, she reckoned was any day now. The years were gurgling down the plughole, and where was she? In the public bar of the Wheeltappers and Shunters Arms, with a half of cider and the barman reappearing to offer her a pickled gherkin.

'No, ta,' she said, with a sweetly tragic smile. 'Give me shocking wind, pickles.'

It was not that she hadn't tried to follow her dream – oh, how poor Lorette had tried. Take art college. How many ritzy, glitzy careers have been launched in art college? Not many, she had soon realized, from a fashion retail course at the Huddlestone Institute. As for marriage, that most traditional of routes for a female-on-the-make, don't even ask. Bill Smith her passport to paradise? She must have been crackers.

And if you were wondering why she hadn't cut and run years back, well, so was she. Too optimistic, that was her trouble. Kept hoping things'd get better. Which of course they didn't, but there was always Mum and Bill persuading her to hang on for the sake of the kids. Besides, if she'd legged it with no money, where was she supposed to go? All very fine if you'd got friends in Chelsea or New York or somewhere. Hers were a stone's throw up the road – well, except for Wendy. Who'd moved to Grimsby. Which only left her mum's, and while Huddlestone was bad enough, Langley was a million times worse. Never mind bright lights, Langley barely had streetlights. Anyway, it was at least a year back that even *Bill* had seen sense, and said they might as well stop flogging a dead horse and flog the house instead. He'd find somewhere else for him and the kids, and split what remained with her fifty-fifty. Only then they couldn't find a buyer, and what with one thing and another . . .

Nevertheless Lorette still couldn't quite believe what he'd told her last night about her share of the proceeds. Nothing. *Nothing.* Five years of marriage and all Bill was offering was her pick of the pot plants and videos – along with her credit cards sliced into ribbons and a load of grief over some old bills she'd forgotten about. He said he was taking the bit of money that remained to look after the kids until he could start earning again, and that was that. Thus, the thirteen pence currently in her purse was her last thirteen pence in the whole wide world.

As she told the barman when explaining why she'd have to wait for her brothers before she had another.

He glanced round warily, and then swiftly refilled her glass. 'On the house,' he whispered.

Lorette hadn't the heart to tell him she wasn't mad keen on cider – not much of a drinker at all, in fact, and was already feeling mildly lightheaded – so she smiled wanly, took a sip and hoped Brian and Col would show up before she fell off the barstool. Not that she could hope for anything from them. Mum had made clear they were under orders to find themselves a home. Small wonder, when she looked down at her magazine, tears blurred her eyes.

To add insult to injury, it had fallen open at a story of life-after-divorce, *Hello*-style. Here was a former model, bravely rebuilding her career after she'd been ditched by some earl with a red nose and short legs. But at least he'd given her the run of a swish apartment in Chelsea, blah, blah, along with a sweet little cottage (cottage? with five bedrooms and a gym?) on the family estate in Northumberland, at mega-expense because he'd had to buy out a tenant from a long lease. And Lorette was just thinking even a lousy cottage in frozen Northumberland with sheep for neighbours beat one rubber plant and a *Pretty Woman* video, when she stopped. Blinking the tears out of her eyes, she went back and reread the paragraph.

Now Lorette would never claim to be the world's greatest thinker. So no one could be more surprised than she at the masterly scheme suddenly taking shape in her head. The more she considered it . . . the more brilliant it seemed. And, right on cue, hearing the pub door open and her name called, she spun round.

'Brian, Col,' she said breathlessly. 'I've had an idea.'

'Don't blame me,' said Bill Smith, smartly manoeuvring the wheelchair back into the waiting area. 'It was your lot made all the cuts in the Health Service.'

'Might have known you'd be a Labour voter,' muttered Teddy.

'Yeah, well, can't go on being a Trot once you're past forty.

Undignified, innit? They said you're allowed a drink now, so d'you fancy a cup of tea?'

'And how am I supposed to down it?' Teddy indicated her swollen, swathed and stitched jaw. 'I've had enough anaesthetic pumped in here to immobilize my mouth until Christmas.' At least, that was the message as it left her brain. What emerged from her benumbed lips was rather more garbled, but Mr Smith seemed to pick up the general tenor.

'Don't,' he groaned, sinking into a plastic chair beside her. 'That needle whizzing in and out – Jesus, Duchess, I'm so sorry.'

'I'll scream if you don't stop apologizing.'

'But it's all my fault, letting Ferdy run off. If it wasn't for you . . . I can't even bear thinking about it.'

'So don't. Ridiculous fuss over a few cuts and grazes.'

'But your poor little face . . .'

'As long as it's better by the thirty-first. Which it will be.' Just so did Napoleon declare that his forces would be in Moscow by Christmas.

'Why the thirty-first?'

'Oh, nothing. Dinner party, sister-in-law's birthday.' She put a hand to her bandages and winced. 'I shall need to be fit for public consumption by then.'

'And in the meantime you don't mind looking like you're auditioning for Bride of Frankenstein?' Bill shook his head. 'You're a one-off, you are.'

'And you're an idiot,' she snapped.

Perhaps a certain tetchiness can be forgiven in one who has spent four and a half hours being prodded and poked, patched and patronized, in the tropically hot, glaringly lit, Dettol-stinking environs of what, in her view, resembled nothing so much as a run-down motorway service station. Bill Smith, at any rate, did not appear to take offence. In fact, he lifted one hand, rather as though he might be about to bestow a comforting pat on Teddy's knee, but then thought better of it. Instead, he stretched his great hulking arms, yawned luxuriously, and subsided into silence.

'If you must know, it's this I'm worried about,' grunted Teddy after a minute, and she stuck out her right foot which had been bandaged to the size of a watermelon. 'How am I supposed to knock out a three-course lunch for twelve tomorrow with this absurd lump on my leg?'

Bill rolled his eyes. 'The doc said rest and elevation.'

'Even that bumptious little schoolboy-in-a-stethoscope admitted there was nothing broken. As if I hadn't told him so all along.'

'Didn't you just?' he murmured, mopping his brow reminiscently. 'And everyone else. I'm only amazed you haven't got us chucked out of the bloody place hours since.'

'No need for you to stay. As I've assured you times without number, I shall be perfectly all right on my own.'

But Bill Smith had been undislodgeable, stubbornly padding after her wheelchair from cubicle to cubicle, department to department. He had even clamped her hand in his hairy fist when a nurse was doing something particularly unspeakable with disinfectant-soaked swabs, although whether this was for Teddy's comfort or his own was unclear. Thus, she wasn't expecting him to rise abruptly to his feet now.

'Where are you going?'

'Back in a tick,' he muttered, patting his pockets.

'Yes, but . . .'

He was already threading a path across the crowded waiting room to the drinks machine.

Marvellous, hissed Teddy to herself. Because, as it happened, she had been on the point of enquiring whether he had any change for the telephone. Much though it galled her, she had at that moment acknowledged that she possibly should attempt to rustle up help with the lunch tomorrow. And since Lily had already declared her unavailability, Audrey was only a day back from New Zealand, and Margaret had all her grandchildren staying, this might not be easy. Her temper was not improved by watching Bill Smith at the far end of the waiting area, slotting a king's ransom of coins into assorted vending machines. She sunk her bandaged chin on to her chest and sulked.

'Here,' he said, hoving back into view with no less than four plastic cups clustered in his fists. These he carefully set down on the floor at her feet. 'You'll feel better with some tea inside you.'

Through her exposed eye, Teddy glared at him. 'I told you—'

'Wait.' From his pocket, he produced two bars of chocolate and a carton of blackcurrant juice.

'A veritable Ascot picnic,' she snapped. 'I hope you enjoy it.'

He didn't answer. He was engaged in ripping the straw off the juice carton with his teeth. Stripping this free of wrapping, he removed the lid from one of the plastic cups of tea, balanced the straw over the rim and handed it to her. 'Didn't know whether you took sugar,' he said. 'So I got two with, two without.'

Most unusually, Theodora Dunstan was at a loss for words. Numbly, she accepted the cup, raised it to her lips, clamped the straw between her teeth, and sucked. Only someone who has spent four and a half hours in an overheated, overlit and overstretched Accident and Emergency Department without so much as a sip of water can begin to appreciate the bliss of that first slug. It might have been machine tea, and sugared to boot, but the finest hand-plucked, silver-potted Orange Pekoe had never tasted better.

Bill watched with satisfaction. 'OK?'

'Thank you,' muttered Teddy stiffly. And she indicated the straw. 'Good of you – to go to so much trouble.'

'Pleasure.' He opened a cup for himself, and settled down into the seat beside her once more.

'No, really. Afraid I've been . . . rather short-tempered.'

'Like a shark with toothache,' he agreed amiably. 'Mind, you've every right.'

Teddy squared her shoulders and tried again. 'Yes, well. Very decent of you.'

At this, to her astonishment and that of several people nearby, he threw back his head and roared with laughter.

'For goodness' sake,' she hissed. 'What's the big joke?'

'You,' he gasped. '*Decent* . . . What are you like, Duchess?'

'Oh, get stuffed,' said Teddy.

Chapter Fourteen

A midsummer moon sailed high in the velvet sky over Langley-le-Moor, silvering the splendours of the Hall, softening the pagan scowls of the church gargoyles, rippling tenderly over the curly red roof-tiles of 3 Meadows Close – and driving Birdie the dog bananas.

'Give over howling,' said Lily Rowbotham. 'You'll wake the twins.'

Lily was in her bedroom. A frothing pile of silky lingerie on the bed suggested, first, that she had never allowed increased girth to inhibit her notions of femininity (which was perfectly true) second, that she might have been retrieving something long hidden at the bottom of her underwear drawer. This also was correct. A slim leather case, silk-lined, was lying open upon her dressing table. She was seated before the mirror, grimacing as she tried to fasten around her ample neck a sparklingly delicate necklace. Five clusters of diamonds and sapphires, intricately wrought into flower-shapes, were linked by the merest thread of platinum chain, which was cutting wickedly deep into the flesh of her throat.

'Sentimental old fool,' she muttered, giving up the attempt. 'Wouldn't hardly fit round my wrist. Any road, things are only things, and it's got to go. I'll not miss what I've never really had.' So saying, she allowed the necklace to crumple into a myriad of twinkling stars in the palm of one hand. The matching earrings still glittered in her ears, however, and a keen observer might note that Lily's eyes, too, were glittering just a little. Blame it on the moonlight. That kindly, waxy globe hovering outside, the honeyed perfume of roses wafting through the window – only human nature, surely, if this were to conjure up the odd bittersweet memory, a stray tear . . .

The growl of a car engine broke the spell. This terminated in a squeak of ancient brakes followed by a burst of high-pitched giggling and a rattling at the front door, unnaturally prolonged, suggestive of difficulty in locating the keyhole.

Lily was already on her feet, yanking the sparklers from her ears. By the time irregular footsteps lurched along the hallway, she had stuffed them and the necklace back into the case and, sweeping up an armful of underwear from the bed, bundled the whole lot back into the drawer and slammed it shut.

'That you, Lorette?' she called. 'Boys? What the bloody hell you been up to 'til this hour?'

'*Hergh*, it's getting awfully late, sweetie,' mumbled Sir Charles Dunstan. Moonlight streamed through the mullioned windows of the stately upper gallery at Langley Hall, causing the Labrador at his heels to whine softly and stare longingly out at the sky. The Baronet, however, was slumped outside his own bedroom door, ear pressed to the mahogany panels. It remained uncompromisingly locked. 'Time to, um, turn in?'

Inside the chamber, Lady Dunstan, still dressed and seated at a small escritoire, did not reply immediately because she was licking the flap of an envelope. 'Feel free,' she called, after sealing the envelope and tossing it onto a pile of others. 'I suggested Mrs B. made up the Blue Room, but of course if you prefer the library floor again, that's up to you.'

'*Hergh*, beautiful moon. Full, by the look of it.'

'Then I dare say your mother is out strangling cats.'

'Just remembering – our honeymoon.' He paused, then continued falteringly: 'Night like this, you said . . .'

'Charles?'

His face brightened. '*Hergh*?'

'Shut up.'

'Oh, Bellsy-Wellsy . . .'

'I'm busy.' She took up her pen again, and began flipping

over the pages of the address book which lay open in front of her. 'Good night, Charles.'

His shoulders sagged. He did not stir immediately but, at length, when it was clear no further word was forthcoming, he lifted himself away from the door. At once, the dog bounded to the head of the staircase, tail flailing hopefully. His master ignored the mute appeal, and shambled off down the gallery in the direction of the Blue Room. The Labrador's tail slowed, halted, then flopped. Finally, the animal turned and followed. It would be hard to say which of the two looked the more dejected.

No one in Langley-le-Moor, it seemed, was in any mood to be swayed by the sweet seduction of a summer moon.

But stay! What stirs in the Market Square? As a taxi pulls away from the shuttered frontage of The Pantry, a burly simian form is revealed – unmistakably that of Mr Smith – knotted in the most intimate of embraces with none other than our doughty heroine. He has one brawny arm locked tight around her waist, while the other is delving . . . Perhaps it would spare our blushes not to examine too closely where his right hand is delving.

'Not in this pocket, you pillock,' he grunted. 'Here, give us your crutches and grab my shoulder while you look in your handbag again.'

And at length, with door key located and house unlocked, there followed another undignified scuffle as Teddy was hoisted up the narrow stairway to her living quarters, protesting at every step that she would do a great deal better unaided, and could he please stop knocking holes in her paintwork with those *bloody* crutches?

'There,' gasped Mr Smith, clapping his hands together as he deposited his recalcitrant charge onto her sofa. 'Anything else?'

Teddy gave him to understand there was nothing else, thank you *very* much. That was to say – she paused, evidently struggling with herself – thanks. She would like him to know that she was grateful to him for delivering her home. However—

'Don't start that again,' he groaned. 'I told you twenty times, Lil's taking the babes on this coach trip to Scarborough tomorrow, and there's no way I'm standing in for her on a Mother's Union outing. Besides, I owe you one. I owe you one big time, Duchess, so I'm helping with this lunch party tomorrow – and that's final.' There was a glint of malice in his eye as he patted her shoulder. 'I'll skivvy and you can sit in the corner with your leg up, doing just what comes natural.'

Teddy glared lopsidedly up at him. 'Meaning what, precisely?'

'Laying down the bleedin' law,' he said. 'Half-six suit?'

'God help us,' she sighed.

During the course of the following morning, however, Teddy was to find herself forced to admit she might have misjudged her new neighbour – and in more than one respect.

The first surprise was the rap at her kitchen door sharp on six-thirty. She had never doubted he would oversleep. Since the whisky and aspirin she had so stoutly predicted would set all her own ills to rights had not, in fact, prevented her stitches twanging her into wakefulness with painful regularity, she had not herself enjoyed a restful night. Moreover, such sleep as she did snatch was rendered hideous by nightmare visions of today's lunch party, featuring incinerated lamb, putrefying salad and shattered tartlets. By the time she cranked herself out of bed she felt as though her entire body had been run over by a fleet of juggernauts, not just a couple of toes by a piffling car, and it was apparent to her – nearly falling flat on the bathroom floor as she attempted to scrub her teeth – that she could no more manage this lunch on crutches than she could fly out of the window. Thus she would have welcomed into her kitchen just about anyone in possession of two functional hands and feet, even this clown who reeled back as she opened the door, gasping that he couldn't hardly bear to look at her.

It should perhaps be explained that Teddy's last act before stumping downstairs had been to unpeel the dressings from her face. Hunched over her crutches, puff-eyed and spectacularly bruised from grazed jaw to spiky stitches tangling bloodily in her hairline, she growled that she hadn't actually relished the prospect in the mirror either.

'No, no,' he protested, 'I meant I can't bear seeing all this damage I've done you.'

'Rot.'

'Shouldn't you be keeping it covered up?'

'Heals better in the fresh air. Even the idiot doctor said so.'

'Yeah, but—'

'Are you coming in,' snapped Teddy, 'or is this just a social call?'

Whereupon, clicking together the heels of his clumping great boots and sketching a salute, the gorilla goose-stepped past her, declaring that this was Private Smith, reporting for potato-bashing fatigues, *sah*!

Teddy unenthusiastically said he might as well chop some garlic while she worked out how to simplify the agreed menu without wasting a fortune in perishable ingredients and offending a lucrative client. After five minutes of fruitless Biro-chewing, as the gorilla tied himself into one of her big white aprons and set to work, she lowered her pen and began watching him instead. After a quarter of an hour, she cautiously announced that perhaps the menu would not need amending so very greatly after all. After half an hour – during which time she herself had done little more than collect half a dozen eggs from the larder and contrived to let two of them smash to the floor – she was content to yield to his proposal that she sit in the corner and supervise, leaving the spadework to him.

It should be said that it was not the blade-twinkling panache with which he decimated a pile of garlic cloves which impressed her (unnecessarily flashy, in her view, not to say fingertip-endangering), nor the rate at which he went on to shell a pan-load of quails' eggs without tearing a white, nor even was it his undeniable touch with mayonnaise, which emerged under his flashing whisk and her wondering eyes as pale, fluffy and alluring as a baby duckling. No, what *truly* impressed Teddy was the speedy economy with which he cleared away the resulting debris. After all, setting aside the likes of her brother Charles, she was aware that many chaps these days seemed to fancy themselves a maestro with a Moulinex (Teddy blamed the television), but none, in her experience, ever demonstrated a matching talent for washing up afterwards.

When she ventured to observe, over the mugs of coffee Bill had brewed while simultaneously reducing a stock and skinning tomatoes, that he seemed unusually handy around a kitchen, he explained he had used to moonlight in a Soho restaurant, proper Frog joint, as much for the free grub as the money.

'Better than the building site, even if the money wasn't so hot.'

'Building site?'

'Gotta earn the dosh, haven't you, one way or another?'

'You have?' croaked Teddy. 'I mean, yes, of course one has, but—'

'Seen too much of my old dad scraping along on the social to go in for that lark. Saps the spirit, know what I mean?'

Teddy, Tory to the azure core, could only agree that she believed she did know what he meant. And learned that the feckless papa in question had walked out when Bill was a mere sprig of nine, leaving him to be reared by a redoubtable mother who cleaned council offices in Brixton, and an even more redoubtable grandmother who appeared to have turned her hand to everything from dress-making to fish-filleting in order to feed and clothe her family. No, there were no brothers or sisters, just him. And to his enduring sorrow, both Mam and Gran had died within three months of each other. Six – no, seven years ago that would be now.

'But at least they saw me earning,' he added.

'Skivvying in a kitchen?' said Teddy, still trying to digest the novel idea that this so-called layabout had never taken a penny from the State – well, excepting Child Benefit, but that, as he rightly said, was different.

He shrugged. 'Come on, what'd you expect in a painter? Gotta do your actual starving-in-a-garret number while you're young and struggling, haven't you? Mind,' he added with a disarming grin, 'I was still struggling and skivvying when I was across thirty. And by the time I hit forty I was a father and broke all over again. Only now it wasn't filet mignon and chocolate marquise I was sweating over, it was alphabetti spaghetti and chicken nuggets for two screaming brats. With tomato ketchup over everything, particularly their lovely selves.' He pulled a comical face. 'You're looking at a full-time kitchen drudge here, sweetheart. I tell you, it's a treat to handle fancy food again.'

Teddy found herself smiling back, agreeing that twins must be jolly hard work. Relations nearly foundered afresh, however, when he added, with a reminiscent sigh: 'Anyway, I shouldn't complain. I had a fuck of a good time in between.'

This at once recalled to Teddy the immoral circumstances in which his children had been conceived. 'By that,' she demanded indignantly, 'do you mean seducing innocent students entrusted to your care?'

He actually choked on his coffee. When he could speak, he informed her with some vehemence that if she was referring to Lorette and the Huddlestone Institute, he would have her know Cuckoo hadn't been a student of his, he never had no students entrusted to him, because he wasn't a teacher, he was artist-in-bleeding-residence, was that clear? Temporary. One-year stint. And, OK, shagging students still hadn't exactly been on the job description, and, OK, he shouldn't oughta have done it, but . . .

'It wasn't quite like what you'd think,' he finished, looking uncomfortable – as well he might, in Teddy's view. Although there rose unbidden in her mind Beryl's observation that Lorette had been no innocent chicken. And she could not but feel it was to his credit he made no attempt to dodge responsibility. He merely grunted that he wasn't going to argue the rights and wrongs of his misbegotten marriage but, for what it was worth, the good time of which he spoke had most certainly not coincided with his brief employment at the Huddlestone Institute. In fact he'd only exiled himself to that dump to try and get his head together after a near-terminal overdose of good times elsewhere . . .

'And look what came of it. Still,' he concluded, his face softening, 'the kids are the best thing that's ever happened to me, so I guess it wasn't all disaster. You want these toms seeding as well as skinning?'

★   ★   ★

There was something undeniably winning about such shining paternal pride, and it became ever clearer, as the morning went on, that Bill Smith's approach to fatherhood was not that of these modern footballing and pop-singing papas who, it seemed to Teddy, grabbed every chance they could to cuddle a naked infant to their hairy chests for benefit of camera, and doubtless handed them straight back while the flash was still fading. Here, beyond question, was a chap who had laboured at the sharp end: potty-training, sick-mopping, the full unglamorous works. When, for example, she enquired how he could claim to have suffered two full years of broken nights, he had begun explaining about Florence's colicky tum and Ferdy's nightmares.

'No, no,' interrupted Teddy. 'I mean, Lorette . . . ?'

Her question withered under his satirical gaze. Domesticity, he observed, was not Cuckoo's strong suit. And again, albeit unwillingly, Teddy found herself recalling Lily's acerbic comments. Until now, she had assumed sweet, dizzy Lorette only abdicated her responsibilities for a well-earned rest while her mum was around. It began to seem she behaved exactly the same at home. Bill, however, referred to his wife's shortcomings with wry resignation. No one, as he said, ever married the likes of Lorette for her talent with a Hoover – and he even murmured she had to be forgiven a certain amount on account of her youth, and the nasty shock of finding what she'd married.

'Not what she was expecting, poor sod,' he declared, as he skewered a final anchovy into an immaculately stuffed, rolled and tied loin of lamb and presented it for Teddy's approval. 'We're as like as candy floss and pig shit, but there you are. We should've called it a day long since, only I kept kidding myself it was better for the babes if we stuck it out. That do you?' He waited a minute. 'Hello?'

'Sorry? Oh, the lamb. Yes, looks perfect.'

What was distracting her was a sudden and unpleasantly vivid recollection of their quarrel the previous afternoon, when she had accused Bill Smith of callous indifference to his family, had laughed to scorn any idea he could rear two children . . .

'Um, Bill?'

'Duchess?'

The moment was lost because Beryl bustled through from

the shop, offering to make a final coffee before they loaded the van. Fortunately Teddy's assistant did not seem to be offended by this unconventional new recruit to the staff, who was scattering curses even more liberally than black pepper. In fact, she'd been bobbing skittishly in and out of the kitchen all morning, and even if this was more hindrance than help, Teddy was touched by the concern it surely evinced for her injuries.

Even more fortunately, Bill's arrival did not appear unduly to disconcert the lady lunchers at Thorpeness Grange either. Teddy was forced to delegate carving and dining-room duties to him, in spite of his earring and the checked tea towel he had insisted on knotting around his head, bandanna-style, in the manner of a trendy telly chef.

'Sweltering day,' he protested. 'Catches the sweat.'

'You look like a particularly disreputable pirate,' she grunted, propping herself on one crutch to hand him a basket of bread.

'Stick a parrot on your shoulder and we'll make it a double act.' He hunched over, squinting back at her. 'Aaargh, Jim lad.'

'Hush, they might hear. Very fussy lot.'

'Obviously loaded,' he murmured, glancing round.

'West Riding,' she said darkly. 'Husband's a car dealer, and they only bought this place last year, but they put a lot of business my way, so for Pete's sake . . .'

These valued clients, however, seemed more than happy to make allowances for her disability. In fact, in a quite unprecedented gesture of sisterly solidarity, they flocked into the kitchen with their coffees and insisted on stripping off their jewellery to help with the washing up. Poor Bill, who was managing perfectly capably on his own, could scarcely get to his sink through the thicket of perfumed female bodies. However, he diplomatically accepted a glass of champagne from his hostess and pulled a comical grimace in Teddy's direction as he soldiered on.

'And to think,' one of the ladies observed to her in an awed whisper, 'he washes up, too.'

Taking this as a well-deserved compliment to Bill's cooking – the tomato and anchovy *jus* he produced for the lamb being every bit as good as her own – Teddy cordially agreed he was indeed an astonishingly useful sort of chap, and, yes, certainly she had a brochure detailing her services and charges. By the time they loaded the last crate into the van she had distributed a half-dozen more.

'I say, good show,' she declared, hauling herself into the passenger seat and flopping back with a sigh. 'That went awfully well. In fact, *miraculously* well. And it's all thanks to you.'

'Piece of cake,' grunted Bill Smith, tossing his fag end into the rose bushes, and clambering into the driver's seat beside her. 'Anyway, least I could do.'

'No,' said Teddy abruptly, and sat up very straight. 'No, that's not true. Look, don't start the car. There's something I want to say to you. Been wanting to say for hours.'

Bill, key in hand, turned in surprise.

'I owe you an apology,' she plunged in immediately, never one to waste time when embarking on an unpleasant task. 'Yesterday afternoon, you only took your eye off Ferdy because, well, quite frankly because I was being a pain in the arse.'

'*You?* Surely not.'

She ignored the satirical tone. 'All that stuff about divorce, not being fit to bring up your children – clearly I had misread the situation, and you had every right to be angry. Particularly – particularly given my own track record in that department.'

'What you on about now?'

'When it comes to divorce, abandoning children, all that sort of thing.' This part was rather harder, but she ploughed on. 'Lord knows, I managed to swallow my scruples in John's case. Was pushing him into the divorce courts, to be perfectly honest.'

'John? Oh, you mean the pillock in the Union Jack drawers?'

'Do you mind?'

'Sorry! Sorry, but I'm not with you.'

'What I'm saying' – she took a deep breath— 'is that I had absolutely no right to get on my moral high horse as I did, and I can quite understand you losing your temper. It was my fault as much as yours that Ferdy ran out into the road, and . . .' Here, Teddy thrust out her hand. 'I'd like to apologize. Sincerely.'

Bill enfolded the hand in his and leaned towards her confidingly. 'Duchess,' he said, 'you're talking a load of old bollocks. But it's *frightfully* decent of you.'

They were friends forthwith.

After a fashion.

Chapter Fifteen

The only worm in this rosily ripening apple, and it began to emerge even during the drive home from Thorpeness Grange, was that Miss Dunstan's concept of friendship was not quite the same as Mr Smith's.

Bill's understanding of that amiable bond comprised a willingness to tolerate the quirks and foibles of one's intimates; to live and to let live, you might say. For Teddy, friendship was an altogether more energetic undertaking. She liked to think of herself as the proverbial friend in need, ever willing to lend a helping hand – particularly in a case such as this, because it was apparent to her, if not to Bill himself, that he was a man in urgent need of help and guidance.

He made no secret of his finances being in as sorry a state as his marriage – witness his fear, yesterday, of debt collectors. Of course, Teddy now absolved him from blame for his poor performance as breadwinner, and only thought the better of him for a certain mumbled reluctance to make an excuse of his children. Privately, however, she doubted that so notoriously unsteady an occupation as painting could ever have earned him much. She still found it difficult to imagine a bruiser like him engaged in such an effete trade, although with rare tact she forbore to say so. Nor did she suggest that hardheaded credit agencies were unlikely to bother distraining his precious daubs. She exercised less restraint when discussing his most recent debts. Bill, again commendably, pointed no finger but a passing joke about a store card statement gave the game away, since no one could suppose he was in the habit of squandering three hundred pounds on underwear. Lorette was a sweet girl, Teddy observed sternly, but very thoughtless. Under the circumstances, she had no right to make such a fuss about emerging from the marriage with nothing. Bill only sighed that his wife would've been welcome to the lot, such as it was, if he didn't have the kids to consider, but what was a guy to do?

He had yet to learn that posing a rhetorical question of this nature to Teddy was unwise. Only too often she had an answer.

'We must *what*?' he gasped, nearly clipping the tail of a tractor he was overtaking.

'I just said, we must see if we can't patch your marriage back together again,' she replied, as though this were the most obvious solution in the world – and indeed, to her way of thinking, it was. With young children involved, reconciliation must always be desirable. She might have sympathized with Lorette's wish for a divorce when she believed the husband in question to be a slavering monster of depravity, but having now detected the heart of gold beating within that unprepossessingly hirsute chest, she realized her duty was to help reunite the Beast with his Beauty. As she pointed out, Bill would need support on the domestic front if he were to return to work and set up a gallery and so forth, and she dared say Lorette could learn to curb her extravagance and shoulder her wifely responsibilities . . .

'Tell me I'm not hearing this,' growled the ungrateful recipient of her wise counsel. 'How can I get it into your head? It's over, Cuckoo and me, gone, dead, extinct – kaput.'

Teddy clicked her tongue. 'What is?'

'It. You know, *it*. The buzz, the fizz, the what-it's-all-about.'

'For a sensible, middle-aged chap you do spout some juvenile claptrap. Buzz and fizz indeed. The divorce courts wouldn't be nearly so busy if people only realized marriage isn't about that kind of nonsense.'

'Sez *Miss* Dunstan.'

'My personal marital status,' she retorted with dignity, 'is both beside the point and below the belt.'

'And lecturing me on my sex life isn't?'

'I wouldn't dream of discussing your sex life. I was talking about marriage.'

'Oh, completely different ball game,' said Bill, with heavy irony.

'Absolutely,' responded Teddy, with no irony at all. 'If you ask me, there's far too much importance attached to sex nowadays.'

'Not when you're not getting any, there ain't.'

'I say, do watch out. That light was nearly red.'

'Who's driving the bleedin' van?'

'Besides, being unmarried is no bar to expressing an opinion. One doesn't have to play cricket to grasp the rules.' Ignoring a snigger from the driving seat, she continued stoutly, 'What's more, if ever I do get hitched, which, as it happens, I trust I may one day—'

'No kidding?'

'—you can be sure it won't be on the basis of some half-baked romantic twaddle. Anyone with two brain cells to rub together can see that a partnership based on common sense, shared interests and mutual goodwill is a damn sight more likely to endure than one based on passing fancy.'

'What about *love*, you cold-blooded freak?'

'Grow up. Second left takes you into the square.'

'This is like arguing with Mr Spock.'

'That American child-rearing chap?'

'That pointy-eared pillock from the planet Vulcan. Hell's teeth, babe, Shakespeare didn't write sonnets to – to common sense.'

'Do you think you could keep both hands on the wheel?'

'Anna what's-her-name didn't chuck herself under a train on a goodwill exercise; *Paris*,' he roared, becoming quite carried away by his own eloquence, 'didn't besiege Troy so's Helen and him could have a quick game of Scrabble.' He glanced round because an odd noise was emanating from the passenger seat.

'Don't,' she moaned, 'laughing's agony with my stitches.'

'Serves you right. Anyway, I don't know what you think's so bloody funny.'

'Who'd ever imagine a hulking great toughie like you could be such a soggy old romantic?'

Bill swung the van into the alleyway beside their premises with vicious precision. 'Anyone ever threatened to tonk
you one?'

'*Frequently.*' She patted his knee. 'But I'm only trying to
help. What are friends for?'

He pulled up behind her kitchen door and stamped on the
brake. 'Look, sweetheart, I'm sure you mean well, but you're
wasting your breath.'

'People often tell me that, too,' said Teddy with unimpaired
cheerfulness.

'Because,' he continued firmly, 'never mind me, now she's
finally made the break, Cuckoo wouldn't come back if I was
the last bloke left on earth.' His mouth twisted. 'Unless I won
the lottery.'

'I feel sure you're doing her an injustice – and yourself.
After all, it can hardly have been for money she married
you.'

He shot her an oddly cynical look as he flung open his door.
'You reckon she fell for my big brown eyes?'

'I can't imagine *what* she saw in you,' declared Teddy before
she'd had time to reflect on her words. Blushing rosily, she
assured him she hadn't intended to be rude. All she'd meant to
say was that she was surprised Lorette had possessed the good
sense to recognize the many sterling qualities inside Bill's . . .
That is, to look beyond the . . .

Bill rolled his eyes. 'I think I'd sooner you stuck to being
rude.'

Fortunately for the continued prospering of good relations,
his wife turned up in person before Teddy could treat her new
friend to any further marriage-guidance counselling.

Lorette announced she wasn't just calling round to dump the
kids – although she had a splitting head on account of the cider
she'd drunk last night and another five minutes of them and that
demented dog would have driven her crazy – but because she'd
had a dead good idea. How long had the twins been back from
Scarborough? Oh, half an hour, but would Bill please shut up
and listen? He was not going to believe how brilliant her idea

was, and she and the brothers wanted to discuss it with him now. Yes, now.

Teddy heard all this from behind her kitchen door. Bill was still unloading the van, but she had mean-spiritedly limped indoors as fast as her crutches permitted the instant she saw rolling into the courtyard that lovingly waxed, sticker-festooned Morris shooting brake, recognizable to any inhabitant of Langley-le-Moor as the cherished chariot of Brian and Colin Rowbotham. Not that she undervalued those worthy pillars of the local community, you understand, but she had, of late, learned more than she ever wished to know about model railways, real ale, digital sound reproduction, Wurlitzer organs, league dominoes and a great deal else besides. Local wisdom held that it took five seconds for Colin to fix a fuse, and five hours for his brother to hand over the bill.

Thus she stumped through to the shop and deliberately dallied with Beryl in cashing up the till and checking the day's messages. These included, to her surprise, a large bouquet of exotic flowers, which, since the blooms were fashionably inter-woven with thistles, curly sticks and assorted veg, had clearly come from far afield and cost a packet. The accompanying card was inscribed: *From Hari, with eternal gratitude.*

'Him what knocked you down yesterday,' said Beryl help-fully. 'Came round lunchtime, full of how he might've ended up with a child's life on his conscience if it wasn't for you.'

'Nonsense,' said Teddy, turning the card over. 'Sweet thought all the same, as I must tell him, only I can't see an address, nor even a surname . . .'

'He seemed to think you'd know where to find him.'

'What?'

'He's away now for a couple of days, but said he'd be seeing you soon. He *said*,' added Beryl, with the air of one who had been saving the best until last, 'all this was meant to be.'

'I beg your pardon?'

'Quite good looking, isn't he?'

'How on earth should I know?' Too late, Teddy recognized a more than usually speculative gleam in her assistant's eye. Cursing afresh the day Bella ever uttered the words 'lonely hearts', she seized the telephone message pad. 'Charlie rang?'

'Twice,' confirmed Beryl, reluctantly abandoning romantic conjecture. 'Sounded like he'd got his knickers in a proper twist. Out now, but please will you call him tomorrow.'

With a sigh, Teddy realized she had barely given a thought to the untangling of Ma's mischief at Mill House. Pondering this as she locked up after her assistant and plonked her mysterious bouquet back in its bucket, she forgot to check whether the shooting brake was still in the yard before limping out of the back door.

'Well, if it isn't the gallant heroine of the hour herself,' boomed an all-too-familiar voice. 'Hail to thee, fair lady!'

Brian Rowbotham was standing by the open doors of the former abattoir from which echoed the happy shrieks of children creating mayhem. He was a shortish, balding man of forty, with a prominent paunch, protuberant blue eyes, and a breast pocket importantly a-bristle with badges, Biros and screwdrivers. A few paces behind him, peering into the gloom of the outhouse, lurked his brother, Colin. He, by contrast, was tall, shy, shock-haired and thickly spectacled, and although a scant two years younger than his brother, possessed still the gangling limbs and spotty chin of adolescence. In his childhood, his anxious mother had feared her younger son must be retarded, so silent was he, until, at the age of nine, he dismantled, repaired and faultlessly reassembled a valve wireless, demonstrating an IQ later assessed at genius level. Colin remained a prodigy of few words, however, interspersing occasional gnomic utterances with a honking laugh and only blossoming into garrulity when seated behind the turntables of his mobile discothèque. Neither bore any discernible resemblance to their lovely young sister, who was leaning on the bonnet of their car, scowling at her husband. Bill, she declared, couldn't do this to her. Bill, feet akimbo, brawny arms laced across his chest, retorted that he bloody well could, just try and stop him.

'Family affairs,' said Teddy smartly. 'I'll leave you to it.'

Brian, however, was already at her side. Lowering his voice and glancing about him in a decidedly peculiar way, he confided that he had been awaiting just such an opportunity for a little chinwag with her good self.

'Oh?' she said. 'Bill, have you brought the green chiller box in?'

Brian was, he continued, a plain-speaking man, and far be it from him to charge in where angels feared to tread, but a little bird (no names, no pack drill) had dropped a hint to him with regard, if he may so express himself, to Miss Dunstan's *personal* life and—

He was interrupted by a squeal from his sister who had spotted Teddy. Breaking off from her quarrel, Lorette offered shuddering sympathy for Teddy's disfigurement along with fervent thanks for Ferdy's salvation and an even more fervent declaration that she deserved to get her picture in the papers for such bravery and self-sacrifice, she did, honest. The heroine's less than gracious retort that this would be over her dead body coincided rather inopportunely with Brian's murmured suggestion of calling round again for a more private chat. Colin, meanwhile, observed to no one in particular that a duck, when swimming, was six times less energy efficient than a ship, and Bill roared that if they'd only belt up and push off home he could get the sodding van unloaded.

'But you won't *listen*,' wailed Lorette, abandoning attempts to persuade Teddy to milk this chance of celebrity.

'I've work to do.'

Brian winked jovially at Teddy. 'How's your new assistant shaping up then? We never see our Billy boy with a paintbrush in his hand, but he's always been a talented artist with the old washing-up mop, eh?'

'Yak-yak-yak,' honked Colin.

'Drop dead,' grunted Bill.

'Now then,' chided Brian. 'Do I detect a short in the old humour circuits?'

'He's a big fat pig,' snapped Lorette. 'Everyone thinks it's a fantastic idea except him.'

'Look,' said her husband, with the air of a man whose patience is wearing thin. 'Not a word against Lil, I love your mum like she was my own, but that don't mean I want to go and live with her.'

'You only came back to this cruddy village to be near her.'

'For a bit of babysitting, not full-time board and lod-ging. Anyway, Lil doesn't want me and two kids packing her place out.'

'There'd be *tons* of room,' declared Lorette, 'once Brian and Col have gone.'

'And it's not just a question of somewhere to live. I gotta work, earn some dosh.'

'You mean paint?'

'Whaddya think I mean?'

'Good question,' she snarled.

'Temper, temper,' murmured her elder brother.

Husband and wife both glared at him, and the brief ces-sation of hostilities gave Teddy the opportunity to enquire why on earth Bill should wish to take up residence with his mama-in-law.

Thus she learned that Lorette's splendid scheme entailed her brothers using their inheritance to buy out Bill's lease, and moving in next door themselves. What was more, as Brian eagerly informed her, with a place as big as the abattoir, they'd been wondering whether they couldn't open their railway to public view once in a while. Colin had already designed a state-of-the-art speaker system to supply digital stereo sound effects. Teddy, he declared, could not begin to imagine the symphonic glories of the Flying Scotsman steaming into a tunnel. Teddy said she was very sure she could not, and eyed Bill with some anxiety.

'They're talking crap,' he sighed, hefting a crate of plates out of the van.

'We're talking *money*,' corrected Brian with undentable good humour. 'Remember what that is, chummy? Crinkly stuff with the swirly patterns?'

Bill's response was succinctly Anglo-Saxon.

'Gently, gently,' tutted his brother-in-law. 'We have mem-bers of the fair sex present. Besides, I'm sure you'll change your tune, when I tell you we're offering a handsome premium.'

Bill paused in hoisting a second crate to his shoulder. 'Premium?'

'Over and above the buy-out of the lease, in consideration of moving expenses, inconvenience, goodwill, et cetera, et cetera. Standard practice in arrangements like this. And for Lorette's sake, I think I can say we're prepared to err on the generous side.'

'And you and me split the lot between us,' she said eagerly.

'Dream on,' said Bill, adding, for good measure, that on top of everything else, he wasn't prepared to pull such a trick on the nice old biddy what'd rented him the joint in the first place. Teddy's attention was straying, however. It had suddenly occurred to her that a deal of this sort might prove the answer to her own family troubles. Could Charlie bribe Ma's tenant into relinquishing the lease on Mill House? And, if so, how much would it cost? She was wondering whether she could enquire the going rate of Brian when she realized the argument had taken a new and rather ugly turn.

'No judge in the world,' Bill was declaring, 'is going to chuck a father and his kids out of their home just to give their mum a bit of pocket money.'

'If I had custody,' said his wife hotly, 'you'd have to give me this place – you'd have to give me everything.'

He glanced uneasily towards the open doors of the abattoir and lowered his voice. 'But you don't want custody.'

She eyed him defiantly. 'I love my kids.'

'Sure you do, so long as some other bugger looks after 'em.' Then, with a visible effort, he controlled his irritation. 'Look, babe, I've heard you out, so go home now, will you? The twins've had a long day and I want to get them bathed and off to bed.'

But Lorette was fast working herself up into a tantrum. 'Say I fight you for custody?'

'And pigs will fucking fly,' growled her husband.

Teddy could not feel it was wise of Brian to intervene at this juncture, whatever her sympathy with his point of view.

Bill swung round to stare at his brother-in-law. 'I beg your fucking pardon?'

'I said,' Brian repeated, folding his hands over his jutting paunch, 'and not for the first time, I may add, that I don't care to hear barrack-room language used in the presence of ladies.'

'Too fucking right, Brother,' snapped Lorette, and turned

back to her husband. 'I'll fight you, I will.' Her voice was rising, with tears threatening. 'I'll go for custody, and then you'll have to let Brian and Col take this place.'

'If you win,' roared Bill, 'and believe me, babe, you haven't a cat in hell's.'

Which was when Brian made an even bigger mistake. Teddy imputed no malice to him. It was with an air of entirely disinterested thoughtfulness he ventured to observe that, although his own courtroom experience was confined to the magistrates' bench, he believed Bill might just find himself on a sticky wicket here, legally speaking. Setting aside the natural judicial bias in favour of the mother–child bond – and Brian had never concealed his personal conviction that the children should remain with his sister – there were aspects peculiar to this case which, he felt, would be bound to carry weight with the gentlemen of the law. He was not referring merely to Bill's, ahem, bohemian mode of life . . .

'Watch it,' breathed the bohemian.

'What's he on about?' said Lorette.

. . . but in assessing whether he was a fit person to take charge of two youngsters, a judge would be bound to consider the respective ages of the parents. Now, were it to be drawn to his notice that Lorette had been a student, barely more than a child herself, when—

Here his musings ceased abruptly because Bill had grabbed him by the collar of his sports jacket. Was practically lifting him off his feet, in truth, and shaking him vigorously enough to rattle several Biros to the ground.

'Listen here, sunshine, and listen good,' he snarled, nose-to-nose, 'no one and nothing comes between me and my kids. Not now, not never. Geddit?'

'Yeah,' whooped Ferdy, unexpectedly hurtling out of the abattoir. 'They're fighting. Bash him one, Dad.'

'I said, *do you get it?*'

'He can't speak if you don't let go,' snapped Florence. 'Oh, shut up, Birdie.'

'If violence is the repartee of the illiterate,' enquired Colin, seemingly of the sky, 'should Kalashnikovs be melted into typewriters?'

Lorette exploded into tears, Ferdy jigged up and down punching the air while Florence hauled fruitlessly at her father's arm and yelled at the hysterical dog, until Teddy – watching this exhibition in stunned outrage – at last recovered her wits.

Hitching up her crutches with the resolution of a Boadicea confronted by a particularly unsavoury rabble of Romans, she swung forward.

Chapter Sixteen

'Gladys Simpson,' declared Bill the following morning, 'that's who you reminded me of, gym teacher when I was a kid. Five feet nothing with a voice like a chainsaw – Glad the Impaler we used to call her.' He upped his pitch to a stentorian soprano. '"*Bill! Put him down this instant, do you hear? Brian, quiet! Florence, control that animal. Lorette, I can only say I'm disappointed in you, deeply*—"' Here, however, he broke off coughing.

Teddy looked up from the list she was compiling at her kitchen table. 'Brian Rowbotham may be a pompous little fart, but that's no excuse for strangling him.'

'I wasn't going to damage him.' He took a swig of coffee. 'Much. God, I feel like death. I should never have got on to the Ouzo.'

'Ouzo?'

'Only bottle I could find in the house last night. Quit scowling, I needed a drink.'

'Not half so much as Brian did, I dare say. I wouldn't mind, but he's only half your size.'

'OK, OK, so I was out of order. I said I'm sorry, what more d'you want, blood?'

'Animal.'

A glint lit his bleary eye. 'You know he fancies you.'

Her head jerked up. '*Brian Rowbotham?*'

He winced. 'Watch it, babe. Sudden noise can be fatal to a bloke in my condition. Anyway, you can't kid me you hadn't twigged. "Hail, fair maiden," all that bullshit.'

'Don't be ridiculous.'

'Know what I reckon? He heard you was advertising for a soul mate and thought he might be in with a – Gawd almighty, don't jump at me like that. I know, I know, there never was no ad, it's all my fault anyone thinks otherwise, and I'm grovelling at your feet.' He eyed her sideways. 'Mind, just think of all those interests you could share. Who needs romance with the biggest train set in North Yorkshire?'

'Buzz off, will you, I'm up to my eyes.' Since Teddy was holding out her cup for a refill, however, she evidently didn't expect him to pay much heed. He had been lured round to her kitchen, as he frankly informed her, by the smell of fresh coffee. The cafetière lay on the table between them, now half empty, while the twins squabbled over toast and orange juice outside. Restored by a good night's sleep, Teddy was determinedly making up for time lost to injury, and the table was also scattered with invoices, orders and lists. She had reduced the bandage on her foot to manageable proportions, swapped the crutches for a stick, and pronounced her face to be well on the way to recovery. Yes, of course it still *looked* a mess, she had responded irritably to Bill's observation that she seemed to be blossoming from a Picassoesque blue period into a full-blown Turner sunset. Any fool, in her view, should know that the worse bruises looked, the faster they were healing. Besides, before he cast any more rude aspersions, he might just glance in his own mirror, and *his* ills were self-inflicted. That twaddle about being driven to the bottle by his wife's threats was the limpest excuse for a hangover she'd heard in years.

'Lorette didn't mean a word,' she stated now, when he glumly wondered whether it was worth putting up shelves in a house from which he might find himself evicted any day. 'Temper talking.'

'You do mind-reading, too?'

'You said yourself she wouldn't really try to take the children.'

'Yeah, but if she gets some shark of a divorce lawyer egging her on?' He grimaced. 'She's well pissed off about ending up broke, that's for sure.'

'So why doesn't she get a job?'

'Joke.'

'I'm perfectly serious. Has she ever worked?'

'Six months part-time in a dress shop, couple of years back. Only she spent more than she earned. Oh, and a stint in the local off licence.' Bill grinned crookedly. 'And I spent more than she earned. No, seriously, you know Cuckoo. God didn't put her on this earth to work for a living. She needs a nice rich man to spoil her silly.' He sighed. 'And I dare say she'll find one, but until then I dunno what she'll do. It wouldn't be so bad if Lily hadn't given all that cash to the Ugly Brothers.'

Teddy had picked up a sheaf of invoices, but she paused, looking up. 'Frankly, I've never believed such a fair-minded woman genuinely intended to dish out thousands to two of her children and ignore the other. I should go and have a word with her, if I were you.'

'No way.'

'Why on earth not?'

He bridled. 'And look like *I* was sniffing round Stanley's little stash? I couldn't stand the bastard, the way he treated Lil. I'd sooner starve than touch a penny of his.'

'No one's asking you to, you clot. This is for Lorette.'

'So? She's still married to me. I'm the one failing to cough up the alimony, aren't I?' He squared his shoulders, looking as nobly heroic as was possible for a hung-over gorilla. Which was not very. 'Down to me to sort it out.'

'Never will I fathom the idiocies of the masculine mind.' Teddy grabbed her stick and hauled herself to her feet. 'Speaking of which, I must ring my brother. By the way, did Brian actually say how big a sweetener they were offering you?'

Bill's eyes widened. 'You're never suggesting I accept?'

'And have the Flying Scot thundering round my back yard?' She limped over to the phone. 'Might have assisted with a little family matter of my own, that's all.'

As he flicked desultorily through the newspaper, she could be heard informing her brother that, yes, this was the only answer and, yes, he would jolly well have to brace up and bite the bullet. He should present himself down here at lunchtime. Why? Because they were going to write a letter on her computer offering to buy out this tenant, that was why. One o'clock sharp.

'Question,' murmured Bill on her return. 'What's the difference between you and God?'

'I beg your pardon?'

'The Almighty took Sundays off. You ever get tired of running the world?'

'When there is trouble in one's family,' replied Teddy with dignity, 'one is duty bound to do one's bit.'

This was a sentiment which would have been heartily endorsed by Lily Rowbotham. It was not until lunchtime, however, that she learned of the latest trouble brewing within her own family.

Lorette, no early riser, commented, as she plonked a magnifying mirror on the kitchen windowsill, that she didn't know why she bothered making up, because the troglodytes round here wouldn't notice if you painted your face blue. She just thanked her lucky stars she'd be off and away soon.

'First I've heard of it,' commented Lily dryly. 'Going anywhere nice?'

Lorette, tracing a fine line beneath one eye, said she hadn't decided long-term, but fancied a fortnight in Marbella for starters. When her mother enquired how she was planning to finance this jaunt, it is surely to the credit of Lorette's natural honesty, if not her native wit, that she did not hesitate to explain exactly how. And when the storm broke, she was astonished her mother should take such exception to her brilliant scheme – a scheme which, as she pointed out, would at the very least even things up between herself and her brothers. And as for being told off for chiselling money out of Bill, money the poor boy didn't have . . .

'He's got more than me,' she squawked indignantly.

'You'd have been getting plenty,' thundered her mother. 'Aye, you may well stare. You daft bat, did you really think I'd treat you any different from Brian and Colin?'

'You mean . . .' She stared at Lily. 'How much?'

'Wouldn't you like to know. But I'm bloody well thinking again now.'

Angry tears glittered in her eyes. 'You're just winding me up. You've given them the lot already.'

'Suit yourself.' Lily pursed her lips. 'But I'll promise you one thing, our lass. Way you're carrying on now, you'll end up not just out of pocket, but out of this house. For good and all.'

'Don't worry,' snapped Lorette, jumping to her feet and tumbling cosmetics into her bag. 'I'm going now.'

'Don't you touch that car.'

'I don't want your lousy car. I'm – I'm going for a walk.'

'Walk?' yelled her mother incredulously. 'You'd tek a bus to the lavatory if there was one running.'

The back door slammed. Breathing heavily, Lily subsided into her chair and groped for a cigarette and the telephone.

'Kids,' she muttered. 'Who'd have 'em?'

Teddy was gratified to learn that Bill had seen sense, and was going to talk things over with his mother-in-law after all.

'Lil's idea,' he retorted touchily. 'It was her phoned me.'

Before she could enquire further, Teddy heard a masculine voice out in the shop, asking Beryl if, *hergh*, Miss Dunstan was available.

'Charlie.' She eyed her watch. 'About time too.' The louvred doors flapped open and her brother advanced with the wariness natural to any right-thinking chap venturing into domestic quarters.

'*Hergh*, sorry I'm late, old thing, but Jeremy finally rolled up a couple of hours ago, and—' He stopped dead and gaped at her. 'Dear God, woman, *your face*.'

''Orrible, innit?' growled a voice to his right. 'And it's all my doing.'

Which was when, wheeling round to discover the source of this basso profundo interpolation, Sir Charles received his second shock, even more unsettling than the first. Not only did his sister look as though she'd gone ten rounds with Mike Tyson; there, perched on the cooker, cool as you please, with a convict crew-cut and a chest hairier than your average retriever, was an ugly great thug claiming responsibility.

'Nonsense, it was an accident,' snapped Teddy. 'Bill, this is my brother Charles Dunstan. Charlie,' she continued, steel glittering in her voice, 'this is my new neighbour and good friend, Bill Smith.' Having watched them shake hands – with palpable reluctance on one side and slack-jawed incredulity on the other – she judged it prudent to dismiss her good friend, cordially instructing him to take a couple more aspirin and give her love to Lily.

'Bugger even wears an earring,' breathed Sir Charles, watching the shorn head pass the kitchen window.

'He's an artist,' said his sister, as though this must explain a great deal. 'Of sorts.'

'Looks a dodgy customer to me.'

'Very likeable, once you get to know him, and quite extraordinarily well house-trained. Anyway, to business. The computer's upstairs.'

And while Sir Charles is put to work, and Bill Smith departs for Lily's, perhaps we can seize our chance to sneak off to the woods for a little romantic interlude. Let's face it, as fairytales go, this one has been pretty thin on the love interest so far, and the time has come to redress the balance.

First, some appropriate scene setting. Imagine, if you will, a sun-dappled sylvan glade, with willows weeping, birds serenading, dragonflies darting, breeze sighing: the full idyllic works. The grounds of Langley Hall (open ten a.m. to six p.m., dogs on lead only) are famously picturesque at all seasons, and on this particular summer afternoon, Home Wood was looking one hundred per cent its mossy-knolled, daisy-strewn prettiest. Nymphs and shepherds would feel quite at home.

Jeremy Dunstan, strolling down a root-rutted path, also felt quite at home, but that was only because he had been born and reared here, not because he was a nature lover. Indeed, with his honey-tanned limbs, Italian shorts and mirrored sunglasses propping back a mane of black hair (of a shoulder lapping length guaranteed to set his sister groping for scissors), he looked much more a creature of the Californian beaches he had so recently quit than a native of this bucolic paradise.

While he mooched along, he was analysing his most recent performance, as any serious actor must – 'The *low* fat spread for you. The low fat spread for *you*' – wondering whether he might perhaps have been over-hasty in quitting LA. Happy, as any serious actor must be, to exchange the tawdry glamour of Hollywood for the more austere challenges of the British theatre, Jeremy nevertheless could not help fretting that around the next corner might have been the offer which would launch his career out of the tawdriness of one-day parts into the glamour of superstardom. Not, to be sure, that he would dream of selling out his art to mere fame and fortune, but lack of money seemed a lame excuse for coming home. A dedicated performer, he reminded himself, should be prepared to starve, at any rate between trust fund instalments . . . At this point in his musings, however, the path twisted and widened into the aforementioned sylvan glade, and *wham!* The world stopped turning. His heart stopped beating. Even the birds stopped singing – not that he'd heard them anyway.

This fabulous creature was sitting on the bank of the stream – here, practically in Jeremy's own back yard – as though dropped like a goddess from Heaven. Her hair glittered in the sun like spun copper; her eyes shone the liquid blue-green of the ocean; her legs . . .

But perhaps we can skip the rest of the eulogy. We've got the picture: red hair, turquoise eyes, long legs, it's got to be Lorette Smith sitting by the beck, and we already know she's drop-dead sexy.

Jeremy Dunstan, however, would have us understand he wasn't thinking about *sex,* Puh-lease. He was undergoing a mysterious and profoundly spiritual experience here. *Oh yes he was.* He was staring into that face, those eyes . . . She was a total stranger, right? He was sure he'd never seen her before, because you couldn't forget a woman like this, not in a million years, but he was looking at her now, and it was as if he'd known her since the day he was born. Can you believe it? He could only suppose their souls must have journeyed together in another life.

(One can understand why Teddy thought it was a mistake for her baby brother to go to California.)

The Goddess spoke first. 'Here,' she said, blowing her nose and stuffing the tissue into her handbag, 'don't I know you from somewhere?'

Amazing, cried Jeremy to himself, she felt it too. Man, this was blowing his mind.

It was blowing his mind to such an extent he even forgot his duty to his Art. An actor, after all, should note his spontaneous reactions at a pivotal moment like this, and tuck that memory away in the emotional archive against the day he is called upon to give his Romeo or his Abelard. However, since theatre audiences are unlikely to be galvanized by a young Montague who, on sighting Ms Capulet, does nothing but stand, glassy-eyed and gulping for air like a handsome codfish, it is possible the loss to British Theatre is not irreparable.

Observing that those oceanic eyes were in fact swimming with tears, our dumbstruck Romeo found words at last. 'You're crying.'

'Yup,' she agreed, with a juicy sniff. 'I'm dead cheesed off, one way and another, plus my feet are killing me—' But then she stopped. And . . . she smiled. It seemed to Jeremy trumpets sounded and a thousand suns broke out at once. 'I know who you are,' she cried jubilantly. 'It was the long hair fooled me. But it's – oh, what were he called? – *Dylan* that's it.'

'Jeremy, actually,' he began, just a shade daunted. '*Jez* . . . Oh, I see.' He coughed modestly, and shook the hair off his shoulders. 'You caught that old thing, did you? *District Hospital*?'

'Every episode,' she assured him. 'Dead good, apart from the creep of a consultant. Did he really kill her?'

Jeremy swallowed. 'Uh, wow, I'm afraid I don't remember. Seems an awfully long time ago, and I've been in Hollywood more or less ever since.'

Her lips parted. Her eyes widened. And when she spoke it was with the reverence of one uttering a sacred incantation. '*Hollywood*?'

Chapter Seventeen

'Silly cow,' grunted Lily. 'Don't get me wrong, I'd stand between my daughter and a bullet any day, but I'll not sit around and let her do this to you.'

'I don't want you involved,' protested Bill. 'It's my own fault for earning zilch all this time.' He stretched, yawning. 'Anyway, chances are she won't do it – fight me for the kids, I mean. That's according to Her Next Door What Knows Everything.'

Lily chuckled. 'How're you getting on with Teddy?'

'Like a house on fire – sparks flying and bloody dangerous. No, no, she's all right. We've had a few laughs.'

They were sprawled in deckchairs on the patio of 3 Meadows Close, with a fringed umbrella overhead and misted glasses of beer on the table between them. Watching his children cavort naked and shrieking under a sprinkler at the far end of the lawn, Bill was feeling rather sorry for himself, if truth be told, and not just because of the lingering remnants of a hangover. Well, look at him, as he said to his mother-in-law after a moment. Forty-two, career in tatters, rented roof over his head, and the next thing to skint with two kids to bring up – pathetic spectacle or what? The surprise wasn't that Cuckoo had jacked him in now; it was that she hadn't done so years ago.

'I do wish you wouldn't call her that,' cut in Lily unexpectedly.

'Cuckoo? Suits her all ways if you ask me.'

To his surprise, she shot him a very sharp look. 'Why's that?'

'Never mind she's off with the fairies half the time, innit

cuckoos dump their eggs for some other mug to do the feeding and rearing?'

'Oh aye,' she said heavily. 'Aye, happen.' She leaned across and patted his knee. 'Well, she knows what I think. I've told her she'll not find another like you.'

'She'd run a mile if she did. If you ask me, one reason she hasn't flitted long since is that she's scared witless of making the same mistake twice. Once bitten, all that.' He shut his eyes, settling back more comfortably into his chair. 'I just hope she doesn't trot off to some sharp-shooting solicitor, that's all, because even if he doesn't twist her arm to go for care and control, she could run up a fortune in legal bills, and I know whose mat they'd land on.'

'She won't, believe you me.'

'I wish I had your confidence.'

'Look, love, I asked you round because it's high time I set your mind at rest. No, be quiet and listen. It's not your fault this kick-up, it's mine – mine for kidding our lass I wasn't giving her any money. It's just I were that mad at her for ditching you and the twins . . . Still, I'm going to set everything straight now. Soon as she gets back I'll be telling Lorette she lays off you or she'll not get her share. And this time,' she added with feeling, 'I damn well mean it.'

Bill turned to squint at his mother-in-law. 'You're taking some back off Brian and Colin? They won't be too chuffed.'

'Don't talk soft. What I've got for Lorette's separate.'

'Here,' he said, struggling upright in some alarm, 'you're not flogging off your pension, are you?'

'Course I'm not. Oh, give over glowering. If you must know, it's a bit of jewellery I'm going to sell.'

And that nearly did for Bill. Bad enough to have your mum-in-law feeling obliged to gallop to the rescue at all, but when she started talking about flogging her trinkets – he didn't know whether to laugh or cry. Still less did he know how to tell her the entire contents of her jewellery box were unlikely to keep Lorette in tights. But she evidently saw his glance flicker to the pin-sized gem in her battered engagement ring.

'Don't fret, it'll fetch enough to keep her happy. Although,

Lord knows, that little madam could fritter twenty thousand in a month if she set her mind to it.'

At this, he nearly toppled out of his deckchair. 'Twenty grand?'

'Same as the lads.'

'But for a bit of . . . Bloody Nora, girl, what've you been up to? Robbing the Crown Jewels?'

'Never you mind.' Staring at her rose beds, she gave an odd, rather sad smile. 'Bit of a pang parting with it, that's all. But I keep telling myself things is only things.'

'Jesus, Lily, you're making me feel terrible.'

'Rubbish. Nowt to do with you. You don't think I'd ever treat one of my kids different from t'others, do you?'

He pulled a face. 'Exactly what she said.'

'Who?'

'Her ladyship next door. And won't she just remind me of it.'

'Here,' said Lily sharply, grasping his hand. 'Not a word where this money's coming from to Teddy Dunstan – nor anyone else. Just say I'm squaring up accounts.'

'Sure. Whatever you like.'

'Promise?'

'Blimey, Lil, what is this? Cross my heart. Mind you,' he continued, after a moment, 'it beats me why you're making these sacrifices. Why didn't you just split the old man's stash three ways in the first place?'

There followed a pause so pregnant Mr Smith is here to tell you it practically gave birth.

'I had my reasons.'

Of course, he should have taken the hint. Should have recognized that this can of worms was none of his business and tactfully changed the subject. 'Like what?' he said.

At which she bent over and began twitching weeds from a crack in the paving stones. 'The lads deserved that money. Their dad never gave them their due.'

'Nor you, mean old sod.'

She looked up, and, to Bill's bewilderment, her eyes were shiny with tears. 'But I did all right by him, didn't I?'

'All right by Stan? You were a bloody saint, girl.'

'Don't you believe it.' And she swept on before he could protest: 'Worried myself sick, I did, when I found how much he'd got hidden away. I always knew he had something in that old box, course I did. Ever since the day the chip pan caught fire, and he ran straight past the baby to grab his precious tin.'

'And you deserved every penny. If you'd any sense, you'd have collared the lot and booked a world cruise.'

'If shrouds had pockets, he'd have taken it with him,' she retorted. 'But there he was, dead, and there was all this money, staring at me. And – and I could only think he'd want it to go to his children.' She fumbled in her sleeve for a tissue, swabbed one eye. 'He might not have had a good word to say for 'em, by and large, but – but—'

'Hey, sweetheart, what is all this? No call for you to go upsetting yourself.'

'You asked; I'm telling you.' She knotted the tissue between her fingers. 'I made up my mind that very night it had to go to his kids. So I counted it up and I split it straight down the middle.'

Bill blinked. 'But what about Cuckoo?'

'You soft ha'porth,' she burst out. 'Can't you bloody guess?'

Our nymph and shepherd meanwhile had exchanged their sun-kissed glade for the beer-scented gloom of the King's Arms, where there was less danger of moss stains to expensive clothing. Behind a barrel table in a quiet corner of the saloon bar, they were gazing into one another's eyes, breathlessly sharing opinions on life, love, Art and hair gels. Naturally they would have preferred to be thus mingling their souls in a finer and more private place – and mingling possibly rather more than their souls, come to that – but they had soon established that they were both cursed with being resident, for the time being, in family homes, beset by mothers and assorted relatives.

This was by no means the only thing they had in common, far from it. There seemed no end to the parallels they were discovering between their lives. A miraculous conjunction of the stars, marvelled Jeremy. Spooky, agreed Lorette. They both hated navel rings, loved cats and avoided cheese and onion crisps, on the identical grounds that one mouthful made your breath stink for hours. But their bond went deeper still. Get this. Not only was each a late arrival in a family with two much older siblings, they had been born in the same village and the same year, a mere three miles and four months apart. And yet – can you believe this? – they had never met. For sure, Jeremy had been dimly aware as a schoolboy home on vacation that the Rowbotham family included a red-haired daughter, and Lorette certainly knew Teddy and Sir Charles had a younger brother, but even so . . .

'"Too early seen unknown, and known too late!"' he declared.

'Pardon?'

'Shakespeare,' he responded, with forgivable pride, given the aptness of the context, '*Romeo and Juliet*.'

'Who was in it?' enquired Lorette.

Even Jeremy, however, felt unable to detect the existence of a long-standing blood feud between their families. Relations between Dunstans and Rowbothams, such as they were, had always seemed mundanely cordial.

'My mum works for your sister these days,' offered Lorette. 'I think she used to cook up at the Hall, too, years back.'

'Lily? Yah, but that was before we were born, of course. I remember her saying to me—'

'Hang about,' she cut in. 'You know my mum? To talk to?'

'Lily? Sure, known her all my life. Love her to bits.'

'You're telling me . . .' Her eyes widened in indignation. 'She knows about you being a famous actor and that?'

His cough was suitably modest. 'She's aware what I do, absolutely. In fact, it was Lily who persuaded me to give Hollywood a go.'

'*What?*'

'At Pa's funeral. She was such a star. I hadn't run into her for yonks, and I was telling her what a fuss the family was kicking up about my idea of going over to the States, whingeing on about proper jobs, the inevitable bourgeois crap. Lily just winked and whispered I should ignore the lot of them, pack my bags and hop on a plane.' Jeremy shrugged. 'Which is what I did, more or less. I remember sending her a postcard to say thanks.'

Bill was having a real problem getting his head round this one. 'Cuckoo? She really is a cuckoo in the nest?'

'Give over,' said Lily, blowing her nose loudly. 'It happens.'

'Who then? I mean, who's her dad?'

'Dead,' she mumbled into her tissue. 'So it doesn't matter.'

But if she wasn't telling him that, she was only too ready to confess the rest. She'd obviously been bottling up her big secret for years and, once the top came off, there was no stemming the flood. Bill wasn't surprised, because it soon emerged that Lorette was not the product of some passing fling, but of a full-blown, rip-roaring affair that had blazed across a quarter of a century and more, ending only when Lily's ageing Casanova finally fell off the perch, a couple of years ago. Dazedly, he realized they must still have been going strong when he first met his mother-in-law – and he, like everyone else, had never suspected a blind thing.

Otherwise, though, the tale she recounted to Bill sounded at first like any old adulterer's saga. The guy was married, natch, kids growing up and away, what a surprise, wife didn't understand him, all the usual tripe, and the bastard had led Lil on by making out he was ready to jack in the missus and skip off with her.

'Which I should've realized was pie in the sky,' she commented wistfully, and Bill agreed, randy men being the liars they are, but, oh no, Lily wouldn't hear a word of criticism. Tried to convince him it was fear of the rumpus they'd kick up that had made *both* of them keep putting off the decision to cut and run. He didn't argue, but he didn't entirely believe her either. Yeah, yeah, this was a country village twenty-five years ago, but it was hardly the Dark Ages. You wouldn't get thrown in the stocks for a bit of the old extra-marital. Whatever the cause, anyhow, they were still shilly-shallying when Mrs Casanova pulled the oldest trick in the book and announced she was pregnant. A real sock in the eye for Lil because – wouldn't you just know it? – Lover Boy had led her on that there'd been no action in the marital bed for years. Told her he must have been so pissed after some party or other he hadn't known what he was doing – a likely story, in Bill's view. But he had to hand it to the mother-in-law. She didn't just get mad, she got even. A few months later, she was up the duff too. One hundred per cent deliberate.

'If I couldn't have him,' she declared defiantly, 'I reckoned I'd have a little bit of him all to myself.'

Bill's jaw had dropped so often, he was getting a crick in it. 'Did he know?'

'What d'you think I am, daft? Only fib I ever told him,' she added sadly. 'But it were for his own good.'

And although she contemplated upping and offing with her unborn babe – after all, she'd been thinking about leaving Stan for years – she never did. Lover Boy was still panting down the road, and so long as Stan was fed and watered three times a day, he wasn't going to notice anything. As she said, the only thing ever made him look up from the telly was the rustle of a fiver. Besides, she had Brian and Colin to consider, too. So the boys kept their mum, Lorette was born into a respectable family, and Lily and her fella went back to romping away like happy rabbits until one day – out of the blue – his heart gave out.

This was the only point in the long story that Lily's voice cracked. And it didn't require much imagination to understand why his dying so suddenly must have been terrible for her. There they were, she and her fancy man, well past silver wedding vintage on their non-marriage, and she couldn't so much as drop a rose on his coffin. Couldn't tell anyone what she was suffering either, and was scared stiff of going to the funeral in case she made a fool of herself. Only, of course, she couldn't *not* go, either . . .

'Sorry,' she gasped brokenly, 'be all right in a tic.'

'You have yourself a bloody good sob,' he urged, wrapping an arm round her shoulders and hugging her tight. 'Time you did.'

Typical Lil, though, after a minute she was pulling away, insisting she'd no cause for moaning. They'd had a damn good run, she and . . . she and her friend, and at least she would always have the comfort of knowing he died with a smile on his face.

'You don't mean—?'

'Sex doesn't stop just because you cross sixty,' she snapped indignantly. 'Or seventy in his case. Anyway, even that weren't quite the finish.' So saying, she hauled herself out of her deckchair and pottered into the house, returning with a slim leather box in her hand.

'Came with a courier, few weeks after he died,' she said. 'He knew I'd never let him give me owt like this when he were alive, so he'd left it in his solicitor's keeping years before. Good thing Stan was asleep that afternoon, because I tell you I wept buckets.'

And Bill could see why. He wasn't looking at the flashy necklace – although Casanova must've been worth a bob or ten if it was real – no, he was studying the little card inside. Tiny, crabby hand: *My Lily needs no gilding*, he read, *but she has this with all my love. Always.*

'It wasn't just sex, you see,' said Lily, wiping a tear from her eye, 'it was the real thing.'

And Bill's not ashamed to tell you his own eyes were on the shiny side, too. In fact he wished Miss No-Romance-Please-We're-British Dunstan could have heard all this. Teach her a thing or two.

Chapter Eighteen

Appropriately enough, Teddy was at the time commanding her elder brother kindly to stop wittering like a lovesick adolescent so that she could check through their letter.

'*Hergh*, all very well, Ted, but she's behaving damned oddly. I'm not imagining it. Charging out to meet the post van, jumping like a terrier in a warren when the phone rings.'

'Nervy, always has been. *Dear Mr Stakinos*, yes, well, the first para's straightforward enough.'

'And Ma said jokingly – at least I think she was joking – Ma said she was behaving just as if . . . God, I can't bear to tell you what she said.'

'Here we go. *Owing to an unforeseen change in family circumstances, I was wondering if there might be any possibility* . . .'

'You don't think she's having an affair?'

'. . . *of your considering* – Bella?' Only an exceptionally acute ear would have detected a half-beat of hesitation. 'Don't be ridiculous. Ma should be ashamed of herself for suggesting such a shocking thing. You must tell her so, Charlie.'

'Bit tricky when she's not speaking to me,' he said miserably. 'Cut me dead after I said we wanted to buy out the tenant.'

'Make the most of it, I would.' Teddy blew a stray hair off the letter.

'Old girl was only doing her bit to help, renting out Mill House.' He tugged his ear. 'You know, with the renovation costs.'

'My arse,' retorted his sister inelegantly. 'Anyway, so long as Bella knows what you're up to.'

'I tried to tell her, but she just said it was too late. And that it was all my fault for letting Ma get away with murder for so long.'

'Well . . .'

'Don't you start, Sis.'

'Where was I? Um . . . *leaves us anxious to regain possession of the property as early as possible.*'

'So nobody's speaking to me up there now.'

'*Naturally the estate would compensate you for—*'

'Even the bloody monkey bit me.'

'God's sake, stop sighing down my ear.'

'You'd sigh if you were me.'

'I give up. Pen.' Teddy handed him letter and Biro. 'See that space?'

'I'll read to the end, thank you,' he retorted, rather huffily. 'I say, any ideas on the birthday present front yet?'

'Do I have to think of everything?'

'Only asked. Tiddly-tiddly . . . *to be negotiated. My sister, Miss Theodora Dunstan, is acting as agent for my mother and myself in this matter, and . . .*' His head jerked up. 'What's all this?'

'You don't imagine I'd leave you to talk turkey with this Stakinos chap when you need a calculator to tot up your own fingers? Never mind having Ma weeping round your neck.'

He cleared his throat. 'Not a pretty business, evicting one's widowed parent.'

'Bro,' said Teddy sternly, 'you do *want* to hold your marriage together?'

His face flushed the purple appropriate to an English officer and gent discussing matters of the heart. '*Hergh,* bloody silly question.'

'Thank you. Sign here.'

The moment Lorette tottered into the garden at 3 Meadows Close, with her sandals dangling from one finger, she scented conspiracy. Her husband and mother were whispering intently in their deckchairs, but their heads sprang apart now. As if she cared.

'Talking about me?' Chucking away her shoes, she flopped

on to the grass and began massaging her red and weeping toes.

'Where've you been all afternoon?' demanded Lily. 'I want a word with you.'

'I want a word with you and all,' retorted Lorette, wincing as her fingers encountered a particularly tender blister. 'Have I got a bone to pick with you or what?'

Never mind that meeting Jeremy Dunstan had turned this into quite possibly the most fabulous afternoon of her life; never mind that the sweet sorrow of parting (as he put it) had been softened by a fervent promise to spend the whole of the following day together; Lorette had been sustained during the weary hike home chiefly by the prospect of telling her duplicitous parent exactly what she thought of her.

Even now, she could scarcely believe the scale of Lily's treachery. For all these years her mother had known full well that Langley-le-Moor boasted its very own home-grown movie star and had breathed not a word about it. Well, OK, maybe Jeremy hadn't actually *starred* in a movie yet, but he'd appeared in smaller parts, had featured on the telly often enough, had modelled in catalogues – no, honestly he had, for thermal underwear apparently – and he'd done radio ads for double glazing and Sunnygold spread, and, oh, loads of amazing things. Plus he already had some auditions for plays lined up in London, even though he only got home today. All of which, in Lorette's book, qualified as celebrity of a spectacular order. So was it remotely conceivable that, in this half-dead village, whose most famous inhabitant otherwise was the winner of the Northern League Giant Onion Challenge, her mother could have *accidentally* failed to mention Jeremy Dunstan's very existence? Exactly.

Lorette couldn't wait to tell Lily about her afternoon. How Jeremy said he knew now why he'd come back from the States. How Destiny had guided him to meet her, he said. How it was a – a consummation devoutly to be wished? Something like that only, as it happened, they hadn't had the chance to do any actual consummating so far. Not that Lorette was bothered. Sex was sex was only sex, wasn't it? Sex she could get at home – far too much of it, until she'd kicked that great hairy beast out of bed. Whereas it wasn't every day you could hear first hand what Madonna's bodyguard said about Warren Beatty's personal assistant. She could have listened to Jeremy's tales of people and parties from here to Christmas. They had parted only because, on his first night back, he felt he ought to join his mum for dinner at the Hall.

However, her lonely hobble homewards had allowed Lorette to do some deep thinking, in the course of which not merely had she established beyond any shadow of doubt that her mother had deliberately concealed the existence of this walking, talking passport-to-paradise, she had even worked out why. Dead obvious really. By the time Jeremy got his first big break on *District Hospital*, she herself had been married for quite long enough to know she shouldn't be. But Lily, of course, thought the sun shone out of Bill's you-know-where, so it had to be her pig-headed determination to keep her daughter on the marital straight and narrow which had stopped her letting drop that dishy Doctor Dylan spent half his weekends down the road at the Hall. Sneaky cow.

Just as Lorette was about to announce that she had uncovered her parent's dastardly subterfuges, however, she was halted in her tracks by Lily breaking the news of her overdue inheritance.

'You what?' she squeaked, momentarily forgetting even Jeremy Dunstan.

'You heard. Mind, you've not got this money yet, nor will you until . . .' Lily hesitated, and caught Bill's eye almost as though challenging him to argue, before continuing firmly: 'until I can arrange to sell summat. And if you go upsetting Bill and your children – in fact if you try any monkey business at all – I can still change my mind. So think on.'

'Twenty thousand pounds,' gasped Lorette. 'Mum, you're a star.'

'That right?' Lily accepted the effusive embrace with a sardonic glint. 'I thought you'd a bone to pick with me?'

'Oh – that.'

And here Lorette would like it noted that she is not the dickhead some people would have you believe. Naturally she wasn't going to quarrel with her mother now. Why, after all, should she care if Lily had tried to stop her meeting Jeremy? They'd met in the end, so nothing else mattered. In fact, she was opening her mouth to announce that this was a fantastic sort of day all round, when she had second thoughts. She looked from her husband, who was staring moodily into his beer glass, to her mother, who was watching him with evident concern. Never mind if she and Bill were as good as divorced, it struck Lorette that Jeremy Dunstan – or any man – was likely to count as monkey business in her mother's book.

So she beamed at her parent. 'Clean gone out of my head,' she declared. And craftily resolved to keep every bit as quiet about their local movie star as Lily had. Until the money was in the bag.

'Splendid,' pronounced Teddy, whisking the pegs off a revolving washing line laden with tea towels and aprons. 'Well, isn't it?'

'If you say so.' As the sun dwindled low behind the rooftops, Bill was squatting on his back doorstep with a whisky bottle and tumbler beside him. 'Oh, I'm pleased for Cuckoo, sure. Haven't seen her so cock-a-hoop for years.'

'But you look as if you'd just lit your cigarette with a winning lottery ticket.'

He shrugged. 'If you want the truth, I'm feeling a prize tosser. Wouldn't you, if you'd had to be baled out of a messy divorce by your poor old mother-in-law?'

'I thought you said she always intended Lorette to have this money.'

'Yeah, yeah,' he responded irritably, 'but she's making it conditional on good behaviour now. Towards me, I mean.'

'Even better. Lord, why do men invariably rush to find the cloud round every silver lining?' Teddy flapped an insect off a cloth. 'I've had Big Bro moaning at me all afternoon, even as I do my damnedest to help.'

'Take no notice of me. Want a drink? I splashed out on a malt by way of celebration.' He pulled a wry face. 'If you can call it that.'

Teddy tucked the last apron into the basket and glanced

at her watch. 'Why not? The custard tarts can wait ten minutes.' She kicked the laundry basket aside and perched on an upturned crate.

'At least I s'pose it's safe to knock up some shelves for the record collection now,' he commented, as he handed her a glass.

'More to the point,' said Teddy, downing a grateful slug, 'you can start fitting out your shop, can't you? I must say it will be nice to see some life in those windows again.'

'My shop.' He actually appeared to shudder. 'Christ, who'd have thought I'd end up as a *shopkeeper*?'

She chuckled. 'You sound like my mother. She can hardly bring herself to say the dread word. I sometimes think she'd rather I dealt in heroin, because at least I'd have to be discreet about it.'

'Sorry.' With a grunt of laughter, he tilted his glass towards her. 'Here's to the noble trade of shopkeeping. God knows, I've nothing against it in principle . . .'

'But?'

'Oh, the gallery was only meant as a fallback. Lil tipped me off about the place and it seemed like a bright idea after a few beers, with her egging me on. I'd tart the joint up myself, track down local painters, sell their stuff on commission so I wouldn't need cash up front for stock . . .'

'Sounds eminently sensible.'

'Sure, sure, steady income, all the rest. But that don't mean I actually want to do it.'

Teddy was just raising her glass to her lips, when she paused. 'Clothes pegs,' she breathed wonderingly. 'Heavens, yes, *clothes pegs*.'

'Pardon?'

'If you're not awfully keen on the idea of starting a gallery,' she explained eagerly. 'Only this afternoon, when I realized I was running short of pegs, it occurred to me there's simply nowhere in this village one can buy them any more, not since Mr Duckworth sold out to those shysters calling themselves antique pine dealers. Antique pine, my foot. Knocked up by the gross in somebody's back yard, if you ask me, but that's beside the point.'

'What point?'

'A general stores,' she said impatiently. 'That's what we need in Langley. You know, the old-fashioned kind stocking everything from budgie mirrors to Rawlplugs; pots, pans, gardening twine, kirby grips, rat poison . . .'

'Am I going crackers or are you?'

'Do you mind? Clothes pegs and lavatory seats are a damn sight more useful than the touristy grot you find in these so-called galleries.'

'Galleries sell paintings,' he roared. 'I'm an artist, not a fucking ironmonger.'

Teddy put her head on one side. 'Ah,' she said, digesting this interesting statement. 'Ah, I see. So you were, um, planning to sell your own work as well?'

'Why the hell else would I be opening a gallery?'

'No need to shout, I'm not deaf. It's just one rather gathered you hadn't painted much recently. Not that anyone could blame you,' she added kindly, 'not with two young children on your hands.'

'Yeah, well,' he muttered, subsiding with a scowl, 'that's been my excuse too long, hasn't it?'

'But you did used to do quite a bit of it?' she continued politely. 'Painting, I mean?'

He stared at her incredulously. 'Frig a pig, am I hearing this?'

'How should I know? All you've ever talked about is slogging away in kitchens or on building sites. I can't recall you've ever so much as mentioned wielding a brush.'

'Listen,' said Bill, with an urgency that startled her. 'The only reason I ever laid a single brick or sweated ten minutes over a cooker was so I *could* paint. Rest of the time, I was at it in the studio all day, all night, for weeks on end, not knowing what year it was, never mind what time of day. You should've seen the place at the end of a work jag, junk knee deep on the floor, rags, bottles, fag-ends, mouldy takeaways, dead rats for all I knew.'

'Dear me,' murmured Teddy, 'and you're so splendidly tidy in a kitchen . . .' Since, as an alternative to ironmongery, the bright notion of his opening a café or bistro next door was already crossing her mind, it was probably fortunate the artist gave her no opportunity to offend his sensibilities further.

'I'd have three, four, a dozen canvases all on the go at once,' he swept on. 'I ate, slept, drank painting, *fucked* painting.'

She cleared her throat pointedly. 'I think I get the general idea.'

'But you don't. Can't. I'm trying to make you understand painting's what I do, what I was put on this earth for, the only *point* to me . . .' But here, as unexpectedly as it had kindled, the fire within him seemed to gutter. 'Well, apart from the kids.' Shutting his eyes, he flopped back against the doorjamb, downing the rest of his whisky in one gulp. 'What's the use? I never could explain it, I just do it, that's all. Did it, anyhow.'

'Goodness,' said Teddy, stunned by this burst of eloquence. And, for a while, they sat without speaking, listening to the distant murmur of a tractor, the raucous chorus of a nearby rookery settling in for the night. 'I suppose,' she said at length, 'I'd better get back to my kitchen.'

'Sorry.'

'What for?'

'Going on.' He reached for the bottle. 'Want another?'

'Thank you, but I've work to do,' pronounced Teddy, watching him pour an alarmingly large measure into his own glass. 'Well obviously, the sooner you clear out that abattoir the better.'

He squinted at her. 'Why?'

'If you're so desperate to get back to work. Isn't that going to be your studio?'

'Oh. Yeah, I guess. That seemed to be the general idea.'

'*Seemed* to be?'

His mouth twisted sourly as he swirled the whisky in his glass. 'Long time since I picked up a paintbrush. Long enough to wonder if I can still do it.'

'Nonsense.'

'Yeah, sure. Forget it.'

'I dare say it's like riding a bicycle,' declared Teddy bracingly. 'Just a question of getting back into the saddle.'

★　　★　　★

143

'Jeremy?'

'Lorette, wow, amazing. I wasn't expecting you to ring tonight.'

'Well, no.'

Lorette had a wary eye on the lounge door, behind which her mother was watching the television. Such was the magnitude of her emotional turmoil, she had very nearly bitten off a fingernail. Of course, there was nothing on earth she wanted more than to keep her date with Jeremy Dunstan tomorrow, nothing. Except – twenty thousand quid was twenty thousand quid. Even so, it didn't seem right to suggest postponing the tryst of a lifetime on account of money.

'Bit of a problem with my family,' she began cautiously.

'You too? The atmosphere up here makes Chekhov seem like a Carry On film. No one's speaking to anyone else, and I've warned my sister-in-law the place will blow sky-high when Big Bro finds out what she's up to. What's wrong with your lot?'

'It's . . . my husband, really,' confided Lorette.

There was a silence. A silence so hugely, operatically meaningful it seemed to resonate out of the phone like the after-toll of a great bell. Belatedly it occurred to Lorette that, in the course of their prolonged soul-sharings this afternoon, she might have forgotten to mention this irrelevant bit of baggage on her life's journey.

'*Husband?*' Jeremy cried. And the thrilling richness of emotion he infused into those two syllables suggested that his histrionic talents might thus far have been greatly underestimated.

'We're divorced,' she cried. 'Or as good as. But . . .'

But what?

And now a veritable orchestra of pain and noble sacrifice throbbed down the line. 'You still love him. Is that it?'

'Blimey, no,' squawked Lorette, before she remembered her mother, and huddled closer to the phone. 'It's all finished, but I can't explain now.'

'I can hardly hear you.'

'Gotta whisper, haven't I?'

Jeremy's voice rose. 'Is he there with you?'

'No, not exactly, I mean—'

'Is he jealous?'

'You don't get it,' she began, and then stopped. Because this, she gratefully realized, could be the answer to her problem. Her thespian gifts might not have been on a par with Jeremy's, but she managed a very creditable shudder. 'That's why I didn't want to tell you about him.'

'Oh my God. Is he violent?'

'You should've seen him go for my brother last night.' A twinge of conscience obliged her to add that she didn't think Bill would ever actually *hurt* anyone, but . . . She halted here only because invention ran dry, oblivious of any sinister implications in that trailing 'but . . .'

'Shit,' muttered her swain, with the pensiveness of an actor mindful of his facial assets.

The upshot was they agreed not merely to postpone their next meeting until Lorette could guarantee the coast was clear, but also that they would exercise discretion all round – villages, as Jeremy pointed out, being small and wickedly gossipy places.

'For your sake, of course,' he continued hastily, 'but we can't risk word getting back to him.'

'Who?' said Lorette, her attention distracted by a creak from behind the lounge door, as of an armchair being vacated. 'Oh, Bill, sure. Yeah, Mum's the word.'

In more ways than one, she reflected, as she softly replaced the receiver.

Chapter Nineteen

———◇◆◇———

Teddy was concerned about her neighbour. He had drunk more than was good for anyone last night. She knew, because this morning his brand-new bottle of malt was sitting in plain view on the kitchen windowsill, almost empty. Worse, he hadn't got drunk – not rolling drunk anyway. When, from her bedroom window, she had seen him let the dog out just before midnight, his gait had been steady, his voice clear. Now, a man putting away that quantity of Scotch, alone, and still managing to appear sober, was a man in trouble, to her way of thinking. And she couldn't quite work out why. He had a home, his custody of the twins was secure, and, in Lily, he would at last be getting help caring for them. His impassioned outburst when she had suggested selling clothes pegs – which she was now prepared to admit might have been a shade tactless – only deepened the mystery. So, he wasn't happy unless he was painting. Well, there was nothing to stop him getting down to work now, was there? But what had troubled her more than his ranting and raving was something she had glimpsed in his face as she got up to leave last night. She was tempted to call it *despair*, and while despair was an emotion with which Teddy had no truck, because one should never abandon hope, she had felt quite uncharacteristically reluctant to suggest he pull up his socks, chuck the junk out of the abattoir and jolly well apply some elbow grease to the easel. She suspected some underlying misery, and his fobbing her off with black jokes and fresh offers of whisky when she tried to probe had touched her more than any cataloguing of woes. She was resolved to investigate further, when the opportunity presented itself. Which, for the moment, seemed unlikely.

Unusually, this morning, she was serving behind the oak and marble counters of her shop, Beryl being at the dentist's. Although Teddy took pleasure in stocking shelves, prinking displays and generally chivvying her premises into gleaming, prosperous symmetry, she did not actually enjoy working in the shop. One's labours were continually being disrupted by customers. She recognized, of course, that customers were a necessary evil in the retailer's life, and could have tolerated their muddy boots and greasy fingers with fairish grace if only they would come in, say what they wanted, cough up their money – and leave. But oh no, most of them expected their tuppenny-ha'penny purchases to be served up with an hour of social chit-chat. This was exactly why she had relinquished front-of-house operations into Beryl's loquacious command, and retreated to the sanctuary of her kitchen.

It was also why, by mid-morning, she was swearing she would never venture this side of the louvred doors again. With so many jobs to do, and problems to mull over – some of them even her own – she had found herself obliged to endure a stitch-by-stitch account of Mr Harrison's triple by-pass, field interminable enquiries into her own injuries, and chair an impromptu debate between two members of the Parish Council on the relative fundraising merits of open gardens versus safari suppers. All for a scant thirty pounds through the till. On top of which, Brian Rowbotham had sauntered in and was now taking a full twenty minutes to purchase a packet of Cream Crackers, while apologizing for what he described as the recent unseemly altercation on her doorstep – at such garrulous length she was tempted to summon round her neighbour to create another. But that would only have given Bill an excuse for more witless flights of fantasy about his brother-in-law's supposedly amorous intentions, so she swabbed down the bacon slicer instead, while pondering her next move if the Mill House tenant refused their offer. Brian, meanwhile, was boring on about a forthcoming social function organized by the members of the Ridings Ring, an association of local traders he believed might interest Teddy

147

in both her professional and, he ventured to hope, personal capacities, dedicated as it was to—

'Telephone,' she cried, with the relief of a Mafeking dweller on hearing the toot of a British bugle.

To her irritation, since there was no chance of her enjoying a chat, she heard the mellifluous, evensong-redolent tones of the vicar at the other end of the line. Thus, while she assured dear Timothy that her cuts and bruises were mending apace – so sweet of him to ring – and that she would certainly be fit for flower duties next week, as per the rota, she was sorry to say she couldn't talk now because . . . Tim had received an invitation to Bella's birthday party, had he? Good Heavens.

'I mean, *good*. Splendid. No, of course you needn't dress up, what on earth gave you that idea?' At which point, her shop door ting-a-linged open and, with hasty apologies, she had to ring off.

'The event of which I speak,' resumed Brian Rowbotham before she could draw breath, 'involves just forty or so kindred souls, enjoying a modest *al fresco* repast with, if I may so put it, an ample sufficiency of liquid refreshment.'

'Ah, an outside catering job,' cried Teddy, reaching for the appropriate leaflet.

'Miss T. Dora Duncan?' There was a fresh-faced police constable standing in the middle of the shop, in a uniform a size too large.

'Up to a point,' she said. Tucking the leaflet into Brian Rowbotham's hand she stumped determinedly over to the door and yanked it open. 'Good of you to think of me, Brian, and normally there's nothing I'd like better than to discuss this do of yours, but as you see I'm run off my feet.'

'Indeed, indeed, but—'

'Ring me,' she commanded, and waited to shut the door behind him before turning to the policeman.

He adjusted his outsize collar. 'Report of a road traffic accident?'

Teddy sighed. 'Can we make it quick?'

'So an *hour* later,' she told Bill, 'I finally got rid of Fabian of

148

the Yard, who turned out to be a raving born-again foodie, and wanted to talk bloody mushrooms. What's more, I practically had to go down on my knees to stop him prosecuting the driver.'

'Why? If this geezer was going the wrong way and speeding?'

'I don't care if he was doing a drunken hundred and ten in a hi-jacked Centurion tank: Ferdy's fine, I'm fit as a flea, and that's the end of it.'

'I still think—'

'If it went to court the newspapers might be there.'

'So?'

'I have an aversion to featuring in the press,' she said stiffly. 'Under any circumstances.'

'What? Oh, I get you. Well, your funeral, I guess.' He gave a grunt of laughter. 'Nearly was, too.' He had been leaning against the counter, but now hauled himself upright, yawning.

'I'm glad you looked in, as it happens,' she said swiftly. 'I've been puzzling over what you were saying last night.'

He froze in mid-yawn. 'Forget it.'

'But—'

'Stinking hot day, innit? Fancy a cup of tea?'

'Are you changing the subject?'

'Would I do a thing like that? Don't you stir, I'll brew up next door, so I can keep an eye on the brats.'

Ignoring her protests, he shouldered off through the swing doors. She would have followed, but the bell of the shop door was trilling again, and she wheeled round to find her sister-in-law framed on the threshold, in a lime-green sundress of startlingly economical cut.

'Bella,' she exclaimed, temporarily shelving Bill's problems in favour of those closer to home. 'Excellent, the very person.'

'*Darling!*' Bella flung a clutch of carrier bags to the floor. 'I'd heard you'd been in the wars, you little heroine, but those dreadful bruises . . . Oh, my poor love.'

'Never mind me, it's you and Charlie we need to talk about.' Before she could deliver a pithy homily on marital relations, however, Teddy saw the bronzed and handsome figure lounging in her sister-in-law's wake. She plunged forward, arms outstretched. 'Jez!'

'Ted, yah, I'm back.'

'Good God, your hair.'

'Shit, Sis, your *face*.'

While fraternal salutations were being thus fondly exchanged – was Jeremy too broke even to afford a haircut? Wasn't Teddy impressed he was already summoned for several auditions? – Lady Dunstan wandered round the shop, sampling a cherry here, a sliver of salami there. Only when Jeremy began urging his sister to get herself some decent concealing foundation in time for the party did she rejoin the conversation.

'My party?' she said swiftly.

'Lord, yes, that's another thing,' agreed Teddy. 'Look, Bella, thanks awfully for inviting Tim—'

'Tim who? Oh, your pet vicar.' Bella stared at her with disconcerting intensity. 'Have you seen him?'

'Phoned this morning, sounding fearfully chuffed – well, I'm sure the poor boy's lonely, rattling around in that barn of a vicarage – but he seems confused about what sort of do this is.'

Jeremy murmured something about others being in the same boat, but was curtly requested by Bella to leave the talking to her. She was going to explain all to Teddy, in her own good time, thank you very much.

'Explain what? You haven't decided to make it a black-tie job, have you? I couldn't give a toss, personally, because I shall wear the same frock either way, but I'll have to ring Tim back.'

'Not black tie, precisely.' Bella was flushing a not unbecoming shade of pink. 'Let's say my plans have blossomed.'

'Oh?'

At this interesting juncture, two things happened at once. The telephone rang, and Bill Smith crashed through the swing doors, rump first, with two brimming mugs in his fists, muttering that nudist tea-making was a dodgy game – the kettle would only plug in at the floor in his primitive doss-hole of a kitchen, and the steam had nearly scalded his bollocks off.

'Still, I done it and lived to tell the tale,' he concluded, turning. 'Oh, sorry, babe. Didn't realize you'd got customers.' And he beamed round, cheerily oblivious of any effect his appearance might be having on the assembled company.

As will have been gathered, the clement weather had prompted him, if not exactly to strip naked, to swap singlet and dungarees for a pair of denims sawn-off brutally short, and not a great deal else, save a dog whistle nestling on a string amid the foliage of his muscular chest. 'Tea up, sweetheart.'

'I'm on the phone,' snapped Teddy, wincing at the spectacle of his unclothed torso. Unabashed, he winked as he plonked a mug beside her.

'My God,' gasped Bella *sotto voce* to her brother-in-law. 'Where did *that* come from?'

'A zoo, by the look of it. I mean, you don't think – not *Ted*?'

'How do?' said the object of their awed scrutiny, propping his mighty haunches against the counter and taking a grateful swig of his own beverage. 'Anything I can help with, while her ladyship's on the blower?'

'I'll say,' breathed Bella. In one flurry, she bit her lips, stuck out her chest and repitched her voice into cello register. 'Have we met?'

'Quiet,' barked Teddy, clamping the phone more firmly to her mouth. 'Certainly, I decorate children's cakes, but I'm not sure about dinosaurs . . . A terra-what-was-it?'

Bill leaned across. 'Pterodactyl, you pillock. Big bugger like a flying crocodile. Look, give it here.' And he twitched the receiver from her hand. 'Pterodactyl, yeah? . . . Sure, you can collect Friday morning . . . Not at all, ma'am, my pleasure.'

'Thanks a lot,' snorted the proprietress after he disconnected. 'Now what am I supposed to do?'

'Cool it, babe, you're looking at a virtuoso performer with the icing bag. I did a dinosaur number for the kids last year. Here . . .' Reaching for phone pad and pen, his hand began to squiggle. 'Choccy body, peppermint jungle, fruit gum flowers. Give us the gear, I'll knock it off in an hour.'

'Incredible,' murmured Bella, and fixed a lambent gaze upon him. 'Don't tell me you work for my sister-in-law?'

Absorbed in his drawing, he barely glanced up. 'Creative consultant, deputy spud-peeler, that kind of thing.'

Teddy rolled her eyes. 'Of course he doesn't work for me, he just lives next door. Sorry, Bill – meet my sister-in-law, Bella, brother Jeremy.'

Bella's eyes widened further still. 'Of all the gin joints in all the world, you've moved to *Langley*?' She purred this so huskily Teddy wondered if she was sickening for a cold – either that or was half cut, which seemed unlikely at this hour, even for Bella. She wasn't surprised Bill appeared lost for words when asked what could have attracted him to this sleepy little village, and did not hesitate to reply on his behalf.

'His mama-in-law lives here. You know Lily Rowbotham, don't you? Well, Bill's married to her daughter.'

'Holy *shit*,' croaked Jeremy – or at least that was remarkably what it sounded like to a mystified Teddy as he practically leaped for the door.

'Jez? Something the matter?'

'I – we – better move. Bella, if we're going to get into town before this costume place shuts, we should shift.'

'Don't be silly, it's open all day.'

'Costume? Is this to do with your auditions?' But Teddy enquired with no particular interest because she was peering round Bill's shoulder. 'I say, that's most awfully clever. Of course, one keeps forgetting you're an artist.'

'An *artist*,' cried Bella. 'Oh my God, how divine, you *paint*. You wouldn't like to do me, would you?' Her laugh gurgled voluptuously. 'So to speak. But I suppose all the girls ask you that.'

'Come on, Bella,' hissed Jeremy, opening the door.

'It's just that I'd absolutely adore to have my portrait painted, something I've always, always wanted.'

'Don't embarrass the poor chap,' snorted Teddy. 'He hasn't time to waste painting you, he's got a living to earn. Jeremy, either come in or go out, because I shall scream if that blessed door trills again.'

'We're going. Bella?'

'Do shut up, Jez. You're the one who's been telling me I must get Teddy on board.'

'Get me on board what?'

'*Bella* . . .'

'Oh all right, Jeremy, I'm coming in a moment. Bill, fabulous meeting you . . .'

'Get me on board *what*?'

'. . . and I hope I'll see you again soon. Jez, be careful, there's a potted hydrangea in that bag, and it's no good glowering, I have to explain *something* to Teddy, don't I?' So saying she beamed radiantly at her sister-in-law. 'Darling, it's all going to be terrific fun and I know you won't mind a bit, now I've invited your sweet little vicar to keep you happy, although I still say you could do better for yourself, and when you hear—'

At this point, however, Teddy, blushing vividly, advised Jeremy to take his sister-in-law away. Yes, now. She and Bella would discuss the party another time. In private. The door slammed and silence fell. She glanced sideways at her neighbour who was bemusedly watching Lady Dunstan blow him a kiss before she disappeared along the pavement.

'Sorry about that, Bill. Mad, of course, but there's no harm in her.'

'And she's married to the chinless wonder I met here yesterday?' He started out of his reverie. 'Sorry, shouldn't be rude about your brother.'

'Feel free. Brainless as well as chinless, but he has his good points. Somewhere.'

Bill whistled softly. 'I bet he doesn't get much kip with that one.'

'Worried sick, poor old sausage,' she agreed, in blithe misunderstanding. 'And I missed my chance to ask her to ease up on him. It's always the same with Bella: getting a word in is like crossing the M25 on a Zimmer frame.' She sighed. 'Still, I'm probably worrying unduly. She and Charlie have always scrapped like a couple of ferrets in a sack. It's just that this row seems to be lasting rather longer than usual.'

'Will I paint her, she says.'

'Take no notice,' snorted Teddy. 'She talks through . . .' But the sentence, begun so briskly, trailed into silence.

'Her hat?'

'Possibly, but . . .' She looked first at Bill, then, speculatively,

153

at the sketch he was holding. 'She did say she'd *always* wanted to have her portrait painted, didn't she? Of course, Bella is forever blurting out the barmiest things, but she rather sounded as though she meant that, don't you think?'

Bill's eyes widened. 'Now, hold on.'

'And there's Big Bro running round in circles trying to dream up the perfect birthday present.'

'Not my scene.'

'And you're desperate to get back to painting.'

'Who says?'

'Besides which, let's face it, you need to earn some money.'

'Never do 'em, portraits. Very specialist line of country.'

'You paint people, don't you?'

'No. Well, maybe, but not in the way you're after.'

'That picture of Lorette out in the abattoir – I mean, I recognized who it was at a glance. None of your three-eyed, square-bosomed modern rubbish, it's the absolute spitting image.' She beamed. 'Heavens, what a perfectly brilliant idea.'

Bill Smith drew himself up to his full six feet four, squared his massive shoulders and thrust out his jaw. 'No way, Duchess,' he said sternly. 'You hear me? No fucking way.'

Chapter Twenty

'So it's all arranged,' Teddy informed her brother the following afternoon, 'Bill will paint her portrait. Of course, it can't be finished for the actual day – when's the party, two weeks today? Dear me, Bella and I must sort out what we're giving these chaps to eat, because I don't think we've agreed anything beyond chocolate pudding.'

'That bruiser next door?' Sir Charles was following the rapid monologue only with difficulty. 'Painting *my wife*?'

'You're very lucky he's agreed.' Teddy crossed her fingers. 'He's a fearfully distinguished artist.'

'Distinguished? *Him?*'

'I had no end of difficulty persuading him to take the commission.' She uncrossed her fingers because this at least was the unvarnished truth. 'Honestly, one would never think he was on his uppers, the way he carries on. Talk about prima donnas.'

'Broke, eh? Well—'

'Messy divorce,' she said promptly. 'No reflection on his talent. His – quite extraordinary talent.'

Sir Charles eyed his sister gloomily. '*Hergh*, gets worse by the minute. How much is he planning to sting me for?'

'As it happens,' retorted Teddy grandly, 'Bill was most reluctant to discuss money.'

Understatement. Bill had refused point blank to do anything of the kind. An hour ago he had still been cursing himself for agreeing to paint the expletive-deleted portrait, and her, for chiselling such a promise out of him.

It should perhaps be explained that Teddy had been driven to clinch their long and wearisome argument the previous afternoon by declaring that one picture seemed a piffling return for the injuries she'd suffered in saving his son's life. And, yes, she did realize such a claim was unjustified, unscrupulous, and – under any other circumstances – pretty unforgivable, and would like to make clear it had caused her a severe twinge in the conscience department. But she would never have stooped to such tactics had she not known, without a shimmer of doubt, that she was acting for the greater good of all concerned, most particularly Bill. Stupid great buffoon.

So if he chose to stomp off and sulk behind a slammed back door, that was up to him. Suited her fine. Life was peaceful again. No interruptions to her work, no shouting in the yard, no cigarette smoke stinking the place out, no fear of unclothed bodies wandering without warning into her respectable shop – no end to the reasons she should let Bill Smith stew in his own juice for as long as he damn well liked. Except . . .

Frankly, after twenty-four hours the silence had become unnerving. Besides, even if he had agreed to paint the picture, they had not settled on a price for the job, and his behaving in this childish fashion was no excuse for her sinking to the same level. Therefore, this afternoon, like the civilized, rational adult she was, she had walked round, knocked on his door, tried to explain – and immediately they were at loggerheads again.

He would do it for nothing, he snarled, which was all it was likely to be worth. She might be able to coerce him into painting the thing, but she couldn't force him to take money. And he was unmoved when Teddy wailed that he was *totally* missing the point, she wasn't looking for a gift, this was a business deal, fair and square. In the end, she was reduced to demanding the sort of figures his work generally fetched. Still he hedged. How long, he said, was a piece of string? Price depended on size, medium, quality . . .

'Say – say something like that picture of Lorette,' she cried in desperation. 'What would that sell for?'

He glowered. 'Years since I flogged anything. Times change.'

'God's sake, just name a figure, can't you?'

'It's a bad joke,' he roared. 'At the last show, a canvas like that, I guess twelve – fifteen?'

Teddy eyed him suspiciously. 'Seriously?'

'Do I look like I'm in the mood for games?'

'OK, OK. Fine, thank you. Leave it to me.'

'Two hundred,' she now informed her brother. Well, why not? Charlie, as she had been assuring herself, would have spent twice that on some frock or trinket, and she could hardly wait to tell Bill the good news. This would teach him to throw tantrums when people were trying to help. Besides, as she virtuously informed her brother, she had taken the trouble of ringing the Royal Society of Portrait Artists. 'And the going rate for the skimpiest chalk sketch is in three figures, so I think we can safely say you're getting a good deal.'

'On top of what I might have to shell out to this foreign Johnny in the Mill House?'

'How do you know he's foreign?'

'Name like Stakinos?'

'I thought you might have heard from him,' she said, disappointed. 'No, well, we have to face facts, he may not bite. This picture's your best chance of softening Bella up in the meantime.'

'*Hergh,* you're sure she'll like the idea?'

'She'd better,' declared Teddy, with feeling, 'after what I've been through.'

Fortunately, Bella did like the idea. She liked it very much. They found her out in the kitchen garden, leaning over the wrought-iron gate of the pigsty, sharing a punnet of strawberries with her Vietnamese pot-bellied pet. She listened with sulky defiance as Sir Charles, after a prod from his sister, apologized, *hergh,* for their quarrel—

'Which he knows is all his fault,' Teddy interpolated.

Which he knew was – mainly his fault. When, however, with much clearing of throat and shuffling of feet, he announced the nature of his proposed peace offering, even Teddy was touched by the transformation in his wife. Bella blinked rapidly for a moment, then, with a chirruping crow somewhere between a sob and a giggle, tossed the strawberries to the ground and herself on to the chest of her startled husband, crying this was the bestest, cleverest present ever – could they hang it in the Gold Drawing Room instead of that horrible fairy-on-the-tree job of his mother? She had been *wretched* not speaking to him, even if he was a naughty boy, the bed had been so cold and lonely, but she would make it all up to him now, she would—

'Spare my blushes,' cut in Teddy. She was, however, smiling indulgently upon the happy couple. 'I'll be out of your hair in a minute, but we really must agree this menu first.'

'Sorry?' Bella's face as she lifted her head from her husband's shoulder was blank. 'Menu?'

'For your birthday dinner, fathead. It's only a fortnight.'

'Oh,' said Bella. 'Oh, that.'

And under Teddy's puzzled gaze she disentangled herself from Charlie's embrace and drifted over to the gate of the pigsty, which she opened to allow her grunting pet out on to the path. 'Chalfont needs his little walk,' she mumbled, in strangely choked tones, keeping her back to them.

'Bella?'

Whereupon she spun back to face her husband and, to Teddy's dismay and bewilderment, erupted into a passion of weeping. 'I was so *cross* with you, Charlie, and it was all – all fine when you were being beastly to me. Jolly well served you right. But now – now you're fixing for some gorgeous artist to paint me—'

'No, only *Bill*,' Teddy felt obliged to interpolate. 'You remember, you met him yesterday?'

Her sister-in-law swept on unhearing. 'It's so adorable of you, and I was going to tell you anyway, of course I was, but now you'll think it's just because . . .' Here she suddenly stopped, and her face contorted. 'Oh my God, *no!*'

A distant voice was calling for Charles. A voice whose timbre had once been likened to that of a crystal goblet struck by a silver spoon.

'Ma,' he croaked, with the air of a schoolboy caught catapult-handed in a greenhouse.

Even Teddy let slip a monosyllable, the pithiness of which

suggested she had been spending too much time in the unedify-ing company of Bill Smith. However, while she might not have a clue about what was distressing Bella, she knew her duty at a time like this, and it was to keep her mother and sister-in-law apart at all costs. Thus, while Charlie froze into his customary impersonation of a pillar of salt and Bella dropped to the ground, burying her tearful face in the dandruff-strewn shoulders of the pig, Teddy seized her stick and stumped forward to intercept the invader. But she was too late.

'There you are!' cried Lady Dunstan gaily, rounding the corner of a hedge and tripping across the gravel towards them on gilt-tipped heels, scarf fluttering like a pennant on the breeze. 'Teddy, I didn't know you were here, too. Oh, darling, *must* you disfigure your legs with those horridly clumpy sandals?' Failing to remark on either the bandage within the offending footgear, or the walking stick, or even the luminescent bruising of the face above, this devoted parent then turned to her son, sighing that she had been so fond of the kitchen garden before it was turned into a menagerie. Not that she would dream of criticizing Isobella's tastes – she dared say a preference for pigsties over parterres was only natural in one reared on a farm – but she had hoped a child of hers would be more mindful of his duties to future generations. 'However,' she continued brightly, 'I didn't come out to lament the loss of my lavender borders.'

'Quite,' agreed her daughter grittily, 'and it's turning rather chilly, so I think you and I should go and find a drink and leave this pair to follow.'

We have to hand it to Teddy. She did her best. No official of the United Nations ever laboured more staunchly in the keeping of a precarious peace. But she was not to suspect there was a grenade – nay, a nuclear missile – nestling in her mother's lilac quilted handbag even as she attempted to take her arm.

'In a moment.' Lady Dunstan stood her ground with an ease which would have aroused profound admiration in the beleaguered Bill Smith, had he been present. 'Charles, darling, I've had a little man at the door with a vanload of champagne. No, no, I *know* you haven't ordered any, this was for *Lady* Dunstan, he told me. Naturally, I said I was Lady Dunstan – so silly of me – but even when we established it must be the other Lady Dunstan, I assured him no one here was likely to have ordered a dozen cases of vintage Bollinger. I think he said Bollinger.'

It was not clear whether the groan emerged from the pig or Bella.

'Twelve *cases*?' ejaculated Sir Charles.

'Exactly.' Her laugh tinkled as deliciously as a carillon of fairy bells. 'I assumed he must mean bottles, too, but he insisted otherwise, and when I couldn't find Isobella, I took the liberty of looking on her desk for a note of the order, and happened to find . . . Now, where did I put it?' Having unclipped her bag, she was probing delicately amongst the contents. 'Ah, here we are.'

Uneasily, Teddy watched as her mother produced a sheaf of papers, much annotated. Wild-eyed, Bella scrambled to her feet. 'How dare you?' she growled thrillingly. 'Give that to me.'

Lady Dunstan, seemingly struck deaf, rustled the sheets into order and smiled the smile of a fox with the key to the chicken coop.

'I'm sure this can all be sorted out amicably,' said Teddy, with more hope than conviction. 'Ma, what is that?'

Bella seized her husband's arm. 'Don't listen to her.'

'Well, darling, it looks to me like a guest-list.'

'For my party. Charlie, I was going to tell you. Just then, before she barged in.'

'*Hergh*, I don't understand.'

Teddy braced herself. 'Oh God, Bella, what?'

She swallowed hard. 'I've – I've invited one or two more people. To my birthday party.'

'I make it three hundred,' agreed her mother-in-law helpfully. 'I wondered if that might explain the champers?'

Sir Charles gazed from his mother to his wife with an expression reminiscent of a rhinoceros at the sharp end of a tranquillizing dart. Bella, perhaps emboldened by his silence, declared that the list ran to a mere two hundred and ninety-eight. Actually.

'You've invited two hundred and ninety-eight people?' he whispered. 'To a party in this house?'

'Not counting the family,' she said conscientiously.

At which point the pig waddled between them, and, with an aptness which surely justified his fond mistress's claims for the intelligence of the species, deposited a steaming pile of ordure at Teddy's sturdily sandalled feet.

'So the shit's finally hit the fan, has it?' commented Jeremy, when he met Teddy by the garages some time later. 'God, I should think they could hear Charlie from the village. I warned Bella he'd go ballistic.'

Teddy, who had been striding across the gravel, stopped dead. 'You *knew*?'

'About her party?'

'Party?' she roared. 'This isn't a party, it's a *ball*. An all-singing, all-dancing, full-blown fancy-dress orgy for half the county. Pantomime indeed. I'll give her pantomime.'

'Cheesy sort of theme, isn't it?' he agreed with a grimace. 'Just imagine all Bella's hearty huntin' chums doing thigh-slapping principal boy in their fishnets, while their husbands thunder out of the closet and into frocks.'

'Jeremy, this isn't a joke. She's spending a fortune. Bands, costume hire, photographers – she even had the gall to use my own printer to turn out the stiffies.'

'Yeah, well, not my problem. Can you lend me a hundred quid?'

'And when she wasn't trying to tell me what a marvellous time I would have, after all she'd invited the vicar especially for me – dear Lord, that's another thing, I shall have to ring poor Timothy – she was assuring Charlie they were saving a packet by keeping the catering inside the family. Oh, yes, a truly *memorable* night I'm destined to have, sweating away from canapés at dusk to bacon butties at dawn with full three-course buffet in between. Well, if she thinks I'm laying on this bonanza at cost, she's got another think coming. I've told Charlie it's full commercial whack plus VAT, and he can thank his lucky stars I'm not stinging him for a late-booking penalty. God alone knows where I'll rustle up the staff.'

'So it's still on? I thought I heard him yelling—'

'Of course it is, Charlie's as big an ass as she is. With

invitations scattered round our neighbours like double-glazing leaflets? We can't pull the plug unless there's a damned good reason, like a death in the family or something. Although at this moment,' she added furiously. 'I wouldn't rule that out.'

'Lighten up, Sis. Look, I'm meeting someone in ten minutes, and I'm totally skint. Fifty would do.'

'Try your mother. She's so pleased with herself she'd probably give you her diamonds to pawn. I could have *screamed*, after all the time and effort I've put into getting that stupid pair together, only for her to trot along and wreck everything. And don't give me any drivel about her not meaning any harm. She knew exactly what she was about.'

'Listen, can't you? It's a woman I'm meeting.'

'You don't say. Damned quick work since you only got home two days ago. Whereupon she deliberately poured petrol on the flames by bleating about the perils of wives deceiving their husbands, how she could never have kept the tiniest secret from our sainted papa—'

'I've already bummed twenty off Ma. Where the hell am I supposed to take Lo − *her* with twenty quid?'

'A Wimpy bar? Anyway, it's twenty more than you deserve, you little toad. If you'd had the common sense − the common decency − to tip me off about Bella's shenanigans, we wouldn't be in this mess. I told Ma the sooner we could pack her off to Mill House, the better − and that,' continued Teddy, barely pausing to draw breath, 'was when she said *surely* poor Charles couldn't still be thinking of buying out the tenant? She rather thought he'd need the rent with this enormous great party to pay for.'

'Ted, *please*. It's really hard for us to be together because − well, never mind why, but the point is, she's just rung to say she can slip out tonight. No, listen, it's our only chance, because I'm going down to town for these auditions tomorrow.'

'You're wasting your breath. I've got about fifty pence in my purse.'

'You're kidding.'

She checked. 'Fifty-two.'

'Shit.' He ran a hand through his hair. 'Can you shift your

van then, so I can get the BMW out? I shouldn't think Charlie's in any state to notice I've swiped it.'

'Move it yourself, the keys are inside. I'm off to Mill House on foot because at this moment, quite frankly, I don't trust myself to drive.'

'Dad's den? Why?'

'Because your cretinous brother swallowed Ma's poison bait hook, line and ten-foot rod, that's why, yelling that of course he couldn't afford the party *and* the lease buy-out. So either the thrash is off, or our offer to the tenant is. And since I'd rather this family ended up figuring as idiots to one anonymous hairdresser from London than the entire bloody neighbourhood, I am going to Mill House to explain that the letter I sweated blood over was a foolish misunderstanding. Bella,' she concluded furiously, 'can scream all she likes about leaving her husband. I just wish I could divorce my entire *sodding* family.'

Not that this vented the full measure of her wrath by any means. And to cap it all, she realized, as she stomped across the park, stick in hand, that Charlie was now about as likely to cough up two hundred pounds for a portrait as he was to paint it himself. Her knock at the shiny blue door of Mill House carried the force of a battering ram.

It was opened by a tall, slender, olive-skinned man she was too preoccupied to recognize, although the streak of silver in the black hair was certainly distinctive.

'Well, if it isn't herself,' he cried, beaming. 'Is this Fate or what? I was just coming to see you again, treasure.'

'Mr – Stakinos?'

'*Hari* – little Hari, don't you remember? Mind, I admit I've changed a bit, whereas I'd have known you anywhere.'

'I'm sorry? Look, my name's Dunstan.'

'Theodora Elizabeth Fortescue, according to the boys in blue, which is a fair old mouthful as the intern said to the president – ooh, hush my mouth. But it was always Teddy, wasn't it?'

'Yes – I mean, was it?'

'Summer of '76, you were my guardian bleeding angel, you

were. And blow me down if you haven't saved me again. Gives me the screaming heebie-jeebies just thinking about what might've happened if you hadn't got to that poor little boy in time. Plus you told that cocky young constable not to press charges. Darling heart, I was in your debt before, but I'm your slave for life now.'

Words rarely failed Theodora Dunstan, but this was one such occasion. She gulped feebly for air. Mr Stakinos eyed her closely. 'My word, we have been getting our little knickers in a twist about something, haven't we?' The next thing she knew, he had draped an arm, weightless as a bird's wing, about her shoulder. 'Psychic, me. Come on in, pet, kettle's on. I'll make a nice cup of tea and you can tell me all about it.'

Chapter Twenty-One

'"In such a night as this,"' cried Jeremy ecstatically, '"When the sweet wind did kiss the trees . . ."'

'You're telling me,' yelled Lorette.

'Sorry?'

'Wind. Nearly blowing my head off.'

'I'll shut the roof,' he said hastily, pressing a button.

'That's better. Nice car you got, mind.'

'My brother's, actually.'

'Well, you haven't had time to fix yourself up with wheels yet, have you?' she said fair-mindedly. 'Go on then.'

'Sorry?'

'What you were saying. Don't tell me: *Romeo and Juliet*.'

'Um, *Merchant*, I think.'

'Makes a change from Shakespeare. What comes next?'

'". . . did kiss the trees, And, . . ." Hell, I forget. Look, you're sure about this? Going to the cinema, I mean?'

'To see a film with you in it, are you kidding?'

'It is, um, only a smallish part.'

'You're dead modest, you are.'

'And you're really not hungry?'

'We can eat after, can't we? Long as I'm home by midnight or so. That's if' – and here, it has to be confessed, Lorette's blue-taloned fingers slid carelessly up his linen-clad thigh – 'we feel like eating.'

'God,' gasped Jeremy, swerving as a passing lorry blasted its horn, 'I can't believe this is happening. It was such a fantastic surprise, you ringing this afternoon. I mean, once I'd seen that Neanderthal walking into Ted's—'

'Pardon?'

'I told you, in the shop, yesterday.'

'Oh, *Bill*.'

'I realized what we were up against. In fact, I began to wonder if I'd ever see you again. Jeez, that guy makes the heavies in a Bond movie look like bunny girls.'

'You reckon?' Lorette seemed to choke momentarily, but recovered herself enough to assure him she too was well chuffed about tonight, that it was a real stroke of luck Mum suddenly deciding to go over to Leeds and see cousin Muriel.

'Lily?' He glanced round as he steered into the car park of the multiplex. 'Why should it have anything to do with Lily?'

Lorette barely missed a beat. She lifted her hand, crossing her fingers. 'Like that, Mum and Bill are.' And she declared this with the conviction of one telling the truth, the whole truth – and a little bit more than the truth. 'If she knew what I was up to, and she told him . . .'

Even if the accompanying grimace was a mite overplayed, it was clear Lorette was getting the hang of her role.

Rather later that evening, her Neanderthal Bond villain of a nearly-ex husband hummed softly to himself as he planted a pink sugar toadstool in a peppermint jungle. He was working alone in Teddy's kitchen and Terry was nearly finished. Terry the chocolate Dactyl, geddit? Not a bad little effort, if he said so himself. He had entered the premises by means of the key her ladyship kept under the geranium tub – honest to God, Bill couldn't believe how innocent these yokels were about security. They seemed to think crime only happened under orange streetlights. Coming home to find her back door flapping wide might just teach Teddy a salutary lesson, in his view. He'd had to prop it open as he worked so he could listen out for his sleeping children next door.

Given the present combative state of relations between himself and his neighbour, you may be wondering why Bill Smith was working in this kitchen at all. Simple. He was doing this cake because he had offered, and he would like you to know he is a man of his word. If he says he'll do something, he'll do it. *Unless* that promise has been extracted from him under duress. By, not to put too fine a point on it, unfair means. No prizes for guessing he was referring here to the portrait of the sister-in-law with the siren eyes and the foghorn laugh. Not that he'd object to showing luscious Lady D. his etchings any old day, because this living like a monk was doing his head in, but that was not the point. The *point* was that he couldn't be expected to perform with brush and canvas just because Teddy Dunstan stamped her autocratic little foot.

He snipped a piece of chocolate fondant to shape and tossed the off-cut to the dog. 'Did Leonardo paint to order?' he demanded grandly. The animal put her head on one side and whined. 'OK, so maybe he did – and don't you get clever with me, sunshine, because I'm telling you the Borgia Popes were a piece of piss compared with Theodora Dunstan. Shove off into the yard, anyway. She'll have a fit if she catches you shedding fleas in her kitchen.'

Sure, Bill knew he owed Teddy. And he knew she *meant* well. What was more, there was plenty he'd do for her even if she hadn't risked her neck for Ferdy, because he liked the little sod. No, he did, honestly. She wasn't nearly such a pain in the bum as you might think. At least, she was sometimes, but – oh, never mind. What he was trying to explain was that he would cheerfully peel spuds and decorate cakes from now to Christmas, if only she would let him off the hook with this portrait.

'And don't ask why,' he remarked to the dog, who was splayed on the back-door step, luxuriously scratching an ear. 'Because you wouldn't get it, any more than she does. Where is she anyway? Should've been home hours ago.'

When the phone trilled, he automatically started towards it, but Teddy's voice clicked in, sounding like the Queen on an awf day, announcing that, much as she loathed these beastly little machines, she would be grateful if callers could bring themselves to speak after the blip. Only when this caller had been rumbling away in the corner for some time, however, did Bill, carefully pressing moistened fruit pastilles into place, recognize the voice as being that of Brian Rowbotham. Sticky hands aloft, like a brain surgeon mid-operation, he leaned towards the machine. Soon, he was listening intently. Because, along with some ramble about unfortunate misunderstandings, and Langley's celebrated queen of cuisine not being required to grill so much as a sausage, it began to sound as though the brother-in-law was – asking Teddy out? To a barbecue, Saturday after next?

'Attaboy,' hooted Bill, deriving considerable pleasure from the prospect of Teddy's face when she heard herself being invited to try her hand – or should Brian say *foot*? – at a spot of informal Morris dancing. Didn't he tell her old Brian was sniffing around? He was still chuckling when a reference to unsavoury neighbours curbed his mirth. How many neighbours did she have? Apparently, Brian would not dream of sullying Teddy's ears with mere sordid tittle-tattle . . .

'I should think not too,' murmured Bill austerely.

. . . but he would not be able to rest easy, unless he warned her that, by all accounts, her new neighbour had carved quite a name for himself in his bachelor days as – how should Brian put this? – a ladies' man.

'Who, *moi*? You sweet-talker, you.'

. . . and while he was tolerably confident Teddy would have nothing to fear in this line . . .

'Dead right, mate.'

. . . Bill being older now, if not (chuckle) noticeably wiser . . .

'Watch it.'

. . . nevertheless, if the fellow should give her any trouble . . .

'You what?' Wiping his hands on his jeans, Bill strode towards the telephone.

. . . any trouble at all, she must not hesitate to call on Brian, because he would be only too willing to—

'Get stuffed,' roared Bill into the receiver.

There was a brief, affronted pause. 'Pardon? Is this a crossed line?'

'No, it's Don sodding Juan from next door. Whaddya mean give her any trouble?'

'*Bill?* What are you doing there?'

'Icing a cake.'

'No call to take that facetious tone with me, my lad.'

'OK, have it your own way. I'm shagging her senseless under the kitchen table – oh, blimey.' He stared at the wheels of the tape recorder, which were chugging quietly and relentlessly onwards. And even as he slapped down the receiver and fumbled for the 'erase' button, car headlights were flashing into the courtyard. Doors slammed and he heard her shouting thanks.

'You're late,' he called over his shoulder as footsteps clattered behind him. 'Someone with you?'

'Bill? Oh – oh, only the gardener from the Hall. I gave him a lift down. At least, he drove, but . . . God no, don't say you've done the cake, too?' If he hadn't been so busy pressing buttons, he would surely have noticed something amiss in her voice. 'You have. And it's brilliant. Work of art. But then, I suppose it would be.'

'Come again?' The tape had at last shunted backwards, but he wasn't budging from this corner until it was safely wiped. A gag like that on the answering machine was no way to re-establish friendly relations with his neighbour, particularly now, when he was bracing himself to turn round and sock it to her that he wasn't, after all, going to paint her sister-in-law. And, yes, he's well aware he said he would. Yes, he prides himself on his word being his bond, all that. But . . .

'Do you know someone called Hari Stakinos?'

'Who?' With a grunt of relief, Bill stabbed the 'off' button, and wheeled round. She was beside the table, staring at the cake.

'Hairdresser. From London. Highly successful, by the sound of it.'

'Do I look like the type to hang out with trendy hairdressers? Quick Number Two down the barber once a month does me. Why?'

'I just wondered—' She changed tack abruptly. 'It was his car. You know, the accident.'

Memories began to filter back. 'Tallish dark guy? Funny white flash in his Barnet?'

'That's him. Inherited from an Irish grandmother. The streak, I mean.'

'Irish, with a name like Stakinos?'

But Teddy seemed lost in a little world of her own. 'Comes from Leeds, actually, huge family. He seemed to think it was terribly significant grandmama being the seventh daughter of a seventh daughter, or something.' She didn't so much sit down as crumple over the stool, letting her bag crash to the floor tiles. 'Can't imagine why.'

'Sounds like a nutter and an accident with the bleach bottle, if you ask me. Read your palm while he was at it, did he?' She stared up, blank-faced. No, more than blank, it was as if she didn't even recognize him. As if she was trying to work out who the hell this was in her kitchen. 'Here,' said Bill, 'have you been drinking?'

'It isn't *that*.'

'You have been drinking.'

'Earl Grey.' She bit her lip. 'Well, we started on Earl Grey.'

A particularly aromatic blend, it had proved to be, leaf not bag, and by the time Hari was straining it into eggshell-fine cups – not the hideous Crown Derby from the Hall attics, she noted – Teddy was no longer the wrathful creature who had stormed up to the door of Mill House. Indeed, as she settled into her armchair, she was cheerily thanking Mr Stakinos for his kind offer of a haircut, but informing him she trimmed her locks herself.

'I can see that,' he retorted, pursing his lips. 'With garden shears?'

And this riposte caused her only to giggle. As one would, with an old friend – because that was what he was. She remembered Hari very well now. Not from the scene of the accident, to be sure. As she apologetically pointed out, she had barely been in a state to recognize her own mother then, but from very much longer ago. That blazingly hot summer of 1976, as he so rightly said. And what she remembered was not the elegantly urbane, expensively-clad, exquisitely-perfumed creature draped across the armchair opposite her now, but a stubble-haired infant of ten, all knobbly knees and gap-teeth, who for ten days had stuck to her side like a shy little shadow. This was when Hari had come to stay at one of the city children's camps in the park.

'And it was the best holiday I ever had,' he sighed nostalgically. 'Well, the only holiday I ever had, back then. Mark you, I sobbed for two solid days 'til you stopped those big lads from Salford ganging up on me – built like brick shithouses they were, but you didn't give a stuff, did you? And once you got me out of all the muddy games, and let me help in the cooking tent, I was happy as Larry. You even let me put some curlers in your hair, remember? You know, I've often thought that's where it all started for me. Fab idea, them camps.'

'I wish Pa could hear you say so,' responded Teddy, touched. 'The camp was always the high spot of his year, for all my mother loathed them. It was one of the few times I can ever recall his standing up to her, insisting we children should be allowed to muck in. I used to have a ball. Those whacking great vats of sausage stew.'

'Sausage stew,' crooned Hari, 'I can taste it now . . .' He kissed his fingers expressively, and beamed at her over his teacup. 'So when I was thinking about a weekend pad, and saw the advert for this place – well, I knew it was meant to be. 'Specially once I found you were still up here. Mind, if looks could kill, I'd be strumming a harp now.'

'I'm sorry?' said Teddy, startled out of her recollections.

'In the garden? Day I come up to view, and you were telling the long-haired Doris with the big boobs about your ideal husband?'

'Good God,' she stammered, blushing scarlet. 'That was you behind the hedge. Well, whatever nonsense I was blathering, kindly forget it.'

'Excuse me,' he said firmly, 'what I heard was music to my ears. Just what I'm always advising my customers, because you would not believe the number of single ladies I get sobbing their mascara over my best towels about how they can't find a man who isn't married, gay or barking. Hairdresser, me? More like a flaming shrink.' He sighed, and took a contemplative sip of tea. 'And I says to them, I says, "Look, petal, forget Mr Universe with a degree in empathy and a banana down his Armanis.

You just keep your eye open for a nice slippers-and-cardi with a bulge in his bank balance." But do they listen?' He leaned forward and smiled invitingly. 'So come on, chuck. Have another biccy, and tell me what I can do for you.'

'Earl Grey, huh?' said Bill.

'We – got talking. He mixed a Martini.'

'Or six.' Well, what was he supposed to think? She was slumped speechless on her stool like she'd dropped from the eighteenth storey. 'No wonder you got a stooge to drive the van back. You and this Hari hit it off a treat, obviously.'

'We did, rather,' said Teddy listlessly. 'Reminiscing about old times, you know, and he was telling me about his life now. Seems to have done terrifically well for himself, I must say. And then, of course, he'd got our letter, so I found myself pouring out the whole nonsense about Ma and Charlie and Bella's blessed party . . .'

But she sounded, to Bill's ears, as if her mind was a million miles away. 'Hell, Duchess, what's this nutter with the spooky grannies done to you?'

She blinked. 'He's a poppet. That's what was so maddening, really, because for all he went on about the stars guiding him back to Langley—'

'Give me strength.'

'—at a word from me, he'd have returned Mill House to us tomorrow.'

'Would he indeed?' said Bill wrathfully. 'On account of your big blue eyes?'

'On account of his cock-eyed notion he owes me some huge favour because of Ferdy,' she retorted, with a reassuring flicker of feistiness. 'Honestly, I do wish people would shut up about it. Hari doesn't owe me a sausage, any more than you do, as I keep trying—' Here, though, she came to a sudden and stricken halt. As well she might, in Bill's view.

He eyed her sternly. 'That right?' he said. 'So how come I got the idea I was in hock to the tune of one bloody great painting?'

'It wasn't just Ferdy,' she began feebly, 'I knew Hari when
. . . Oh Lord, why am I such a fool?'

Straight up, that's what she mumbled. And instead of her
usual cheery jack-booting self, she was sounding almost tearful.
Still, that wasn't going to stop Bill saying what had to be said.
'Look, sweetheart. About this portrait—'

Before he could get another word out, however, she had
lurched to her feet, hissing determinedly that, for *once* in her
life, she was going to get her facts straight before making an
even bigger ass of herself. After all, it was a pretty commonplace
sort of name, wasn't it?

'Pardon?' said Bill.

And she didn't suppose he'd mind her taking a quick look
at the picture in the abattoir.

'You what?'

'You know. Of Lorette.'

'It's pitch black out there.'

'I've a torch in the car.'

'Jesus H. . . . *Why?*'

She was already on the doorstep. 'Just something Hari
said.'

'*Hari?*'

Her answer floated back faintly across the dark yard. 'But
then he doesn't know anything about art either.'

'Heavens,' she had said, squinting at the wall above his dining
table, 'how frightfully *rude*.'

And she was not studying one of Hari's handsome Hockney
boys, grappling on a swiftly pencilled bed: by the third Martini,
it should perhaps be explained, he was giving her a guided tour
of his little treasures. No, what had caught her eye was a still life.
A still life of a dish of peaches. However, in Teddy's defence,
it must be admitted that this was a most remarkably un-still still
life. The small canvas exploded with colour, positively throbbed
with tropical vigour. And Hari, for one, was not offended by
her critical judgment.

'Three bums on a plate, dear,' he agreed briskly. 'Gives
me a hot flush every time I look at it. My friend Michael

made me a present of that, couple of years back. Must've been drunk.'

'Michael?' said Teddy, fishing the lemon peel out of her glass and sucking it thoughtfully.

'One I was telling you about, bigshot film producer in the States, neurotic cow? Marries one bimbo after another, then weeps on my shoulder about the alimony?'

'Oh, *him*,' said Teddy, just a shade woozily. Hari mixed a strong Martini. 'Silly ape.'

'You said it, cherub. I love him to bits, mind, but he's enough to make you tear your hair out. I used to do his, when he still had some. Now I just flash the comb and chat, more of a spiritual cut and dry, if you know what I mean. His guru, he calls me, but does he listen?' Hari sighed and topped up their glasses from a misted jug. 'Number of times I've told him to forget the floozies and stick to movies and paintings – at least he makes money on *them*. Complete genius when it comes to sniffing out next week's talent, actors or painters. I mean, take these peaches. A Bill Smith original, and he paid less than a grand, can you credit it?'

'Bill – Smith?' said Teddy, articulating the two syllables with exaggerated care.

'Don't worry, I can't tell my Botticelli from my *Beano*, neither, I just know what I fancy. Anyway, it's not much like them big bosomy nudes he's famous for, is it? You know, on all the greetings cards?'

Teddy, however, did not appear to be listening. Spilling the contents of her handbag along with her Martini in searching for her spectacles, she perched them on her nose, and peered intently at the corner of the painting. 'Oh my giddy aunt,' she breathed. 'Bill Smith. Except, no, can't be the same . . .'

'Not that I'm a great one for the naked ladies personally,' continued Hari, tracing one velvety curve of peach with an admiring finger, 'but Michael's never stopped kicking himself for not grabbing a couple before the prices went galactic. He reckons . . . Teddy? Something the matter, chuck?'

Chapter Twenty-Two

In such a night as this, when the sweet wind did gently kiss the trees and they did make no noise; in such a night as this, when the lights of the Huntley Manor Country House Hotel did glow gold upon the dusky air; in such a night as this, was Sir Charles Dunstan's shiny BMW parked under the said noiseless trees in a lay-by up the road from the hotel, as Jeremy and Lorette polished off quarter-pounders and fries with Diet Tangos.

'Of course the bastards cut my best bit,' said Jeremy. 'I had a really significant reaction shot, holding that door for her. But you saw my hand?'

'Recognize it anywhere,' said Lorette, rather indistinctly because she had a mouth full of sesame bun. 'And I spotted you behind the horse and all. You looked great.'

'You really think so? You're not just saying that?'

'Honest. Got another thingy of tomato sauce?'

'What? Oh, on the dashboard with the drinks.' Jeremy bit the corner off a sachet and tenderly squeezed it over her remaining bun. 'Shit, this is terrible, isn't it?'

'What?'

'Burgers – ending up in a lay-by – everything.'

'Yeah, well . . .' Did Lorette's gaze stray wistfully in the direction of the Huntley Manor Country House Hotel? 'Nice chips, any road.'

'It isn't how things should be for us.'

'No,' she agreed, and heaved a pensive sigh. 'Life's a funny old box of chocolates, innit?' So saying she swallowed the last corner of burger, dabbed her mouth with the paper serviette and shrugged. 'D'you want to get in the back then?'

Sure enough, Bill found her out in the abattoir. A wobbly puddle of light spilled over his wife's naked body, but Teddy, to his mystification, was aiming the torch down at the right-hand corner.

'Checking I can spell my own moniker?'

The torch jerked round. 'Why didn't you *tell* me?' she demanded. And she flung this at him as though he'd forgotten to mention her house had burned down.

'Tell you what?'

'That you're a famous artist, you great fat fool.'

'And you're the Queen of Sheba.'

'Don't play any more games with me, Bill Smith. Your pictures sell for a fortune.'

'I did tell you,' he said indignantly. 'You asked what a piece this size would've gone for, and, OK, I might've been a bit under the mark when I said—'

'Twelve or fifteen, and that's exactly what I thought you meant.'

'Twelve – quid?'

'It's not funny.'

'Too right it's not, it's downright fucking libellous, but . . . hey, hey, what's all this?'

Her face was knotting up in exactly the way his daughter's did when tears were on the way: brow crumpling, mouth letterbox-square, chin all a-quiver. Indeed, before he could say another word, Teddy erupted into hacking sobs. 'I'm so sorry,' she wailed. 'I went on and on at you to paint – paint Bella, I even screwed Charlie up to' – she could hardly get the words out – 'up to two hundred pounds. *Two hundred pounds.*'

'Yeah, well, very kind of you.'

'Kind? It's an *insult*. Not to mention telling you – telling you to sell clothes pegs. You obviously thought I was a complete and total idiot, which I am, and I'm not surprised you were angry. Serves me – serves me right if—'

She had to shut up, because he was hugging the silly sod to

his chest, stroking her quaking shoulders, murmuring soothing nonsense into her ear, just as he would if he'd had Florence weeping in his arms. And after thirty seconds, exactly as Floss would have done, she was wriggling away.

'Sorry.' She gave a ferocious sniff. 'Sorry. Bad enough already, without blubbing all over you. Just – just glad we've sorted it out in time. Least you hadn't started work.'

'Look,' he began uneasily, 'when I say I can't paint your sister-in-law, you mustn't think—'

'Dear God, of course you can't,' she burst out, staring at him in horror. 'Out of the question. Even if Charlie weren't spitting tacks, there's no earthly way we could pay your sort of prices.'

'It's not the money, pillock,' he cried, outraged. 'How many times did I tell you I didn't want paying? Oh blimey, babe, don't start spouting again. I feel enough of a bastard already.'

'Not your fault,' she gasped, tears coursing down her cheeks. 'Not any of it. Very – very long day, that's all. My family's at each other's throats, and I've drunk too much gin. And – and this afternoon I thought I'd been so *bloody* clever, thought I'd got everything sorted out so brilliantly . . .'

'Oh, sweetheart,' he sighed, gathering her against his shoulder again.

'Don't sweetheart me. I'm a pig-headed, pea-brained, interfering busybody. I shall never do it again. Meddle in other people's lives, I mean. And if – and if Bella divorces Charlie, because I know they've always fought but this is – this is different, so if the whole family – falls apart, God knows what will happen to the children, the house – well, too bad. Not – not my fault. I tried. Just made a – a complete and total muck-up.'

All this gasped into his chest, with her little heart hammering twenty to the dozen. So what does Bill do? What do you bloody think?

'Look, Duchess,' he finds himself saying, 'if it means so much – if it'd really help, I guess I could have a go at this sodding picture.'

Him and his big mouth.

*   *   *

'Charlie?' called the younger Lady Dunstan softly, drifting noiselessly along the upper gallery in a very smart silk négligé. 'Charlie, are you in there?'

The door of the Blue Room opened. Her husband was revealed in dressing gown and slippers. 'Bellsy?'

Her face worked soundlessly. 'I'm . . .' The word was forming. Slowly but unmistakably: *sorry*. That was what she was struggling to say – and almost getting there.

Sir Charles simply stretched out his arms, and she stumbled into them. Neither spoke for a long time. Just stood entwined, rocking gently to and fro, until . . .

'Charlie?' Cautiously his wife pressed herself closer. 'Is that – what I think it is?'

'*Hergh* . . .'

A tentative watery chuckle. 'Really?'

'Missed you – old thing.'

'Oh, my poor, sweet love.'

A door opened at the far end of the landing. 'Ah, Charles, darling. I was just putting my light out and I thought I heard – *Isobella?* Dear me, I hope this isn't an inconvenient moment?'

'Oh *God*,' gasped Jeremy. 'That was just so – *God!*'

'Uhuh,' murmured Lorette, extracting what turned out to be a dog lead from under her shoulder blade. 'Very nice.'

And if she sounded a mite abstracted, that was not because there had been anything wrong with their coupling, as far as she was concerned. Fine. Lovely, all that. Although the back seat of a car, even of a car of this size, was hardly what Lorette would call ideal for a spot of the old how's-your-father. No, she was subdued only because she was . . . thinking.

Thinking, strange to say, about a tatty old studio couch at the Huddlestone Institute, every bit as cramped as this car seat, and much less opulently upholstered, upon which she and Bill Smith had first consummated their union. So devoutly had Lorette wished for *that* consummation, she had pulled every string in the book with the college authorities to let her pose in the altogether, only to suffer three weeks of boredom and arctic draughts round her bum before she managed to lure the artist away from his interminable fretting and faffing behind the easel and on to that selfsame couch with his model. Now she was pondering, and not for the first time, just where all that effort had got her.

Not, as she would be quick to assure both us and herself, that there was any comparison to be drawn between Jeremy Dunstan and Bill Smith, none at all. Jeremy was an actor, which was a million times better than an artist, wasn't it? Even a supposedly famous artist, with a huge great flat in London, a roaring new Porsche, and rock stars, models and millionaires by the limo-load turning up to his exhibitions. Because that, believe it or not, was what everyone had been saying about sexy Mr Smith when he rolled up at the Huddlestone Institute – in, fair enough, a Porsche. Lorette, too, found it hard to credit the rest these days, but she had been younger then. Younger and a whole lot dumber. Dumb enough to decide this was the husband for her and cast aside contraception by way of insurance policy. That, as she had long since freely admitted to all concerned, had been a reprehensible move – not to say dick-brained – but even she couldn't be blamed for conceiving twins. You may be sure she had not missed a single pill in the five intervening years. No danger of history repeating itself on that score, no thank you.

Besides, Jeremy Dunstan was a totally different kettle of fish. You couldn't imagine him striding into the labour ward like Marlon Brando and emerging as Mary bloody Poppins, could you? He was ambitious, he really *was* going places – and the right places at that. Paintings were only paintings. Movies were the real thing. OK, burger and chips wasn't exactly what she'd been expecting tonight, but . . .

'So is there any chance? Because the workshop as well means I'll be there for nearly a fortnight.'

Lost in her thoughts, Lorette hadn't realized the man of her dreams was addressing her. 'Pardon? I mean, chance of what?'

'Cooking up some excuse and coming with me to London tomorrow, when I go down for these auditions?'

London? Lorette's heart skipped several beats. Oh, how she longed to taste the heady, sophisticated delights of the capital city. How passionately had she striven to persuade Bill to return to his former stamping ground. It had been his decision to put his flat on the market – on the piffling grounds that a Docklands warehouse conversion two hundred-odd miles away from her mother was no place to rear a family – that had rung the first, faint warning bells in her head. That ringing had intensified when the Porsche was swapped for a family saloon. The din was deafening her by the time the saloon was itself traded down to the present bucket of rust. As for the ritzy, glitzy exhibitions, don't make her laugh. Not a single show since she met him. But now? With Jeremy to introduce her to the high life?

'I'm dossing down at a friend's flat in Shepherd's Bush,' continued her passport-to-paradise eagerly. 'I'm sure he wouldn't mind.'

'Shepherd's Bush?' she responded cautiously, running through the Monopoly board and drawing a blank. 'Is that nice?'

'Terrific. The council's done up the block recently, and it's really handy for the tube. I'm afraid it'd only be a sofa-bed in the sitting room but at least, you know, we could be together.'

'Yes,' she said wistfully. 'Yes, we could. Only . . .' It was a question of twenty thousand pounds in the hand *versus* a bonk in a Shepherd's Bush council flat. 'Better not,' she said, sadly but with resolution. 'Can't take any risks with – you know who.'

Bill Smith was a trouper, sighed Teddy to herself, gulping back her second pint mug of water along with two paracetamol and clambering unsteadily into bed. An abs'lute, through-and-through, one-hundred-per-cent good egg. Because she'd tried to talk him out of painting this portrait – *course* she had. Friendship was one thing, thass what she'd tried to tell him, but it was simply too much, his offering them free, gratis and for nothing, a work of art worth zillions.

'Crap,' he'd said. 'The silly prices were years ago. I had my fifteen minutes in the limelight, but it's history now.'

They were in her kitchen, drinking whisky. Of course Teddy knew she should not have been doing anything of the kind, not on top of Hari's gin, but she had jolly well needed a drink, and a zonking big one at that. She had felt as wrung out as an old dishrag after her outburst, when the frustrations of the whole long day had suddenly surged up and exploded in such an undignified fashion all over poor Bill. And his insistence on keeping his promise to paint Bella only made her feel more wretched still.

'I *should* do it,' he declared, stubbornly. 'Can't piss around frying fish fingers for ever.'

''Sterrible,' Teddy remembered saying. 'Downright criminal. All that talent, success, all thrown away, 'cause of your children.'

His half-hearted attempt to persuade her, again, that his ceasing to work wasn't the fault of the twins, or even of his wife, only showed what a fine and generous soul he was. Facts were facts and, as he had himself admitted, that picture of Lorette out in the abattoir was the last thing he'd painted – or the last he'd finished. Ever since then, they'd been living off the fat of his glory years while he painted skirting boards instead of canvases and played full time househusband. Teddy was shocked beyond measure that such a promising, nay glittering, career had guttered to nothingness in a dump like Huddlestone. She couldn't imagine what had attracted him up there in the first place.

'Don't ask,' he'd said, wincing. 'Here, gimme that whisky bottle.'

'Tragedy 'bout you and Lorette, too,' she sighed. 'Don't *pounce* on me. Wasn't going to say what you thunk – thought I was.'

'That right?'

'The marriage's over, I know, I know, you told me hundred times already. Thank you, yes, I'll have another one, too. Small one.' She scowled. 'Not *that* small.'

'Your funeral,' he murmured, adding another slug.

'What I *was* going to say—'

'I knew we'd get back to it.'

'Ish – is that none of this would've happened with the right sort of wife behind you. Not dizzy, dotty Lorette, but someone to support you. You know what they say, behind every succ-shessful chap is—'

'Shouldn't you eat something to mop up the booze?'

'A woman. 'Swat you need.'

'Too right I need a woman.'

'Don't be vulgar. A wife to help you with.' – Teddy waved a hand and nearly toppled off her chair – '*everything*.'

'Wanna job?' he enquired. 'Likes of you on the job, I expect I'd be in the Royal Academy, knighted, with the kids at Cambridge and the dog trained to catch pheasants by tomorrow teatime. Go on, Duchess, stiffen the upper lip and lie back and do what England expects.'

'I am '*stremely* serious. But if you insist on making the tick, I mean . . . Oh, stop sniggering. Anyway, dogs don't catch pheasants. And if Birdie tries it, she'd better watch out for Charlie's twelve-bore.' Teddy swallowed the contents of her glass, along with a discreet hiccup, and rose to her feet. 'I think I had better retire,' she announced carefully. 'Be so kind as to drop the latch behind you. And, Bill?'

'Sweetheart.'

'I am – more grateful to you than I can say.'

'Piss off.'

'You're – a good chum.'

'State you're in, any minute now you're going to tell me you *will* marry me.'

Clutching tight to the door handle, she had wobbled round. 'I may be drunk,' she declared with dignity, 'but I am not *that* drunk.'

There was no denying her inebriated condition, however. When she settled back on the pillow, closing her eyes, the bed lurched nauseatingly. Outside, she heard Bill whistling softly for the dog. Silly chump. If only he'd listen. Except she was not going to meddle in other people's lives any more. If he insisted on painting portraits for free when he had two children to rear and a living to earn, well, that was his funeral. As he was so fond of saying. Naturally, one would try to help – in so far as one could. When there wasn't a sledgehammer pounding the base of one's skull.

Abandoning, for the moment, any attempt to find refuge in sleep, she sat up and groped for her water glass. At least she understood now his reluctance to run a gallery. A man of his potential piddling around in a shop? Any fool could operate a till. But Bill, perverse to a degree, was now maintaining this was the only answer. The galleries that once used to deal in his work, he said, had long since given up on him. Yes, the dealers had pestered him for a bit – well, OK, for quite a while – but not any more. He was yesterday's news, cold potatoes, dead in the water, finished down in London, finished in the big wide world, finished full . . . At this, however, he had caught himself up, and stubbornly reverted to stating that the gallery was his only answer. He had to start flogging his own stuff, make a fresh start, right here in little old Langley.

Which, as Teddy reflected hazily now, wasn't exactly Bond Street. A businesswoman herself, she could appreciate the advantages of dispensing with the middleman, particularly when Bill told her the outrageous cut demanded by those smart dealers, but she couldn't help reflecting that he would have to lower his prices substantially in this neck of the woods. Even so, once word got around, he might do quite well for himself, provided he could attract the right sort of customer. There was no shortage of money if you knew where to look. And there was the rub. Because she frankly doubted he had the first clue about setting up a retail outlet. Sweet man, and highly practical in some respects, but she saw no evidence of commercial acumen.

He might be capable of fitting out his shop, although it would take time, and the abattoir, too, would have to be cleared of junk and transformed into a habitable workplace before he could start painting something to sell. But that was only the start. She was very sure Bill had not so much as given a thought to drawing up a business plan for the bank, setting up an accounting system, registering for VAT, researching an appropriate customer base, organizing mail shots – Lord, the list of what needed to be done ran from here to Christmas.

Poor old Bill, she thought, settling cautiously back on to her pillow. Small hope of election to the Academy at this rate – anyway, Bill Smith RA sounded distinctly unconvincing. *William* Smith, perhaps. Sir William Smith RA, if he wanted to be facetious, silly fool. Oh, he could snigger all he liked about the glorious pinnacles he might scale with a woman like her bolstering his career, but she stood by what she said. He'd be a million times better off with a wife, of course he would. With two young children on his hands? Not to mention a delinquent dog. Good-natured, but totally feckless, that animal, rather like her owner. In fact, a spot of dog-training was one small offer of assistance she could make immediately. It would give Teddy real satisfaction to take Birdie's education in hand. And, while she was about it, she might also—

At that instant, her eyes flipped open and she sat bolt upright as though several thousand volts had passed through the mattress.

'Glory Moses,' she gasped.

And Glory Hallelujah say all of us. Because, surely, Miss Theodora Dunstan has recognized her destiny at last. Must have done. She might be drunk, but she's not *that* drunk – is she?

Chapter Twenty-Three

She wasn't – and then again she was. That is to say, she was quite drunk enough to conceive the crazy notion of marrying Bill Smith – but not nearly drunk enough to suppose she meant it. However, even in the cold and leaden-skulled dawn of sobriety the next morning, she was not dismissing the idea out of hand. In fact, she was giving the idea detailed consideration.

At a quarter past nine, she was seated at her kitchen table when, inevitably, the object of her deliberations put his head round the door. And, equally inevitably, observed that he hadn't expected to find her about so bright and early.

'I rose at six,' she replied, swiftly whisking a clipboard over a sheaf of papers. These papers featured, amongst other things, her ruminations on the pros and cons of becoming Mrs William Smith. Note that, *William* Smith. She had, in fact, drawn up two neatly tabulated lists. In favour of the motion: he was a likeable chap – she had gone so far as to score out 'likeable' and substitute 'good', which conveyed a wealth of admirable qualities beyond mere amiability; on past performance he evidently had the potential for a distinguished career (the only area in which he outscored the vicar); and he even more evidently needed a wife to help him realize this potential. And that, on a quarter page, seemed to be the sum total of arguments in favour.

Arguments against ran to three A4 sides and were by no means comprehensive. Suffice to say they ranged from earrings to nicotine addiction with much in between, including congenital laziness. This, admittedly, was annotated with a question mark, but sobriety had led Teddy to realize that

Bill had completed his last work, the painting of Lorette, some considerable while before assuming the burdens of fatherhood – at least nine months before, since it did not take a genius to deduce that the one had led to the other. One therefore had to ask oneself why he had painted nothing in between, and there was an asterisk reminding her to do just that. Cons also encompassed the twins themselves (delightful infants, but did any sane woman choose stepmotherhood?); his hairy chest; his presently insolvent condition; and so forth. Not forgetting a gorblimey accent one could cut with a butter knife. Teddy trusted she wasn't a snob, but these things had to be considered. Imagine Charlie's face giving her away at the altar – except they might not qualify for a church wedding, Bill being a divorcee. That minor consideration, too, had gone on the list. Naturally, she was too old for the tears-and-tulle routine, but she would still infinitely prefer to proffer her vows to a representative of the Almighty than of the Civil Service. She had even, without a qualm of self-consciousness, listed 'drinking?', her own binge the previous night being quite different from habitual overindulgence.

'Writing your life story?' enquired the query alcoholic.

'In the future tense, possibly,' murmured Teddy, without looking up, because she was discreetly rummaging for a different sheet of paper altogether. 'And before you ask, yes, I feel like death. No, worse than death. I may be experiencing an intimation of eternal damnation. Thank God it's Sunday.'

'My word, the tongue's getting round the old syllables again, isn't it?' He pulled up a stool opposite hers, and plonked himself down on it. He was sporting the indecently sawn-off shorts again. They would have to go. 'Any coffee on offer?'

Repressing a shudder, Teddy invited him to brew his own. She herself would have tea. Milkless.

'Bad as that? You know, what you really need—' Before he could suggest some disgusting and probably forty-per-cent-proof cure-all, however, he broke off, goggling. 'What the bloody hell's she doing in here?'

'She' being his wife, the painting of whom was now propped across the top of the fridges.

'We can't leave a valuable work like that to rot in the

outhouse.' Teddy had located the correct list and glanced up. 'Have you got a dinner jacket, by any chance?'

'You got a pet iguana?'

She sighed, and scribbled *Moss Bros.*

'Here, what is all this?'

Ignoring his question, she posed one of her own. Why, she wondered, had he not sold this canvas to raise some much-needed capital? Unless – and she tactfully cleared her throat – there were sentimental reasons for holding on to it? Well, she had only *asked*, there was no call for him to snap.

'Even if there was a dealer still interested in me,' he grunted, avoiding her eye, 'they'd want a run of work, not a one-off.'

'But surely—'

'Besides which,' he burst out, 'it's crap, can't you see?'

This took her aback. Removing her reading specs, Teddy craned round for another look. When she had carried the painting indoors earlier, and was able, for the first time, to study it properly in decent light, she had been rather impressed. Not that she pretended to know anything about art – as had become mortifyingly clear over the past few days – but any fool could tell this canvas showed rare technical accomplishment. Lorette's skin shone with pearly luminescence, every coppery strand of hair seemed individually defined, and one felt one could almost pluck the rusty old springs out of the couch on which she lay.

'Not got it, has it?' said the artist flatly. 'I don't know why I haven't chucked the thing. Maybe I kept hoping one day I'd look and actually see something.'

'See what?'

'It. Don't ask me for words. *It.*' He shrugged. 'Like my old teacher used to say, if what's on a canvas is all that's in the picture, you're fucked, sunshine.'

Teddy, who was reminded of him holding forth on the subject of love in an equally half-baked fashion, enquired whether this 'it' might be like beauty. 'You know, in the eye of the beholder?'

'Balls. It's like *life*. You can't see life, can't touch it, but that doesn't mean it isn't real. No, listen to me. You've got two bodies side by side, identical down to the last fingernail –

except one's alive and the other's a stiff. You telling me they're the same?'

'I should think the corpse would be paler,' she said prosaically. 'Anyway, Lorette looks chock-full of beans to me. Rather like my father when one of his precious no-hopers was romping towards the winning post. In fact' – she chuckled – 'now I come to think about it, there really is the most extraordinary look of Pa round the eyes. What a hoot.'

'Hilarious.'

'*But*,' she said, abandoning art criticism for the business in hand, 'what I've been wondering is how you came to paint it at all. When I asked last night how a successful chap like you ended up at the Huddlestone Institution—'

'Institute. Of Applied and Fine Arts.'

'Whatever. Not exactly the Slade, is it? Anyway, you said—'

'I'm amazed you can remember what I said, state you were in.'

'You said, with the most peculiar expression, "*don't ask*".'

'Correct.'

'Sorry?'

'That's what I meant. Don't ask.'

'Oh, for goodness' sake, don't be so prickly.'

'I thought last night's sweetness and light wouldn't last: you're such a chum, Bill, such a trouper.'

'Perfectly reasonable question. Is it too much to expect an answer?'

'I'll kill her,' snarled Bella, lighting a cigarette and sucking furiously. They were seated side by side on the shallow stone surround of the lily pond, and a blazingly hot midday sun was causing Teddy's head to throb unpleasantly. 'Truly I will. I'll kill her first, then divorce him. Last night, just when we were getting somewhere for the first time in ages, because I could feel that Charlie had a really solid—'

'I don't want the clinical details,' shuddered Teddy, 'and not another word about your hangover, either, because however bad yours is, mine's worse. Can we please get back to your party?'

Her sister-in-law blinked at her dazedly. 'God, how weird,' she breathed. 'History's repeating itself. Hangover; us out here by the pond; me swearing to strangle the old bat; you wanting to invite men to my party.'

'Not *men*,' cried Teddy, in a near-paroxysm of exasperation. 'I'm asking you to invite *Bill*.'

'Well, if he isn't a man, I don't know who is.'

'We were talking about partners for me, then,' she said crossly. 'This is quite different.' And Teddy said this without a blush, because whatever her motive in securing an invitation for Bill to this event, it was certainly not with a view to improving their acquaintance.

They had had a most enlightening conversation this morning – in the end. Blood out of a stone, certainly, but she had at least established that Bill quit London for Huddlestone after suffering – rather alarmingly – some sort of nervous breakdown.

'I went gibbering bonkers,' he added helpfully.

Teddy's pencil quivered. 'Does it run in the family?'

'Pardon?'

'Sorry. I mean, what actually happened?'

The full story somewhat mitigated her alarm. Indeed, given what she had already learned about his working methods – who could forget that ghastly vision of him labouring round the clock, knee-deep in mouldy tikka masala? – one could scarcely wonder the strain had taken a toll on his health. In truth, his very success had contributed to his undoing, by freeing him to paint uninterruptedly. It had, moreover, arrived with startling suddenness. After all those years of subsidizing his art in kitchens and on building sites, one of his paintings had caught the fancy of a journalist, who had run a spread in a glossy Sunday supplement on this talented brickie – conveniently ignoring, as Bill said, that he'd served his stint at art college like everyone else and was only hod-carrying in order to eat. But the tag captured the popular imagination – Teddy even dimly remembered reading something about it herself – and his pictures did, too. To a staggering degree. One day, Bill was pleading with the bank manager for an extension to his overdraft, the next, he was being offered lunch and investment advice. The latter, inevitably, he ignored, and one could only be grateful he had been painting too manically to squander the money as fast as he earned it. Although, by his own account, he made heroic efforts.

'I can imagine you must have felt tempted to let rip a bit,' she conceded austerely.

'The likes of you couldn't begin to imagine the stupid stuff I got up to,' he retorted. 'Sex, drugs and rock'n'roll was the least of it. About the only thing I never found time for was sleeping, so once in a while I'd take pills to knock me out, too.'

'Dear me,' she murmured, wondering whether she should add narcotic dependence to her list.

'Only, after a bit, when I'm making these filthy piles of dosh, the critics start putting the boot in. From being God's gift, every canvas roaring with raw, brute sex—'

'I'm sorry?'

'Oh, that's all they reckoned I ever painted: sex. Didn't matter if it was a bottle and a couple of apples, they saw sex.'

'Do you know, I said something of the sort about Hari's picture,' she exclaimed, rather gratified. 'Wasn't that clever of me?'

'Don't ask me, I only paint the buggers. But the next minute, I'm supposedly becoming mechanical, predictable – *commercial*. The poor old brickie's still pulling the same cheap tricks, they said; no soul, no brain, just painting with his prick – well, maybe they didn't use those exact words,' he added irritably, 'but that's what they meant.'

'And that made you crack up?'

'Nah,' he sighed, squinting as he lit himself a cigarette. 'No, not really – I mean, if you worried what those dickbrains said, you'd never pick up a brush in the first place. Besides, the work was still selling faster than I could turn it out. Problem was, I stopped believing in myself that my stuff was good any more. I looked at it – and I just didn't know.'

After five years of manic work and still more manic debauchery? Teddy, frankly, was amazed he could see at all, and said so. But instead of doing something sensible like taking a holiday, he had just redoubled his efforts on both fronts. With the result that he had come to consciousness one grey morning, stark-bollock-naked, as he so elegantly expressed it (really, he'd given her a very graphic description of that fateful dawn), splayed on the floor in front of his easel, upon which rested a glisteningly fresh canvas, and it looked, to his bleary eyes, as though a drunken spider had been doing a tap dance across it. In interestingly assorted shades of pink.

'That was what got to me,' he commented wryly. 'It wasn't as if I'd sloshed paint around, those colours were carefully mixed. Every last tint from pearly fingernail through corset salmon to flaming magenta. I looked at it, and I thought, that's your brain on that canvas, you wanker. So I had another slug of vodka and I said to myself, you get off this merry-go-round, old son, or you're dead. So I found a doctor, got some pills, stopped drinking, and' – he sighed – 'I stopped painting, didn't I? Seemed no big deal at first, because the doc warned me some people can't work on anti-depressants. Still, before I could chuck myself off a bridge, the letter from Huddlestone arrived. Old tutor of mine was principal there, would I consider a year as artist-in-residence. I thought maybe a change of scene, chance to put something back, all that kind of crap . . . Anyway, the rest you know. End of glittering career. Happy now?'

'I just—'

'Because there ain't no more to tell.' He whistled. 'You know, we've got to keep you off the bottle, babe. I only paint pink spiders, you turn into the Spanish friggin' Inquisition.'

'You appear,' said Teddy, ignoring this jibe, 'to have made an admirable recovery.'

'You reckon?'

'Well you're not bonkers any more, are you?' she said with some asperity.

'Not painting neither, in case you hadn't noticed, although I stopped taking the tablets years ago. And if you say one word about bicycles and getting back in the saddle,' he added grimly, 'I won't be responsible for my actions. What were you asking about dinner jackets for, anyway?'

'But it isn't just Bill, you said you wanted *two dozen* invitation cards,' insisted Bella stubbornly, 'and a copy of the guest-list.'

Teddy clicked her tongue. 'Have you got spares?'

'Of course. I didn't invite nearly as many people as I could.'

'The merest two hundred and ninety-eight, as I recall. One can only pray, at such short notice, half will scratch.'

'Well, no, that's the lucky thing,' said Bella with a flicker of animation. 'If you can call it lucky, because it was supposed to be the Hartlepools' silver wedding do that night, to which *everybody* was invited, only of course Johnny's gone and run off with the stable girl now.'

'Lord help us.' Teddy scribbled an appropriate adjustment to the figure at item 9: *anticipated attendance*.

'Anyway, you're talking about inviting more.'

'Not necessarily. I just want to make sure you're asking the right people.'

'Meaning what?' squeaked Bella indignantly.

But Teddy had no intention of explaining. It had been a mistake ever to confide so much as a hint of her marital aspirations to her sister-in-law in the first place. Under no circumstances was she going to confess that those vague notions might now be assuming a concrete shape – one might even say the shape of a concrete mixer, although decent tailoring should work wonders here. Bill's eligibility would also be improved by a less brutal haircut, the jettisoning of his earring, some respectable footwear, and . . .

Sorry, what was that? Did someone have the temerity to ask whether Miss Dunstan, amidst all this meticulous cataloguing of her intended's shortcomings, had spared a thought for the likely views of Mr Bill Smith – sorry, of the future Sir William Smith RA – with regard to herself?

Good God, Teddy would cry, of course she had. What sort of a totty-headed nincompoop do we take her for? She would have us know she doesn't suppose for one moment Bill wants to marry her. If he didn't rupture himself laughing, he would probably faint with horror. Well, she rather hoped 'horror' was overstating the case, but we may rest assured she was not counting on his enthusiastic participation. Why else would she be going to all this trouble? Surely we cannot be naïve enough to suppose she has driven hotfoot, hung-over and clip-boarded to the Hall merely to argue the trivia of a family party. Of course she hasn't. Men, as is well known, are a witless breed, unable to recognize what is good for them, and she has devised a strategy for the re-education of this particular specimen, guaranteed to open his eyes to the matchless benefits of marrying someone like herself. It is a highly ingenious strategy, if you will forgive her immodesty. So ingenious, in fact, that she is putting it into operation under our unsuspecting eyes at this very moment.

'Did you include the Huntley-Pinkers? You know, with the socking great hacienda place down towards Boroughby?'

'Thought you couldn't stand the Stinker-Pinkers,' said Bella, bemused. 'Anyway, I can't remember.'

'Hopeless. We must go inside and find that list.'

'I haven't finished my fag, what's the rush?'

'I,' said Teddy sternly, 'have a vast amount to do.'

Which indeed she had. For while another woman's strategy aimed at helping a chap see the marital light might involve a plunge bra, large gins and a wash of Puccini on the record deck, it must be apparent Theodora Dunstan's campaign plan is of a different order altogether. Be honest. Can you see her playing *femme fatale*? Exactly. Not that she would ever argue sex cannot be a means to an end – of course it can, that end being the procreation of children, and although she hadn't yet had time or inclination to give much thought to the sex side of their putative union, she dared say she and Bill could toddle through the requisite nonsense well enough, if and when the time came. That time was not yet come. Forget Wonderbras, subtlety is the key to her plans, and if anyone is inclined to suggest that subtlety has never seemed to be her strong suit, she can assure such doubters that she has learned a thing or two since she proposed to John Blackwell over the marmalade pots. *Oh yes, she jolly well has.* She intends to be as a swan, floating serene and inscrutable, while her little legs paddle like fury under the surface.

She was paddling pretty furiously already. 'Crock-hire, car-parking?' She looked up from her clipboard. 'I want details of everything you've planned for this jamboree so far.'

'Planned?' said Bella blankly. 'Well, I've jotted a few notes, but—'

'Typical. Just as well I'm ready and willing to take over, isn't it?'

'Awfully sweet of you, but—'

'Ah, and the old ping-pong room, that's terribly important. You don't use it these days, do you? You know where I mean – far end of the attics?'

'I thought we were talking about my party?'

Teddy clicked her tongue again. 'We need somewhere for Bill to paint you.'

Bella's eyed widened. 'The portrait's still on?'

'Certainly, but with the best will in the world we can't turn the abattoir into a studio in time. It's vital he makes a start before your party.' She was talking more to herself than to her bemused sister-in-law. 'Work in progress, you know. Guests – might like to see.'

Bella heaved a sigh. 'I suppose Charlie thinks a painting will be something to remember me by when I've gone.'

'Charlie doesn't know a thing about it – yet. Anyway, it's no longer his concern, Bill's painting you as a favour to me, and will you please stop talking drivel? When you're gone indeed.'

'You don't realize—'

'Ah, Jeremy!' Teddy had espied a mane of black hair over a hedge. 'I was hoping to catch you before you left for town.'

'Sis, hi,' he responded, with no great enthusiasm. And even less when he was informed he was detailed to preside over drinks supplies.

'You'll be back from London by then, won't you? Quite, so you might as well make yourself useful. I'll supply the white jacket.'

He stared at her with outrage. 'Run a bloody bar? I wasn't even thinking of coming to this geriatric knees-up.'

'Did I invite you?' enquired Bella tartly.

His sister rolled her eyes. 'Forty quid, cash.'

'But he'd be hopeless. Why can't we have a proper bar-man?'

'We're economizing.' Teddy was flipping through the lists attached to her clipboard. 'And it's murder getting reliable staff at this notice. The children can do their bit, too, with coats and cars and what have you. Ah, here we are . . .'

Bella pouted. 'I'm going off the whole idea.'

'Too late for that. And if Charlie's not going to blight the evening by stomping round like a six-foot thundercloud, he

194

needs convincing it isn't bankrupting him. I've scribbled some ideas here on cheapo food, drink – we'll be cancelling that fizz, naturally, vintage Bolly, my foot; fancy dress is *not* going to be compulsory, black tie will be fine; now, *music*. Was it a ghastly dream or do I recall hearing you'd booked a band?'

'I'm trying, but—'

'Good, that can go. Cost the earth. Don't goggle, Bella, I assure you nothing would suit me better than to lavish a king's ransom on this shindig, hire the entire London Symphony Orchestra along with the Rolling Stones – make my job a damn sight easier to boot – but I happen to have a conscience about frittering my brother's lolly. Don't worry, it will all be splendid, but it's strictly high-gloss, low-cost from now on. I'm thinking of your marriage as well, you know.'

There was a pause.

'As well as what?' said Bella.

Chapter Twenty-Four

Indeed. Good question. This proved to be only the first of many occasions when Teddy found that a master strategist needed an inventive tongue if she were to maintain her swan-like serenity. And she had never been clever at fibbing.

She wriggled off that particular hook because her sister-in-law, without waiting for an answer, began complaining afresh about the imperative need for music at anything claiming to be a party. In relief, Teddy agreed to book a discothèque herself. No, Bella wasn't to stir in the matter, she would arrange everything, and square the plans with Charlie to boot. Trust her, *everything*. Whereupon Bella, with swimming eyes, whispered brokenly that it was too sweet of Teddy, going to such enormous trouble, just for the sake of her silly old birthday.

'Nonsense,' muttered our heroine, feeling a bit of a heel, because, of course, her labours had precious little to do with Bella's birthday. This party had become the central plank in her own grand strategy and, for any slower wits who have failed to divine what she was up to, her thinking ran as follows.

Say what you like about Bella's cronies – and Teddy could say a great deal – they included most of the local filthy rich. Once it had occurred to her, therefore, that such a gathering offered a once-in-a-blue-moon opportunity to introduce a struggling artist and would-be gallery proprietor to a wide and decidedly up-market clientele, she had seen her way clear. Not so much a party, more a fat and juicy public relations opportunity. When she wasn't steering around her protégé (smartened up and strictly sober) to press the appropriate flesh, she would be navigating potential customers up to the attic to admire his emerging portrait of Bella. That was why she had commandeered the old ping-pong room as his temporary studio – a smart touch, don't you think? Furthermore, if Bella's guest-list lacked any of the fatter-walleted local art-fanciers, such omissions would be rectified by means of a little research and the spare invitation cards. Thus, with God's grace and a following breeze, the evening would kickstart the transformation of Bill Smith from amiable layabout into eligible mate, and demonstrate to him the benefits of linking his future fortunes with hers – all in a single, dazzling coup.

Along the way, she had toyed briefly with the notion of disclosing to him at least those parts of her scheme concerned with the relaunching of his career, but decided against doing so. Surprise, as some canny old soldier once said, is the essence of attack. And if anyone feels inclined to counter this wisdom with rather more famous saws about tangled webs and Scottish mice, they can jolly well put a sock in it. Still less does Teddy wish to be reminded of her impassioned vow last night to cease interfering in other people's affairs. She was drunk. And this is *different*.

Besides, Bella was more than happy to hand over the reins, even if she did burble on rather hot-makingly about finding a way to reciprocate such generosity, and all that remained for Teddy to do was convince Charlie he should stump up the spondulicks with good grace for the sake of his marriage. This further economy with the truth also tweaked her conscience, but she staunchly reminded herself that the thrash would have gone ahead anyway, and her efforts were saving him a great deal of money.

'Whatever you say, Sis,' he muttered dolefully when she bearded him in the Estate Office. 'Don't suppose it will make any odds. Fact is . . .' His mouth worked soundlessly for a few moments before producing a strangulated croak to the effect that his wife didn't seem to love him any more. '*Hergh*, can't say I blame her.'

'Tommyrot. I've had Bella saying practically the same about you, not half an hour ago. And looking miserable as sin.'

'Was she?' The poor sot stared up from his desk, pathetic as a kicked bloodhound.

'Why is it the pair of you have to carry on like a pair of moody moonstruck teenagers,' she wailed, 'instead of settling down into middle-aged married peace?'

'Like the parents, you mean?' retorted her brother with an unexpected flash of defiance. 'Never argued because they never bothered to speak for twenty-odd years?'

'Perfectly satisfactory marriage.'

'You think so?'

'Did they ever complain? Anyway, that's beside the point.'

But Charlie's cavils were as nothing compared to those of the other pawn on her carefully plotted board. The most important pawn of all.

'Me, get tarted up in a tux for a party at your family's poncey joint?' cried Bill Smith. 'You got to be fucking kidding.'

When she had mentioned dinner jackets earlier, Bill had apparently assumed she was recruiting him as a waiter. Which job – at a pinch – he had been prepared to undertake.

'Tell you what,' he offered now, 'I'll work the doors.'

'Doors?' said Teddy, holding on to her temper with difficulty.

'Don't tell me you haven't thought about security? Big do like this? Ten to one you'll have the scaff and raff from miles round sneaking in. And don't say it doesn't happen, because the parties I've crashed are legion. What's more, I've earned a few quid in my time with the old dicky-bow and walkie-talkie keeping undesirables like me out, so if you're looking for a bouncer . . .'

Teddy assured him, with a moue of distaste, that she could easily imagine him in such a role, but would not require his services at this occasion, thank you very much. She was, however, moved to jot a note that some sort of security on the gates might be advisable – a gardener with a guest-list should do the trick – and secured Bill's reluctant agreement to attend by wimpishly claiming she was without an escort and needed his moral support. Dear God, the depths of dishonesty one had to plumb in pursuit of the greater good.

'Well, if you put it like that,' he sighed, shrugging, 'I guess a free drink's a free drink. But there's no way you're getting me into a dinner jacket.'

The upshot was her amending of *Moss Bros* on her list to *Fancy dress hire x 2*. The second costume was required because Bill, sniggering, said that if she was prepared to make a fool of herself, too, he was game – always provided, of course, that Lil could babysit. This presented another hurdle, because Lily was detailed to supervise the kitchen operation – even if she did not yet know that her twenty-two sit-down diners had swelled to three-hundred-odd all-night revellers. A hasty phone call secured an assurance that the redoubtable Mrs Rowbotham felt herself up to the job. A big do at the Hall, said Lily, would be quite like the old days. As for the twins, they would be entrusted to the care of their mother.

'For once in their lives,' she added sardonically. 'But never fear, Lorette'll do it. Just now I've got that lass right where I want her.'

Over the following week, Teddy booked two equally sporting grandmothers to support Lily behind the scenes, and pieced together a tolerably reliable assortment of skivvies and waiting staff, which was itself an achievement at such short notice. During planning and reconnaissance sorties to the Hall, she briefed the head gardener on his security duties, which he embraced with slightly disconcerting gusto and talk of mobile phones, dogs and reinforcements; and, with a judicious mixture of cajolery, threats and cash bribes, recruited her nephews and niece as car-parking stewards and cloak attendants. She also sent out a couple more invitations, although by and large she was disposed to approve her sister-in-law's guest-list. Bella's invitation to the photographer from the *Ridings Life* magazine, however, caused her some soul-searching. In the end, she elected to let the arrangement stand, nobly subsuming her own wariness of the press – even of such a frippery, parochial rag as this – in favour of her protégé's need for publicity. It may even have crossed her mind that Bella would be bitterly disappointed if her birthday were to pass unrecorded in the local glossy annals, but this is by no means certain. She had, after all, a great deal else on her mind.

You see, it was not just the party itself she had to consider. If only. There was little point in embarking on a public relations exercise for an artist and his soon-to-be-opened gallery unless that gallery was indeed to open soon. Which brought her inexorably back, once again, to her neighbour.

Teddy would like you to know she was not unsympathetic. She perfectly understood Bill's ambivalence at the prospect of setting himself up as a shopkeeper – but he was the one who had insisted a gallery was his only option. Indeed, he regularly assured her that he was applying his mind to the matter. She just wished he would apply something more than his mind. And although her tact and patience were exemplary, there were times, during those frantic days, when she would glance out from her seething kitchen to see Bill sprawled peacefully in the sunny yard, fag in one hand, beer in the other, children gambolling around him, and wonder why she was going to such trouble. Then she would sternly remind herself that the slob-like hulk concealed a rare and precious talent, and her appointed mission was to help it re-emerge glittering into the world.

Early efforts at burnishing the outer shell did not, to be honest, meet with much success. A delicate hint that an earring was perhaps an unnecessary accoutrement for a chap of his years was countered with an equally friendly suggestion that a bit more jewellery might do wonders for her own appearance – and, while Bill was on the subject, did Teddy so much as possess a make-up bag? Not that he was a great one for the painting lark – clearly, she hissed, momentarily forgetting herself – but she had a sweet little face, she had, honest. Well, when she didn't have a socking great black eye. Only she didn't seem to make the best of herself, know what he meant? Similarly, she had scarcely touched on the virtues of a well-cut suit before Bill began pondering whether she herself should wear more yellow – not some washy, babywool lemon, he hastened to explain, but a real, blazing butter-gold. He thought she ought to give it a whirl; trust him, he knew a thing or two about colour. It was around then she decided to abandon sartorial issues, and concentrate her energies on business plans. Employing the softest of kid gloves, naturally.

With studied casualness, then, over coffee one morning, she enquired whether Bill had yet fixed on a date to begin the refurbishment of his retail premises. And, like a mother hen watching a chick peck its own tottering way down a path long since mapped by mama, she let him burble on about the job needing more than brute labour and a Black and Decker. First off, he'd need to rustle up cash for fittings, equipment, lights – good lighting, after all, was key and central to anything claiming to be a gallery, and that kind of gear wasn't cheap.

Did Teddy tartly enquire where he thought he was going to get this cash? Whether he was expecting it to rain from the skies? Not a bit of it. Having anticipated just such a procrastinatory response, she assumed an air of wide-eyed innocence as she pondered aloud whether selling that painting of Lorette, now adorning one corner of her own sitting room, might not raise a handy lump of working capital? Yes, she remembered what he'd told her about dealers being uninterested in single works, but supposing it were possible to locate an admirer of his, who might be interested in a private purchase?

'You mean if his guide-dog takes a fancy to it?'

Interpreting this as a free hand, Teddy promptly went off to telephone Hari Stakinos at his salon in London, exactly as she had planned.

'Theodora, my little treasure,' he exclaimed delightedly. 'I *knew* you were going to phone today, I had a feeling in my water.'

He professed himself equally unsurprised to learn that the artist responsible for his peach still life actually lived next door to Teddy and was, moreover, father of the little boy who had so nearly come to grief under his car wheels. Such things were always happening to him.

'*Carmen*?' said Teddy. 'Sorry, the music your end of the phone's a bit noisy, and I'm not terribly well up on opera – oh, *karma*. Well, I dare say. The thing is, Hari . . .'

The thing was, Teddy remembered his mentioning that the friend who had given him the selfsame painting rather regretted

201

not having acquired one of Bill's, um, naked ladies . . . Indeed, yes, the producer fellow . . . Michael *Splitz*, was it? No, she couldn't say she recognized the name, but then she was as dim about films as she was about opera . . . He was over in this country now, was he? Due to walk into Hari's salon any moment? Heavens, it was enough to make one believe there might be something in this karma lark after all.

'Casting a movie,' Hari confirmed, 'or chasing a nineteen-year-old on the make, or probably both, because if it's not his money they're after, it's a starring bleeding role. Beats me why he can't see it. I mean, if you were a teenage blonde with tits like missile cones and legs up to your armpits, you'd really fancy a pot-bellied, frog-faced dwarf who's practically due for his bus pass, wouldn't you? Not that there isn't a warm and wonderful soul inside, but don't try kidding me that's what excites them. And I've warned him he'll be needing the flaming bus pass soon, if he ends up in another divorce like the last, because helicopters don't run on lemonade. "Settle down, can't you?" I says to him, "act your age for once in your—" *Michael*, cherub, fabulous seeing you, love the shirt. Hang on a tic, Teddy.'

But Teddy was herself distracted by a hairy arm suddenly wrapping itself around her waist. 'I'm on the phone,' she yelped, wriggling free. The last thing she needed when about to embark on negotiations for selling a picture was the presence of the artist. 'Go away, can't you?'

'Any sec,' Bill assured her. 'I'm on my way into town with the brats, and I thought I'd take a look in at this costume place you was on about.'

'Sorry?'

'For this party of yours, fancy dress?'

'Oh, that,' she said, and since Hari was still chirruping to his friend, she lifted the receiver away from her ear for a moment. 'Kind of you to take an interest,' she said acidly. Thus far, Bill's response to any mention of the event had been a martyred sigh of resignation.

'Yeah, well, I've had this ace idea.'

'Oh?'

'Pantomime cow. You know, you and me. I don't mind doing the back legs,' he added generously.

'Over my dead body,' she squawked. 'Oh, sorry, Hari, not you.'

'We're only in this for the laughs, aren't we?' protested Bill. 'Unless, no, don't tell me you was planning to tart up to the nines so's you can pull yourself a bit of local talent?'

'I *beg* your pardon?'

'Well, that's nice, innit?' he cried, grinning. 'No wonder you wanted me as your expendable bloody escort.'

'I haven't the remotest interest in the local talent, as you so disgustingly phrase it,' hissed Teddy. 'I have never *pulled* a man at a party in my life, and I certainly don't intend to start now.' At this, she heard a faint intake of breath from the telephone receiver and bit her lip. 'Sorry, Hari.'

'Don't be sorry,' he breathed. 'I believe I might just be seeing the light . . .'

An attentive listener must have caught a note of wonderment – one might almost say of *mysticism* – in his tone, but Teddy was not listening attentively and, besides, would be the first to acknowledge she wouldn't recognize mysticism if it jumped up and bit her. Instead, she began rapidly to explain that Bill Smith was with her now – breaking off to glare at him as he whispered something about a horse if she didn't fancy the cow – indeed, it was he who had been distracting her from . . . from the little matter she and Hari were trying to discuss, with asinine suggestions about fancy dress for Bella's party. She would get rid of him in a minute, but—

'A party,' crooned Hari, in apparent ecstasy. 'Talk about two birds with one crystal ball! Am I a genius, or what? Look, cherub, don't go away. I'll just have a quick confab with Michael.'

'No,' said Teddy to Bill, lowering the phone to her chest again. 'No horses, no cows, no nothing. Leave the costumes to me.'

'But I'm going into town, the kids are already in the motor. Least let me suss the job out.'

Teddy stared at him for a moment, brain ticking over furiously. God knows what he'd come back with. And she was *not* presenting to the world a protégé dressed as Widow Twankey. 'I'm coming too,' she said tersely. 'I'll be with you in five minutes. Now buzz off and let me finish my telephone call.' She waited until his bulky figure had vanished out of the door.

'Hari?'

'That's settled then.'

'He's interested in the picture?'

'What? Oh, I shouldn't wonder,' said Hari. 'You can show it to him when we come up for the party – OK by you, isn't it? I love fancy dress, me, and I've told Michael he's been working too hard, needs a weekend in the country to untangle his spiritual wires.' Briefly, his voice shifted away from the phone. 'You listen to your guru, blossom. Hari knows what's good for you.' The volume upped again. 'In more ways than one. Besides, what do you know? He thinks some old git he's making a movie about stayed at your place once. Synchronicity isn't in it. Look, have a word with him.'

'Miss Dunstan?' The breathy, high-pitched words tumbled out at a speed suggestive of a man for whom time is money. 'I wonder, does the name *Hugo Magulvey* mean anything to you?'

'Who?' said Teddy bemusedly. 'Look, Mr – Mr Splitz, isn't it? If you'd care to come to my sister-in-law's party, you're terrifically welcome, of course, it's one big free-for-all, but what I was really hoping—'

'Poet, novelist, playwright, belletrist? Only I'm sure he passed what was nearly the last weekend of his life at some joint called Langley. With old friends of his, name of Blaydon-Shawe?'

'Oh, you mean that old soak who pinched my bottom? How extraordinary, I was talking to my mother about him only the other day.'

'You actually met Hugo? Miss Dunstan, I shall be *honoured* to make your acquaintance. When's this party?'

'Give her back to me,' cut in Hari's voice. 'Leave the arrangements to the Fairy Godmother, eh?'

Chapter Twenty-Five

Teddy's only response was to assure Hari that fancy dress was absolutely not mandatory—

'It is for you, sunshine,' bellowed a voice from the door. 'And we're sick of waiting. On yer bike.'

Terminating the conversation in such haste, therefore, she had not the least suspicion she might no longer be the only spider at work in this web. Nor, a couple of days later, did she trouble to enquire what had moved Bella to send out a further seventeen cards of invitation. Assuring herself that, with these numbers, another dozen here or there made no odds, she just spun innocently and industriously on.

If the idea of marrying Bill Smith – which had, after all, been the starting point of her schemes – seemed to recede in importance, well, she wouldn't be the first general to lose sight of the ultimate objective in a determination to win each cut and thrust of a complex campaign. Because that was how it was beginning to seem to her. A war of wits between herself and her neighbour. The costume round she claimed as a comfortable victory, with an anodyne shepherdessy number for herself, and an opulently oriental set of robes for her friend.

'What's the bleedin' Sheik of Araby got to do with pantomime?'

'Aladdin,' she'd stated firmly, having worked out that the flowing headdress would nicely conceal both earring and convict crop. 'Or do I mean Ali Baba?' And with that, she steered him out of the shop.

She only began to feel that events might be slipping a *little* out of her control when it came to the installation of the artist in his studio at the Hall. Admittedly, Bill raised no objections to the idea in principle. Fine by him, he said, if she wanted him to do the job *in situ*. He exhibited an admirable absence of artistic temperament as Teddy conscientiously described north-facing skylights, generous strip lighting, plain white walls and so forth. She refused to countenance that what he was exhibiting might be a very much less admirable absence of interest. Still, he didn't argue when, taking matters into her own hands, she backed her van up to his premises, flung open the rear doors and mendaciously announced that, since she was delivering some plates to the Hall, she might just as well ship his gear up, too. She did, however, begin to get just the faintest sense he might be amusing himself at her expense as the piles of equipment began to emerge. Great steel tool-boxes of paints, flat wooden cases of pastels, tubes of brushes, reams of paper, boxes of Heaven knew what – all, she grimly noted, thick with the dust and spider webs of long disuse. There followed a couple of easels, and canvas after pristinely-primed canvas, board after board, of every size and shape . . .

'Eight canvases?' enquired Teddy, red in the face with her exertions, and finally growing suspicious.

'Don't know what I'll be needing 'til I start, do I?' Bill beamed innocently. 'Pastel, acrylic, oils; big, small – sitting, lying. Be prepared, that's my motto. Attic job, you said this room was?' Only now did his mirth begin audibly to quiver. 'Good few stairs the other end?'

Teddy eyed him measuringly and announced he could count those stairs for himself, because he was coming with her to offload. No, she would not hear any excuses, the twins were with their gran, and he could spare half an hour from his vital work of – she glanced into his kitchen – reading the *Daily Mirror*. Besides which, she added crossly, once again forgetting the kid gloves, it would give him a chance to fix a time for his first sitting with Bella.

'You're a hard woman,' he grunted, stubbing out a fag and lumbering towards the passenger door.

She was soon to wish she had not press-ganged him along. Bella, espying the bulge of a cigarette packet in his pocket, immediately proposed they repair to the lily pond together, and even as Teddy declared their filthy habit could wait until the van was unloaded, her mother shimmered in with outstretched hand and enquiringly arched brows. She had no choice but to make the introductions.

'And you're to paint my daughter-in-law?' murmured the dowager. 'Heavens.'

'Bit of a bummer, innit?' agreed the artist cordially.

Teddy hastily reminded Bella of her promise to show their guest the lily pond.

'Bill Smith,' mused her mother, rather as though tasting an exotic fruit, and was later to be heard in the kitchen yard informing her son that she admired his sweet nature in thrusting such brawnily brazen temptation into his wife's path.

Charlie, who was hosing down his Labrador after a couple of hours venting his miseries on the local rabbit population, glanced round in bewilderment.

'Take no notice,' gasped Teddy, heaving a viciously angular metal chest to the threshold of the van. She had already made several lone and limping trips up five staircases, each a little steeper and narrower than the last, and was not in the sunniest of humours. 'Brawny temptation, *Bill*? I've heard you talking some hogwash, Ma, but that takes the biscuit.' She was glad to observe that her mother, after trotting out some self-justifying tripe about forty being a dangerous age for women, had the grace to blush under her withering gaze.

Teddy then turned to Charlie, asking if he would give her a hand with this easel, since its owner had sneaked off into the garden with Bella for a – for a breath of fresh air, she concluded lamely. This resulted in her brother growling that bloody Bill Smith could shift his own bloody gear, Sir Charles was going to find his wife, and he marched off cradling his twelve-bore.

He had it cracked open across his knee and was rubbing the barrels with an oily rag and stony purposefulness when – having delivered the last of the equipment to the attic, bitterly wondering why she hadn't had the wit to commandeer ground-floor premises – Teddy found the three of them grouped around the lily pond. Bill grinned at her, Charlie glowered at Bill, and Bella, with a throaty giggle and a *wickedly* provocative pout in her husband's direction – really, she was every bit as bad as Ma – wondered aloud what she should wear to pose for her picture, if anything. 'A fig-leaf and a dab of Chanel?'

'You giving me danger money on this job?' enquired Bill as Teddy drove home in glacial silence. 'Bullet-proof vest?' When this elicited no response beyond a faint grinding of teeth: 'Got all the gear installed then? Shame I never got to check the place out – you did say east-facing skylights?'

'North,' began Teddy worriedly, before catching sight of his smirk in the mirror. 'Oh, very humorous.'

She was even less amused, the following day, by a telephone conversation with Brian Rowbotham. She had rung to confirm her booking of Colin's discothèque – Colin Rowbotham might not be anyone's idea of a groovy king of the turntables but he was at least cheap and available which was more than could be said for the previous four DJs she had approached – and then found herself being handed over to his brother.

'Who promptly sprang an invitation to some ghastly barbecue and Morris-fest on me,' she informed Bill furiously. 'By pure luck, it's the same night as Bella's do, otherwise God knows what I'd have said. I'm hopeless at instant excuses. And he told me he was recording a message on my machine about it when you butted in.'

'Don't you start. I've just had lover boy yelling down my phone.' Bill's face split into a delighted grin. 'Didn't matter what I said, he's obviously convinced I'm hatching a deep, dark plot to wreck his chances.' There was a frigid silence from Teddy. 'You know,' he prompted, 'he thinks I'm after getting off with you myself, can you believe it? Well, *I* thought it was funny . . .'

A lesser woman might be daunted. Might even feel she should pack up and leave the Bill Smiths of this world to moulder in their self-appointed gutter. But how would England have fared if such a craven spirit had reigned on the eve of Agincourt? On the beaches of Normandy? In the village hall, the chaotic morning before last year's jumble sale? Exactly. Teddy soldiered on.

Was she deterred when Bella threw a tantrum over the

booking of Colin Rowbotham? Or when her mother, demonstrating the infallible scent for trouble of a pig for truffles, chose this moment to draw out her sample books with the declared intent of redecorating her bedchamber at the Hall – well, it was so *tired*-looking, and since she seemed unlikely to be vacating it in the immediate future . . . ? And even when Charlie, instead of stepping in as he damn well should and chucking those samples books out of the window, morosely announced his own intention of taking a few days' fishing in Scotland, and leaving them all to enjoy the jamboree in his absence, *still* Teddy did not give up. Not merely did she return her brother to a proper sense of his duties as head of the family, she lectured him to such inspiring effect he began talking of inviting his old chum 'Sparky' Gryce-Hampton to lay on a firework display. Moments later, she was describing to her mother with relish the amenities of an old people's home recently opened on the York Road. She even reconciled Bella to Colin's disco by holding forth at length and with entirely spurious authority on the incomparable qualities of the Rowbothams' sound-reproduction equipment – clinching the deal by pointing out that they had offered to install festive lighting round the garden at minimal extra cost.

'With my luck it will rain,' muttered Bella. Then, making a palpable effort: 'No, no, I shouldn't say so, when you're working so hard. Anyway, don't worry, my angel. This may be the end of my marriage, but you are going to have a *triumphant* evening, I promise.'

'Let us trust so,' said Teddy, but with more doggedness than confidence, because, even as she steamrollered along, one obstacle remained unbudgeable in her path. She was discovering, as with horses and water, that you can take an artist to the most magnificently appointed studio imaginable, but you cannot make him pick up his bloody brush.

It was the same story as the gallery. Of course Bill was going to start work on the portrait, it was just a question of finding the time. His excuses were annoyingly plausible: there was the new school to be inspected for the twins; a potentially devastating leak in the water tank (so he claimed, vanishing into the loft for a whole afternoon a-bristle with spanners); the dog needed to be taken to the vet for worming – and it was no consolation to Teddy that she herself had diagnosed the cause of Birdie's dragging her backside along the ground. The final straw, however, on the Thursday morning, with but two days to go to the party, was learning he had promised the twins an outing to the Funtastic Adventure Park.

'Fancy coming along?' he enquired.

Teddy's mouth fell open. 'Are you *mad*? The party's the day after tomorrow, I'm feeding the five bloody thousand, I've got chairs and tables arriving at the Hall any minute, and a million jobs to finish here first.'

'Need a hand shifting anything?'

'All I need—' With a heroic effort of will, she curbed herself. How could she coerce Bill into setting promptly to work when, as far as he was concerned, this portrait of Bella was no more than a favour to herself – and a jolly generous favour at that? She eyed him measuringly, questioning afresh her decision to present him with the launch of his career as a *fait accompli*, wondering whether she should come clean. She resolved to risk one last attempt at persuasion first. 'If you did happen to have time on your hands,' she said, with studious gentleness, 'I'd be most awfully grateful if you'd make a start on Bella's birthday present.'

A shadow crossed his face. 'Yeah, well, I was thinking she'll be so tied up with the party, I'd better leave it until after.'

'No! Bill, look, I really think—'

'Can we talk about it some other time? The kids are champing at the bit, and if you're sure you don't want to join us—' He recoiled. 'Cool it, sweetheart, cool it, I get the message. I just thought you needed a break.'

'Very likely, but—'

'They've been on at me to invite you. They'd like you to come.'

'Very sweet of them.'

'They haven't hardly seen you these past few days.'

'Do you wonder?'

'Anyway, it's not just the kids. I'd like you along, too. I've been missing you.'

He disclosed this with a bashful sincerity which might have been touching, had Teddy possessed either the inclination or leisure to feel touched. She did not. Her battle-fatigued brain was already rejigging tactics. She was calculating that the painting of Lorette could be installed in the ping-pong room to show evidence of past work, and if she erected an easel, spread a few paints around . . .

'A few preliminary sketches,' she said rapidly. 'That should do the trick. Charcoal, pencil, anything you like. Just so the guests can see work in progress, you know, on . . . her birthday portrait. Could you manage that for me?'

He stared at her. 'It's so important?'

'Would I be asking otherwise?' She drew a deep breath, acknowledging, finally, that the time for dissimulation had passed. 'Maybe I should explain. The truth is, Bill, this isn't just any old common-or-garden birthday party. It's—'

'The be-all and fucking end-all, far as you're concerned,' he snapped. 'Spare me, I've already had this party up to here. See you.'

'Fair lady, I insist. It is your privilege to throw the master switch.' Brian Rowbotham, glinting with perspiration, signalled across the rose garden to his brother, and presented Teddy with a thickly taped adaptor socket. Tucking her pen behind her ear and her clipboard under her arm, Teddy pressed the button indicated. Nothing happened. The strings of bulbs nestling along wall-tops, through trees, across arbours, remained uncompromisingly black. A fanciful woman might find this symbolic.

'Ah,' murmured Brian. 'A little gremlin in the works, it seems. But never fear, all will be well soon.'

'You think?' said Teddy.

This was the eve of her Agincourt, half past five on Friday afternoon, with barely twenty-four hours to the commencement of battle. The terrace was ranked with tables and chairs; a hired refrigerated van, bulging with food, growled softly to itself in the kitchen yard; fathoms of cable snaked hither and thither; giant speakers loured black in corners; white-damasked trestles in the breakfast room glittered with glasses; and the home pasture, emptied of sheep, was roped and marked, ready for an invading horde of cars. Distorted mutters crackled from the direction of the lily pond as Harold, the head gardener and self-styled security supremo, rehearsed radio communications with Andrew, the head keeper, who was far away by the potting sheds. From further afield still, there echoed the odd crack of gunfire. Charlie was occupying himself in the Home Wood. And overhead, in the former ping-pong room, an easel stood bare, a stack of paint boxes lay cobwebbed and unopened, and only a cheerily grinning portrait of Lorette Smith broke the stark white of the walls. So much for work in progress. Teddy had not so much as clapped eyes on Bill since he stomped out of her kitchen yesterday.

'Fault located,' carolled Brian, puffing past with screwdriver in hand, 'and be not afraid, our installations are fully waterproof. Noah could have used these lights on his Ark with total confidence, if I may say so.'

Because now – and a fanciful woman might also find this symbolic – after weeks of cloudless, smiling sunshine, the sky was like sodden granite. No rain had fallen – yet. There had been heard not a murmur of thunder – yet. But the air was as heavy and smothering as an old face flannel. Lily, sweating in the kitchen, had observed to Mrs Boardman in Teddy's hearing, not ten minutes ago, that it was weather for turning cream to butter.

'That sky's rather spooky, isn't it?' remarked Bella, stepping out onto the terrace beside her, monkey nestling in the crook of her neck. There was another crack from the woods. 'Hush, Mungo, don't be frightened, my sweet. Only Daddy blasting at a poor little bunny. He must be allowed some pleasures in life.' Her laughter had an edge. 'I think it will actually be a relief when the storm breaks.'

'I suppose it must rain,' said Teddy dully. Truth to tell, she was beyond worry. 'Doesn't matter, we've got contingency plans for the wet.'

'Knowing you, you've probably planned for blizzards and plagues of frogs, too.' Bella sighed irritably. 'Oh, I'm sorry. I'm just feeling like a spare part, the only unemployed ant on the heap.' She screwed up her eyes, leaning forward slightly. 'I say, that funny little chap with the screwdrivers, over by the ha-ha, what's his name?'

'Brian?'

'He keeps staring at you in the doggiest way.'

'Really?'

'Charlie used to look at me like that. Once upon a long-gone time.'

Teddy registered the rattle of nerves in her sister-in-law's voice, but she was past caring. Any last-ditch chance of enlisting Bill's witting participation in her plans had gone, stymied at half past nine this morning. This was when Lily had popped into the kitchen at the Hall to say she was free all day to lend a hand if required, because she'd persuaded her big-hearted son-in-law to drive over to Leeds in her stead, to tie up a bit of business she had with cousin Muriel's son – did Teddy remember Mo's boy? Little tyke, he used to be, but doing very well for himself in the jewellery trade these days.

Bella yawned. 'Shall we have a gin?'

'Actually,' said Teddy dispiritedly, 'I might peel off. There's nothing more I can do until tomorrow.' And what, precisely, could she do tomorrow? Because it could not realistically be supposed that a sitting for even the sketchiest of sketches could be squeezed between the hairdressers, beauticians, manicurists and other nonsense Bella had lined up for herself. 'I might try for an early night.'

'I suggested just that to Charlie yesterday,' commented her sister-in-law sourly. 'I actually thought he might faint. But no, he simply took care to drink himself comatose and snored like a tractor all night. He's back in my bed, you know. Only because we need all the guest rooms tomorrow.'

'Countdown to blast-off imminent,' called a distant voice.

'Maybe my trouble is that I don't have enough to do, not since my babies grew up.' She gave another jagged trill of laughter. 'At least, I'm always doing *something*, but . . .' The sentence withered away into dejected silence.

Teddy, for once in her busy life, was doing nothing at all. She was just standing here on the terrace, staring at the leaden clouds, wondering why she couldn't stir herself to go home. Wondering, to be perfectly honest, why she had bothered working herself to a frazzle over the past fortnight. Not that her efforts would be wasted, entirely. Bella would enjoy a nice party, she supposed. Bill could meet a few people, for what that was worth, and there was always Hari's wealthy friend. He might take a fancy to the painting of Lorette. Although the more Teddy had looked at that canvas, the more she had found herself wondering whether Bill wasn't perhaps right, whether it wasn't a shade – lacklustre? It certainly didn't compel the eye in the curious way Hari's still life did. However, that was neither here nor there. Still less relevant at this moment were any barmy notions she may once have had about this party leading to a blossoming of relations between herself and Bill – she must have been crackers. As things stood, they weren't even friends any more. Not that she gave a fig for that. All his fault, silly fool.

'Shall I do the honours with the switch this time?' called Brian, peering up from the lawn. 'Fairyland, I promise, any minute.'

'Teddy?'

'Sorry?'

'I said, let me see the bruises on your face.' Bella's smile was brittle. 'Must have you sparkling tomorrow.' Unresisting, Teddy let her sister-in-law angle her chin towards the light. 'Not bad. Nothing we can't lose under concealer.'

'If you say so.'

'Darling, you seem rather down-in-the-mouth.'

'Yes, well . . .'

At that moment, however, a small red-haired figure hurtled round the corner of the house and lunged at her knees. 'Teddy, is it going to thunder and lighten? Nanna says so.'

'Stop it, Ferdy,' interrupted a shrilly autocratic voice, as his twin followed, dog on lead. 'Teddy's busy. You know what Dad told us.'

'Dad?' Teddy turned. Indeed, a familiar bulky figure was shambling along the terrace.

'Well, hello, stranger,' cried Bella, brightening immediately.

'Billy boy?' growled Brian Rowbotham, scrambling up from the lawn, scowling. 'May one be so bold as to enquire what brings you here?'

Bill winked at Bella, ignored Brian and looked at Teddy. 'Lil said I'd find you out here. Duchess, I've come to say I'm sorry. Been wanting to say it all day. Ever since yesterday morning, in fact.'

She shrugged, trying for a smile. 'Why should you be sorry?'

'Storming off like that, taking it out on you. I bashed on your door last night and first thing today.'

'Did you? Yes, well, I've practically been living up here. So much to do.'

'Sure, sure. That's why I thought I'd come up now.' He looked down, bit his lip. 'See, you know, if you could use a bit of muscle.'

Bella giggled. 'Best offer I've had all week.'

'Sounds like a case of too many chefs around the old consommé to me,' muttered his brother-in-law, busily clamping plugs into sockets. 'Now, if you'd all like to stand by?'

'Or . . .' Bill spoke so quietly, Teddy could barely catch his words, 'if there's anything else I can do to help. I'm free all evening.' His gaze met hers steadily. 'Mind, you'll have to take the kids off my hands.'

Her eyes widened. 'Anything?'

'*Geronimo!*' roared Brian Rowbotham.

Bulb by bulb, strand by strand, the garden was blossoming into light – dazzling, multi-coloured light, blue, green, yellow, red, all the shades of the rainbow. There were silver cascades rippling up and down the cedar tree, gold spangles flashing over the gazebo, violet search beams dancing through the fountain . . .

Bill's head jerked round. 'Fuck a duck.'

'Wow,' whooped Ferdy, wide-eyed. 'Better than Blackpool.'

'My God, it'll kill her,' breathed Bella ecstatically. 'The old witch'll have a heart attack when she sees this.'

'*Sit!*' ordered Florence. 'Only some pretty lights, you silly dog.'

They were all turning towards Teddy, each confident she must be sharing their jubilation or hilarity, their round-mouthed wonderment or gleeful horror. Teddy, however, said nothing. She was not even looking at the illuminations. She had turned back to the house and her gaze was directed upwards – not quite to the heavens, but to the ornately carved roof parapet, behind which lay the former ping-pong room.

'"Once more unto the breach,"' she whispered, resolution thrilling afresh through every syllable, '"dear friends, once more . . ."'

Chapter Twenty-Six

Well, he'd asked for it. Bill had walked into this with his eyes wide open, knowing exactly what Teddy would say. And she had. Heigh-ho, he murmured to himself, anything for a laugh. Mind you, the wicked glint in her sister-in-law's eye suggested there might just be more than a laugh in it for him. Who said virtue had to be its own reward?

Bet your life he'd like a drink, he declared, as he followed Bella's opulently swaying bottom up the stairs – with a monkey pulling rude faces at him over her shoulder. 'Up yours and all, mate,' he muttered. Pardon? Oh, yeah, gin, terrifico. He'd sort out the gear while she went back for the booze.

The first thing he did was shift the painting of Cuckoo out of his sightline. He didn't bother puzzling how the bloody thing came to be here at the Hall. God's ways might be mysterious, but He didn't have a patch on T. Dunstan. Besides, Bill's was not to reason why, his was but to doodle and die, and the only question interesting him at this moment was whether the condemned artist would be granted a last request. Heigh-tiddly-ho, better arrange a couple of chairs then, and find the right box of tricks . . .

'Strewth, Teddy seemed to have shunted everything up here bar the kitchen sink – including a crate of car tools, now he came to look inside the lid. Poor old Duchess, humping this lot around. He deserved to be shot, and it wasn't such a bad little studio she'd found for him, either. Plenty of light, even at six o'clock on a piss-awful day like this. As if it mattered.

'What? Oh, sure, ice, lemon, anything.' He was glad to see

her ladyship had brought up the full works on a tray because he reckoned a job like this would need plenty of anaesthetic. Quick swig for starters . . . He blinked. The lady mixed a mean drink.

'You don't mind Mungo, do you? Only storms make him rather jumpy. There is going to be a storm, don't you think?'

'Shouldn't wonder. No, feel free, the more the merrier.'

'Actually' – Bella eyed him coyly – 'I wondered if it might be fun to have him on the picture, too. Can you do monkeys?'

'About as well as I can do anything else.' He stuck a fag in the corner of his mouth, then took it out again. 'Sorry, OK by you if I smoke?'

'Absolutely, so long as you let me have one, too, only for goodness' sake don't include that in the drawing.' She giggled as she leaned confidingly towards him for a light. Bill found himself goggling into a cleavage on Grand Canyon scale. 'My husband hates me smoking. Maybe we'd better open the window.'

Which he duly did, and nearly torched her nose with the lighter because a gun blasted below.

Hoot of laughter. 'Only Charlie.'

'You don't say.'

Another high-pitched giggle. 'At least we know he's safely occupied.'

Hello, hello, did Bill just hear what he thought he heard? More to the point, had she just *meant* what any red-blooded, chronically sex-starved male might be pardoned for thinking she meant? Nevertheless . . .

'Business before pleasure,' he whispered, meeting her jittery little smile with the long, slow, wraparound grin he thought he'd forgotten how to do. Probably had forgotten, because the only practice he'd had at playing wolf in recent years was of the huffing, puffing and blow-your-house-down variety. 'Madam wants some sketches,' he murmured. 'God knows why, but she's going to get them.' He reached for a pencil. 'In spades.'

'You mean Teddy?'

'Who else?' He'd found his pencil knife. Hullo, old friend, haven't seen you for a long time.

'Are you doing this just for her?'

Was that a shimmer of pique he detected? He had already

begun shaving his pencil to a stiletto point, but halted, mid-curl. 'No,' he felt obliged to admit, because this was no time for kidding anyone, least of all himself. 'No, I guess if I'm being honest, it's sod-all to do with your sister-in-law. Whatever she thinks.'

However, he wasn't going to tell Bella it had even less to do with her lovely self, was he? Particularly when, with another giggle – he was beginning to think that laugh could seriously do your head in – she asked how he wanted her. So to speak.

'Any old way you like,' he responded, dripping the words like honey from a spoon, what a lad he was, 'so to speak . . .' Hang about, hang about, first things first. 'Maybe if you could look towards the window?'

Few sketches. Easy or what? Pencil, pad, attaboy.

After five industrious minutes she whispers, out of the corner of her mouth, 'You'll be kind about my double chin, won't you?'

'What double chin?' So saying, this old smooth talker adds a swift smudge of strategic shadow under the jaw, and *rip*. Completed half-profile hits the floorboards along with artistic integrity. Maybe a full-length now – with monkey? With monkey, why not. 'Towards me, good.'

'Top up your glass?'

'Don't even bother to ask. Intravenous drip'd suit me.'

His pencil's shifting faster by the minute. This rate, he could make a living doing lightning caricatures on street corners. Now there's a thought.

'You look . . . rather stern.'

'Uhuh?' Tender angle of monkey's arm, like a scrawny, plucked chicken wing.

'Sorry, should I shut up? Do you prefer to work in dark broody silence?'

'Actually . . .' He thinks back. He thinks back a long, long way to another life, to what seems like a different guy altogether. 'Mainly people used to moan about me singing.'

There is a pensive pause before she observes: 'You're not singing now.'

Wisp of chain round her neck. Dot and flash of dangling diamond. 'No, well, there you go. Think yourself lucky.'

Rip, number two goes down. 'Want to sit back in the chair now?'

The only sound is the soft hiss of lead on paper, the sneck of a lighter, the sighing exhalation of smoke. Then there's another rip and flutter, with a squeak of chair legs on bare wooden boards as Bella obediently shifts again. From time to time the monkey yatters sulkily – novel this, reflects Bill, working in a safari park. Rip, flutter; where are we? Four, five? How many does she want? And quietly – very quietly – thunder begins to stir.

'Is it me?'

'What?'

'I mean, is that why you're looking so fearfully bleak?'

Bill bites back a snort of irritation. Does she have to talk? Give him paid models any day.

'Having the time of my life,' he responds, cross-hatching with the speedy precision of a sewing-machine needle. And he is, because there's nothing like proving to yourself, once and for all, that what you've suspected for years is one hundred and ten per cent correct. Rip – there goes another little masterpiece, along with half a tumbler of hooch. He's really getting into his stride now. 'Other side. Look beyond me, hold it – beautiful.'

'I wish.' Her focus sharpens on a point over his shoulder. 'She is, though. That's your wife in the painting, isn't it? Terribly good.'

He doesn't argue. Know what he's thinking? He's thinking he might even paint Bella Dunstan tonight, strip lighting and all. In for a penny, in for a pony – if he doesn't slit his wrists with his pencil knife first. Only joking. Life might sometimes seem one big waste of breath, but we mustn't forget he's a father. Never mind if that's all he is. He is a loving and responsible father.

'Are you happily married?'

'Fucking deliriously,' he ripostes merrily, about to add *I don't think*, except for some reason her head jerks round, and he has to remind her to sit back. Eyes fixed in that corner, yeah?

'I used to be,' she sighs, after a couple of minutes.

'What?'

'Happily married.'

'That right?' He catches the gleam of an earring with a swift curve and a dot. You can see why he was gold-medallist twice in a row in the old life class, can't you? 'Yeah well, happens to all of us. Cuckoo's—'

'He doesn't find me attractive any more,' she suddenly bursts out. 'Obviously.'

'Uhuh?' Scribble, scribble.

'Do — do you think I'm attractive?'

'What? Sure, knockout. Face up.'

'Sorry, I suppose I shouldn't ask questions like that. Look, would you give me — give me a minute, I just need to blow my nose.'

'Don't worry, nearly done.'

'Only — only it's rather upsetting. When one's husband doesn't love one any more.'

'Dear oh dear.' Rip. What next?

'Of course, he says he does.'

And if, by any chance, you're thinking Bill isn't listening, you're absolutely bloody right. The words may be going in at the earhole, but the brain's well out to lunch.

'But the awful truth is — is he can't *make* love to me any more.'

And Bill has outlined brow, jaw and shoulder before he finally twigs where this conversation might be leading, and before he can stop himself . . .

She bounces to her feet. 'It's not funny.'

'Sorry,' he splutters. 'Not — laughing at you. It's *me*.' Course he's laughing at himself. Wouldn't you, if you'd panted up here, randy as any old hound dog, with drawing the last thing on your mind — when you'd spent years making excuses for not picking up a pencil — only to get so obsessed in your lousy, pointless scribbling you don't even twig you're being given the big come-on? No, well, she obviously doesn't get the joke either. In fact, now he comes to look at her — really look at *her*, not just at a collection of planes and angles, highlights and shadows — he's suddenly seeing a raw mass of quivering human misery, unstable as fucking dynamite . . . And can he get a sensible word out? 'Oh God,' he gasps.

The Almighty is on the ball. He rends the heavens with a bloody great crack of thunder right outside the open window at the exact same moment Bella Dunstan asks if *Bill* could make love to her.

Electric pause.

'I didn't mean—' Both say it at the same time.

'Darling!' shrieks Bella, and lunges forward.

And that, as Bill will later conclude, is where the fun really begins.

'Daddy's *frightfully* busy,' explained Teddy brightly, gathering up the Snap cards from her sitting-room floor and sneaking a glance at her watch. 'He's obviously working jolly hard, drawing lots of lovely pictures.'

Teddy has no problem handling children, no problem at all. Heavens, with three nephews, one niece and godchildren beyond counting, she's been doing this kind of thing all her life. It's perfectly straightforward, just like handling dogs. One simply has to be kind but firm. Perfectly straightforward.

'Drawing's not *work*,' snorted Ferdinand.

'It is for your papa. You know, like painting?'

She might *just* be prepared to concede, after two hours in the exuberant company of Bill Smith's offspring, in a once pristine sitting room now knee-deep in playing cards, crisp packets, board games, discarded clothes, mugs, half-eaten biscuits and a tennis racquet – *tennis racquet?* – that she was beginning to understand why he hadn't done much in the way of drawing and painting in recent years. The only wonder was he hadn't turned into a terminal alcoholic. Resolutely she averted her own gaze from the whisky bottle.

Ferdy eyed her expectantly. Fog-eyed and frog-voiced with weariness after their outing to Great-aunt Muriel's in Leeds, he was nevertheless stubbornly battling on. 'Can we have a bonfire then?'

And on to her pale lemon, newly upholstered sofa had crawled a hairy, grinning spaniel. Again.

'*Off!*' Teddy roared, and watched Birdie's flailing tail send a cushion crashing onto a Coca-Cola can, blessedly empty. At least – almost empty. 'Sorry, darling?' Fortunately, she had a cloth to hand. From when Florence had trodden on the

Kit-Kat. 'Bonfire? Goodness, I'm afraid Guy Fawkes night isn't for ages yet.'

'Before we came here,' explained Ferdy, as though she were being exceptionally dim-witted, 'we had a huge great bonfire of Dad's pictures.'

'You did what?' began Teddy.

But he had raced over to the window with a squeal of glee. 'Lighten!' he whooped.

That was all she needed. For while Teddy knew it was shameful, indefensible and totally potty, and she would have died rather than own up – especially to two tender infants, one of whom admittedly was jigging up and down, cheering as a jagged zipper of lightning tore across the sky – she had a bit of a thing about storms. As in, they scared her witless. But would she show it . . . ?

'What fun,' she gamely cried, when the lights blacked out and a thwack of thunder set the dog careering and barking its silly head off. Lunging for Birdie's collar in the dark, feeling something soft and sticky yield under her foot, she even managed to stifle her shriek as an icy hand closed on her arm.

'Will – Dad be back soon?' quavered a small voice.

'I damn well hope so,' snapped Teddy. The power flickered back to life and light, revealing a squashed apple core under her heel and a solemn and distinctly anxious face at her elbow. Breathe deeply, Teddy told herself. Rearrange face into smile of Madonna sweetness. 'I'm sorry, Florence darling. Yes, of course Daddy will be back soon. It's quite dark now. He can't be long.'

'Bill, you're wonderful. Totally and utterly fabulous.'

'Hush, not much longer.' Bill utters this in a hoarse whisper. 'We're nearly there. Don't worry, it'll be all right.'

'But I feel so horribly guilty.'

'No point crying over spilled milk. Anyway, my fault too. Should've seen – what was coming.' He lowers his voice further still, to a sweet croon of seduction. 'That's my baby, easy now.'

'Are you all right?'

'Me? Oh, I'm on top of the bleedin' world, I am.'

And Bill Smith would like it known he is speaking entirely literally – just in case any dirty minds have come up with the kind of scenario which was so unaccountably not in his when he abandoned sketch numero whatever, an hour or more back. By 'on top of the world', he means he is crouched in monsoon rain and hurricane gales on a dodgy stretch of lead flashing about five hundred feet above North Yorkshire – at least, that's what it looks like in the bleached panorama snapshots he gets from time to time, courtesy of the lightning. Otherwise, it's pitch black out here, and he is holding bloody tight to a shallow parapet along the edge of the roof, hoping Charlie Dunstan keeps his stately stonework in good repair. And what is he doing? He's glad you asked that.

'I'm not tired,' said Ferdy stubbornly.

'I am,' said Teddy. With feeling. And, thank you, no, she did *not* need reminding that, according to her once-cherished plan, this battle of wills was destined to be the shape of bedtimes to come from now to bloody eternity. Plans, she was reminding herself, could be unmade as easily as made.

It had gone like this.

Bill had laughed.

The celestial timps issued the adultery alert.

At which the monkey went bananas, grabbing a Sable Number Ten on the way.

'Darling!' shrieked its besotted owner, leaping after it.

'Forty quid a pop,' Bill roared, also leaping, quite forgetting he wouldn't ever be needing a paintbrush again. 'Give it here.'

Whereupon the monkey dropped the brush and bit a thumb (Bill's); he swore; she screamed; it catapulted out of the window.

Cue Sir Galahad. Who has been balancing here ever since, twig of grapes in outstretched hand, while Bella sticks her head out of the skylight offering advice, apologies, small talk and fruit supplies. Her sodden, gibbering pet clings to a television aerial and basically tells Bill to get stuffed. At least the thunder and lightning have stopped. There is only the rain beating down now.

Besides, all things come to he who waits. Even monkeys. Very slowly, three skips forward, two back, little Mungo is tiring of his great adventure. Very slowly – 'Come on, sweetheart, come on,' breathes his pursuer – he's skittering down towards Bill's outstretched hand, until . . .

'Isobella?' said the elder Lady Dunstan, raising her eyes from the crossword. 'Vanished upstairs hours ago with a bottle of gin on a tray. Darling, you're dripping on the carpet.'

'Cats and dogs. *Hergh*, silly of me, but I tried to sit it out in Home Wood. Early night, eh, Bella?'

'Oh, I don't think so. She streaked through the kitchen rather later screaming for grapes, just after the children took their sandwiches through to the television. Odd, really, because it's very dark now, isn't it?'

'She's outside?'

'Dear me, no, darling, she's upstairs with Mr Smith – you know, the artist? Although what they've been doing all this time, with gin and grapes, I really cannot imagine.'

'We're going to bed *here*?' said Ferdy.

'Daddy's obviously working very hard,' replied Teddy, tight-lipped, because if Daddy wasn't working his bloody socks off she would personally flay him alive, 'so we'd better not interrupt. Florence, my love, it's terribly sweet of you to offer to clear up, but . . .' She sighed and averted her eyes from the sitting-room carpet. 'I think we'll forget the mess in here until the morning. Now then, *nightclothes*.'

'Out of those wet togs at once,' commands Bella Dunstan, 'before you catch pneumonia. I'll go and find something of

Charlie's for you to wear. No, no, I insist. It's the very least I can do, you great *hero*, you.'

And she's gone before Bill can argue, with the monkey shivering around her neck. So he strips off to his boxer shorts, and lights the best cigarette he's tasted in twenty years. Then he hears footsteps in the corridor, and thinks, blimey, that's quick.

'Look,' he calls, adjusting his underwear, which, as his late grandmother would have said, is more holey than reverent, 'are you sure your husband won't mind?'

The door opens. And guess who walks in?

Chapter Twenty-Seven

This felt, ominously, as though it were only the eye of the storm. The sky hung heavy, black and silent, while the rain was reduced to a gauzy mist, thick with the promise of more downpours to come. In the distance, trees grumbled in a fretful wind, and an owl's call quavered long and low.

Tossing a cigarette stub into the darkness, Bill stepped back from the window. It must be late, but he'd long lost track of time. Still up in the attic, he was at least dressed now, in too-tight corduroy trousers, roped together with a belt, and a hairy pullover the colours of a peat bog. His own jeans and T-shirt lay sodden and filthy in a corner. They looked pretty much as he felt, if you want the truth. And the fact that he was cradling a glass in his hand made nonsense of his being here at all, because the idea, as he'd tried to explain to her ladyship, was that he would hang around until he was sober enough to drive home. She wasn't to worry about him, he had added helpfully, he could see himself out – kitchen door, yeah?

Bella hadn't answered because, by then, she was already halfway down the corridor, wholly entwined with her husband, and had seemingly forgotten Bill's very existence. Fine by him. Mind, he was grateful to her for barging in when she did. Old Charlie boy had been bunching his fists, sticking out his non-existent chin, growling that Bill was, *hergh*, a cad and a bounder. Well, maybe he hadn't used those exact words, but you get the picture. Yeah, yeah, very funny, farce of the wackiest trouser-dropping variety and Bill, too, would have been splitting his sides if he hadn't happened to be the mug without the trousers. And just as he was wondering whether another sharp exit out of the window might not be called for, Bella had bustled through the door with an armful of clothes, only to drop them on the spot.

'*Darling!*' she had shrieked. Which, now he came to think about it, had been her catchphrase all evening, and at just such a hysterical pitch. 'Darling, you're *jealous*. You're really, really jealous.'

Well, give the lady a gold star for observation. Fists up, face puce, smoke practically coming out of his nostrils; yup, it seemed fair to conclude this was one seriously jealous husband, who was, moreover, ignoring his missus and continuing to advance purposefully on Bill. That was when she had flung herself on her spouse – and we're talking a big woman here – locking her arms round his neck, plastering him with kisses, dragging him towards the door and practically tearing off the clothes he was wearing, never mind the heap she'd dumped on the floor. Do you wonder Bill had mumbled his excuses and shuffled into the background? If you asked him, it was touch and go whether they reached the marital bed in time.

Still, nice to see someone happy. More than he was. Know what he'd been doing for the past hour – or however long it was since they'd gadded off on their second honeymoon? He'd been pacing round, psyching himself up to take a look at his own lousy sketches. That's what had driven him back to the bottle, just as it always did. He'd spent a long time putting off the moment of truth, and he wasn't just talking about tonight.

Brilliant, the drawings were, Bella had assured him, having gathered them up while he was performing the acrobatics on the roof, totally amazing. Bill was a genius as well as a hero.

Great truth of life – which, pardon him, he used to share with the students at Huddlestone during his fleeting time as artist-in-residence – if your subject likes what you've done at first glance, it's ten to one you're in deep shit. Rest assured he hadn't imparted this twopenny gem of wisdom to Lady D., he'd already offended her quite enough for one night by bursting out laughing at such a delicate moment. He'd offered grovelling apologies for that since, of course, because they'd had plenty of time to chat, while he was squatting out there on the tiles like a spare gargoyle. He'd made up some tale of an old joke, too daft to repeat. And she, poor baby, had been just as anxious to apologize to him, to convince him that she hadn't meant *would* he make love to her, only *could* he . . .

'You know, as in, am I getting so horribly fat and old no one would look at me any more?'

Bill had gallantly assured her any man in his senses would leap on her like a hungry tiger, adding for good measure that he'd never for one moment dreamed she could have meant anything else. Which in his view was no small feat of diplomacy with rain lashing down from above, a fifty-foot drop yawning below, gin coursing round his veins, and a monkey sticking two fingers up at him.

However, here he found himself now in warmth and safety, with the monkey rescued and a pile of drawings face down on the floor beside him. And, great hero that he was, he couldn't even bring himself to turn them over. He was too afraid of what he'd see – and of facing up to what that would mean. Call him a snivelling coward, but he'd sooner go on kidding himself a bit longer. Not that he cherished many illusions about himself, not really.

The brutal fact was, since the day he'd flipped off his rocker with a canvas full of spiders, he hadn't turned out a single decent piece. Oh, of course he'd *painted* since the twins rolled along, for a while, anyway – God's sake, women artists have always managed to mix work and family, haven't they? – but he'd produced nothing worth the effort of finishing. Half-painted canvases had piled up like dry leaves in his dusty studio until, just before they left Huddlestone, he and the kids had built a bonfire of them and a load of other old junk. Hell of a good blaze. Of course, the babes didn't even remember him painting, because they were barely more than two when he'd finally packed away his gear, telling himself he'd wait until they started at school – until the house sale was sorted – until he was settled in Langley. One excuse after another. Only now there wasn't a shred of an excuse left. No wonder he was shit-scared. A million times more scared than he'd been clambering along that dodgy guttering.

Actually this evening had proved one thing to him at least:

he didn't want to die. Wisecracks about pencil knives and sticking around for his children's sake were as dishonest as they were pathetic, because with real death inches away on that roof, he'd clung on for grim life, and not out of fatherly altruism, either, but out of healthy, sane gut instinct. Salutary lesson: tragedy is reserved for your tortured geniuses, Bill's level was clearly knockabout slapstick. Suffering artists cut their throats. Bill Smith loses his trousers. Oh God, yes, this was a night to face the facts.

'Come on, you creep,' he muttered to himself. 'Look at the bloody drawings or we'll be here all night.'

He lowered his bum onto the stool, bent down and gathered them up. Even so, it took a terrible effort of will to turn them over, and . . . There you had it: the truth in black and white. He didn't bother flicking beyond the first couple, just grabbed his cigarette lighter, and had the flame cocked and dancing when—

'*Hergh*, hullo?'

Drawings and lighter went flying. He hadn't heard a step in the corridor, hadn't heard the door open behind him, nothing.

'Ah, good. You're still here.' Sir Charles stood on the threshold in pyjamas and a towelling dressing gown. 'Afraid I owe you an apology. *Hergh*, slight misunderstanding.'

Bill's muscles unbunched. They unbunched so far he nearly keeled off the stool. He managed to right himself, but he could no more have got to his feet than walk on the ceiling. He searched for a voice. 'Forget it. I mean, kind of thing anyone might think.'

'Decent of you. Bella explained. Whole business – rescuing the beast, all that.'

Whereupon Sir Charles seemed to have run out of small talk, but did he go? Did he hell. He just hovered in the doorway, shifting from slippered foot to slippered foot. And belatedly it dawned on Bill that this geezer was looking pretty despondent too. Terrific. Couldn't a guy have a nice cosy mid-life crisis round here without some other screwball muscling in on the act? But the moment Charlie caught Bill's eye on him, his features refroze into polite English gent mode, and he shuffled over to the drawings scattered on the floor.

'Mind if I, um, take a quick look?'

That was all Bill needed. He knew he should be laughing – hell, the whole night had been a farce, start to finish – so he hauled himself to his feet, kicking the stool aside. 'Help yourself.' Last exhibition you're going to get, Billy boy, he murmured to himself, better make the most of it.

'Oh, I say, jolly good.' And Charlie managed to sound like any old punter at any old exhibition, except he happened to be wearing his jim-jams. This wasn't just comic, it was surreal. 'First class.'

Bill had to get out of here. Get out and – well, fuck knew what he was going to do next, but get out of this madhouse for starters. He lumbered over to the corner and began to rummage in the sodden pockets of his discarded jeans for keys and cash.

'Enjoy it, do you, this art business?'

The question, trite and meaningless as it was, nevertheless caught him on the raw. What was he supposed to say? No, no, it's just my life blood, the only thing I ever wanted to do, total obsession, body and soul, Heaven, Hell, the reason I was born, the beginning, middle and end of my universe – bar two kids, who deserve better than this for a father. He managed to crank his features into a smile. Two can play the stiff-upper-lip game. 'It's had its moments.'

'I *say* . . .' Oh God, he'd found the painting of Lorette. Lot of throat-clearing here. 'She's a bit of a cracker, isn't she? Wouldn't mind that on my wall.'

And that, finally, was a joke too far. Why had the Duchess shipped that piece of crap up here? The last painting with his name on it, the first he'd been ashamed to sign, the only one he hadn't quite been able to chuck on the bonfire . . . If he couldn't make a break for it now – well, he didn't know what he might do.

'*Hergh*, strikes me as a jolly sort of way to earn a living, standing there with a brush, gorgeous girls getting their kit off for you.'

Pull yourself together, you wimp. 'Dead right, mate. Only problem is . . .' Three steps and he would be through the door, but it was already too late. Bill squeezed his eyes tight shut, because for one excruciating moment he thought he might start crying, and before he could stop himself, he heard a voice – his own voice – gasping: 'Only snag is – I can't do it any more.'

There, it was out. He'd finally said it, finally admitted it. He slumped against the wall, eyes closed. He couldn't move, speak; nothing. Then he felt a hand on his shoulder. A strictly masculine, all-chaps-together sort of hand. 'My dear fellow,' mumbled Sir Charles Dunstan, deeply moved. 'You too?'

Peace. Silence. Deep, dark, black silence. Teddy lay back on her pillow and breathed out slowly. It would be too much to say that she was contemplating the hitherto unappreciated blessings of a spinster's lot – or at least the lot of a childless woman – because, of course, it was different with one's own offspring, well-known fact. But that she was contemplating with renewed doubt her grand scheme of taking over Bill Smith's life and family was undeniable. Unlike the first wife's curtains or cooking pans, children could not be discreetly discarded after six months, and any half-formed optimistic notions that Florence and Ferdy would spend a substantial amount of time in their mother's keeping had been comprehensively whacked on the head by four hours of their conversation this evening. Lorette figured less centrally than an Aunty Grace who ran a corner sweetshop in Huddlestone. With a very fat cat called Benny.

Not that the twins had been naughty, exactly. Florence hadn't been a scrap of trouble all evening; sweet child, hardly a peep out of her. Ferdy, too, was sweet, bright, adorable, funny, just – *relentless*. Made one wonder if there was anything in this E number business. Maybe the Coca-Cola had been a mistake, and not just because of the carpet. Still, with young children, one wouldn't elect to have a plain carpet. A plain carpet in duck-egg blue.

Three bedtime stories. According to young Ferdinand, Dad always told them three. One for Ferdy, one for Floss, one for Birdie. But Birdie wasn't here, as Teddy had grittily pointed out, Birdie was in the sitting room. Which was bad enough, but not quite so bad as having the beast moulting and farting all over her elegantly appointed spare bedroom. Even Teddy, however, had felt unable to banish the creature to the abattoir on a filthy night like this. At least, she might have done so, but there was still a tingle of electricity in the air, and frankly she couldn't face the walk across the yard. So Birdie, duly let out to relieve herself and remuddy her paws, was back in the sitting room, and almost certainly on the sofa.

And then there was a fight over the T-shirts Teddy had unearthed for the twins to wear in bed – a garment too girly for Ferdy's notions of seemly night-gear, apparently – followed by the inevitable tussle over tooth-scrubbing . . .

Oh God, was that a flicker in the window? After an agonizing interval, there was a soft menacing rumble, which growled on and on as though it would never end. Tears stung Teddy's weary eyes, and she actually clapped her hands over her ears, only to drop them again when some sixth sense alerted her to a noise closer to hand. The creak of a door – footsteps? Unmistakably, she caught the rattle of her own bedroom door handle and, with a scowl, groped for her bedside lamp. 'Ferdy?' she barked as she found the switch. 'Ferdinand, I've told you . . .'

But it was not Ferdy who stood at the end of the bed, blinking in the sudden light.

'*Florence?*'

The window bleached brilliant white with lightning. The child whimpered, twisting her hands together, and suddenly Teddy – roundly cursing her own stupidity – realized why the poor mite had been so subdued all evening. In that square and solemn little face she was seeing a mirror of her own terror – and exactly the same dogged refusal to admit to it.

'Birdie – might be frightened of the storm,' the girl gasped. 'Dogs are so silly, aren't they?'

And when the inevitable crack of thunder exploded, she leaped across and hurled herself into Teddy's startled arms.

'Thing is – *thing is* – just because you find you don't wanna die, as such, 'fyou get my drift—'

'Shhtarting 'gain,' grunted Sir Charles Dunstan from the depths of his wing chair.

There was a long silence, punctuated only by the ticking of a venerable long-case clock.

'What is?' croaked Bill, sprawled full-length along the Chesterfield.

Between them stood a decanter of malt whisky, empty. Also a bottle of the same, half empty.

'Thingy. You know.'

The thunder, comfortably muffled by thick stone walls, heavy brocade curtains and softly gleaming ranks of leather-bound books, supplied the answer.

'Oh, get you, the storm.' Bill reached for his glass and missed. His hand flopped to the carpet. He was feeling no pain. No pain at all.

'*Hergh*, sorry.'

'What?'

''Nterrupted you. Rude. Saying something important. 'Fore – before thunder.'

Tick, tock. Tick, tock.

''Sright,' agreed Bill. 'I was, too.'

This time he found the glass. Empty. And it was too far to the bottle, 'bout a mile and a half, but never mind. 'Yeah. What was it? Oh, I know, 'swhat I worked out tonight. You see, funny thing is, Charlie, my ole friend, what I realized is, just because you don't want to die – and I don't, course I don't, never did, bloody silly. But somehow, just because you don't wanna die, it doesn't mean – doesn't mean, I exactly want to, you know . . .'

From the wing chair trickled the slow, shuddering crescendo of a snore.

'*Live*,' sighed Bill, and slid off the Chesterfield to the floor without opening his eyes.

In the crook of her right arm, Florence's breathing was slow and steady. Cradled against her other shoulder, Ferdy was snorting softly like a little piglet. Across her feet, a comatose spaniel sprawled. The sky outside the window was calm, cloudless, and starlit. A faint spangling of dawn lightened the far horizon. The world was at peace. Teddy lay there, also at peace. With herself, with the twins – with the future. She'd been right all along, of course. Children were just like animals. Dammit, one didn't have to give birth to puppies to love them. And she'd always been fond of this pair. She would learn the rest.

'All right now,' mumbled Florence, not waking.

'Indeed it is, sweetheart,' whispered Teddy, and as she closed her own eyes she was still smiling. 'Indeed it jolly well is.'

In the principal bedchamber of Langley Hall, in a vast and opulently draped four-poster bed, Bella Dunstan curled round a balding teddy bear, and sobbed and sobbed as though her heart must break.

Chapter Twenty-Eight

'What a *spiffing* day for a party,' declared Teddy, glancing out into the sunshine, as she cracked open the top of a second soft-boiled egg and gave the contents a stir. 'There you are, Ferdy, love. Help yourself to toast soldiers.'

'Party?' he said hopefully. The twins were perched on high stools either side of her kitchen table.

'Oh, darling, I didn't mean a party for you. Very boring grown-up sort of do. It's for Aunt Bella.' Experimentally, she endowed her sister-in-law with this soubriquet and was rather pleased with the effect. 'Tomorrow's her birthday, she's going to be forty.'

'That's dead old,' Ferdy observed, excavating deep into the egg. 'Will she die soon?'

Florence rolled her eyes. 'Dad's forty-two, twit.'

'Mum's twenty-four,' he retorted indignantly. 'How old are you, Teddy?'

'Thirty-seven and far too busy to die today. I should be at the Hall already, and if your papa's still asleep next door, I might just have to drop you round to Meadows Close on my way, because you're staying with Mummy tonight, aren't you? So that Daddy can come to the party with me.'

'We like it here,' announced Ferdy, appointing himself official spokesman on an issue evidently discussed with his sister.

'And I like having you here,' responded Teddy with all the complacency of one who began the night in Castle Doubt and awoke on the sun-kissed slopes of the Delectable Mountains. 'Nevertheless, I fear—'

'He's not home.'

'What was that, Florence?'

The girl dunked a finger of toast and, unlike her brother, aimed it neatly into her mouth. 'Dad. The car's not there.'

Teddy walked to the door. Sure enough, the spaniel was stretched voluptuously across the warm tarmac on the spot where Bill's vehicle was more usually to be found. Scarcely had she begun to wonder where he could be, however, than he lurched into the courtyard – although, at first glance, she honestly failed to recognize him. Not merely was Bill on foot, and in strange clothing – that is to say, in quite characteristically decent clothing – he was tottering and tripping over his feet like a very old man. Dear God, don't say he'd crashed his car. She started towards him. '*Bill?*'

The gust of breath halted her a yard away. Moreover, his eyes were red-rimmed, his chin blue, and his hand quivered like a pheasant's tail. 'Ah,' she said thoughtfully, and stood back to let him enter the kitchen.

'Dad!' A stool clattered over as his son scrambled to the floor. 'We all went in Teddy's bed last night, and Birdie.'

'There was a storm,' said Florence, following more sedately. 'Only I wasn't frightened.'

''Course you weren't, babe,' muttered their papa, slumping a cashmere-clad shoulder against the doorjamb – surely that wasn't *Charlie's* pullover? The trousers, too, now she came to look at them. 'Duchess, I'm really sorry. Should've rung.'

'Don't worry,' said Teddy calmly, 'we were fine, weren't we, darlings? Had a lovely time. Now back to the table, you two, and finish your eggs.' She surveyed Bill. 'I suspect Daddy might appreciate some quiet.'

He didn't so much sit on the doorstep as dissolve earthwards, like a punctured hot-air balloon. 'The tea's already brewing,' she observed, as she filled a pint mug with water. 'Here's a couple of Alka-Seltzers to be going on with.'

Pouring the fizzing liquid down his throat, he failed to suppress a belch, which provoked noisy hilarity from his son, and a worried enquiry from his daughter whether he was poorly.

He managed a grin of quite ghastly cheeriness in their direction. 'I'm fine, don't you worry.' Turning back to Teddy, he lowered his voice. 'Whatever you're going to say, don't. I'm in no state. Worst hangover of my entire life, and I'm still pissed as a fart. Tried to unlock the car and couldn't find the bloody keyhole – thass when I realized I'd better walk back. Gin with her ladyship, whisky with your brother.' A reminiscent quiver contorted his features. 'Jeez, can that man drink.'

'Dear me.' Just in time, Teddy rescued the glass dangling from his limp fist. 'I won't ask how you appear to be wearing Charlie's clothes . . .'

'You wouldn't believe it if I told you.'

'But, amid the carousing' – and, oh, how diligently our little heroine strove to cloak the eager anxiety in her voice – 'did you, by any chance, manage a few rough sketches?'

'Rough sketches?' Bill's mouth twisted into a sneer. 'Excuse me, madam, *masterpieces*. Your big brother's talking about framing the whole bleeding bunch.'

Yes! Teddy could have leaped skywards and punched the air, as Ferdy was so fond of doing. The last plank in her grand strategy was secured: she would have something to show to the world tonight. And if the world proved even half as enthusiastic as Charlie . . . ? Naturally, she paid no heed to the contempt with which the artist spoke of his work. She remembered how grim she'd felt after a night on gin and whisky – a particularly noxious combination. Not for her to cast a stone in this glass house. She bustled away in search of further palliatives, calling bracingly over her shoulder that he had plenty of time to sleep off his sufferings before the party tonight. 'Because, as I was just saying to the twins when you rolled up, I can drop them round to Lorette on my way to the Hall, if that would help.'

'Oh, Duchess.' He shut his eyes and leaned back against the doorframe with a groan. 'I think I love you.'

'Don't want to go to Mum's,' said Ferdinand, sticking out his lower lip. 'Why can't we stay here?'

'You'll be back soon, poppet,' responded Teddy absently, rifling through a cupboard in search of her largest mug. 'No time at all.'

The children began whispering and, as she leaned over for the teapot, Ferdy peeped at her from under his outrageously flirtatious lashes. 'Have you got a husband, Teddy?'

She felt a faint flush warm her cheeks, and glanced towards the door, but Bill appeared to have relapsed into coma. 'You know I haven't, bird-brain.'

'Do you want one?' he asked slyly.

One must never lie to children. Teddy raised her chin. 'I'd like to be married one day, certainly.'

At which Florence chipped in. 'You could marry Dad.' And, while this made her brother choke with mirth, the child continued with a breeziness so palpably assumed it put Teddy rather disconcertingly in mind of herself in recent dealings with Bill: 'We wouldn't mind.'

'Very sporting of you,' Teddy said brightly, and just missed pouring scalding tea over her hand. Sloshing in some milk, she walked over to the doorway. 'Tea?'

One unsteady hand stretched up and fastened round the mug without a word. A disinterred corpse might have looked healthier.

'Children,' she said, watching him raise the trembling mug to lips, 'if you've finished your breakfast, I think you should run next door and dig out what you want to take to Nanna's. I'll come and help with knickers and socks in a moment. Bill, key?'

Having unlocked the neighbouring door, she returned and waited until they had clattered out before carrying her own tea over to stand beside the sorry heap of their parent on the step. 'Charlie's a menace pouring so much booze down you,' she remarked. 'I suppose I needn't ask why he was on the toot. Another row with Bella?'

Bill grunted a sad assent. 'Poor bastard. He *loves* that woman.'

'So I should hope,' she murmured, rather amused. 'He's been married to her long enough.'

He grimaced, fumbling for words. 'No, really loves her. Only . . .' With evident pain, he craned forward to check the yard was clear of children. 'Sex problems. I gather.'

'Lord, not that old chestnut again.'

'I mean, last night, they went off like a pair of newly-weds, only when it came to the crunch . . .'

'Still, as long as it wasn't anything serious, like Mother.'

239

'You don't get it, the guy can't—'

'Of course I get it, although I should infinitely prefer to be left in ignorance. I've told Bella to water his whisky if she's so concerned. However, that's their affair.' She smiled proudly down upon him. 'I'm far more interested in these drawings of yours.'

He squinted up. Bleary-eyed, stubble-jawed, slack-mouthed, foul-breathed. Even if this were Michelangelo reincarnated, did Teddy falter just for a moment at the prospect of waking up with that on the neighbouring pillow for the rest of her natural? Well, if she did, the wobble was momentary because, as she reasoned with herself, he was unlikely to drink himself into a stupor every night. Besides, twin beds had always struck her as a more sanitary arrangement.

'They're crap,' he said flatly. 'Complete and total crap.'

'Oh, come on, Charlie wouldn't talk about framing pink spiders.'

'Worse. At least those spiders said something. Like, they told me I was going round the twist. Maybe that's the answer, maybe I can only work when I'm halfway to the funny farm.'

Honestly, men. One tiddly hangover and they thought it was the end of the world. 'Cheer up,' said Teddy. 'Everything will look a whole lot rosier after a good sleep.'

Rather unwisely, given his condition, he attempted to shake his head, only to flinch and shut his eyes. Patiently, she waited until he was fit to speak again, and then had to strain her ears to catch the words. 'It's no use,' he mumbled. 'I've been kidding you all along – you and myself – leading you on I'd paint your sister-in-law. Plain truth is, I can't. I knew it all along, really. Why'd you think I've been dodging the job, day-in, day-out? Because I didn't want to face the reality, which is that I've lost it.'

Teddy snorted. 'First time back in the saddle, that's all. Bound to take a while for you to find your stride.'

He wasn't hearing a word. 'Let's be honest, I lost it years ago. I've obviously said whatever I had to say, and now I'm through. Washed-up, screwed-up, painted-out. Time to move on. What was it you reckoned I should be selling, clothes pegs?'

'Idiot,' said Teddy, but not unkindly because the wretchedness in his voice – in every inch of his dejectedly slumped body – would have touched harder hearts than hers. She lowered herself to the step beside him and clasped her hand over his. 'Of course you're not going to be reduced to selling clothes pegs, don't be absurd. As for leading me on, well, I'm afraid the boot's rather on the other foot. I never gave a hoot about your painting Bella *per se* . . .' She hesitated for only a second. 'Look, I think it's time *I* came clean with *you*.'

He blinked round at her. 'What about?'

'Oh, the reason I've been making such a song and dance about this blessed party. The point is, I worked out ages ago that anyone who's anyone round here will be coming, and it was obviously the perfect opportunity to put you and your gallery on the map.'

Hard though it was to imagine, his face seemed to turn an even paler shade of grey. 'Oh my God.'

'Don't panic, you can leave all the legwork to me. I'll be introducing you to the right people, telling them what a brilliant chap you are and all that sort of tosh – hush, trust me, I've thought it all out. You just have to smile nicely, and I'll have them eating out of your hand in no time, queuing up with their big, fat chequebooks – at the door of your gallery.'

'For Christ's sake,' he burst out, 'I am not going to run a bloody gallery.'

'Well, I've always said manning a till would be a shocking misuse of your time,' agreed Teddy promptly. She had intended only to disclose part of her strategies, just to put some heart into the poor sap, but one thing seemed to be leading inexorably to another. 'The answer to that, as I've told you before, is a partner to take over the administrative side – and the house, children, dog, all the domestic nitty-gritty.' She laughed, a shade uncertainly, before plunging on: 'Of course, I know you were only joking about the amazing things you could achieve with a wife like me – Lord, you probably don't even remember, and I certainly can't guarantee membership of the Royal Academy, let alone a K. – but the one promise I can make is that I'd leave you totally free to lock yourself away and paint from morning 'til—'

'Fuck, *no*,' roared Bill, throwing off Teddy's hand with an expression remarkably akin to horror. One might even say – revulsion. 'Anything but that. No, no, *please*, no more. Gotta go. Sleep.' At which, lurching to his feet, he staggered off to his own door and plunged inside without a backward glance.

Now this, you might think, presented something in the nature of a sock in the eye to one who had, to all intents and purposes, just proffered her hand in marriage. Even Teddy was a little . . . taken aback. But then, as she very soon began assuring herself, the silly ape was horribly hungover. Still half-cut, in fact, he'd said so himself. And since he was visibly incapable of walking straight, his thinking capacities were unlikely to be in steadier shape. He would see things quite differently this evening, when she could actually *show* him the glittering prospects she had mapped out – wouldn't he? Well, of course he would. If nothing else, she should have realized it was barely eight o'clock in the morning . . .

'And you'd think I'd have learned my lesson on that score by now, wouldn't you?' she sagely observed to the dog, which had slouched over to squat on her outstretched foot. 'Breakfast is *not* the time for issuing proposals. Just as well he's too pickled to have a clue what I'm on about.' So saying, she briskly drained her mug of tea, shoved the dog aside and rose to her feet. 'Florence, Ferdy?' she bellowed up at the windows of the adjoining house. 'Five mins, and I'm off to the Hall.'

Langley Hall has been described as one of the most perfect small houses in the North of England – 'small', of course, being a relative term in the glossy periodicals which publish such pronouncements. On that day, the day of the party – the day when all Teddy's plans were due to ripen to triumphant fruition – the old place looked as glorious as she could ever remember. The stonework basked mellow and creamy in the bright morning sun. The gardens, refreshed by the night's torrents, sparkled green and luscious. The kitchen yard, which had been designed to accommodate the to-ings and fro-ings of regiments of servants but which, in this democratic age, was generally deserted, once again bustled with vehicles, people and activity. The very air fizzed with excitement and was as exhilarating as champagne – to Teddy's mind, at any rate. And speaking of champagne, she must check when the ice was being delivered.

That no one else appeared to share her exuberantly high spirits she did not allow to trouble her. She was far too busy to worry about Charlie's ashen face or Bella's reddened eyes. Still less was she perturbed by Jeremy's lack-lustre greeting when he wandered into her seething kitchen mid-morning, having travelled up from London on the overnight coach. Which was the most uncomfortable economy he'd ever been reduced to, he bitterly said, pouring himself coffee and dodging a passing washer-up, particularly since no one here would come and meet him, forcing him to wait two hours for a connecting bus to Langley. Still, he added, brightening, he was pretty sure he'd got the part he wanted.

'And it's an incredibly powerful piece, set in a psychiatric ward, Broadmoor sort of place, and this character I'm playing, ex-SAS guy—'

'Not now, thanks.'

'I thought you'd be pleased.'

'Ecstatic, but busy. Would you mind not leaning on that pile of cloths?'

'You'll be happy about one thing anyway,' he retorted huffily. 'They told me I'd have to get my hair cut.'

'Kitchen scissors in the drawer,' said Teddy promptly. 'Short back and sides while I fill you in on what you're doing tonight?'

'Very funny. Jeez, I wish you hadn't twisted my arm about this party, you don't know what it means. I'll hardly get a chance to see ... *Lily*,' he stammered, as Teddy's trusty lieutenant bustled in from the yard with a plastic crate of radicchio clutched to her bosom. 'I mean – hi. Good to see you, must catch up ... soon. But I gotta go have a bath.'

While Teddy found nothing to wonder at in her brother's hurried exit, she did notice, after a moment or two, that her assistant seemed to have taken root where she stood. 'Lily? Is the watercress there, too?'

'Sorry, love? Oh – oh, fetch it in a minute.' But she did not stir. 'So young Jeremy's back from America then?'

'Didn't you know? Ran out of money, surprise, surprise. Actually, probably better to leave the cress in the coldstore in this weather. Yes, the prodigal bro's home, not that we've seen much of him. Not likely to, either, because he's been down to London and actually seems to have found himself gainful employment. Wonders will never cease. Now, where shall we put the strawberries?'

'Crashed straight into your ma,' muttered Jeremy into the library telephone, glancing round and grimacing. 'Phew, this room smells like a doss house. I nearly dropped dead with shock. She's actually here in the kitchen, working for Teddy.'

'You think I don't know?' responded Lorette's voice sourly. 'Ferdy, how many times do I have to tell you to put that ball down?'

'Ferdy?'

'Got landed with the kids, haven't I? Because of your sister's flaming party.'

'Whose kids?'

Ah yes, this was another trivial detail Lorette had somehow overlooked in regaling Jeremy with her life's history. But she was quick to assure him now he mustn't worry about the twins, their dad was getting custody. Not that she didn't love her children, but— 'Florence, get that dog out of here.'

'Just – the two?'

'Do me a favour. So you're back?'

'Sorry? Oh, yah, absolutely.' If Jeremy sounded a little *distrait*, this was perhaps forgivable in a man suddenly confronted with the possibility of stepfatherhood. Twice over. 'And – and longing to see you again,' he added doggedly. 'But if you've got a houseful of kids . . .'

'I could maybe farm them out next door for a bit,' offered Lorette hopefully. 'And they're only here for today.'

'Thing is, though, it looks as if I've got a job.'

There was an immediate sharpening of interest from the other end of the phone. 'You're a star, you are.'

'Thanks. I mean, yup, I'm really knocked out about it, too, but the downside – honestly, I can't bear to think about it – is that I'll have to go straight back to town next week for rehearsals, and with this ghastly party tonight . . .'

'Yeah, yeah. All right for some.'

Jeremy blinked a couple of times, once again having to readjust his ideas. 'You don't mean you'd actually like to come to the thing?'

'Are you kidding?'

'Ask Bella.'

'She said to ask you. Said it was your party now.'

'Dear me, is she still playing tragedy queen? However, I don't see why not. Swing left a bit.' Teddy was supervising the shunting of the baker's van into the yard. 'Since the guest-list I've just handed to Harold ran to three hundred plus, I dare say one more won't be noticed.'

'Yeah, that's exactly what I said,' agreed Jeremy. 'Not in a crowd that size.' There was a short pause. 'Lily's going to be out of the way – I mean, working in the kitchen, isn't she?'

'No, mowing the lawns, what do you think?' She nipped forward and bashed the side of the van. '*Stop!* Any further and you'll flatten Bill's mobile scrap-heap.'

'That car belongs to Bill Smith?' Jeremy glanced this way and that, lowered his voice. 'He's not here too, is he?'

'He had to ditch it after falling foul of Charlie last night, and several gallons of whisky, by the sound of it. Now, where's my note of the bread order?' Abruptly, Teddy stopped flipping the pages of her clipboard and turned back to her brother. 'You'd better find Harold, though, and get him to put your lady-friend's name on his blessed list. I've done my best to persuade him this is not the Kremlin, but he's quite unstoppable. Probably planting barbed wire and landmines along the boundary even as we speak, and I don't want you leaving your duties at the drinks table for as much as five minutes to get her through the gate, do you hear?'

'Fine. Can I take your van?'

'Down to the Lodge? Honestly, you've spent too long in

America, we still remember what legs are for over here.' Nevertheless, in her present sunny humour, she handed over the keys and had begun counting out trays of buns when she heard him give a cry of disgust. A red and white courier Transit had pulled up, blocking in Teddy's own van. Jeremy strode over to the driver, scribbled impatiently, and returned to deposit a large and heavy white-wrapped box in her arms. 'Take that, will you? I want to get a move on.'

He had roared away by the time Teddy read that the package was addressed not to Langley Hall, but to Mill House, Langley Hall Estate, for the attention of one H. Stakinos, Esq.

'*Sender, M. Splitz.*' She glanced up. 'Crikey, I must get upstairs and make sure the ping-pong room is ready for Mr Money-bags Splitz and the rest. *Same Day Delivery – Urgent . . .*? Yes, well, better ring Hari, too.' So saying, she hoisted the box under one arm and hastened indoors.

Chapter Twenty-Nine

'What?' snorted Hari Stakinos, having ripped open his parcel. 'Does he seriously think I'm wearing this?'

He had swirled into the kitchen yard minutes earlier in a filthy temper and a fabulous white Mercedes: 'It was that or a turd-coloured Fiesta with a broken wing-mirror and, as I said to Miss Kwik-Hire at the airport, if you think I'm getting into that jalopy you've got another think coming, flower, give me the bloody wedding wagon . . .' This was after flying direct to Yorkshire from a fashion shoot in the Outer Hebrides, and both temper and limousine were the result of Mr Michael Splitz failing to meet his plane as arranged. That his friend had conscientiously arranged delivery of Hari's fancy-dress attire, from a very grand-sounding film and theatrical costumier's in London, did not appear to be assuaging his wrath.

'Thanks for collecting it,' said Teddy, distractedly. 'I'd have run it up to Mill House, only, as you see, life's rather hectic here.'

A twang of distorted electric guitar assaulted their ears, seemingly from all directions.

'Howdy, howdy, testing, testing,' boomed Colin Rowbotham's North Yorkshire accents, intriguingly overlaid with a patina of Wild West. When last Teddy had spotted him, he was sporting an outsize Stetson, with horns protruding. 'Hi there, pardners, everything's gonna be fine and dandy on the sound systems tonight.'

'I shall go mad if I hear that man's voice again.' Bella's shriek soared out of the kitchen window. 'Totally mad.'

'The birthday girl,' explained Teddy. 'A little over-excited.'

But Hari was not listening. He was staring at a fistful of some silvery fabric with evident revulsion. 'Typical American,' he declared, flinging the offending parcel into the boot of the Mercedes, and slamming it shut. 'Not a clue about pantomime. "Sure, I get it, Hari," he says to me, "*Commedia dell'arte* meets Benny Hill, right? Transvestites telling mother-in-law gags and throwing custard pies, right? I just love your quaint little British customs." And what does he come up with? After I told him to find summat magical and mysterious?' Fishing a mobile phone from his pocket, he began stabbing in numbers. 'Just as well I packed my new tux.'

'I say, Bella,' called Teddy in the direction of the kitchen window, 'have any of the house guests shown up yet, because I'm leaving them to you, remember?'

No answer.

'And a happy birthday to you, too,' she muttered.

Not that she was losing her cool, you understand, absolutely not. Everything was under control; fine and dandy, as Colin would doubtless express it. She would be feeling a mite less stressed, however, if she hadn't had to waste a whole hour spring-cleaning the ping-pong room – sorry, studio. Studio as it now was; – complete and utter shambles as it had been when she walked in. Bottles, sticky glasses, trails of ash, cigarette stubs, pencils, pencil-shavings – these, at least, she could understand, as she swept, hoovered and polished them away. But fruit bowls, rotting grape twigs – what appeared to be Bill's damp and dirty clothes strewn across the floor? She had never supposed drawing to be such a filthy occupation. However, the room was now fit for public inspection. The painting of Lorette was exhibited on the easel, and scattered hither and thither, with cunning artlessness, were the new drawings. Jolly flattering they were, too. Bella barely looked thirty, never mind forty. Teddy was prepared to concede that they were possibly a tad lacking in animation, but nothing to justify Bill's histrionics this morning, silly chump. As a final touch she had concertinaed open a tool-box of paints and fanned out a few brushes. The result, she thought, was rather charmingly Bohemian.

'Teddy, love.' Lily puffed out into the yard, her elder son

beside her, 'I'm running Brian home, because he's leaving the big van up here with our Col, and if you can spare me for half an hour, I'll have a word with Lorette while I'm there. Time I handed over what she's due. I'd have done it yesterday after Bill got back from Muriel's only I were that jiggered. Still, it'll cheer her up tonight for babysitting when everyone else's out on the tiles.'

'Mr Splitz is in *Paris*?' shrieked Hari into his mobile. 'What the fuck's he doing there?'

Brian winced pointedly at the bad language as he leaned towards Teddy. 'Time for me to depart to my own modest jollifications,' he murmured. 'Unless I can be of further assistance here?'

Another brain-numbing guitar riff exploded across the air.

'You could ask your brother if he's got any Victor Sylvester,' shouted Teddy, clapping her hands to her ears. 'Sorry, Hari?'

'I said, did the old git who stayed here ever go to Paris?'

'What?'

'That poet, you know, Michael's movie – oh, hang about.' He pressed the mobile more firmly to his ear. 'Meeting an *actor*, is he? That's all right then.' He grimaced expressively in Teddy's direction. 'Just so long as it isn't a woman.'

'But he's welcome to bring a friend . . .'

'He left a message for me, you say? Fine, I'll ring in for it now.'

'Because,' persisted Brian doggedly, 'if I can be of service here, I'm happy to be a little late at my own barbecue.'

'Absolutely not. I mean, noble of you, Brian, but we'll cope. Oh, Bella, there you are. What was that?'

From an upstairs window now, her sister-in-law screamed that if she heard one more twang of Meatloaf, she was going to hurl herself out.

'Don't worry,' Teddy yelled back. 'I'll speak to Colin. You just make sure you're ready to greet the overnighters . . . Yes, I did hear, and yes, of course I shall be going home to get changed. Plenty of time yet.'

'Want me to do your hair, pet?' Hari was busily tapping more numbers into his phone. 'Turn you into the belle of the ball? Mind, it'll take some doing, the way you look now.'

'Miss Dunstan,' declared Brian Rowbotham, bristling, 'needs no artificial aids to beauty.'

'Brian?' called his mother exasperatedly. 'Are you coming?'

'Pop up to Mill House later, pet?'

'No,' said Teddy, wiping her damp fringe off her forehead as she rechecked her list. 'I mean, thanks awfully, but maybe some other time when I'm not quite so busy.'

'What's the use of – Oh, here we go, message timed at sixteen-forty-two. Yes, yes, hi there to you, too, Michael . . . Give over blathering, you gabby cow, and tell me when you're arriving.

'Ah, Jez,' called Teddy, as a slim and suntanned figure appeared yawning at the kitchen door. 'You've got the corkscrews?'

'You've asked me three times already.'

'Mangoes?' squawked Hari at his phone. 'Frigging passion fruit?' He spun round. 'Can you believe it? Not a dicky bird about when he's deigning to show up, but he remembers to leave a bloody great shopping list for his latest diet. Where does he think I'm going to get tropical fruits at this hour on a Saturday in the middle of nowhere?'

'Mr Splitz?'

'Who else? Flaming Californian health-freak.'

'No problem,' said Teddy instantly. 'I've at least two mangoes, a box of kiwis and a couple of pineapples at home. I'll pick them up when I go to get changed. Anything to keep him sweet.'

'I should be thanking my lucky stars it's only a fruit kick,' grumbled Hari, dropping the phone back into his pocket. 'This time last year it was fermented goat yoghurt . . .' He broke off, eyes widening. 'Well, hello, pretty boy. Where'd you spring from?'

'Oh, sorry, this is my baby bro, Jeremy. Jez, Hari Stakinos.'

Jeremy's eyes widened. 'Hari Stakinos? I mean, wow, as in Hari?'

'Gorgeous child, have a word with your sister, will you? Girls've been known to murder their grannies just to get on my waiting list, and here I am, scissors snapping, and she won't let me near her.'

'Ted, are you crazy?'

'Don't you start.' All at once, however, her flustered gaze focused on her brother's tousled mane, before wandering, speculatively, to the man standing beside him. 'On the other hand, Hari, if your scissors really are at Mill House . . .'

'I said, turn that hairdryer off,' shouted Lily. 'I want a word.'

'Mum?' Lorette spun round on her dressing table stool so violently she nearly tumbled off. 'What you doing home?'

'I've run our Brian back and I thought it was time I put you out of your . . . misery.' The sentence was tailing away as she took in the room. Her eyes shifted from the hairdryer, to a dressing table littered with cosmetics, from the floor, where flopped a talon-heeled pair of gold sandals, to the bed, across which was draped a white dress: a short, white and spangled confection with marabou trim and spaghetti fine straps. 'What's going on here?'

Lorette had rehearsed this, had even squared the story with her brothers, against just such a contingency. 'I'm going to give old Col a hand with the disco,' she parroted fluently, 'being as how Brian's off at his barbecue. Don't worry, it's all fixed up at the Hall, my name's on the guest-list.'

'I'll give you guest-list. Where's Ferdy and Floss?'

'Next door. I asked Gwen if she'd have them for the night and she – *Mum?* Mum, where are you going?'

'Next door,' snapped Lily. 'To get them kids back.'

There comes a point in the masterminding of every operation when a clipboard is no longer enough. Teddy was now inscribing *Fruit Asstd.* on the back of her hand, glancing at her watch as she did so. Seven-forty-five: an hour and a quarter to go. Plenty of time still to drive home, bath and change – and, much more importantly, to ensure that Bill was awake, sobered and fit for public parade. And she supposed she'd have to do something with her hair. Dear Hari had still been pressing her to accept his services even as he ushered Jeremy into his limo, which was very generous of him. Embarrassingly generous, in fact, if what

Jez had hissed in her ear were true, about the going rate for a few snips of Hari's scissors. Lord, one would expect a diamond tiara thrown in at that price. She would *never* have suggested he gave Jeremy a trim if she'd realized what she was asking, and the least she could do, by way of return, was ensure supplies of fruit for his diet-conscious friend. Only first, she must double-check Charlie had the safety arrangements in hand for the firework display.

'Lorette?' Washed, shaved and clad in appropriately bucolic checked shirt and golfing slacks, Brian Rowbotham strolled into the kitchen at Meadows Close – and stopped short.

Picture the tragic scene which met his eyes. Admittedly, this kitchen was a sunny apartment of cream melamine and chintz, with a fan-adjusted oven and vacuum cleaner in one corner, rather than the more usual gloomy cavern featuring the statutory twig broom and black-leaded range, but no Cinderella had ever slumped on her lonesome stool and wept more desolately than Lorette was doing at this moment. Instead of a cat and assorted mice as her companions, she had two small children and a spaniel, who were watching with not unsympathetic interest.

'I can't go – to the party,' she gasped, in the best traditions of her role. 'Mum's wrecked everything.' Between sobs she explained that their heartless mother – who didn't want her to have any fun in her life, not ever – had decreed she must stay at home with the twins. According to Lily, the poor mites had been farmed out to strangers the night before – and been scared witless by a storm – and they were going to sleep cosy in their own little beds tonight, watched over by their own parent. At least, they were if Lorette wanted twenty thousand pounds.

'You're not their only parent,' cried her brother indignantly. 'What about your husband?'

'Ex-husband,' snapped Lorette, emerging briefly from her wad of Kleenex.

'No go,' intoned young Ferdinand, with the melancholy relish of one enjoying the drama. 'Dad's going too.'

'With Teddy,' added his sister.

At this, Brian turned. 'I beg your pardon, young lady?'

''Swhy we're here, silly.' Florence folded her little arms in the manner of one stoically resigned to suffering in a good cause. ''Cause Dad's going to the party with Teddy.'

'Is – he – indeed?' breathed their uncle slowly, and a strange light entered his eye. Under their wondering gaze, he pulled back his shoulders, hitched up his trousers, and slicked his scant locks more securely across his shining scalp. 'Dry your tears, Cinderella,' he commanded sternly. 'And get yourself back into your glad rags.'

'You look proper bonny, love,' declared Lily, as Bella swirled up in billowing crimson harem trousers and a plunging bodice, thickly encrusted with gold sequins. 'Real knockout.'

'My mother-in-law doesn't think so.' Bella, fumbling to open the satin purse that dangled from one shoulder, was becoming entangled in multiple strings of beads.

'Here, have one of mine.' Lily handed her both cigarette and lighter. They were standing beside the refrigerated van in the yard.

'You're an angel.' Bella tucked her yashmak behind one ear and lit up thankfully. 'God, I hate her. Truly, madly, deeply.' She pinched her nose to achieve the appropriate timbre. '"How extraordinary, Isobella, I never realized the Mata Hari figured in pantomime." Bitch.'

'Twenty-two carat, always was,' chuckled Lily. 'Tek no notice.'

'"Good grief, Charles, you appear to have imported enough alcohol to float the *Queen Mary*. Now, when I held my parties, they were small and civilized gatherings of kindred souls."'

'Arseholes, more like. Listen, I was running this kitchen for *her* fortieth, and some of her precious cronies were that pissed they were crawling round the carpet before the pudding.'

Bella gave a crow of laughter. 'No, really? I wish you'd told me before.'

'Or over anything in a skirt. By, there was a drunken old Irishman who got me behind the dining-room door. I had to clout him round the ear before he'd let go, but he were that pie-eyed, I doubt he'd have felt a sledgehammer. Your own pa-in-law wasn't in much better shape, neither,' she added darkly. 'It's a party I'm not likely to forget, one way and another – What's up?'

Bella was peering round the corner of the van. 'Surely that wasn't Teddy heading for the gardens?'

'Shouldn't wonder.'

'But she ought to have gone home to change *hours* ago.' Bella's beads rattled in agitation. 'People will be arriving.'

'You know what she's like for scratting up to the last minute. She was counting forks, last time I saw her.'

'Sod the cutlery,' cried Bella, 'I want her back here dressed, so I can see to her make-up. It's no good leaving it to her, she hasn't a clue.'

'She doesn't change, does she?' Lily chuckled reminiscently. 'I remember her at five years old, screaming blue murder when I tried to tie a ribbon in her hair. If you can get near with a lisptick, you're a better woman than me.'

'She's no choice,' declared her sister-in-law forcefully, 'because I'm not having her looking like a frump tonight, not with all the gorgeous hunks I've lined up for her.'

Lily choked on her cigarette. 'Come again?'

Bella started guiltily, and she peered once again round the van before leaning towards Lily. 'Not a word to her, promise?'

'What? I mean, yes, cross my heart.'

'I had to do something, didn't I?' Bella whispered rapidly. 'There she was, working her fingers to the bone, pouring her heart and soul into this party for me, and she never has parties of her own – hardly even goes out, poor soul. You've got to admit she needs to meet a nice man before it's too late.'

'Well, maybe, but—'

'Exactly, and I realized it was my duty to lend a hand. Gracious, she told me so herself. So I racked my brains, and then sat down and zapped off cards to just about every man in the area I could think of with two legs and no wife. Some I've barely so much as shaken hands with, so Heaven only knows what they made of the invitations plopping onto their doormats.' Bella giggled nervously. 'Probably think I'm crackers.'

'How many?' enquired Lily faintly.

'Well, seventeen at the last count, although I can't imagine they'll all turn up. But, good God, if we don't do something, she might end up marrying the vicar, who's queer as a coot, whatever she says, and then where would we be?' Bella snatched another hasty puff from her cigarette. 'Sorry, am I babbling? Nerves, take no notice. And what thanks do I get? Teddy's still slobbing around in her jeans, and my bloody mother-in-law inspects the guest-list and trots straight off to Charlie, wondering in that sickly-sweet voice she reserves for being *particularly* poisonous, why dear Isobella seems to have invited so many more chaps than girls – unattached chaps galore. Which means I have to tell him they're not actually for my benefit, thank you very much, but for his poor unmarried sister's.'

'Well, that's all right then.'

'I shouldn't need to justify myself.' Bella dabbed one eye. 'Hell, mustn't blub, not with this amount of mascara. But I mean, *honestly*.'

'Anything for a quiet life, your husband, eh?' Lily shook her head, sighing. 'Just like his dad.'

'He never sticks up for me, never.'

'He loves you, though.'

Bella pouted. 'He used to.'

The older woman smiled rather sadly and patted her shoulder. 'Don't fret yourself, sweetheart. He's like his dad in that, too. More heart than brain, but faithful through and through.'

Shiny-eyed, Bella stared at her. 'You really think so? I have to say, looking at my mother-in-law, one somehow can't imagine . . .' But a youthful voice was calling for Mummy, and her youngest son rounded the corner of the van holding out a telephone. 'Clever Harry, finding me here. Now, don't tell Papa about the ciggy, will you? Excuse me, Lily.' Sweeping yashmak and jangling earring aside, she clamped the implement to her head. 'Hello, Bella Dunstan . . . Oh, *hi*.' She listened, examining her nail varnish. 'Gosh, what a bore. Of course I'll tell her – when I find her, that is. Last seen vanishing into the garden, talk about the Scarlet Pimpernel . . . OK, sure.' So saying, she tapped a button to disconnect. At the same moment, Teddy recrossed the yard at a brisk canter.

'There you are, you monstrous creature,' shrieked Bella. 'Now will you *please* go home and change?'

Teddy's stride did not falter. 'One minute – just one minute, then I absolutely swear I'm away.'

'I should jolly well think so. Oh, and by the way,' she called after the retreating figure, 'that was Bill. He's had to drop out.'

Her sister-in-law halted as though she'd been shot on the spot. Then very slowly she wheeled round. 'I'm sorry?'

'You know, Bill Smith? Just phoned, full of apologies, can't make it tonight.'

Chapter Thirty

'Give us a break, babe,' he protested miserably as Teddy's voice screeched out of the telephone, 'it isn't my fault.'

Truly, it was *not* Bill's fault. Admittedly, he felt like partying about as much as he felt like taking a chainsaw to his leg, but he'd said he would go, and, to that end, had dutifully kicked himself out of bed and into a bath. Only to be interrupted, mid-way through shaving, by the arrival of his children and their Uncle Brian, who – when Bill stumbled through to the living room with a towel round his waist and a faceful of foam – breezily announced that Lorette had also been invited to this party, so dog and twins were being returned with her compliments.

'Grievously though it pains me to toss this spanner into your own plans for the evening,' Brian had added, with a canary-swallowing smirk. 'However, you will understand that I could not find it in me to desert a fair lady in her hour of need. At the cost, I may say, of making me rather late for my own barbecue. Still, my duty is done and I must away.'

For a moment Bill could only gape at him. Our hero was not, to be fair, at his brightest. Still in recovery from a hangover of galactic ferocity, he might have managed to obliterate most of the events of the past twenty-four hours in an alcoholic fog, but remembered only too well the final burial of his career in a pile of drawings on an attic floor. On top of which misery, he was three-parts naked and spitting bubbles. In the nick of time, he summoned the wit to thrust himself between Brian and the door. 'You can't do this.'

'Already have, old son. So if you'll kindly step aside?'

'Wait.' And for all Bill was tempted to bash the little toe-rag one, shove the kids in the car and drive them straight back to their mother, he realized there was a snag: no car. The motor was still at the Hall, and a bloody nose was unlikely to persuade Brian to do the honours – even if it wasn't already too late? He risked dodging over to the mantelpiece for a squint at the invitation. Nine p.m. kick-off, eight-fifteen now. Cuckoo wouldn't have left – but her brother was already halfway out of the door, when Florence unexpectedly stuck her oar in.

'Teddy will be *furious*,' she stated firmly – and that, at least, gave Brian pause for thought.

'Too right,' agreed Bill promptly. He could have added Teddy was likely to string him up on piano wire only he didn't suppose the prospect would unduly distress his brother-in-law.

Brian twinkled indulgently down at his niece. 'Now why on earth should Miss Dunstan mind whether your dad goes to this party or not?'

'Why do you think?' retorted Floss, and turned expectantly to her father, who – floundered. Matter of fact, Brian's question struck him as pretty reasonable. Why *should* the Duchess give a toss whether he showed his mug at a ritzy job like this? Except she would. She most definitely bloody well would.

'Exactly,' grinned the Ugly Brother-in-Law.

'You tell him, Dad,' commanded his daughter, fixing him with a steely gaze disconcertingly reminiscent of Teddy's own.

'She – needs me there,' he stuttered, clutching at straws. 'For – for moral support, that's what she said.' Which she *had* said, hadn't she? And even if, now he came to think about it, the idea of the Duchess needing moral support was about as likely as Bill Gates needing to bum a fiver, he wasn't going to let that stand in his way. Never mind if he was knackered, nauseous and at the bottom of his own private pit, she wanted him there, and that was enough. He'd messed her around too much already. Straight-faced, then, he proceeded to draw a moving picture of his shy little neighbour, shrinking at the prospect of attending this great jamboree without an escort, and having to call upon his unworthy self to step in. Growing in eloquence by the minute, and determinedly ignoring the frank incredulity in his daughter's face, he pointed out that Teddy had even gone to the length of selecting his fancy dress outfit herself – Brian could see it, there on the sofa. Was all her trouble to go to waste?

'In fact, I'll be honest with you,' he added, in a cunning shift of tactics. Nothing like a sliver of truth to disguise a big fat lie. 'I actually do not want to go to a party. I feel like death and nothing'd suit me better than a quiet night in front of the telly with a few beers, but,' – Bill drew himself up, wrapped the towel tighter round his loins and squared his foaming jaw to deliver the clincher – 'you said it yourself, Brian, old son. A gent can't desert a fair lady in her hour of need.'

Bingo. The brother-in-law, visibly moved, plucked the invitation from the mantelpiece, stared at Bill's name inscribed in her own fair hand, and gruffly agreed that leaving Teddy without an escort was out of the question. However, it was equally unthinkable that his little sister should be disappointed. Shaking his head sadly, he declared there could be only one answer: his own barbecue would have to be sacrificed.

'Straight up?' Bill glared at Ferdy whose face reflected only too vividly what he felt about being handed into his uncle's keeping for the night. 'Well, I call that bloody generous of you, mate.'

'My pleasure and privilege to step in,' responded Brian as he tucked the invitation card into his breast pocket. 'I'm grateful to you, in fact, for pointing me in the right direction.'

'Think nothing of—' Bill stopped short. 'Here,' he cried, 'what d'you think you're doing with my sodding costume?'

'He *what*?' yelled Teddy, ignoring the startled glance of a passing waitress. She was clutching a phone to her ear in the passageway outside the kitchen. 'Why didn't you stop him, you numbskull?'

'I couldn't force him to take the kids, could I? And as long as they're here, I'm hamstrung.'

'Ever heard of babysitters?'

'In case you've forgotten, I've no car.'

'I'll be home in a minute.'

'Besides which I hardly know a soul in this village, my outfit's been half-inched, and . . .' A weary sigh gusted out of the receiver. 'Blimey, babe, does it really matter?'

'*Matter?*' Her voice rose to a shriek. 'Are you crazy, or have you forgotten what I told you this morning?'

There was a bemused silence. 'What about?'

'Give me strength.' Teddy was dancing from one foot to the other. 'About meeting people here tonight: nice, rich, potential-customer-type people, to patronize your gallery, relaunch your whole bloody career, everything I was telling you . . .' Only at this point did it occur to her that the conversation in question had, albeit unintentionally, culminated in something approximating to a proposal of marriage. She cleared her throat. 'Well, possibly not *everything*.'

This time the silence lasted much longer. It lasted so long, she had time to feel the blush spreading like a bush fire from her solar plexus, around her neck, right up to her ears. Eventually, she gave the receiver a tentative shake. 'Bill?'

'Oh, Christ. Yeah – yeah, I'd forgotten. You saw the state I was in.'

Her and her big mouth. 'Look, I didn't mean—'

'It's not on.' That was all he said. Absolutely flatly.

'Sorry?'

'So am I. Really, really sorry. Oh sweetheart, I know you mean well, I dare say you'd try and convince me anything's possible if only I'd be sensible, put my back into it, all that kind of crap.'

'No I wouldn't,' she squawked in an agony of embarrassment, 'at least, well, I suppose I might have been known to say something of the sort, but . . . For pity's sake, do we have to talk about this now?'

'I think we'd better get it straightened out. I mean, I don't want to, I hate doing this to you.'

'Then don't.'

'No, listen, I've got to make you understand some things are beyond willpower and grit. They are, love, honest. They need more. Don't ask me what, spark of divine grace very likely, and, well, it isn't there. Not in me. Hell, I wish I could say different, wish with all my heart and soul I could, but I know there's nothing inside, and pretending won't get either of us anywhere.' His voice had dwindled to a wretched whisper. 'Thanks for everything, Duchess. I mean that, you're a real mate, but it's not going to happen. So, let's face it, probably as well I don't come tonight, eh?'

'Was she mad?' enquired Ferdinand.

'Wasn't pleased, that's for sure.' Bill was still gazing at the dead telephone. He could tell she was spitting tacks by the way she'd been so fast to assure him that no, she wasn't in the least angry; no, he hadn't offended her; no, she perfectly understood. *Perfectly.* Did she hell understand, he reflected sadly. How could any sane and normal person be expected to understand that for years and years, practically since the day you were born, your soul could flow straight out onto a canvas, and then one day – bang – the tap just turn itself off?

'So you won't be getting married?' asked Florence.

'Sorry?' said her father, lost in thought. 'I mean, who to?'

'Teddy.'

In spite of everything, Bill let out a roar of laughter. 'Whatever gave you that idea, you daft bunny? Teddy Dunstan wouldn't marry the likes of me in a million years.'

'Never in a million years,' snarled Teddy, striding into the library and crashing the telephone back on its base. 'Me, marry a brainless, useless thug like that? I must have been mad even to think about it. Which was all I ever did, *think* about it. I'd never have done it, of course, not likely, not *bloody* likely . . .' She had to fight for breath. 'And then to go blurting it out this morning, making a complete fool of myself. Again. Oh-God-oh-God-oh-God, will I never learn?' There was a Meissen figurine on the davenport beside the telephone. She actually had to tuck her hands into her armpits, so strong was the urge to smash something.

Not that she was angry with Bill. Much. Well, all right, yes, she was angry. A bit. Just a little bit hoppingly, pot-chuckingly, incandescently, *homicidally* furious with him, but also with herself, chiefly with herself – dammit, with everyone. Not least her mother, who chose the moment Teddy stomped out of the library again to sail along the hall in diamonds and a perfect column of black devoré, and was unwise enough to enquire, with a quizzical smile, whether her daughter was planning to grace these proceedings in jeans and apron?

For a moment, Teddy couldn't trust to herself to respond. But her face must have spoken volumes because her mother's smile unexpectedly froze into a grimace of glassy dismay.

'Terrific frock, Ma,' echoed a voice down the hall. 'Ted, hi, what do you think?'

Turning, she registered her younger brother striding across the tiled floor, twirling to a halt beside her. 'Sorry?'

'The hair, dimbo. He's a genius, that guy.'

'Oh no, Hari,' she exclaimed despairingly, and plummeted back into the library.

'What's eating Ted?' he enquired as he continued over to a gilt-framed mirror.

'Jeremy, darling,' said his mother faintly, 'you look – so different.'

'Pretty amazing transformation, huh?' He was studying his half-profile intently. 'All thanks to you and your man.'

'I'm sorry?'

'Your tenant at Mill House. Smart move, letting the place to Hari Stakinos.'

'Ah.'

'Met him yet? Seriously nice guy. Anyway, he's coming tonight.'

'Really? My love, if you'll forgive me, I might go and see if anyone's opened a bottle. I feel – rather in need of a drink.'

After a few moments, it evidently occurred to Jeremy he was responsible for popping the corks, because he called vaguely over one shoulder that he would be along shortly, and returned to contemplating his image. Even he scarcely recognized himself. For the first time he could see how his features had changed and matured during the last couple of years – hell, the last time he'd had hair this short was when he was a kid. He experimented with a lean, mean sneer appropriate to a former-SAS, schizophrenic wife-batterer, and was not displeased with the effect.

Naturally, he paid no heed to his sister, who could be heard barking apologies into the library telephone for some catering hitch, along with instructions for finding her back door. Only the mention of Bill Smith's name caused him to glance round sharply, but he relaxed again on hearing her declare that her neighbour was sure to be at home, and would know where to find the spare key – something about fruit being on the right of the larder.

With a last tweak to his coiffure, Jeremy peeled himself away from the mirror and strolled off to undertake his duties.

'The photographer's here already,' called Bella, exploding into the kitchen some twenty minutes later, in a blaze of crimson and gold. She looked rather reminiscent, thought her sister-in-law without interest, of an expensive Christmas cracker. She halted, mouth agape. 'Teddy? What are you *doing*?'

'What does it look like?'

Teddy was scattering parsley over a salver of canapés. Bathed, wet-haired and opulently scented – searching for some common-or-garden shampoo, she had inadvertently knocked over one of the forest of crystal bottles stacked around Bella's bath – she was clad in snowily immaculate chef's jacket and regulation check trousers. Fortunately, after an incident with a gravy boat last Christmas, she had taken to keeping a spare set of whites in the van. The donning of them tonight should have made it blindingly obvious to anyone – not least her witless sister-in-law who was nevertheless trying to wrest the bowl of parsley from her clutches – that Teddy was no longer intending to grace this party as a guest. The idea was unthinkable in her present mood. She might bite someone. She was remaining at the Hall, naturally, because – much as she would love to slam home and shoot Bill Smith – she was honour bound to ensure the evening passed off smoothly. But she would be remaining in the place where she could do least damage and most good, her natural habitat: the kitchen.

'You told me,' said Bella hotly, 'you *promised* me, hours ago, you were going to get changed.'

'I am changed, in case you haven't noticed. Couldn't face a night's sweated labour without a freshen-up – I used your room, I knew you wouldn't mind. Oh, stop screeching at me, you idiot. Who gives a fig whether I join the merry throng or not?'

That Hari Stakinos, for one, might notice her absence had not prevented her fabricating a staff shortage, and inviting him to go and help himself to her fruit racks. Some distant twang of conscience about thus cavalierly abandoning her personally invited guests had stopped her informing him that the supposed crisis was destined to confine her to the kitchen all night. That could wait until she slipped out, at some appropriate moment, to meet him, and she was still hoping Mr Splitz was coming – 'So am I,' snapped Hari crossly, 'but there's no sign of the little bleeder yet' – because she fully intended showing him the painting upstairs. It would give her great satisfaction to fling a large cheque at Bill Smith. Teach him a lesson. Demonstrate exactly what he was turning down.

'Teddy, have you been listening to a single word?'

'Frankly—'

'What's all this shouting in aid of?' Lily trundled in from the yard. 'Here, Teddy, give over fiddling with them savoury balls. Already looks like you've emptied the bloody lawnmower on the plate.'

'Look at her,' yelled Bella. 'Just *look* at her. She says she's not coming to the party.'

'Pardon?'

'Correct,' barked Teddy. 'And at twenty to nine, with a costume I wouldn't wish to be seen dead in three miles down the road at home, I suggest there's little point arguing. So you toddle off to greet your guests, Bella, and leave me to take these canapés to the pantry.'

She did not suppose that her sister-in-law would give up without a fight, but she couldn't have cared less – in fact, was positively ripe for a screaming match. Any excuse to vent her spleen. Thus she returned from kicking aside the wine-crates some fool had stacked in the middle of the pantry floor with the merry bounce of a mongoose in a cobra farm. 'Well?' she cried.

But Bella was deep in muttered conversation with Lily, who was instructing her to run upstairs and find the black tights, boots, curling tongs and stuff. 'Herself and me'll join you in a tic. And never you fear,' she continued, shooting a very beady look in Teddy's direction, 'I can deal with this little madam.'

This *what*? The little madam's entire five feet two inches quivered in magnificent outrage. 'I *beg* your pardon?'

'Give over huffing,' snapped Lily, glaring back. As two of her assistants bustled in chattering with armfuls of bread, she lowered her voice, took a firm grip of Teddy's wrist and began pulling her towards the door. 'This way, Cinderella,' she growled. 'Like it or not, you are going to this sodding ball.'

Chapter Thirty-One

'I'll wait,' said Bill, on being told by a youthful voice that Aunt Teddy was up in Mummy's room. 'I've got to talk to her. Tell her it's important.'

Bill was feeling like a bum. A pea-brained, self-pitying, drunken bum who couldn't see beyond the end of his nose, and who didn't deserve a friend and would-be champion like Teddy Dunstan. The more he'd been thinking about it, the worse he felt. It was no wonder she was mad with him, after the mumbling hash he'd made of telling her he was finished in this business. All that pressure to get him to the party, to make a start on Bella's portrait – 'work in progress', he could swear she'd used those very words. But, as he plaintively rehearsed his apologies, waiting for her to be summoned to the phone, how the hell was he supposed to have guessed she'd embarked on a crazy, one-woman mission to rescue his lousy career? Talk about lost causes. The only mystery was why she should bother. It brought a lump to his throat just thinking about her wasting so much time and effort on a useless toe-rag like him.

'She there, Dad?' enquired Florence, looking round from the television.

'They're trying to find her.' He glanced at his watch. 'Nearly nine. Guests'll be rolling up.'

Among them Brian in his stolen costume, he reflected savagely, Rowbotham of bloody Arabia. That was another reason he had to speak to Teddy, to tip her off that, thanks to his own misguided eloquence, the Ugly Brother-in-law believed he was rolling up as her substitute knight-in-shining. He didn't suppose she'd be any too happy about that, either.

There was a welcome click in his ear. 'Yes?'

'Duchess, thank God.'

'I'm sorry?'

'Oh, Bella, is it? Bill again. Teddy about?'

'Yes – *no*.' Her voice sank to an urgent whisper. 'We're nearly done with her, but my God it's been a race against the clock.'

'Quick word.'

'Absolutely not, you'll have to ring later.' Her tone changed. 'What, Lily? Oh, hairspray's over there, by the mirror. Don't worry about the phone, nothing important.'

'Yes this bloody is important,' shouted Bill. '*Listen* – listen, I'll phone back if I must. But you've got to tell her I'm sorry.'

'Fine.'

'Wait. And you'd better warn her Brian Rowbotham will be making a beeline for her. My fault, because . . . What's so funny?'

'That makes eighteen for her to choose from, then,' she hooted merrily, 'with a bit of luck. Gosh, nineteen, because I keep forgetting the vicar.'

'*What?*'

'Just tease a bit of body in,' grunted Lily, whipping the comb up and down in Teddy's hair as Bella shuffled off into the bathroom with the telephone, her voice shrinking to a giggling whisper. The words were inaudible, but the pitch was too nervy for Lily's liking. Tears before bedtime with that one, if she wasn't mistaken. Didn't Theo, fond as he was of his daughter-in-law, always say the lass was strung tighter than a ukulele? In fact, at this moment, Lily almost fancied she could sense the old rascal's ghost cheering Bella and her on in their endeavours.

'Finished yet?' growled his daughter.

'Quiet, if you don't want a gobful of lacquer.'

Teddy reverted to the mute woodenness of a shop-window dummy, but there remained, as her harassed *coiffeuse* noted, a truly wicked glint of temper in her eye. Enough to send any chap screaming over the horizon, thought Lily, tweaking a strand of fringe. Not that she entertained much hope of Teddy finding herself a soul mate among the cavaliers lined up for her tonight – only Bella Dunstan, as soft in the head as she was in the heart, could have come up with such a crackpot idea. No, Lily was toiling with tongs and spray simply for the pleasure of sticking a spoke in the elder Lady Dunstan's wheel. The old witch had dripped enough poison into her son's ear already about the guest-list, and she'd have a field day if, after Bella's explanation about inviting all these fancy-free fellas for Teddy's benefit, Teddy didn't even show up.

That was why Lily had shunted young Theodora up to her sister-in-law's bedchamber with the no-nonsense efficiency of one who had handled her as a recalcitrant three-year-old, sternly declaring she neither knew nor cared what had put her in such a strop, but that it was no excuse for spoiling someone else's birthday. Teddy should be ashamed of herself. Her sister-in-law wanted her at her party, and that was that. Teddy had given in, but no one, looking at her thunderous face, could suppose she was doing so gracefully.

'Cheer up,' cried Bella merrily, casting aside the phone as she hurried back to join them. 'Anyone would think you were going to a funeral. Now, where was I? Lipstick, yes. Mouth still, Teddy.'

'Who was that on the phone?'

'Nearly smudged it, idiot. No one. Blot with this tissue while I get your sash.'

The costume, in Lily's opinion, was a miracle of improvisation, all credit for which she freely ascribed to Lady Dunstan. As they'd feverishly debated ways and means of rendering Teddy fit to attend a party, it was Bella who had suddenly observed that her white chef's tunic could almost pass for a dress uniform. If they added a belt, the sash from her own red taffeta, Charlie's sword – gosh, yes, and his medals – but they would have to get rid of those silly check trousers.

'Black tights,' offered Lily.

'Pelly's new riding boots,' Bella cried – and they had been away. To such good effect that now, barely twenty industrious minutes later . . .

'Bugger me,' breathed Lily, stepping back to admire their handiwork. 'Talk about a transformation scene.'

Indeed, this dashing creature with scarlet lips, bouffant curls, glossy black legs and an hour-glass silhouette enhanced by the ruthless tightening of Bella's best Hermès belt, bore startlingly little resemblance to our commonsensical heroine.

'Teensy touch more mascara?' But Bella lowered the wand when a voice they both recognized drifted along the landing. '. . . can't understand it, darling, because she changed into her harem kit hours ago, and cars are pouring up the drive.' A tinkling laugh operated on Lily's ears like tinfoil on a filling. 'Although I hardly think even Isobella would choose a moment like this to walk out on you.'

The bedroom door flipped wide – and so did Lily's eyes, because a giant goose was revealed on the threshold. A seven-foot-tall goose with magnificently fat, foam-filled, furry body, diving-flipper feet, wrinkled yellow legs – and Sir Charles's anxious face peering out from a hole in the neck. 'Bellsy? You ready?'

'Charlie!' cried his wife, standing back and gesturing him triumphantly towards his sister, 'what do you think of this?'

'*Hergh*, stunning,' he stammered – except, bless him, thought Lily, he hadn't so much as noticed Teddy. Only got eyes for his wife. 'Too lovely for words. God, I can't bear it.'

Bella blinked. 'Bear what?'

'Thought of all those other chaps – looking at you.'

Bella's eyes brimmed up. Lily beamed fondly, willing the great soft lump to stick his wing around his missus, give her a smacker – but the silvery laugh was trilling again. From the doorway, the dowager Lady Dunstan sweetly assured them that her own dear husband had never been troubled by the admiration his wife excited – if she might be permitted such immodesty. 'Doubtless because, in my case, he could be quite certain—' But they were not destined to learn of what the late Sir Theodore could be so certain. His relict was staring across the room, open-mouthed. 'Good God. *Teddy?*'

Two would-be Fairy Godmothers stiffened. 'Not quite Cinderella,' quipped Bella gaily, 'but the next best thing. Well, Charlie?'

To Lily's exasperation, however, Sir Charles, knocking over a side table with his undercarriage as he lumbered round to inspect his sister, seemed interested only in the sword dangling from her waist. '*Hergh*, not mine, is it, Ted?'

'Don't blame me,' she growled.

'Did you use it to apply your make-up?' enquired her mother tartly. 'Or just a trowel?'

Bella's face reddened as though she had been slapped. 'I think she looks *gorgeous*,' she declared hotly. 'Charlie?'

'You'll, *hergh*, look after it, won't you, Sis?'

'Charles, darling, had we better go down? I hear voices in the hall.'

'And the gongs, not that they're anything to write home about, *hergh*, all other chaps' efforts, of course, but—'

'*Charlie?*' wailed his wife. And Lily, for one, could hear tears frothing under the merriment. This birthday girl was perilously over-excited – and all she was after was a bit of praise for her efforts, a bit of attention. Lily looked to Teddy for support, but she was scowling down at her boots, lost in her sulks. Meanwhile, the dowager sailed across and tucked a proprietorial hand into the goose's wing. Goose was right and all, muttered Lily to herself. At that moment she could happily have trussed and roasted the gormless berk.

'By the by,' cooed Lady Dunstan, steering Sir Charles inexorably towards the door, as the grandfather clock began to strike nine, far below in the library, 'Jeremy tells me our tenant from Mill House is coming this evening, delightful man, apparently. I thought I might take the opportunity to explore an extension to the lease.'

That did it. Bella's face, which had seemed to be crumpling into tears, jerked up with a look of utter horror.

'Another year, do you think, or . . . Oh, Isobella, are you coming down, too? You seem in a tearing hurry all of a sudden.'

'You bet I'm in a hurry.' And to Lily's dismay, if no one else's, Bella's cheeks were now as crimson as her trousers and her eyes more dangerously glittery than all her necklaces put together. 'It's party time,' she snarled. 'And I give you fair warning, Charles Dunstan, I am going to *party*.'

*   ★   ★   ★

'Heigh-ho,' sighed Bill, 'a man's work is never done.'

On his hands and knees, our long-suffering hero was scrubbing the floor of his scullery. This dingy chamber, unlike Lily's spotless kitchen or even the vaulted magnificence of the domestic regions at the Hall, could serve only too plausibly as a back-cloth for that well-loved pantomime tale prominent in so many minds this evening. Twig brooms might be lacking, but an ancient coal-fired range, rusted and filthy as it was from years of neglect, glowered centre-stage in quite the approved manner. A tangle of wire-wool and a canister of noxious-smelling chemical suggested Bill might be contemplating the restoration of its antique glories. That some vigorous housework was long overdue cannot be denied, but it is perhaps significant that he had felt inspired to roll up his sleeves tonight. To be sure, having slept all day, he was unlikely to feel ready for an early bed, and – given his consumption last night – was probably wary of lulling himself back into the arms of Morpheus with alcohol. If asked, however, he would freely have admitted that he had set himself to work chiefly as a means of distracting his addled brain. Nothing like a scrubbing brush for washing troubles away, as his mum used to say, and at this moment Bill Smith felt beset with troubles.

The last straw – the icing on the whole lousy cake – had been Bella Dunstan gleefully reeling off the names, charms and track records of some of the rogue males she had invited for Teddy's delectation tonight – the emphasis, as she made clear, being on 'rogue'.

'Are you off your head?' Bill had bellowed down the phone. 'Does she know what you're up to?'

'Don't be silly, it's a surprise.'

'She'll go bananas.'

'Oh, I hope so, lucky girl.'

'I didn't mean *that*. 'Strewth, let me talk to her, will you?'

Bella, however, had remained implacable, insisting that their prinking session was not to be interrupted and Bill must ring back. So, a quarter of an hour later, he had duly done so, by which time there was music blasting down the line, along with a crowd roar worthy of Wembley Stadium, and whoever had answered the phone and promised to find Teddy obviously got lost in the stampede. In the end, the line had just gone dead. He would have summoned a cab there and then – assuming such conveniences could be summoned in these benighted parts – and gone up to find her himself, only, once again, he was stymied by the kids. He could hardly turf them out of their beds and cart them along, too.

Anyway, as he assured himself, adding another squirt of Flash to his bucket, he had no real cause for worry. Apologies would keep until the morning. She might even be more amenable to reason with a hangover. But explaining his own conduct to her wasn't quite *all* that was troubling him . . .

'Look,' said Bill to the dog, who was curled into a tight knot in the corner, eyeing the wet floor with disfavour, 'we both know she can handle the likes of Brian Rowbotham with one hand tied behind her back, but these chums of Bella's strike me as a different kettle of shark, wouldn't you say?'

True, a geezer calling himself Piggy Gloucester did not sound like your average sex god, but if he'd got through three wives already? And, as Bella hadn't hesitated to explain, her poor sister-in-law was *longing* to find herself a chap, was *desperate* to settle down and make babies and all that sort of thing, although – another high-pitched giggle – one trusted she wouldn't be applying herself to the baby-making business immediately. Still, who could say? The moon was high, the night was young . . .

'Bollocks,' grunted Bill, scrubbing harder. He wouldn't have minded so much had his own children not piped up to the same tune as he put them to bed. He had been on the point of switching off the light when Floss observed: 'She wants a husband, you know.'

This time, he hadn't needed to ask who. 'How'd you know?'

'Told me. And I said we didn't mind if she married you.'

All very well for Ferdy to lie there laughing like a drain, Floss wasn't kidding. 'And what'd she say to that?'

'Not much,' his daughter admitted.

'What she was thinking was probably too rude for your ears. Anyway, sleep, you two.'

'But, Dad—'

'No. I'll be down in the kitchen, OK?'

And here he still was, at half past ten, with the moon even higher and the night not quite so young. Was it worth phoning again? Hardly. Let's face it, Teddy wasn't what you'd call wolf-bait. Although he'd found himself thinking recently, as her bruises faded – or maybe it was just as he got to know her better – what an appealing little face she had. Kind of heart-shaped. And if she was getting all tarted-up for this thrash? Oh, for God's sake, she could take care of herself, course she could. Even if she was about as streetwise as Floss – less so, in fact. Because, for all she'd the bark of a Rottweiler, there was no matching bite. Underneath, she was as soft-hearted and trusting as Birdie here, and a damn sight braver. She'd rescued his son's life, done her damnedest to perform the same trick on his own career – only for him to turn round and kick her in the teeth. Oh shit, groaned Bill, he'd *got* to talk to her, try to make her understand he wasn't ungrateful, just—

'Hang about,' he muttered, tossing down his brush and scrambling over to the back door. 'Headlights. She coming home early, then?'

It was not Teddy's van purring to a halt, however, but a socking great stretch limo, Mercedes by the look of it, white. He watched, baffled, as a tall figure unwound gracefully from the driver's door, snowy shirtfront gleaming through the gloom.

'Bill Smith?' the figure called, fishing into the back seat and producing a natty wicker basket.

'Last time I checked. And you?'

The guy grimaced as he strolled across, one thin hand outstretched. He was sporting a wing collar, cummerbund, dicky bow – belatedly, Bill recognized the flash of silver in his elegantly sculpted hair. 'The Fairy frigging Godmother, dear,' he snorted. 'With a touch of menopausal wand fatigue.'

Teddy had never realized it was possible to remain quite so angry for quite so long. Until now, she had naïvely believed temper to be a transient phenomenon, come and gone as swiftly as a camera flash. And, speaking of camera flashes, if that leering cretin from

Ridings Life magazine pointed his lens in her direction just one more time, she would smash his Nikon over his stupid head. Either that, or find practical employment for Charlie's sword, which was clunking into her Lycra-clad thigh at every step.

She did not want her appearance recording for posterity. You must be joking. One glimpse in a mirror through an inch and a half of hairy black mascara had been more than enough – and as for these idiots exclaiming at every turn how different she looked, how marvellous . . . She could only comfort herself with the reflection that they looked quite as ridiculous as she did, and most – she devoutly trusted – a great deal more so. At the last count, she had spotted two pantomime cows; one cat; one horse – already split into its component halves; a Tinkerbell in glittery leotard and roller skates who was fifty if she was a day; and enough Ugly Sisters to found their own branch of the Women's Institute – along with a veritable battalion of fat-bottomed, wobbly-thighed Principal Boys, every Tom Thumb, Dick Whittington and Aladdin of them parading around, honking with mirth, declaring this to be the most delicious idea for a party, such a hoot, such *fun*. Fun? She'd give them fun.

She would have a few pithy words to say to Lily Rowbotham, too, when she got the opportunity. How dared Lily blackmail her out of the kitchen by claiming her absence would spoil Bella's night? Bella, giggling like a schoolgirl, soaking up booze like a dehydrated camel, and kissing everything that moved, clearly couldn't give a tuppenny cuss about her sister-in-law. Within the first three-quarters of an hour, Teddy had observed her being photographed in the arms of five different men – in ever more compromising clinches – and frankly wasn't surprised she hadn't seen hide nor yashmak of her since. In her opinion, the hostess was very likely comatose under a rosebush by now. That was if anyone could sleep with this appalling racket pounding out of the speakers and lights flashing everywhere with a brashness more appropriate to Las Vegas than a respectable English garden. Teddy must have been out of her tiny mind, letting the Rowbotham brothers loose. Her only minor consolation in the whole giant fiasco was that she had, thus far, managed to evade Brian, whom she had several times spotted stumbling around the place like a mobile clothes horse in robes twice his size. Initially, she had escaped by dint of his failing to recognize her, thereafter only by prowling the terrain with the wariness of a fox on Boxing Day.

Why was she still here at all? Why do you think? Because, after his kindness in inviting his friend Michael up at her behest, she felt obliged to see Hari. Ten minutes of civilities would suffice – she had long since ditched any notion of selling paintings – if only she could locate the bloody man.

Hari Stakinos, as it happened, was not merely in Teddy's kitchen at that moment, but in a temper almost as volatile as her own.

This was *totally* unlike him, as he had been explaining to her neighbour, who was helpfully ransacking the larder on his behalf, because, as anyone in the biz would tell you, Hari Stakinos was the cuddliest bundle of sweetness and light this side of Shirley Temple – but not tonight, Josephine. He had, he grumbled, spent the past three hours receiving a variety of conflicting messages from assorted minions in the Splitz empire about their employer's whereabouts and intentions – the latest to the effect that Michael was as keen as ever to visit the noble establishment once graced by the mighty poet, but a late-running casting conference meant he would have to make his own way, direct to the party . . .

'Some time after midnight, can you believe it? I'll just have to make sure Teddy's still awake and flaming sober. Honestly, there's no reward for trying to spread a little happiness round the place, is there?'

Thus far, the artist had merely been contributing vague grunts of sympathy, as he carried out one box of fruit after another and opened them on the kitchen floor. Hari's mistake, while minutely inspecting a proffered mango for ripeness, was perhaps to specify precisely the nature of the happiness he was planning to spread this evening.

'What?' bellowed his confidant, swivelling round on his haunches.

'Talk about a marriage made in heaven.' Hari, engaged

in sniffing a melon, was blithely unaware of the effect of his revelations. 'Came to me in a flash.'

Bill had scrambled to his feet. 'Tell me this is a wind-up, that it's one big joke and you're all in on it except me. First there was Bella—'

'Who?'

'—with bloody Piggy Gloucester, now you're talking about shipping up some fat old tycoon, probably bald as a coot—'

'Lovably chubby,' retorted Hari indignantly, whisking a pineapple out of Mr Smith's grasp. 'And who's going to worry about a thin patch on top with fifty million dollars sprouting in the bank? Not my sensible friend Theodora, I assure you.'

'*Your* friend?'

At this juncture, Hari took refuge on the far side of the kitchen table and glared at Bill with the outrage of a sensitive soul who had been expecting sympathy from a fellow creative spirit. 'Teddy wants a husband,' he began.

'Oh my God, not that again.'

'And I owe her a big favour, one way or another, and it suddenly came to me: Michael. They'd be so good for one another. She'd settle him down, give him a nice home, a little Michael Splitz Junior, or two.' Hari beamed fondly. 'And I dare say she won't flap about the odd bimbo on the side – fair play, if you've been mainlining on teenage nymphos for thirty years, you can't go cold turkey overnight, but he's pushing sixty now, so she shouldn't have to put up with it for long.'

'I never heard anything so bloody disgusting in all my life,' yelled Bill. 'What on earth gave you the idea she'd look at this old satyr?'

'*She* did,' retorted Hari crossly. 'Right out of the blue, when she asked me if he might be interested in buying a painting of yours.'

'*My painting?*'

'You know you want to be careful, pet,' Hari tutted, edging towards the door. 'Bust a blood vessel if you carry on like that. Anyway, I must be off, because when himself finally condescends to put in an appearance, I've got to be there to waft the old fairy dust, haven't I?'

'No,' gasped Bill, lurching forward. And for the second

time that evening he was blocking a doorway with his not inconsiderable bulk.

Hari crossed his arms and pursed his lips. 'Don't you come the heavy with me, big boy.'

'No, I mean . . .' All at once, Bill's features cranked into a smile: a smile which anyone at all acquainted with Mr Smith would recognize as being quite uncharacteristically crafty. 'You reckon you owe Teddy a favour, right?'

Hari, eyeing him suspiciously, nodded. 'Several. Over the years.'

'And your chum isn't arriving until after midnight?'

Hari, more warily still, agreed to this, too.

'Then,' said Bill, 'if you want to do our mutual friend Theodora an extra big favour while you're waiting for Mr Wonderful to show his ugly mug, will you lend us your motor and babysit for half an hour?'

Chapter Thirty-Two

'It's like this constant battle between the whole fame and fortune thing and artistic integrity, you see?' continued Jeremy, handing a bottle without a second glance to two nappy-swaddled gents with dummies in their mouths and leafy garlands about their necks. 'Of course, I realize now I was right, turning my back on all that—'

'Oh, I get it,' exclaimed Lorette, whose attention was wandering. 'You two are Babes in the Wood, yeah? That's really clever.'

'—Hollywood stuff, which is a dead end, artistically, whereas a big-issue, cutting-edge drama like this – sorry? Sure, I'll find more ice.'

'It's a nice haircut you've had for it anyway,' Lorette called to his departing back, smoothing down her spangly frock and sighing. She was quite content to leave others to make twerps of themselves in fancy dress, less content to prop up this corner of the drinks table all night.

'But is it, you know, *brutal* enough?' he resumed, handing over a refilled ice-bucket, 'for a former Para, ex-con, with a mother fixation and neo-Nazi tendencies?'

'Sounds a great part,' she muttered.

'Once-in-a-lifetime,' he responded, with utter sincerity. 'I mean, why the pet rat? Does it really exist? I'm seriously beginning to think . . . More fizz? Coming up.'

'Can't we go and have a dance?' She allowed her skirt to slip a further couple of inches up her thigh, and peeped flutteringly up through her lashes. 'Or something?'

'If only,' he said fervently, but nevertheless continued to swathe the bottle in label-concealing cloth according to the precise directions of his sister. What else could a struggling actor do, with a trust fund which barely covered his dry-cleaning bills, and the prospect of twelve weeks of profit-sharing starvation on the road? He needed his forty quid pay tonight, and Ted, stomping past in a filthy temper earlier, had actually threatened to halve it if he took so much as a breather. 'She said I could knock off after midnight, when supper's out.'

Lorette stifled a yawn. 'What time is it now?'

Eleven o'clock and Teddy was still cross. In fact, crosser. The information, courtesy of Brian Rowbotham, that Bill did not even *want* to attend this party, had sworn he would prefer a few beers in front of the telly – a sentiment so redolent of her neighbour she could not doubt its provenance – was maintaining her wrath at a satisfactory sizzle. She had made no attempt to shed her poisonous mood. On the contrary. For once in her conventional life, instead of skipping around like a badge-hunting Brownie, with a cheery face and a helping hand for all the world, Teddy was tasting the exhilarating pleasures of behaving badly.

To be sure, she had not thus far actively insulted any of the gift-wrapped baboons around her – with the possible exception of Charlie, that is, who had waddled up in plaintive search of his wife, anxious she should not miss her birthday fireworks. He had also been unwise enough to enquire, by way of afterthought, whether his little sis was having a good time, *hergh*, meeting lots of nice chaps? Snarling that she'd had a better time at the dentist's, Teddy added for good measure that he looked more like a dead duck than a pantomime goose. Being rude to brothers, however, did not count. One could insult them any old day of the week. More temptingly, she had yet to vent her spleen on either of her two gentleman companions, even now pursuing her with the unslappable persistence of flies in a cow field. Not only was she being dogged by Brian, who tripped over his too-large robes at every third step – Teddy for this reason maintaining, indeed increasing, her habitually brisk pace as they perambulated around the glittering, bustling, beat-thumping gardens – but also by the Reverend Timothy Lighthope, in the well-upholstered guise of Friar Tuck. He, at this moment, was burbling some particularly fatuous nonsense about the pleasure of meeting her at a social gathering of this nature, because, although they were forever bumping into one another in the course of parish business, that was not quite the same, was it? In fact, if she would forgive him for saying so, Tim had for some time entirely failed to recognize his churchwarden in her, ah, dashing ensemble. Dared one hazard a guess as to the character she was representing?

Before Teddy could utter a most unchurchwardenly retort, the Sheik of Langley chipped in, chuckling as he recalled his own astonishment on finally locating Miss Dunstan.

'And I'm sure Teddy won't mind my repeating the little joke I made at the time?'

'On your own head,' she hissed, upping her pace still further.

'Because,' persisted Brian archly, panting to keep abreast, 'we mustn't forget why that fairytale King and Queen threw a ball for their so-charming son, must we? It was for the Prince to choose himself a—'

But Teddy, triumphantly reaching the end of her tether, had whipped round like a panther for the kill – only for Brian to plummet into her, trip and fall headlong. And since his nose fell foul of the ornate pommel of Sir Charles's regimental sword on the way down, his punch line, sadly, was obliterated in a gush of blood.

'Pande-fucking-monium,' breathed Bill.

He could not believe the crowds packing this place out, glugging liquor like it was lemonade, and braying with all the dignified restraint of English football fans on the Costa del Grot, egged on by brother-in-law Colin's amplified exhortations to live it up and boogie on down. Even now he had elbowed his way out of the house to the terrace he could hardly move. However, he wasn't going to let a giant goose cannoning across his path stop him tracking Teddy down, not after the monumental effort required just to get here.

Putting the squeeze on Hari Stakinos had made Bill wonder whether he mightn't have a future in double-glazing sales. The sod had argued every inch, whingeing that he didn't *do* children. Bill had retorted that he himself wasn't used to dumping his children on total strangers, but that they were dead to the world upstairs, and besides, anyone of whom Teddy spoke so highly was clearly a fine, upstanding member of the human race, as trustworthy as he was golden-hearted. Which had done the trick – almost. Until Hari, tetchily asking whether there was any gin in the house, advised Bill to look sharp about changing because he wasn't hanging around all night.

'Changing?'

'You don't think you're going up there in your jeans?'

So he'd begun to explain he wasn't planning to hit the dance floor, just sneak in for a quick word with herself.

'You'll never get through the gate dressed like that. Took me all my time to get out with Stalin's grandson manning the checkpoint.'

'Crap, I've got an invitation. At least' – Bill rolled his eyes – 'I did have until the bloody brother-in-law swiped it along with my costume, but that's neither here nor there.' Which it wasn't – nothing short of loaded sub-machine guns would stop him talking his way into the Hall tonight. No, what suddenly hit him like a ton of the proverbial was the prospect of confronting Teddy in the midst of her posh cronies. Dressed like this? After the hoo-ha she'd already kicked up over what he was supposed to wear? One look at his jeans and, far from listening to his apologies, she was more likely to belt him one. His eyes wandered speculatively to the beautifully cut dinner jacket presently adorning the back of his own kitchen chair.

'No chance, big boy. Anyway, it wouldn't go near you. Dig out your own tux.'

Bill, through clenched teeth, admitted he did not possess such a garment. No, not even a whistle. Clean pair of trousers, maybe, but . . . 'I gotta get up there – hey, stop. You can't just walk out on me.' Because the guy was already gathering up his jacket with the complacency of one who has neatly wriggled off a very nasty hook. 'One minute, that's all. I'll think of something in a minute.'

On the very doorstep, Hari – hesitated. Slowly, he drew out his car keys, studied them for a moment, then glanced back at Bill. And his face began to curl into a smile. It was not what Bill would call a pleasant smile, more like the smirk of the tiger calling time on a riding lesson, but who cared?

'Yeah?' he said eagerly.

Now, trudging down into the gardens, scanning the faces at every turn, he just hoped Teddy would appreciate the tortures he'd suffered for her sake, not least nearly pranging the Mercedes on account of not being able to find the pedals. Right now, he could hardly breathe, had something jabbing viciously into his left armpit, and his scalp was itching like an ant hill. This was because the bloody costume he'd been dispatched to retrieve from the boot of the limo came complete with wig, and Hari, sniggering every step of the way, would permit no half-measures. Bill got the distinct impression that the vexations of a long day were being vented on his innocent self. What was more, while lacing him up with quite uncalled-for zest, the bastard had treated him, with every heave on the strings, to a rundown of his mystical gifts – *tug* – ran in the family – *yank* – he'd had this gorgeous little vision – *wrench* – of the happy couple.

'Vision?' yelped Bill, suddenly soprano.

'Clear as I'm seeing you.' Hari's eyes became dreamy. 'There's a pink marble fireplace, with one of them pretend log fires in the grate, which is a bit tacky but that's California for you.'

'You're strangling me.'

'Got to suffer in the cause of beauty, petal, that's what I tell all my girls. And if you ask me, it's bloody vulgar to keep your Oscar on your mantelpiece, but we'll let it pass.' Hari, tying a final excruciating knot, paused theatrically. 'The point is, on one side of the fire sits Michael, happy as a sand boy in a bathrobe far too short for legs like his, because he's got shocking veins. But smiling back at him – mind, I'm being honest with you, Bill, because I *never* tell more than I see, I couldn't make out exactly where she was sitting – still, beaming straight at him like she's won the lottery is your friend and mine Theodora.'

'Bullshit.'

'It's written.'

'I tell you—'

'And I'm telling you, chuck, I have the sight.' Hari spoke with serene certainty. 'It never lies.'

And although Bill hadn't believed a word, even now, as he lumbered down towards the lily pond, he felt a mite unsettled. Barmy, of course, because this podgy lech with the dodgy legs wasn't even due here until midnight – *after* midnight. Bill would have found Teddy long before then, and they could laugh together about the loony schemes cooked up by her family and so-called friends. Although, he thought, glancing round with a flicker of anxiety, if he didn't locate her soon, it'd be time for him to get back in the motor. He had just paused under a tree which was flashing like a Belisha beacon, to see if he couldn't adjust whatever was biting his armpit, when his eye was caught by a couple at the far end of the hedge.

Didn't he recognize those oriental robes? Although the wearer of them was wrapped in the intimate embrace of some female with a very nice little bum at the top of her shiny black tights. She was far too tasty to be wasted on the Ugly Brother-in-law. At any other time, Bill would have been over there pronto, shoving a spanner straight back in whatever plans Brian Rowbotham might be brewing for *his* evening, but right now he had more pressing business in hand. At least, he thought he had, and was pacing off round the pond, dodging a drunken Captain Hook, when a familiarly strident voice assaulted his ears.

'How many times do I have to tell you? Head back, you fool. Ah, Timothy, and about time too. Have you got the ice?'

Bill wheeled round, paced back. Stared. And stared again. It was . . .

'Duchess?' he cried, in scandalized tones worthy of a maiden aunt. 'What the bleedin' hell do you think you look like?'

'*Bill?*' squawked Teddy, abandoning Brian and his bloody nose

283

to the mercies of the vicar and hopping back along the line of the hedge, gazing this way and that. But there was no sign of her neighbour. A lurching Captain Hook, a couple of chaps at the far side of the lawn, and by the lily pond a horrendously bewigged and bejewelled pantomime dame in sparkling silver crinoline with starry wand and – *hairy chest?*

'Titania with rubber tits,' Hari had snorted, adding acidly that only Michael could come up with a drag Fairy Godmother. Ignorant flaming Yank. As for the cheek of supposing Hari would ever stoop to the indignity of donning skirts . . . 'He'll be sorry next time he wants a scalp massage. And so will you,' he had added, fixing Bill with a basilisk eye, 'because, believe me, big boy, if you don't get yourself and this car back by midnight, I'll stuff that wand right up your—'

Silence! Enough of such tomfoolery.

Let us dismiss Hari Stakinos, and pause here, just for an instant, to savour the magic of the moment. After all, if this were one of Mr Splitz's popular screen epics, an entire symphony orchestra would be raising their bows now, ready to let rip with the soupily-soaring love theme we have been anticipating for so long – for so *very* long. Because, after their little ups and downs, their tiffs and trials, their mishaps and misunderstandings – in short, their jointly pig-headed refusal to recognize their inevitable fate – our hero and heroine are at last coming together. And, in this most romantic of settings, under a gloriously star-spangled sky, we must surely be permitted to assume the veils are about to fall from their eyes. Could Bill's disquiet over packs of rogue males have been inspired by mere friendly neighbourliness? Would Teddy be so incensed at her seeming rejection if Bill were nothing more to her than a promising meal-ticket? Ah, but there, perchance, lies the rub. For while it is merely probable Teddy feels more for Bill than that, it is absolutely undeniable she is, at this moment, in the biggest strop of her life. Besides which, in quitting Hari Stakinos thus cavalierly, we have overlooked the small stumbling block of his vision. Which – never lies? Absurd, surely, as Bill says, and yet . . .

Gentlemen of the orchestra, on second thoughts, perhaps you had better rest your bows for the time being.

'*Me?*' roared Theodora Dunstan, sword bouncing against her black Lycraed thigh as she thundered over to the pond. 'What do *I* look like?'

'I mean, flashing your knickers, painted like a hooker—'

'You *told* me to wear make-up.'

'Not a foot thick, I bloody well didn't – oh, hell, that's not what I come here to say.'

'I can't think why you bothered to come at all, frankly. Let alone in that disgusting rig.'

'Now, hang about. I only got into the bloody kit for you.'

'A likely story. Who d'you think you are, you – you big *nancy*.'

'Well, that's nice, innit?' snarled Bill, forgetting he was here on a peace and reconciliation mission. 'Particularly when I walk in to find you slobbering all over Brian Rowbotham.'

'*What?*'

'Pardon me if I spoiled your fun.'

With a shriek, she hurled herself at him.

'Prince Charming?' he jeered, grabbing her flailing fists in his own. 'Oh, *very* charming.'

'And I s'pose you, you hairy great gorilla,' she panted, squirming and jerking up her knee at an angle which might have inflicted grievous injury but for the padding of multiple petticoats, 'fancy yourself as Cinder-*bloody*-ella?'

'Ow!' yelped Bill, nevertheless retaining his manful grasp of her wrists. In order to avoid a further and possibly more telling assault from her writhing lower limbs, however, he hopped a prudent couple of steps backwards, unaware that the shallow parapet of the lily pond lay immediately behind him. A viciously sharp coping-stone crashing into one calf inevitably caused him to stagger. For a moment, locked furiously together, they swayed on the flagstones as he struggled to regain his balance – and failed. Thanks to his billowing crinoline, however, their descent beneath the twinkling fairy lights was slow and graceful, indeed one might say almost *balletic*. Their thrashing immersion in the muddy waters was rather less poetic. As such ornamental features go, the pond at Langley Hall was unusually deep, and richly infested with weed as well as the eponymous lilies.

'Great steaming idiot,' gasped Teddy, the first to splash to the surface, Bill being hampered by his acreage of skirt. 'Sword – Charlie's.'

And by the time he'd righted himself and spat away a mouthful of slime, she was plunging under again, face first. 'Daft bat,' he spluttered, lurching forward and snatching a handful of tunic, only to feel it rip.

'Lemme go,' she coughed, squirming away to dive afresh. 'Gotta find it.'

'What?' he roared, grabbing again, but all he got for his pains this time was a fistful of red sash. Cursing, fighting for breath, he flopped back, staring across the heaving waters. And before he'd had time to gather such wits as were left to him, he saw, right over in the middle of the pond amid the spangled reflections of the fairy lights – like a scene from bloody *Camelot* – a palely naked arm poke up through the lily leaves, triumphantly brandishing a sword. That arm was followed, more slowly, by a weed-bedraggled, mascara-splattered face, gasping and choking.

'Oh, God, *help*,' coughed Teddy, clutching her throat.

'Serves you right if you drown, you little monster,' he yelled, battling to rise through sodden petticoats sucking at his legs like treacle. ''Sall your fault.'

'No, I mean – oh, *God*. What do you look like?'

Which was when he clocked she was actually laughing – laughing so much she couldn't stand up. 'I'm glad you find it so funny,' he bellowed, snatching up a stray bosom which was bobbing away on the tide and pushing the wig up from his nose, 'because your chum Hari's going to want my head on a platter after what I've done to his gear.' With a final mighty effort, he heaved himself to his feet, and thrust a hand towards her. 'Quit pissing yourself, and cop hold of this, you mad tart.'

Tossing Excalibur with a clang onto dry land, she staggered upright – only to let out a squeal of horror because she realized that her tunic was dangling round her waist, her bra had come unstuck, and just about the only covering on her top half was a lacing of pond weed.

'Well don't just stand there,' she shrieked, clapping her hands to her tits. 'It's not funny.'

'No,' Bill breathed – except he didn't quite seem able to breathe, still less speak. In fact, if this were Hari Stakinos, you might be forgiven for supposing he was having a vision of some sort.

'Bill?' she says uncertainly.

'Fuck,' he whispers. 'Holy *fuck*.'

And now, quite unaccountably, he's stretching out both arms, and Teddy is flinging herself into them, and he's wrapping her tight, kissing her black-caked eyes, her muddy nose, her scarlet mouth, while she shoves off his wig, knots her arms around his neck . . .

'Teddy?' There floats from beyond the hedge a curiously muffled cry, suggestive of a nose swathed in several handkerchiefs. 'Dear lady?'

Their faces part the barest reluctant inch.

'Inside?' hisses Bill.

'Back stairs.'

'You're navigating, sunshine.'

So saying, our gallant Cinderella bundles his skirts over one arm, and hoists up to his lop-sided chest our dripping Prince, along with sword, medals and assorted pondlife. Pausing only to plant a kiss on her neck and with a growl rather deliciously redolent of a hungry wolf, he bears her off into the night at an urgent gallop.

The darkness was sudden and all engulfing, the silent gropings and blunderings punctuated only by a stray whisper, an occasional sugary giggle. The surge of mounting excitement was becoming gorgeously, almost unbearably thrilling . . .

'Sorry, too late, can't hold back any more.' One instant of throbbing silence. '*Hergh*, chocks away then.'

Whoosh. Myriad showers of ruby, emerald and sapphire sparks fizzed and glittered across the blackness.

'Just have to hope, *hergh*, she's out there somewhere.'

Whizz. Silver Catherine wheels whirled in a delirium of white-hot ecstasy.

'Oh, hullo, Ma. Haven't, um, seen Bellsy, have you? *Hergh,* hate to think she's missing all this. I say, first of the big brutes coming up. Hold onto your hats.'

With a mighty roar, a rocket surged, up and up, impossibly high into the heavens, before – *pow!* – it shattered in a blinding shoal of gold, fiery darts shooting wider and wider, higher and higher until – to a shuddering collective sigh – the last spark melted into the darkness.

'*Wowee!*' whooped Miss Theodora Dunstan. 'I mean, crikey. Is it always like that with you?'

'No,' said Mr Bill Smith lovingly. 'Generally it takes a bloody sight longer and it's not compulsory to shout your head off all the way through.'

She blinked a couple of times. 'I say, there really are fireworks out there. I thought they were all in my head.'

'You say the nicest things.'

'But—'

'Might've known there'd be a but.'

'Do you think we could make it as far as the bed before we have another go?'

With immense tenderness, he kissed her soot-streaked, weed-encrusted cheek. 'Some people are never fucking satisfied.'

'Got to be nearly midnight,' yawned Lorette.

'Fireworks end at twelve,' said Jeremy, handing out trays of glasses to the waitresses. 'The lights go back on, your bro plays "Happy Birthday" over the PA, they all troop in for supper—'

'And we,' she said, stroking his smartly shorn head, 'have some fun.'

'Can't wait. I've got the script to show you.'

★   ★   ★

'Course it's overrated, this sex lark. Like you always said. Load of fuss about nothing.'

'Get stuffed,' murmured Teddy and, finding one of his chest hairs between her teeth, tugged hard.

'Pack it in, you abandoned hussy.' Bill lifted her away from him, grinning up at her naked body through the firework-flickering twilight. 'If your sister-in-law could see you now . . .'

'So?'

'And if she takes it into her head to trot up to her room and powder her nose?'

'Everyone's out there, silly, I told you. Any moment now they'll be toasting her birthday, all that nonsense. In fact,' she added thoughtfully, 'if we get a move on, we might just have time for—'

Bill pulled her back down to the bed, hugging her close. 'You're amazing, you know that? Completely, totally, gorgeously unbelievable.'

'Can't you ever shut up?' This was whispered rather indistinctly into his ear which she was exploring with her tongue.

'Help,' he moaned. 'God, babe, I dunno if I can stand this sort of pace long term.'

Teddy, ignoring him, began nibbling a path down his neck. 'You know Floss said – Floss *and* Ferd said – we oughta get married?'

'Is that nice?'

'Bloody hell, Duchess, are you listening?'

'Married, yes. Oh, bliss, do that again.'

'Only I'm beginning to think—'

'*Isobella?* Isobella, surely you're not up here?'

Teddy's squirming body jackknifed into the air. 'Mother,' she screamed, and plummeted under the bedclothes.

'Only your poor husband is quite distraught.' Light from the landing flooded into the room, revealing a floor strewn with wet garments, a quaking mound of quilt in the middle of the splendidly curtained bed and, alongside the mound, Bill Smith's large and very naked person, one hand splayed demurely over his fast-detumescing organ.

He smiled politely. 'Evenin', Lady Dunstan. Fancy meeting you here.'

Chapter Thirty-Three

'About time too,' cried Lorette, on hearing her brother's amplified voice urging all these good folks to charge their glasses for the birthday toast. 'Nearly there.'

'Nearly . . .' echoed Jeremy and, thrusting a last trayful of opened Cabernet Sauvignon bottles into the hands of a waitress, he turned and threw open his arms. 'Shit, darling, what a marathon.'

Lorette was returning his embrace with ardour, and an even more fervent concern he shouldn't snag the sequins on her expensive dress, when she espied a face framed in the far window, which gave on to the kitchen yard. That face also apparently saw her, for, in the act of exhaling smoke, it contorted, broke into a violent fit of silent coughing — and instantly vanished.

'Mum,' she squealed, disentangling herself at spangle-endangering speed. 'And she's coming in.'

'Cheer up, my little passion flower,' said Bill. 'She can't eat you.'

With an uncertain giggle, Teddy risked a nose out of the bedclothes. 'Did she see me?'

'Not unless she's got X-ray eyes.' He ruffled her hair. 'Anyway, she obviously found it highly amusing.'

'Ma? Are you *crazy*?'

'Straight up. She was smiling all over her face. I just hope it wasn't my prick giving her such a good laugh.'

In the distance, a raucous choir was carolling 'Happy Birthday, dear Bella . . .'

Teddy bounced upright. 'Oh, my giddy aunt,' she cried. 'I'll bet she was smiling. She thought I was Bella.'

'Lily, hi there,' said Jeremy. 'How's tricks in the kitchen?'

'Where is she?'

Not for nothing had Jeremy devoted his life to his art. 'Sorry, who?'

'Don't play games with me, young man. Lorette.'

'Um, *Lorette?*' He returned Lily's furious stare with one of politely vacuous bewilderment. Bertie Wooster, he fancied, when confronted by a particularly ferocious aunt.

'My daughter, Lorette Smith. *Mrs* Lorette Smith.' Her mouth twisted this way and that as she eyed him suspiciously. 'If you – happen to bump into her, tell her I want a word. Urgently.' And she added meaningfully: 'Don't worry, she'll know what it's about.'

'Jesus H. she'd really do that to her own son?' Bill was slumped on the edge of the bed wistfully toying with a saturated packet of cigarettes as Teddy scrambled into her long-discarded jeans and sweatshirt. 'Toddle straight off and tell the poor bastard she's found his wife having it away with yours truly?'

'You don't know my mother.'

'Do I want to?' He gave a grunt of reminiscent laughter. 'She certainly picks her moments.'

'Oh, Bill, I'm so sorry. Wait here, I won't be long, I promise.'

'Blimey, don't worry about me, babe. You just scoot off and put your brother out of his misery.'

'You're so sweet, I love you so much.' Hopping across the floor, tugging the laces of one plimsoll, Teddy suddenly halted. 'I do,' she breathed wonderingly. 'I absolutely, utterly do.'

'Bloody hope so, the way you've been carrying on. Anyway, I thought we didn't believe in juvenile rubbish like that?'

She was not listening. 'Gracious, you'll never get back into that,' she muttered, giving a kick to the soggy mountain of crinoline. 'Look, the door over there, Charlie's dressing room.' She pressed a hurried kiss to his mouth. 'Help yourself.'

'Seems a bit rich, stinging the guy for two outfits in twenty-four hours . . .' But she was already gone, and through the open doorway Bill heard, unmistakably, the sonorous chime of a grandfather clock.

It was striking midnight.

Lily met her thundering down the back staircase, hopped forward and smartly caught hold of her arm.

'Not now,' Teddy panted.

'One minute, that's all.' At any other time, Lily would be asking what had got into the lass. Never mind if she was back in her jeans, and mucky as a street urchin, Teddy was radiant with happiness, blazing like a little beacon of joy – and wriggling like a ferret in a sack. But Lily had no intention of letting her escape. Hauling her into the crook of the stairs, she glanced round nervously.

'I hate landing this on you, love,' she whispered rapidly, 'truly I do, but you're the only one with half a brain in this family and someone's got to be told.' Even so, she could hardly bring herself to put her fear into words, the one catastrophe she had prayed all these years would never happen. She took a gulping breath. 'I think – no, I'd *swear* – I've seen my Lorette with your little brother.'

'Jez?' Teddy's eyes widened. 'You don't mean Lorette's his mystery guest?' She began to laugh.

'You're not telling me Jeremy *invited* her? They didn't just meet tonight?' Lily clapped a horrified hand to her mouth. 'Don't laugh,' she wailed, 'you wouldn't credit what people can get up to at a do like this.'

At this, Teddy positively hooted. 'Wouldn't I just? Sorry, sorry, Lorette and Jeremy. What's the problem?'

Lily bit her lip. 'Your dad,' she began unsteadily, 'your dad and me . . .'

'Pa? Where's he come into it?'

This was even harder than Lily had envisaged. She tried a

different tack. 'Do you remember, love, at his funeral, I told you he didn't suffer – at the end?'

'Jolly sweet and comforting of you it was, too. I mean, one will never *know*, but—'

'*I* knew,' Lily cut in before Teddy could say another word. 'I knew because I were there with him. When he passed on – and often before.'

'Sorry?' That little face was just like his, clear as plate glass, and you could practically see the cogs whirring inside. 'Does this mean . . . Are you saying, you and Papa . . . down at Mill House?'

Lily hung her head. 'Over twenty-odd years,' she mumbled.

'*Twenty years?*' Fiercely, she clutched Lily's shoulders. 'Was it love? Did you love him?'

Lily couldn't meet her eyes, but she wasn't going to lie, wasn't going to pretend that some mucky, drunken, one-night tumble had produced Lorette. That might have been the only way her ladyship could get Sir Theodore to sire little Jeremy, and on just such a night as this, but not Lily. Her daughter had been conceived in sobriety and love and, whatever the consequences, she wasn't going to tell the tale any other way. She shut her eyes. 'I'd have died for him,' she whispered – and nearly fainted with shock when she felt a warm kiss planted on her cheek.

'No wonder he was always so bright-eyed and bushy-tailed, the old devil,' cried his daughter exultantly. 'How amazing. How simply wonderful!' All at once her head swivelled. 'I say, was that Ma? Going towards the dining room?'

'Yes, but—'

'Another time, bless your heart. I've got to sort out my bloody mother.'

'Charles used language to me I never expected to hear from a son of mine.' Lady Dunstan had two pink spots burning high on her cheekbones and eyes as bright as her diamond collar.

'Serves you damn well right.'

293

'So I told him, if he refused to believe his own mother's testimony, he could go upstairs and see for himself.'

'And did he?' demanded Teddy. 'Is that where he's gone?'

'I'm afraid so.'

'Well, thank Heaven for small mercies. Bill will soon set him straight.' Mirth bubbled up afresh. 'Just so long as Charlie doesn't tonk him one first and ask questions later. Dear me, I'd better go armed with a first-aid kit.'

Her mother eyed her witheringly. 'You seem to be taking a remarkably sanguine view of your sister-in-law's adultery.'

'Bollocks, Ma,' Teddy snorted, borrowing from Bill Smith's vocabulary to satisfying effect. 'That lump in the quilt you saw wasn't Bella, it was me.' She took even greater pleasure in observing the effect of this revelation on her parent.

'You? In bed with that – that *animal*?'

'I don't think that's any way to speak of your future son-in-law.'

At this it almost seemed as though her mother might swoon. 'He's asked you to *marry* him?'

'Well, I think he was just about to,' said Teddy, subjecting the matter to brief consideration, 'only I'd other things on my mind at the time. Anyway, I did the job myself this morning – proposed, you know.' She chuckled reminiscently. 'Although as I recall his answer was something along the lines of "*Oh fuck, no . . .*"'

And with a cordial recommendation that her mother take herself off to bed – she looked quite washed-out and, besides, had made quite enough mischief for one night – Teddy hastened away.

'Teddy!'

'Sorry, Lily, I've simply *got* to find Charlie.' She giggled. 'Mission of mercy, life or death.'

Lily followed a few paces, but had to give up, because, for all the lass was laughing her silly head off, she was shifting like greased lightning. Out of sight before a despairing and harassed Lily could even begin to tell her that, while one brother was in imminent danger of committing incest, the other, whom she seemed so keen to find, was actually behaving exactly as his dad had always done when he got fed up with parties and wanted a quiet snooze. Lily had not been in the least surprised to see Sir Charles sneaking into the gunroom a couple of minutes ago.

Although why he had a clonking great black shoe tucked under his wing was anybody's guess.

'Back,' carolled Teddy, bashing open the door.

She wasn't quite sure what to expect, a bloodbath or, with luck, gales of shared hilarity, but certainly not this echoing emptiness. She knew the room was deserted the moment she walked in, but for some reason she trotted round, flinging open the doors to the dressing room, the bathroom – even to the wardrobes – calling, Bill? *Charlie?* There was no response.

This caused her to feel a mite crestfallen, but only for a moment. 'The little swines have gone to find themselves a drink, I'll bet,' she said wisely to herself. Pausing only to sluice her face – what, with the mud and the remains of Bella's make-up she looked like some ancient tribal warrior and had probably ruined a perfectly good towel, but too bad – she hurried out.

Thus, once again, Teddy finds herself combing the crowded rooms and gardens of Langley Hall, only now she is in search of a face very different from Hari's. Well, she's looking for two faces, in truth, although it seems unlikely her brother figures prominently in her thoughts.

This perambulation differs from the last in other respects. We, as dispassionate observers, might be forgiven for thinking she is actually grinning up at the lights strung round the trees, almost as if she is discovering a wacky charm in their very vulgarity. Certainly, she chuckles aloud as a green-clad gent encased in something resembling a gigantic teapot stumbles across her path.

'The genie in the lamp?' she cries. 'Oh, good show.'

She, of course, would be innocently amazed at our amazement, would pity us as mean-spirited kill-joys – where's our sense of fun? Frankly, she is entranced by the cleverness, the invention, the *wit* demonstrated by so many of Bella's friends in the devising of their costumes. And how splendidly happy they all seem: everyone she looks at is smiling at her. Surveying the buffet with proprietorial pride, she threads a path around the candlelit supper tables as people settle down, in twos and threes, with their brimming plates and glasses – no, no, thanks awfully, she'd adore to have a drink with Piggy and his chum, but just at this moment . . . Her costume? Oh, a slight mishap in the lily pond, yes, what a hoot. Incidentally, they haven't seen Charlie? Comical white goose outfit? Not since the fireworks. Oh, Piggy can bet his sweet life she enjoyed those fireworks. In fact, she believes she can claim to have derived more enjoyment from that part of the evening than everyone else put together. Yes, isn't this *indeed* a heavenly night?

We cannot argue with that. It is a summer night of rare perfection. A pale crescent moon flirts with chiffon tatters of cloud, a zephyr breeze wafts the heady scent of roses across the lawns, even the music has lulled to some gently rippling piano serenade.

Teddy, setting out to traverse the near-deserted gardens, registered a particularly dazzling flash at the end of the terrace. She was just reflecting that the *Ridings Life* photographer was proving himself to be a most admirably conscientious young man and wondering whether a line of thanks to his editor might not be in order when she recognized the present object of his attentions. Bella – *Bella!* With heart overflowing, Teddy realized that the one person in the whole wide world she most wanted to talk to at this moment – save the obvious – was her beloved sister-in-law.

'You've changed,' stated Bella, with a distinctly cross-eyed stare. She herself had shed a yashmak, several yards of beads and one earring along with all of her lipstick. She had, on the other hand, acquired a silver bow-tie around her neck, a rose at her bosom, and a new gentleman companion at each elbow, one of whom sported a monocle and cane, the other a doublet and hose. Teddy recognized neither swain, although she nodded to them with sunny good humour before turning back to her sister-in-law, who wagged a stern finger in return. 'Where's your lovely cozzy, you naughty girl?'

'Darling, have you a moment?'

'You met my friends, yet?' She hiccupped. 'Sorry, forgot their names. Anyway – anyway, 'smy sister-in-law, chaps. Best sister-in-law a girl could wish for, even if . . . Teddy? What you doing?'

Teddy wrapped an indulgent arm around her shoulders and steered her a few discreet steps away before asking if she had seen her husband at all? Bella's face clouded as she replied, no, she *bloody* well had not, and what was more didn't want to.

'Let's hope Bill's with him, then, because I've simply got to tell you this, it's so funny.' Teddy lowered her voice. 'Ma came charging into your room during the fireworks, looking for you, and you will *never* guess what she found.'

'Too late, old cow,' muttered Bella darkly. 'Got down just in time, obviously. You hear everyone singing "Happy Birthday" afterwards?' Unexpectedly, tears welled in her eyes. 'Wasn't it sweet of Charlie, all that?'

'Wonderful. But the point is Ma was convinced she'd caught you in, you know, flagrante whatsit.'

'During the fireworks? I told you—'

'Because there was Bill, starkers on the bed, with this heaving lump in the quilt next to him.'

'Anyhow, 'dultery doesn't count, not at a party. Well-known fact. 'Slong as everyone's too drunk to remember.'

'Goodness, are you hearing a single word? I'm telling you, Ma looked at Bill, saw the lump, and not unnaturally assumed—'

'Bill?' Bella cut in. 'Big, sexy, built-like-a-brick-shithouse Bill?'

'Isn't he *just*?' gurgled Teddy with a reminiscent shiver.

'In my bed, the cheeky monkey? Who with?'

'Who d'you think, stupid? Well, aren't you happy for me? Heaven knows, you've been telling me long enough to get myself laid.'

Bella gave an uncertain giggle. 'You're having me on. You wouldn't – *he* wouldn't. Course not, he's happily married.'

'Nonsense. Practically divorced.'

'Fucking *deliriously* happy. Told me so, when I asked him whether he'd . . .' The tears were glistening up again. 'Only I didn't mean it, not really, not *then*. But at least that'd've been better than . . . Oh, Teddy, why'm I such an idiot? Why can't I be sensible like you?'

'Marvellous.' Teddy rolled her eyes. 'The one time in my life I really want to talk to you, and you have to be half-cut.'

Bella blinked. 'Talk about what?'

'Sex, as it happens. Amongst other things.'

'Bad for you. I'm giving it up.'

'Dear me, you must be drunk.'

'Think I must be.' Her shoulders began to wobble. 'I mean, pink rats, maybe, but you and Bill Smith bonking away . . . Was he drunk, too?'

Teddy's chin came up. 'No, he jolly well was not, and I don't see what's so damned amusing.' Only Bella seemed to be weeping as well as laughing. 'Oh, forget it,' she snapped.

The odd thing was, after that, people stopped smiling at her. No, odder still: they seemed to stop seeing her altogether. Extraordinary. It was as if she had dwindled into a ghost, and was drifting around quite invisible to the laughing, chattering crowds. Even Brian and Timothy, whom she nearly fell over at a table in the corner, intently debating the finer points of pneumatic as opposed to electronic tracking in the organ, quite failed to notice her squeezing past their chairs. Only Lily actually *saw* her, and began signalling urgently, but she was at the far end of the long gallery, so it was easy for Teddy to slip away. She felt bad about doing so, but somehow she didn't want to hear any more about Lily and Pa just at this moment. It was wonderful, to be sure; *miraculous* even; she could not be more enchanted to learn her dotty old father had known what it was to feel as she felt now, had not simply settled for trudging on in civilly silent cold war with Ma, but . . .

She was being foolish. Everything was OK. Bill felt exactly the same as she did, course he did, she couldn't be mistaken. He'd just – just gone off for a drink with Charlie, maybe some food, anything. In fact, at this moment, he was most probably wandering around looking for her and they were missing one another at every turn. So the sensible course of action — the *only* course, now she came to think about it — was to return to Bella's room, where he was bound to loop back sooner or later. After all, she had told him to wait there, that she would be returning, as soon as ever she could . . .

On entering the room now, she noticed, as she hadn't before, that the pile of crinoline had gone. Also the wig, the wand, the petticoats — everything. Not only was Bill himself absent, but there remained not a trace or sign he had ever been here at all. This realization rather knocked the wind out of her. She found herself kneeling on the floor where his costume had lain, feeling for wetness. The carpet was damp, she was sure it was damp — and here was a scrap of silver thread, fallen from his frock. Or trodden in from any one of a dozen other glittering costumes? But what did it matter? She was being silly beyond measure, she knew full well he'd been here — dear Lord, was she ever likely to forget?

For an instant, she was overtaken by a longing for him so dizzyingly fierce, she let out a cry. And then started, glancing guiltily around, feeling a fool. Resolutely, she clambered to her feet, strode over to the window, yanked aside the curtain, and planted herself on the padded window seat. This was the best plan. From here she could watch the gardens below, look out for — for *what*? What was he wearing? A sodden crinoline? Something borrowed from Charlie? Nothing at all? Not that it made any odds. She would recognize Bill Smith whatever he was wearing, wherever he appeared, however far away — if he were marooned out on that star, a million light years off, she would somehow know he was there. And besides, he would be toddling back here to find her in no time at all.

She couldn't imagine why she was crying. Must be going potty. She'd never been so happy in her whole damn life.

Chapter Thirty-Four

A pale glow silvered the eastern horizon, painting the treetops of Home Wood in jagged, inky relief. One blackbird piped a lonely trill and was answered by a warbling descant, then by a rich chorus as the flimsy moon melted into the brightening sky. Gaps yawned now in the ranks of cars in the meadow, but there were still costumed figures to be seen wandering the lawns and gardens, a little bedraggled perhaps, some not entirely steady of foot, but all evincing a dogged resolve to see the revels out and the new day in. The kitchen, however, was echoingly hushed. Plates, dishes and cutlery were packed gleaming back into their crates; the flat surfaces shone empty, save for the big refectory table where were arrayed a battalion of mugs for breakfast tea, and — Lord help me, thought Lily — two trays of bacon ready to be grilled and sandwiched into buns for mopping up the collective hangover. But not yet awhile. Stripping off her apron with a weary sigh, she gathered up her handbag and headed off into the house. Maybe, this time round, she'd find someone.

Even if occasional snores were growling from sofas and the more secluded corners of the floor, there were bursts of laughter and the odd clink of glasses still to be heard, while Ella Fitzgerald quavered soulfully and softly from the speakers. Colin Rowbotham, although nobly remaining at his console, had plugged in a long tape, stuck his booted heels up by the turntables, and was quietly snoozing under his Stetson.

So muted was the music, it barely percolated up to the first floor landing, along which crept Jeremy Dunstan and Lorette Smith. And while Jeremy had about him the lusty glow of a young animal in love – in love with life, with Art, with his new haircut and, not least, with his beautiful companion – that companion looked rather less exuberant. In fact, if anyone bothered to examine her closely, she looked fed up to the back teeth.

Well, what do you expect? Fine old night Lorette'd had. Three hours propping up a bar, followed by a panicked dash aloft to Jeremy's room. Which was where she'd been holed up ever since, not having the nerve to try losing herself in the crowd with Mum on the hunt for her. It was all very well for Jeremy to swear Lily wasn't sure of having spotted her daughter, he didn't know there was serious money at stake.

'Anyway, I can't believe she'd betray you to that psychotic maniac,' he had protested.

'She'd do worse than that,' muttered Lorette, so darkly he had stopped arguing.

Besides, he hadn't in the least objected to skipping the rest of the party. Bella's friends, he said, reminded him exactly why he had bolted to the States, to escape these braying morons who thought Hamlet was a cigar and Stanislavsky a – a trendy vodka label.

'Is it?' had enquired Lorette, with a flicker of interest. 'Mind, I'm not a spirit drinker.'

But once he'd joined her upstairs they'd, you know, which she would concede had killed half an hour pleasantly enough – made a nice change to be doing it in a bed at any rate. Better still, he'd had the sense to bring a tray of supper with him. It was perhaps a shame he didn't have a telly up here, but then, as Lorette had wisely said to herself, there was no point watching some sad old late-night movie on the box when you were in the company of one equipped to supply the juicy lowdown on the film world first hand. Except all Jeremy could go on about now was his new play. Don't get her wrong, Lorette had been dead interested. At first. She got a real kick out of imagining herself perched like royalty in a plush box, watching proudly as, to cheering and encores, her very own star swept out through red velvet curtains to take his bow. Only . . .

Hatchet Job, that was the name of the company he was joining. And they weren't touring round theatres, she learned, no, more community centres, canteens, *prisons* – taking the message out to the people, he said. Meeting the challenge, he said. What was more (he said), by an amazing piece of luck, although rehearsals were in London, the tour actually opened up here in the North, first venue not too far away at all, in Huddlestone. Did Lorette know the town at all?

A cold hand had fastened around her heart. Nougat, that was what she was thinking, don't tell me I've picked the flaming nougat all over again. Yeah, yeah, Jeremy was fantastic, gorgeous, dead good fun – well, fun when he wasn't ranting on about the psycho-whatsit significance of pet rats – but Lorette had served five long years in Huddlestone, and was in no hurry to return. Still less was she inclined to grace communal digs already fixed, fantastically cheap, in Corporation Road – oh yes, she knew Corporation Road all right. Sunset Boulevard it was not.

'You hurt your leg?' she had enquired.

Jeremy, limping up and down the bedroom carpet, muttered something about fascinating parallels with Richard III. Listen, in the big speech, in the mortuary . . .

When she had finally woken up he was still poring over his script, pulling faces at himself in the mirror, and while she was in no frame of mind for contemplating plans in the long term, one thing she knew with absolute certainty in the short: it was home time for her now – yes, right this very minute – and if Jeremy could spare ten minutes from his rehearsing she would appreciate his borrowing a car, any car, and running her back to her own bed. With luck, she could be tucked up before Mum returned and no one any the wiser.

It was not to be her lucky night. As they reached the head of the main staircase, who should be trudging up towards them? And there was no chance of skipping away half-recognized this time. Her mother stopped dead and, never mind seeing her daughter, she looked as though she were seeing her own tombstone.

'Oh my God.' That was all she said.

'I've not dumped the kids on anyone,' protested Lorette instantly, 'they're safe at home with Bill.'

'You been with him all night?'

She risked a glance over her shoulder – but the landing behind her was deserted. 'Who?'

'Who'd you think? Him what dodged into her ladyship's bedroom two seconds ago.' Lily's features twisted and she clutched the banister, almost as if she might keel over. 'I won't ask what you've been up to. It were written all over his face.' And, to her daughter's bewilderment, she let out a moan.

'Mum?'

'That's it, then,' she whispered, in seeming desolation. 'God forgive me, but I'll have to do it to her.'

This, for Lorette, was the last straw. She burst into tears. 'You can't,' she wailed. 'You can't: you promised me.'

'Promised you what?' And Lily's face was blank, as though she really didn't know.

'The money, of course, you said I could have it, promised me.' The sobs were coming so thick and fast Lorette could hardly get the words out.

'Oh, that.'

'I'm divorced, as good as. You can't expect me to – to live like a nun.'

'Love, I don't, but—'

'And after the lousy rotten night I've had, it'd just be the icing on the cake, if you – if you—' She stopped because her mother had plunged forward to grip her shoulders, and was staring intently into her face.

'What do you mean, lousy night?'

'Whaddya think? Everything. I've had it. Had it up to here.'

'Listen to me, sweetheart.' Lily spoke softly, with a passionate urgency. 'Don't you believe for one minute I want to stop you having a good time, because I don't, course I don't. There's nothing in this world I want more than for you to be happy. In fact, that's all I've ever wanted, to see you comfortably settled, nice fella, nice family—'

'Don't tell me to go back to Bill. I won't. Can't.'

'I know that. Lord, d'you think I don't blame myself for trying to make you stick it out? But only because I thought that were best for you. It's just . . .' Lily glanced round and lowered her voice further still. 'Young Jeremy. He's a nice enough kid, I grant, but he's not right for you.'

Lorette gulped. 'Why?'

Her mother did not reply at once, and when she did, she spoke gruffly, rapidly. 'He's a loser, that's why. Oh, I know this acting lark sounds glamorous, but it doesn't earn him owt, does it? Look at him now, piddling round here, cadging off his family – what way is that for a grown man to carry on? Don't tell me you want to spend another umpteen years scraping from hand to mouth – and Bill was swimming in money when you wed him, which is more than you can say for yon lad.' She snorted. 'Do you wonder I don't want to go dishing out thousands of pounds just for you to waste it on a no-hoper like that?'

'No-hoper?' choked Lorette, squinting tearfully over her shoulder.

'You should hear his sister on the subject.' As Lily leaned forward, her tone softened again. 'I've got your money for you, love. There's a big fat cheque tucked safely away in my fancies drawer, right this very minute.'

Lorette caught her breath. And if a cock crowed over in Bella's poultry yard, she didn't give it a thought. Day was breaking outside, what else would the blinking cockerels be doing? 'Twenty thousand pounds?' she whispered tearfully. 'Honest?'

Teddy, frozen in her corner of the window seat, was not quite awake, drifting still in a tangle of dreams – wretched, horrible dreams. Not sure where she was, bewildered by the black misery which seemed to be engulfing her, she thought the murmured voices must belong in that melting dream world.

'You can't mean – you're finishing it? Us?'

With a convulsive twitch, she opened her eyes. She registered pale shards of light in the sky outside, aching numbness in her shoulder where it was slumped against the window frame, and realized that the whispering was real, inside this room, on the other side of the thick curtains.

'I really like you and all.' The voice was Lorette's, surely, and she sounded to be in tears. Only – Teddy blinked bemusedly – she also sounded, in some strange way, to be play-acting. 'Really, really like you, but if he ever found out . . .'

'Once you're properly divorced, though?'

'Won't make any difference to – to *him*. It's no good, Jeremy, we can't be together.' Only now she wasn't play-acting. The unhappiness – despair – in her voice was heart-wrenchingly authentic. 'I'm sorry, but I just *can't*. You don't understand. I've got too much to lose.'

This isn't happening, thought Teddy, dashing a hand over her face, I'm still dreaming. In a moment, I'll wake up properly.

'But, darling—'

'Mum says if I go home now she'll – she won't tell Bill. She's going to get one of my brothers to run me back. Look, I can't keep her waiting, she's out there on the landing.'

Teddy was already beating aside the heavy brocade, but emerged to find the room empty. On cramped limbs, she lunged across to the door, telling herself she must have misunderstood or imagined what she'd heard. But there on the landing stood Jeremy, ashen-faced, while Lily was guiding her tearful daughter to the stairs.

'Lorette!' she called imperatively, and then faltered. She had been about to demand what the girl meant by spouting such tripe, but, in a sickening rush of apprehension, she was no longer sure she wanted an answer. She was remembering Bella hooting at the very idea of her and Bill – her and Bill *bonking* as she'd sniggeringly put it – insisting he was happily married, deliriously happy . . . But that was rubbish, and Bella had been drunk, out of her tiny mind. Only there was the image of Bill himself, shuddering, yes *shuddering* away when she'd blurted out her proposal – hell, that seemed like a lifetime ago. It *was* a lifetime ago, before . . . Before what? Before tonight, of course, when they'd careered along this very landing, her arms locked round his neck, him panting curses as he tripped over his skirts, when they'd collapsed breathlessly, joyously behind the slammed bedroom door and then . . . A quick bonk – an even quicker exit? 'No,' she whispered, feeling her legs buckle, 'no, it wasn't like that.'

She didn't realize Lily was addressing her until she felt herself being hustled to one side, with the older woman trilling something about Charlie, that she knew Teddy had been looking for him.

'What?' she murmured. 'Lily, what's the matter?' Because

Lily wasn't talking naturally either. The feeling of being trapped in the remnant of a bad dream intensified, where nothing made sense. And then she heard a rapid whisper in her ear.

'All that stuff I told you, about your dad and me, let's keep it as our little secret, eh?'

'Sorry?'

'These things happen, and what no one knows can't harm them, can it?' After which Lily immediately upped her pitch again to unnervingly artificial brightness. 'Sir Charles, yes, don't you remember asking me about him? Only you went tearing off that fast I never got a chance to tell you I'd seen him sneaking into his gunroom, and I'll lay you ten to one he's there still, snoring his little head off. I certainly haven't seen him round the place since.'

'Gunroom?' echoed Teddy stupidly. She was wondering, momentarily, why she had ever wanted to find Charlie at all, then remembered, in a fresh surge of bewilderment and hurt, exactly why. 'Oh yes. I should've thought of that, Pa's hidey-hole.' Which was all the gunroom could be described as, barely more than a cupboard. Charlie couldn't have spirited Bill there, could he? 'I suppose I should go and look.'

Lily eyed her more keenly, and the synthetic laughter softened into concern. 'You look done-in, chuck. Shall I go and check for you?'

'Mum,' hissed her daughter, avoiding Jeremy's lovelorn gaze. 'You want to get me home, remember? We've got to find Brian or Colin. Anyway, Sir Charles isn't here. I saw him go out with his gun ages ago.'

Her mother barely glanced at her. 'Don't talk soft.'

'I *did*, hours back. I looked out of the window when I come upstairs, and he was down on the lawn with a gun over his shoulder.'

'You're dreaming. What'd he want with a gun in the middle of a bloody party?'

That was when, for Teddy, the bad dream began to merge into a far more nightmarish reality. 'No,' she breathed, 'no, surely . . .'

'I'm telling you it was him,' continued Lorette defiantly. 'You can't exactly mistake him in that goose outfit, can you?'

'Bill? Has anyone seen *Bill*?'

'Bill?' squawked Jeremy and Lorette in dismayed concert.

But no sooner had Teddy uttered the name than she realized, with a sick sense of dread, that it was not Bill she need fear for. 'Charlie?' she whispered tremulously. No one heard. They were too busy arguing as she stood there, frozen, imagining Charlie charging up to his own bedroom, with Ma's wicked stories ringing in his ears . . .

'Course Bill's not here,' Lily was snorting, 'I've been searching the bloody house top to bottom all night, haven't I?'

He'd found the room deserted, just as she had, the bed ripe and rumpled from love-making, the sheets probably still warm . . . She grabbed Jeremy's arm. 'We've got to find Charlie.'

'Why?' He shook her off, his eyes not so much as wavering from Lorette. 'You know Big Bro, never happy unless he's shoving lead up some poor animal's backside.'

'No,' she stammered, 'no, not this time, I don't think so . . .' Only the terrifying thing was she didn't *think*, she knew. At this moment she knew exactly what might have driven Charlie to his gunroom, driven him to – with a shudder, she blocked out the picture. She mustn't assume the worst, mustn't assume anything. Most of all, she mustn't panic. Unforgivable. She locked her shivering hands together and forced herself to draw a long slow breath. Dear God, if ever in her prosaic, unimaginative life she had needed to be calm, practical, *organized*, that time was now.

'On second thoughts, Jeremy, you can go and find Bella.' She was distantly surprised at the composure in her voice. 'Don't argue, do it. Tell her to remember what I said about—' Remembering the presence of Lorette and her mother, she caught herself up, struggling for an innocuous form of words. 'About Ma barging into her bedroom earlier. Have you got that? And . . .' Again she had to stop and think. 'Yes, you'd better tell her Charlie's gone out with a gun. She needs to know.' She spun round on Lorette. 'Where was he headed?'

'Who?'

Lily, evidently scenting trouble, snapped: 'Sir Charles, who d'you think? Where were he going when you saw him?'

The girl shrugged. 'Side lawn – towards the woods, I suppose.'

'Woods. Home Wood, yes.' Somehow, Teddy managed a sketch of a smile. 'I'm probably making a fuss over nothing, but he was quite drunk. And, you know, firearms and so forth. Could have tripped up, goodness knows what, clumsy ape. So, Lily, would you mind going for a quick scout round the house? I'll make a start on the grounds.'

It didn't take her long. With heart thudding, chest heaving and blood roaring in her ears, Teddy pounded along the path through the wood, crested the first shallow rise – and saw him at once. A great, fat, muddy white bird was sprawled on the bank of the stream, with an empty whisky bottle and a glinting black shotgun beside him.

Chapter Thirty-Five

A raw animal howl ripped across the still air. Teddy didn't even know it came from her own throat. Blundering down the slope, she sprawled headlong over a tangle of briars, and crawled the last few yards to clasp his limp hand between hers.

'Charlie, I'm sorry, so sorry.' She clutched his fingers against her cheek, mumbling kisses into his wrist, rocking jerkily to and fro. 'Oh, my poor boy. I never knew. Never understood.'

His face was turned away from her, half buried in the neck of his absurd, undignified costume. Lowering the hand tenderly back to his chest, she leaned forward to tuck the fabric away from his features. There was no blood. Just a smear of mud across his forehead, and he looked so peaceful, he could almost have been sleeping. She supposed, if he'd put the barrels inside his mouth . . . A retching wail of horror convulsed her; she crumpled forward – and felt something nudge her knee. She gasped. Stared. His poor lifeless hand had flopped down, that was all – wasn't it? He couldn't possibly be alive, not after . . .

Dear God, one read wild stories about people surviving such things, and here she was, blubbing like a fool while time and maybe even lifeblood ebbed away. Without hesitation she thrust her hand inside the neck of his costume and pushed round to the back of his skull. It was damp – *wet* – still warm, but she could find no gaping wound, no injury at all. She flung herself forward, cheek pressed to his face, listening, praying, for a breath.

A lusty, popping snore reverberated into her ear.

'Charlie?' She seized his shoulders, jolted him half upright. '*Charlie?*'

One bleary eye opened. 'Ted?'

She got as far as a half-cough of incredulous laughter before tears erupted with the force of a tidal wave. Letting him slump back to the grass, she collapsed across him, racked with sobs. 'So – awful. Thought – you were dead. Saw the gun, and I thought you'd—'

'I did.'

'No. No, you mustn't say it.'

'Can't even get that right, can I? Too stupid to shoot myself.'

Face buried in his shoulder, she couldn't speak, just beat her fists feebly against his chest.

'Tried to wedge the bugger between my knees, but it kept slipping. *Hergh*, drunk, of course. And the bloody costume got in the way.' A tear squeezed out of his eye. 'Sorry, wicked thing to do. Don't tell me off.' Teddy gasping for words, could only shake her head passionately against his shoulder. 'Coward's way out – children, everybody. But when Ma told me—'

'No,' she choked, 'it's not true.'

'I didn't believe her either. Told her so, but I went up to the room. Found this by the bed.' His hand flapped around in the nearby grass, and he held up a large black shoe. 'Not mine.'

'*Bill's*'.

He recoiled as though she had hit him. 'I know who the bastard is.'

'He was with *me*.' She managed to hoist herself up on one elbow. 'Me, not Bella. When our bloody mother walked in, I was in your bed with Bill and I was so – so happy.' She snatched the shoe from him, face crumpling afresh. 'Sorry, doesn't matter now, nothing matters, 'cept you being alive.' But, mightily though she strove, she was as helpless as a piece of driftwood on a roaring floodtide of misery. 'Oh Charlie,' she wept. 'You know – you *know* what it feels like. What'm I going to do?'

'A gun?' echoed Bella drunkenly, and clutched her brother-in-law's arm for support. 'Don't be silly.'

'That's what Ted said.' They were in the hall, and Jeremy,

who frankly felt he had wasted more than enough time already in tracking down his sister-in-law, saw Lorette totter past the open front doors, calling to her mother. He hastily shook himself free. 'Gotta go. Shit, no, hang on. You're to remember what Teddy told you before. Don't ask me, something about Ma charging into your room. Make any sense?'

'But it was a mistake.' Bella swept the hair out of her flushed face and stumbled after him. 'It wasn't me the old witch found, it was her, Teddy said. Her in my bed with Bill.'

Jeremy was already at the door, but this made him wheel round. 'Ted with that thug? Christ, you really must be pissed.'

'But if Charlie thought . . .' All at once, she lurched forward, breaking into a run. 'Oh no – *no!*'

'*Hergh*, maybe all for the best, eh?'

As the sun inched blindingly over the horizon, brother and sister were seated side by side on the grass, Sir Charles's arm tight round Teddy's shoulders. He gave her a bracing squeeze.

She glanced round dully. 'What's for the best?'

'Chap's a bit of a dead loss, let's face it. Told me so himself. Hasn't earned a bean in years.'

'So?'

Her brother blinked. '*Hergh*, couldn't support you.'

'Do you think I care?' She snorted. 'I wouldn't give a damn if he never earned a penny piece the rest of his life.' Her voice was rising. 'I'd keep him, work my fingers to the bone, anything, crawl over broken glass on my hands and knees, *happily*, if only—'

A cock pheasant, startled by the tirade, exploded indignantly out of the undergrowth.

'Don't you see?' she swept on passionately, cradling the shoe tight to her bosom, 'for the first time in my pig-ignorant, pig-headed life I know what it feels like, I understand how you felt, why you didn't think you could go on living. I *love* him, Charlie. I love him so much, I wouldn't mind if you took your gun now and put me down like a sick dog, because he obviously – he obviously doesn't . . .' Tears were crowding into her throat again. 'I mean, one minute, there we were making love, and everything was bliss and I thought, I just somehow took it for granted . . . Only he's gone. Vanished, and . . . Oh, I'm sorry. Ignore me. Be all right in a minute.'

She slumped forward, weeping softly into her cupped hands. For a time her brother just sat beside her, staring down at the beck as it danced and chuckled heedlessly over the pebbles.

'Heigh-ho,' he breathed. 'Heigh-jolly-old-ho.' With a final comforting buffet to her shoulders, he began lumbering to his feet.

'Not yet,' she mumbled. 'I'll come, very soon. Just need to pull myself together.'

'Don't worry, Sis. You sob your little heart out.'

Dimly she became aware he was groping around the grass, picking up his gun, cracking it open, slotting in fresh cartridges.

'Charlie? Charlie, what are you doing?'

'*Hergh*, just getting the kit in order.'

'But—'

'Ready to march? Or shall I advance and you follow up the rear?'

Teddy squinted up at her brother. Never mind the ungainly costume, the wrinkled yellow legs, or the comical bird's head now dangling forlornly down his back, standing before her, with soldierly erectness, was Major Sir Charles Dunstan, Bart. His gun was hoisted over his shoulder at an angle precise enough to warm the heart of any drill sergeant. Such chin as he possessed was resolutely squared. His eyes, fixed on the distant horizon, shone with a light strongly suggestive of death or glory, and it does not seem too fanciful to suppose that in his ears was sounding the rousing toot of the old regimental bugle.

'Going to find this bugger for you, Sis,' he growled. 'Going to find the bugger and make him grovel at your bloody feet.'

'I don't get it,' said Jeremy bemusedly. 'I mean, she's pissed for sure, but Bella swears your husband's screwing my sister.'

Lorette, suspecting she might be pushing her luck by claiming Bill combined ruthless womanizing with murderous jealousy, scanned the gardens for a rescuer. But mothers were never there when you needed them. 'What's that noise?' she cried, snatching at any diversion. 'Sounds like a helicopter.'

'Forget about Bill,' panted Teddy, cantering to keep abreast. 'It's Bella you should be worrying about, showing her you can stand up to Ma.'

'Taking advantage of you. Wham, bam, *hergh*, I'll give him bloody thank you, ma'am.'

'Anyway, I don't know where he's gone.'

'I'll find the blighter. Can't get far on one shoe.'

'And it's not his fault, not if he doesn't love me. I know that now. Like catching flu. You can't choose.'

'*Hergh*, that a chopper?'

'Besides, you can't seriously – I mean, the gun. You wouldn't . . . ?'

'It is. A damn great helicopter. Hell does it think it's playing at?'

'Look,' cried Teddy desperately. 'Far end of the lawn, turning this way, Bella. Has she seen us?' She stuck two fingers in her mouth and let out a shrill whistle. 'What's going on down there?'

A crowd was amassing. Harold, the head gardener, with what appeared to be a mobile phone clamped to one ear, was frantically windmilling with the other arm, ushering people off the grass.

'Bloody thing's circling, as if it's planning to land.'

'She's coming, good. Who's that behind her?' Teddy hurried forward, only to stop short with a cry of disgust. 'Hell's teeth, I thought I'd packed her off to bed hours ago.'

Beyond Bella, silken dressing gown streaming in the downdraught, a small but indomitable figure had determinedly thrust Harold aside and was striding across the lawn, gesticulating up at the sky as, with an ear-splitting roar, the helicopter see-sawed gently down to squat on the dewy grass.

'Charlie?' bellowed his wife, staggering to a breathless halt in front of them. His reply was drowned in the commotion but he stretched out a hand. Bella did not take it, however. She was staring in wide-eyed horror at the gun over his shoulder.

Meanwhile, a voice behind her was already slicing through the dwindling engine roar as the helicopter blades circled to rest.

'I *said*, who gave permission for that vulgar contraption to land on my lawn?'

Bella started. 'Her lawn?' she echoed dazedly. '*Her* lawn?' Wheeling round, bosom swelling, she seized her husband's arm and began dragging him forward. '*I* gave permission for that helicopter to land,' she yelled furiously. 'On *my* lawn.'

'Charles?' Her ladyship shielded her eyes against the sun. 'Thank goodness you're here. Go and tell them to take it away at once. No one is to disembark.'

'Charlie,' snarled Bella, steel-eyed, 'come with me to welcome our guest.'

Sir Charles looked helplessly from one outraged face to the other, a rabbit between two cobras, both with tails a-rattle. 'But – who is it?'

Mr Michael Splitz, for this could only be he, framed in the doorway of the Sikorsky, proves to be short and balding as per our expectations, but not entirely disagreeable to the eye. His face was handsomely bronzed, his jawline expensively tightened, and his figure, as he meticulously fastened one button of a snazzy pale pink tuxedo preparatory to alighting, a positive advertisement for the benefits of mango-consumption. His thoughtful expression, however, as he surveyed the motley crowd assembling below, was perhaps suggestive of a man who, having dispatched a minion to research this quaint old British theatrical tradition, was only now recalling the alternative definition proffered by his conscientious employee.

'Pantomime,' he mused to himself. 'Also denotes a confused or farcical situation, huh?' Because, as he leaned out to enquire whether he had the pleasure of addressing Lady Dunstan, two glaring viragos swept forward, one in bedraggled houri garb, the other in her négligé, both raucously claiming to be the female in question, while behind them a muddy goose with a shotgun under its wing vainly flapped away assorted transvestites, animal impersonators, fairies, medieval knights, sheiks, a pot-bellied monk . . .

'Fellini on fucking ice,' he hissed through teeth clenched in a grin forced on him by the popping of a flashgun stage right. 'OK, son, you got your shots, I'm coming down.' No sooner had he carefully placed one patent-leathered toe on the helicopter steps, however, than a piercing shriek nearly caused him to plummet headlong. It seemed to emanate from a diminutive broad he had not even noticed until now, so unremarkable were her homely jeans and sweatshirt amid this exotic throng. What had apparently excited her was the arrival of a milk cart – yes, an ordinary, workaday dairy van – rattling and clattering up the drive. And when she hurtled away towards it, screaming like a banshee, first the gun-toting goose, then the ancient négligé and Miss Eastern Promise, then just about everybody else, took off after her. By the time he reached the grass with politely outstretched hand there remained only the spotty youth with the Nikon round his neck to shake it.

'Don't tell me,' drawled Mr Splitz, never one to miss a chance of demonstrating his familiarity with the vernacular, 'the Milky Bar Kid is here?'

'Florence, Ferdy!' yells Teddy, her tear-stained features now radiant with hope, because what had inspired her shriek a moment ago was the sight of two small faces pressed to the windscreen of the float, and a wild and woolly tail flailing out of the side window. 'How could I have been such an idiot?' she cries exultantly, as she pounds up to the passenger door. 'Of course he had to dash off home because of you two, didn't he? So where is Daddy? Round the back?'

But the reptilian hiss which emanates from the rear of the vehicle as it squeaks to a halt does not sound like Bill.

'That, my treasure, is what we all want to know.' Resplendent still in evening dress, Hari Stakinos uncoils himself from his undignified perch amid the milk crates. With immense hauteur, he stalks round to thank the chuckling driver for the ride, sorry only that he cannot express his gratitude in more concrete terms, but then, had he been carrying money when he so innocently left home last night, he would have been able to avail himself of a more conventional form of transportation long since.

The light is fading pitifully from Teddy's face. 'Have you seen him?' she falters. 'Bill, I mean?'

He swings round on her. 'Not since the bastard hi-jacked my car,' he snarls, 'and left me with two juvenile delinquents and the Hound of the frigging Baskervilles. More to the point, have *you* seen the little skunk?' Fortunately, at that moment, the sight of the disembarking helicopter passenger distracts him, because a violent quivering in Teddy's chin suggests she is unlikely to be capable of an answer. 'So the Queen of bloody Sheba's finally arrived, has she?' he mutters, and raises his voice as he waves to the pink-tuxedoed figure. 'Hi there, Michael, treasure. Come on over, there's someone I'm *dying* for you to meet.' At which his gaze whips back to Teddy – to her grass-stained jeans and sagging sweatshirt, her tear-swollen face, the muddy shoe she is clutching to her bosom – and he shuts his eyes in a grimace of exquisite anguish. 'Why do I bother?' The eyes snap open again. 'But what is written, is written. Come, Theodora.'

If she hears at all, Theodora pays no heed. This fresh disappointment has seemingly turned her to stone. Lost in misery, she is as oblivious of the people clustering round her as is a rock of the winds and waves. Charlie is the first to arrive, pursued by his furious wife and mother. Lily, clucking, hastens to gather the twins to her side. Lorette glances back at the helicopter with undisguised envy, while her unhappy swain has eyes only for her. As the elder of her brothers assures a solicitous Friar Tuck that the brisk walk has not in the least exacerbated his nasal injuries, the younger announces to other assorted revellers who, sheep-like, have trundled along with the flow, that a Sikorsky consumes as much fuel in an hour as seventy-five Ford Fiestas. This fascinating snippet of wisdom bypasses Teddy. As for Mr Michael Splitz, it seems certain, much to Hari's palpable frustration, she has forgotten his very existence.

'Hari, don't you look just great?' cries the great producer, nimbly side-stepping the silver-haired dame in the nightdress who has, for some unaccountable reason, hopped in front of him. 'Looks like I've missed one helluva party, and I'm sorry, but the goddam movie goes into production in ten days—'

'Is that your machine disfiguring my lawn, you stupid man?'

'Nanna, Teddy's got a shoe.'

'That lawn was laid by my late husband's ancestors in the year of Waterloo.'

'—and the little jerk we had lined up to play him as a kid snuck off yesterday and signed with Fox, can you believe it?' Unaccustomed as he is to heeding any voice but his own, Mr Splitz nevertheless feels obliged to turn. 'Beg pardon, ma'am?'

'Why has she got a shoe?'

'I said—'

'Charlie, stop her, this is *our* lawn – *our* house.'

'Only I believe my people contacted yours about landing, and I surely understood—' But here, mysteriously, Mr Splitz breaks off, and his mouth opens to dimensions endangering several thousand dollars' worth of plastic surgery. 'My Gaaard, am I hallucinating?' The question, it seems, is not entirely rhetorical, but he is unlikely to get an intelligent answer in this scrum, even his friend Hari being too busy digging an unresponsive Teddy in the ribs to attend. He has to resort to grabbing the nearest arm, which happens to belong to the elder Lady Dunstan. 'The boy over there, who is he?'

Jeremy half turns, with no interest. The sunlight falls full on his handsome, wretched features, 'Sorry?'

'Hugo Magulvey,' moans Michael Splitz as one in a delirium. He casts aside the dowager's arm and paces forward. 'The young Hugo to the life. This is *incredible*.'

The shock, it seems, is not his alone. Lady Dunstan, blenching, presses a thin hand to her mouth to stifle a cry, although, in the general hubbub, no one is likely to have heard. No one, that is, except Lily Rowbotham, whose eyes widen into saucers as they shift across to Jeremy. He, however, unaware that Fate is approaching in a pink tuxedo, is shaking his sister by the shoulder. 'Ted, is it true? What Bella said about you and that gorilla?'

This, interestingly enough, proves to be the talisman which at last brings the statue to life. 'Gorilla?' Teddy's bosom and voice swell. '*Gorilla?*' she repeats, in outrage so strident other conversations falter.

'Teddy,' pipes up Ferdinand, smartly profiting from the lull and his grandmother's suddenly slackened grasp, 'why've you got that shoe?'

For perhaps the only time in her life, albeit unintentionally, Teddy rises to the drama of the moment. She holds aloft the muddy piece of footgear. 'Because I love the man who owns it,' she proclaims into the sudden, shocked silence, baring her heart, her soul, her entire despondent essence to the world without a second's hesitation, 'and I was foolish enough to think I was going to marry him.'

Even Michael Splitz is temporarily sidetracked, narrowing his eyes as though assessing such a self-evidently pivotal moment for the right camera angle. And before anyone else can utter a sound, there drifts faintly across the hushed morning air the sound of singing – wince-inducingly tuneless singing, as it happens, although the melody is just about recognizable as that popular fifties ballad 'Mona Lisa'. As the well-briefed Mr Splitz could doubtless inform you, one of the eccentricities of pantomime is that productions rarely feature a decent original score, tending instead to cannibalize and adapt music from an eclectic variety of sources. True to form, the lyrics of this particular serenade now celebrate the enigmatic charms of one Theodora – an alternative which does at least scan. Up to a point. The spaniel stiffens, pricks up her ears.

'Bill?' chokes Teddy, disbelievingly.

'Theodora, Theodora, do you love me?'

'Yuck-yuck-yuck,' groans Ferdinand, clutching his sister and pretending to be sick. 'Dad's *singing.*'

'Were you sent to guide me by the Lord above?'

'He's here?' squeaks Jeremy to Lorette.

'Bill?' cries Teddy, more loudly now, looking round desperately.

'Action stations,' grunts Sir Charles, shaking off his wife's hand and hitching up his gun. 'Sounds to me the bugger's holed-up in the attic.'

'BILL!' roars Teddy, and takes to her heels. With the entire company in hot pursuit.

The final flight of stairs at Langley Hall was never designed to accommodate a stampede. The dog plunging across her path, which gave her panting elder brother the chance to grab a fistful of her sweatshirt, delayed even Teddy.

'Let me *go*!' she snarled, raining blows to no avail on his foam-padded belly, as the slower members of the party clustered up behind.

'Major budget Hollywood biopic, into production twenny-ninth – you have an agent?'

'Charles, tell this vulgar little man to get out of my house at once.'

'Charlie, he's our guest, even if I don't know who he is—'

'Ow!' roared Sir Charles, as his sister sunk her teeth into the hand gripping her sweatshirt and, with one triumphant bound, was free.

'Out of my way!' she yelled, shoving bodies aside. Still clutching the shoe, she scrambled up the last couple of stairs, plunged along the corridor to the small attic door, flung it wide, and staggered to a halt, open-mouthed.

Happily, the photographer arrived just in time to capture the moment for posterity.

Epilogue

One Year Later

You probably don't remember the story.

At least, Teddy devoutly hopes you do not, although, that being a typically slack summer week for news, the photograph was featured in a wide range of papers amid non-sightings of Nessie and further exploits of the Beast of Bodmin. Indeed, one can only admire the enterprise of the fledgling snapper from *Ridings Life* magazine, who did not merely point his camera, but had the wit to suspect there might be a wider market for this particular shot – as indeed there was, at a profit which enabled him to splash out on a serious telephoto lens and a candle-lit dinner for two with leggy Samantha from Advertising.

'TEDDY BARES ALL NOW', was a typical tabloid caption, over a text amounting to little more than a rib-tickling reminder of Miss Dunstan's earlier scantily-clad moment of stardom. The broadsheets, naturally, felt obliged to justify their publication of full frontal posh totty with references to art and suchlike. One or two even managed correctly to identify the artist – for it was, of course, Bill Smith who was responsible for a naked Teddy once again being catapulted into the public eye, and was thereby doubtless also responsible for many an elderly gent choking on his cornflakes.

Not that this is to suggest it was all Bill's *fault*. As he has been protesting ever since, he was a mere tool in the hands of Fate. And if Teddy doesn't believe him, she should bloody well ask Mr Stakinos. What was written, was written.

320

Just for the record, however, Bill would like you to appreciate that when he crept out of the master bedroom at Langley
Hall with the clock striking twelve and a sodden crinoline
clutched around his nether regions, he had but one simple and
perfectly sensible object in mind: to reclaim the garments he'd
left in the attic the previous night. On reaching the former
ping-pong room, however, he had found those garments gone,
tidied away, he soon deduced, by the fastidious Miss Dunstan.
Fortunately, she had only tucked them into one of the many
boxes neatly ranked rounds the walls. By the time he found the
correct box, however, Bill had gear scrambled all over the floor,
a loose brush in his hand and suddenly – this was, anyway, as he
described it – that brush began to twitch. More than twitch, it
quivered, surged with life, begged, implored, *demanded* to be
put to use. And here was a studio, canvas, easel, every last paint
tube he had ever possessed. No model, perhaps, but if ever an
image had been etched on his brain, imprinted through his very
being . . . He didn't consider what he was doing, just got on
with the job, as natural as breathing.

Thus proving, as he was later generously to admit – if rather
fruitlessly at the time – that the Duchess had been right all along.
It was just like riding a bike. And oh how he pedalled through
that short summer's night. A man possessed, he gave no thought
to the passage of time, to Hari Stakinos, even to his children –
but for Teddy to claim, as she did at ear-splitting length, that he
spared no thought for her either, is a gross calumny. As far as he
was concerned, she was there in the room with him, imbuing
his heart and soul, inspiring his every brushstroke. Naturally it
never crossed his mind that she might actually be wandering
around downstairs like a tearful little ghost.

Within a few frantic hours, then, our heroine was immor-
talized arising from the lily pond, rather in the fashion of Venus
from the waves – but what a lily pond, what a Venus. The
waters erupted with blooms of tropical exuberance under a
sky riotous with glittering, shattering pyrotechnics. It cannot
be denied that Bill allowed himself a certain artistic licence
here, because the blue touch paper on Charlie's fireworks had
not even begun to smoulder when Teddy emerged from the
pond – but who are we to quibble? What Teddy did rather

more than quibble about was the artistic licence he had also taken – 'diabolical bloody liberty' were her exact words – in stripping her person of every last shred of clothing, leaving her not so much as a blush-sparing frond of pondweed. On top of which indignity, he chose to depict her clasping a sword in a distinctly lascivious fashion. Under such circumstances, you may find it hard to believe (as Teddy certainly did) that the primary feature of the painting to strike anyone looking at it was her smile. But that smile was a distillation of purest bliss, a smile which out-dazzled every firework in the sky, a smile to warm the cockles of the cockliest heart – and we must all be accounted the poorer for being unable to bask in its glow in some public collection, the work having passed at once into private ownership. Plenty more, as the artist cheerfully said at the time, where that one came from.

Happily, he was right; there have been plenty more. A full calendar year has elapsed since Bella's famous birthday party, and today Langley Hall is again *en fête* with a family celebration – albeit on a smaller scale. Once more, however, the splendid salons ring with happy chatter and clinking glasses, which are hurriedly being refilled as the grandfather clock tolls noon, because this is the appointed hour for the drinking of toasts. And to whom or what, you may wonder, are we raising our glasses?

It should be stated at once that, if you are preparing to drink the health of Mr and Mrs Bill Smith, you are to be disappointed. Miss Theodora Dunstan remains a spinster of the parish, and at this moment is circulating one of the bottles of bubbly – the real thing, please note, no label-concealing cloths round these bottles – while keeping a beady eye on waitresses and brothers. She is, in other words, carrying on much as ever. Perhaps this is because today's gathering marks the christening of a bouncing, blossoming three-month-old infant, to whom Teddy – after such mighty time and effort neither bride nor mother herself – stands merely as Godmama. Again.

'Brought a bit of a lump to the old throat,' remarks Bill Smith, squeezing past her with a packet of cigarettes poorly concealed in one hand while, with the other, he niftily relieves her of the champagne bottle, 'seeing you at the font with the sprog. Never mind, next time, eh?'

'Not bloody likely,' she retorts. 'And don't even think of sneaking out before the toasts, you loathsome little shirker. Charlie's already up on his hind legs.'

'You haven't got a glass, babe.'

'No,' says Teddy, sounding all at once strangely hesitant. 'No. Don't worry, I'll – find myself one.'

'*Hergh*, my wife and I,' begins Sir Charles Dunstan, which provokes the traditional hoots and whistles, no one seeming to care that this is not, in fact, a wedding, 'would like to welcome you to our home on this, um, happy day . . .'

Behind him, Bella is semaphoring to Bill that if he's going out for a sly ciggy after the toasts, she's coming too. She has already spent most of this past year in virtuous nicotine-deprivation, and now Charlie has reacquired the knack of the reproductive mechanics, he's talking about trying for a round half-dozen. Bella thinks five children are quite enough, thank you very much. Pregnancy at forty was no joke, her ankles were elephantine – and quite frankly she doesn't know how to cope with her dangerously rejuvenated husband. Crumbling Mogadon into his cocoa has crossed her mind.

'Marvellous to have, *hergh*, the whole tribe gathered again here, back from our various globe-trottings . . .'

Globe-trotting, for Charlie and Bella, was a four-week cruise round the Aegean last summer, by way of second honeymoon, marred only by Bella's beastly seasickness, which turned out not to be seasickness at all. Other family members, however, have ventured further afield.

The elder Lady Dunstan, standing by the window, averting her eyes from the plastic playpen adorning an Aubusson rug, has spent the past twelve months on an extended tour of friends and family connections in the Far East. She had long contemplated such a holiday, it transpires, although one might be forgiven for wondering why she only chose to disclose those plans at Bella's birthday party last year, after a brief, whispered conversation with Lily Rowbotham.

Bella, naturally, ascribed all credit for her mother-in-law's departure to her husband's stammered declaration at the time that he would listen to no more of Ma's mischievous tittle-tattle and that he would, moreover, have her remember she was no longer chatelaine of this establishment.

'My hero,' Bella had cried, flinging herself into his arms. She murmurs something of the sort now, as Charlie pays blushing tribute to his beautiful wife, more precious to him than . . .

But Sir Charles cannot call to mind exactly what Bella is more precious than – besides, this sort of stuff is going it rather for an Englishman, so he clears his throat and hurries on to welcome home his younger brother, on a fleeting visit from the other side of – of the pond, is that the expression?

'Fearfully jolly to have a film star adding lustre to the old name. And, of course, even jollier to welcome dear little Lorette, the newest Mrs Dunstan.'

The pair of them certainly add lustre to the room, making everyone else look undercooked and over-nourished. It is the turn of Lily's heart to overflow, seeing Theo's daughter, here in his house, part of the Dunstan family in the end. Not that the world will ever know Lorette belongs here in her own right. As Lily pointed out a year ago, to a person standing not a million miles away now, these things happen, and, as that person and she have long since agreed, there's no harm to anyone provided folks've got the sense to keep their mouths shut. She nods cheerily at Lady Dunstan, who does not appear to see her.

Lily is looking notably glamorous, not least because of the sapphire and diamond flowers twinkling in her ears. Hanging on to the earrings had been Bill's idea, the big softy, since the necklace alone fetched enough to square up Lorette, and she wore them for the first time at her daughter's Beverly Hills wedding earlier this year. Glorious colour photographs of the star-studded event, courtesy of *Hello!* magazine, are framed on every available surface in her lounge at Meadows Close. Lorette, naturally, looks heart-stoppingly beautiful in every shot. Lily just wishes she could be confident this is the last of her daughter's weddings she will be called upon to attend.

'And who knows?' Sir Charles harrumphs loudly, looking significantly in a certain direction. 'We may have another marriage to celebrate in our family before too long . . .'

Is there a minatory note in his voice? Does Charlie still suspect Bill Smith of leading his sister a dance? If so, he is quite wrong. Teddy is fed up to the back teeth with Bill pestering her to do the decent thing and make an honest man of him. As she points out, with *four* businesses to run – her shop, the catering, the gallery, and the sole agency for his work – she cannot possibly find time to organize a wedding. God understands she will be getting round to it as soon as she has a moment. Anyway, his earthly ambassador in Langley-le-Moor is too busy playing trains to conduct marriages, now that the Rowbotham brothers have installed their set in two rooms of his vast and underused vicarage.

'No romance, that's your trouble,' mutters Bill austerely. 'If not for my sake, you might spare a thought for the brats. Children like to feel secure.'

'Phooey,' she retorts, scooping Ferdy into her arms to silence him, and sharing a conspiratorial wink with Florence. She has become quite used to people discerning a likeness between herself and her unlegitimized stepdaughter.

'Poor child,' she is wont to say. 'Still, plenty of time to grow out it.'

Subscribing wholeheartedly to the Lily Rowbotham school of thought, she is equally blasé in discussing her brother's remarkably lifelike portrayal of the late Hugo Magulvey, agreeing that it's amazing what cinematic make-up artists can do. She has not, however, discouraged him from re-growing his hair.

As for children of her own, she just wishes Bill and everyone else would shut up on the subject. Once his big exhibition is out of the way, and the new bathroom installed – oh, and the abattoir reroofed if she can ever turf him out of there for long enough – then, and only then, might she give the matter serious consideration. That is why, as staunch a believer as ever in the efficacy of mind over matter, she is determinedly ignoring her sudden aversion to alcohol and the lurch of nausea provoked by so much as one whiff of a smoked salmon sandwich . . .

'And there's nothing like, *hergh*, a baby to make one feel young again,' asserts Sir Charles Dunstan, gazing down at his new daughter with dewy pride. However, as he says, he'll stop rabbiting now, because if everyone would care to raise their glasses, it's time to welcome into the world little Alice Charlotte, the apple of his eye. *Hergh*, not quite sure who she looks like – general laugh – maybe the milkman, but can we all drink her health?

A camera clicks. Hari Stakinos, stylish as ever in pale blue linen, is behind the lens. Having relinquished the lease on Mill House in time for Lady Dunstan's return, he is staying for the weekend with his dear friends Bill and Teddy – and now points the camera in her direction with a disconcertingly wise squint in the direction of her midriff. Hari has long since staked a claim to stand as godparent to their first child, since he naturally sees himself as being solely and personally responsible for their union. Did he not foresee this happy outcome? Was it not prefigured in his vision? *Oh, yes it was*. Because when that fateful flash camera exploded a year ago, as the crowd pressed into the attic room, and a variety of cries went up, not least from our heroine, one strident American voice roared:

'How much?'

There might have been an uproar reminiscent of a rugby club on a Saturday night, but Mr Michael Splitz had not survived forty years in the clamorous babel of Hollywood without learning to make himself heard.

'Have it,' the reckless artist cried.

'For fifteen thousand, no VAT, that's pounds not dollars,' said Teddy smartly, and the new gallery was launched in two scribbles of a pen. The ink on the cheque was dry before the painting.

And since, as we have been told, Hari's visions never lie, we can be pretty safe in assuming the work now hangs over the pink marble mantelpiece of the producer's Californian mansion. What the latest Mrs Splitz feels about her husband's taste in voluptuous nudes is not recorded.

Nor, for that matter, have we set on record precisely what Miss Theodora Dunstan felt when first she clapped eyes on her portrait. To do so, we must abandon the christening, the champagne, the merriment – the whole happily-ever-after scenario – and return, finally, to that moment of truth when she charged into the attic room to find the artist pensively cleaning a brush, and herself revealed in unclothed splendour.

Was she thrilled? Moved beyond words by having inspired such mighty creative endeavour? Not quite.

'*FUCK ME!*' she bellowed.

And this was not an invitation, notwithstanding the fact that she was flinging herself at the artist at the time, this was quite definitely her spontaneous critical appraisal of his work. Bill Smith, it may be remembered, has claimed before now that enthusiasm in a subject on first viewing their portrayal is an indication that the artist is in deep ordure. By this admittedly questionable criterion, he would appear to have produced a masterpiece. And indeed, as the critics have been noting of late, his new work seems to be expressing hitherto unsuspected depths of emotional force and maturity. He takes this to mean he is now painting with his heart as well as that other less mentionable organ.

Which was *exactly* what he tried to tell Teddy at the time.

'Give us a break,' he roared, fending off her furious assault. 'I love you, you daft pillock, can't you see? This is how I feel about you. I LOVE YOU.'

A sharp-eyed newspaper reader who cared to study that widely disseminated photograph featuring the painting with the happy couple locked together beside it, might have observed that, far from embracing, our heroine appeared to be attempting to punch our hero on the nose with a gent's black shoe.

And there's a very curious thing. Fortunately − at least it is fortunate if we too share Lily Rowbotham's robustly commonsensical view of such matters − the shot is cut off at knee level, leaving no record for posterity of our hero's footgear. Nor, in the general happy uproar, were Teddy or her elder brother ever likely to spare a thought for anything as trivial as the ownership of a size eleven shoe. Only in fairytales do shoes take on such absurdly disproportionate significance.

But the plain fact remains, recorded or not, that on the morning in question, one year ago, Bill Smith's feet were encased, as ever, in clumping great size thirteen boots. Both of them.